What Reviewers Say About B

Kim Baldw

"'A riveting novel of suspense' seems to be a very overworked phrase. However, it is extremely apt when discussing Kim Baldwin's [Hunter's Pursuit]. An exciting page turner [features] Katarzyna Demetrious, a bounty hunter…with a million dollar price on her head. Look for this excellent novel of suspense…" – **R. Lynne Watson**, *MegaScene*

Ronica Black

"Black juggles the assorted elements of her first book with assured pacing and estimable panache…[including]…the relative depth—for genre fiction—of the central characters: Erin, the married-but-separated detective who comes to her lesbian senses; loner Patricia, the policewoman-mentor who finds herself falling for Erin; and sultry club owner Elizabeth, the sexually predatory suspect who discards women like Kleenex…until she meets Erin."– **Richard Labonte**, *Book Marks, Q Syndicate, 2005*

Rose Beecham

"…her characters seem fully capable of walking away from the particulars of whodunit and engaging the reader in other aspects of their lives." – *Lambda Book Report*

Gun Brooke

"*Course of Action* is a romance…populated with a host of captivating and amiable characters. The glimpses into the lifestyles of the rich and beautiful people are rather like guilty pleasures.…[A] most satisfying and entertaining reading experience." – **Arlene Germain**, reviewer for the *Lambda Book Report* and the *Midwest Book Review*

Jane Fletcher

"*The Walls of Westernfort* is not only a highly engaging and fast-paced adventure novel, it provides the reader with an interesting framework for examining the same questions of loyalty, faith, family and love that [the characters] must face." – **M. J. Lowe**, *Midwest Book Review*

Radclyffe

"…well-honed storytelling skills…solid prose and sure-handedness of the narrative…" – **Elizabeth Flynn**, *Lambda Book Report*

"…well-plotted…lovely romance...I couldn't turn the pages fast enough!" – **Ann Bannon**, author of *The Beebo Brinker Chronicles*

THE EXILE AND THE SORCERER

ISBN 1-933110-32-5
This Trade Paperback Is Published By
Bold Strokes Books, Inc.,
Philadelphia, Pa, USA

New Revised Edition, February 2006

Originally published as Part One and Part Two of *Lorimal's Chalice*,
by Fortitude Press, 2002

Credits
Editors: Cindy Cresap and Stacia Seaman
Production Design: J. Barre Greystone
Cover Image: Tobias Brenner (http://www.tobiasbrenner.de/)
Cover Design: Julia Greystone

The Exile and The Sorcerer

Lyremouth Chronicles Book One

by

Jane Fletcher

2006

Acknowledgments

Thanks go to everyone at Bold Strokes Books, especially Rad, Stacia and Cindy, for their support, professionalism and for being great people to work with. I would also like to thank Pam and Ads for helping with earlier drafts of this novel.

DEDICATION

In memory of my father

Tom Fletcher

the one who first talked me into reading a book
that had no pictures

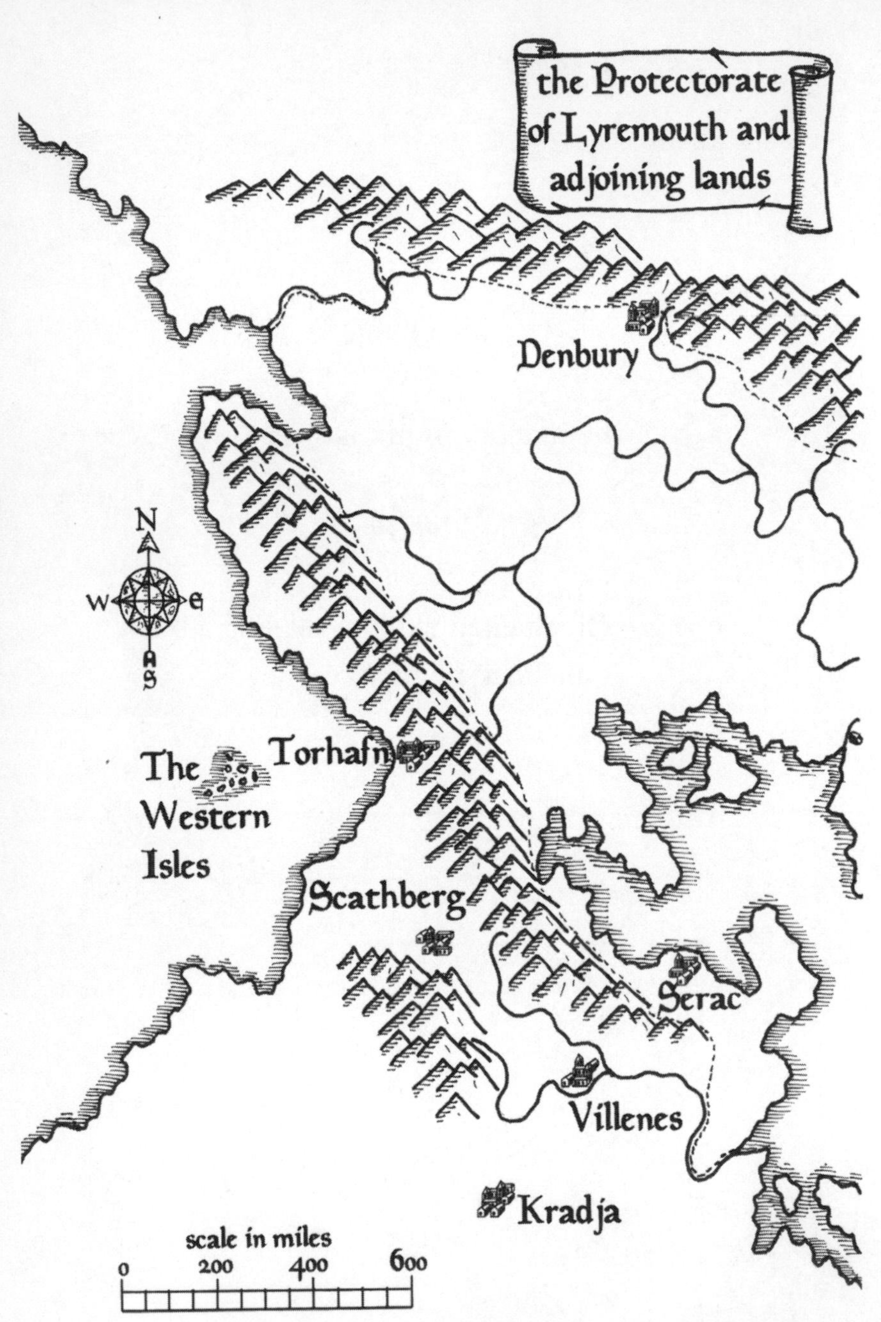

the dotted line markes the border of the Protectorate

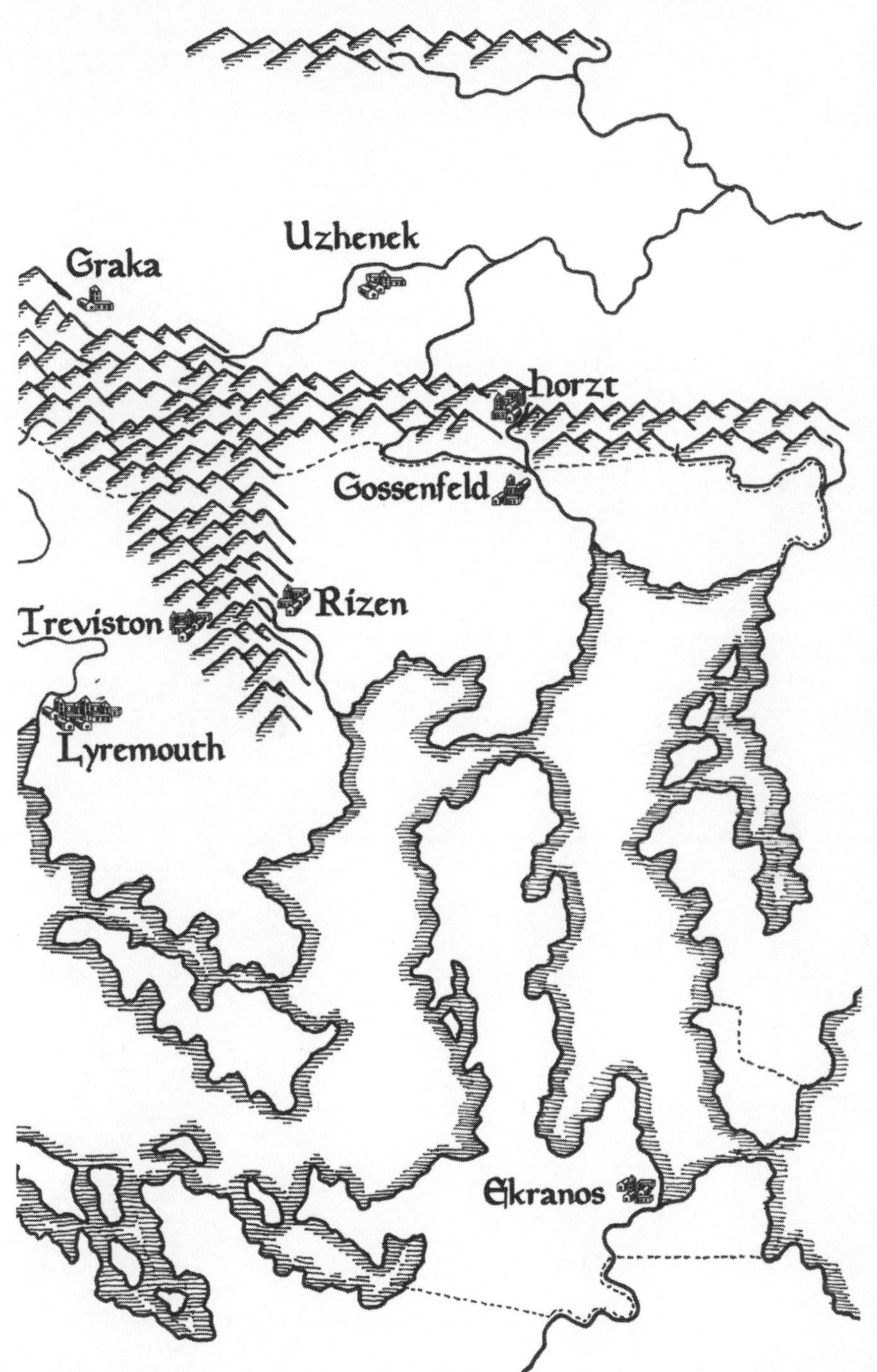
Uzhenek
Graka
Horzt
Gossenfeld
Rizen
Treviston
Lyremouth
Ekranos

Part One

The Exile

Chapter One—A Bad Joke

Predawn light filtered through chinks in the stone walls, so faint it did little more than hint at the sleeping figures. Tevi lay awake on the earthen floor, staring bleakly at nothing, tormented by memories of a dozen miserable events over the past month. A hard day's work loomed ahead, yet sleep eluded her. She felt utterly alone despite being surrounded by her family. A grimace crossed Tevi's face at the thought. Her family. She was an enormous disappointment to them. How could she not be? She was an even greater disappointment to herself.

The light strengthened slowly. Then came the wailing of seagulls. Tevi rolled onto her back. There was no point trying to sleep now, and as if hearing her thought, several bodies stirred. A woman by the hearth sneezed and sat up. Whispered words rippled around the hall.

"Hey, who's taken my boots?" The first loud voice of the morning belonged to Laff. It always did. The question provoked several retorts; the wittiest were greeted by laughter.

Tevi closed her eyes. She did not for a moment think her sister's boots were missing. It was just Laff's excuse to be noisy and claim everyone's attention. What Tevi never understood was why people were so tolerant of her sister, and so irritated if she tried similar childish ploys herself.

A man stepped over Tevi's legs. She watched him weave towards the hearth, between shifting bodies. He knelt and began coaxing the fire back to life. All around, people were getting to their feet, brushing dust from their clothes, rolling up blankets and sleeping mats. Noise in the hall rose. The double doors were pushed open. A sudden shaft of daylight glittered on eddies of smoke rolling under the thatched roof.

At the centre of the hall, Laff was standing by the hearth, making a show of stretching her muscles while teasing the men preparing breakfast and exchanging boisterous good mornings with the women. Everyone seemed to like her. It was a trick Tevi had never been able to master, no matter how much she tried to emulate her sister.

The differences between them were not in their looks. Both were tall, with brown eyes and straight black hair, hacked short. They had small, oval faces, on the bland side of good-looking, with thin noses and wide, straight lips. But that was where the similarity ended. Laff was loud and assertive, quick to argue, quick to make friends. Tevi was unsure of herself, subdued in company, uncomfortable with the swaggering bravado that other women put so much effort into. *"Weak and soft"* were their mother's words to describe Tevi. The comparisons with her sister made it worse. Maybe, if Laff had been the firstborn, it might not have mattered that she was the natural leader, but at nineteen, Tevi was the elder by two years.

Tevi sat up and looked around. She was not the last to rise; a few still slept at the edges of the hall. One couple lay nearby with their arms around each other. The man was sprawled lazily on his back. The woman, one of Tevi's many aunts, was up on an elbow looking down on him. Tevi's movement caught the aunt's notice. For a moment, Tevi was subjected to a critical stare before the aunt bent to whisper something in her companion's ear. The man's eyes brushed over Tevi as he twisted to giggle into the aunt's shoulder. Tevi felt a flush rise on her cheeks. She scrambled to her feet and hastened towards the hearth, but she knew she was being oversensitive. Judging by the noises last night, the couple had plenty of topics to laugh about.

Laff had her arm around the waist of the young man she had spent the night with. A selection of cousins were matching her in good-natured banter. Something Laff said made the man blush and raised a howl of laughter from the women. He smiled shyly at Laff, who hugged him closer.

Despite Tevi's attempt to join the group unobtrusively, Laff noticed her approach and yelped, "Watch out! Don't tread in the porridge!"

Tevi froze and looked down, but her feet were nowhere near the pot. It was a joke. Laff sniggered.

"You fall for it every time."

Tevi met her sister's eyes. "Yes, I know. It's sad. I always forget that you still have a toddler's sense of humour and haven't grown up yet."

"Oh, I'm quite grown up." Laff squeezed the young man and asked him playfully, "What do you think?"

"Everywhere except between your ears," Tevi said.

Laff's face twisted in a scowl, but their mother's approach stopped the argument before it could escalate. Red was tall, a trait inherited by both her daughters. Her body had once been strong and agile, before an ill-fated skirmish four years previous. Now she hobbled across the hall, leaning heavily on a wooden crutch. Never again would Red lead the war band to victory. Her naturally stern face was creased in pain, but she managed to smile indulgently at Laff. If Red noticed her older daughter, she gave no sign.

A slight bustle announced the emergence of Tevi's grandmother. As Queen of Storenseg, her status was marked by a wicker partition around her sleeping area. It was the nearest thing to a private room on the island. Two of Tevi's cousins hovered in attendance while the Queen settled herself on a bench. People paused to nod respectfully in the Queen's direction before picking up their conversations again. The hubbub flowed from group to group, the friendly family chaos binding everyone in the room from laughing grandmothers to squealing babies—everyone except Tevi.

The group around Laff had subtly closed ranks so that Tevi stood outside. Her mother and grandmother were in conversation. They glanced once in Tevi's direction, but their expressions were not warm. Nobody else in the hall even looked in her direction. The whole family was happy to ignore her existence.

Tevi considered the porridge heating over the fire. It would be some minutes before it was boiling, but she had no wish to hang around. A nearby basket held several loaves of dark rye bread. She tore off a chunk, dipped its corner in a bowl of honey, and headed for the doorway.

At the entrance, Tevi paused and glanced back. The Queen's eyes met hers briefly in shrewd appraisal. Once her grandmother had been an ally, but that had changed. Tevi was not sure when, or why, she had lost the Queen's favour. Now, of the whole island, only Brec was ever on her side. Tevi ducked through the doorway and escaped.

The sky to the east was awash with pink. Sunlight hit obliquely on the surrounding hills. Seagulls overhead called raucously as they wheeled around the valley, and pitched below the sound of their squabbling, the hissing roar of surf carried cleanly on the crisp air.

Tevi rested her shoulder against the stone wall of the hall and breathed in deeply, tasting salt. The smell was comforting. Soon she would be on the water, with the solid timbers of her boat beneath her feet. Captaining a fishing boat was the only thing she was good at, and the women respected her ability even if they did not respect her.

Thinking about her boat eased the knot in Tevi's stomach. She lowered her gaze and began eating the bread. Abrak's chapel stood in the middle of Holric village square. An armed woman was posted at the door. Tevi allowed herself a cynical smile. Setting a guard after the chalice was gone served little purpose. Obviously, a sorcerer had wanted the artefact and had sent an enchanted bird to steal it. Nothing now remained in the chapel worth taking. In truth, even the chalice had been purely symbolic. Abrak's legacy lay in her potion, the magic brew that gave the women their strength. Without it, they would be even weaker than men.

Unconsciously, Tevi grimaced at the memory of being forced to take her daily dose throughout childhood. The potion tasted foul, but it had done its work. Her enhanced strength would stay with her forever. Typically, Laff claimed to like the taste, but Tevi was pleased she would never need to take it again. However, at that moment, it was the only thing in her life that Tevi could think of to be grateful for. Her situation was hopeless. The friends of her childhood had deserted her until only Brec remained. Even her family scorned her—not that anyone thought she was a bad person, just a bad joke.

The round chapel marked the spot where Abrak had been burnt many years before. Now the ancient sorcerer stood, in spirit, at the side of Rangir, goddess of the sea—or so the myths claimed. Tevi was sceptical, but she needed whatever help she could get. On impulse, her lips moved as she silently offered a prayer. *"Please, Abrak, speak on my behalf to Rangir. Give me the chance to prove myself, so people will speak of me with respect. Show me how to end the scorn."* Was it too much to ask?

Around the square, clusters of people stood by doorways, soaking in the spring sunlight before beginning their day's work. One group was looking in Tevi's direction, although it was unclear whether she, or her grandmother's hall, was the topic of conversation. Either way, Tevi felt self-conscious. She was about to walk away when the focus of attention shifted abruptly. Voices were raised in shouts, and heads turned.

Tevi moved away from the wall just as a running woman burst from a pathway between two buildings. It took a second for Tevi to recognise the runner: Anvil, a senior member of the war band. It took less than a second longer for the significance to dawn. Anvil was due to be on lookout duty on the Stormfast Cliffs that morning.

"Rathshorn," Tevi whispered. It had to be the explanation. The season was early for raiding, but Anvil would not be running so frantically just to bring a report on the weather.

Tevi spun back through the doorway. People looked up, startled, from their breakfasts. "Anvil, from the lookout...she's coming."

While most leapt to their feet, the Queen remained impassive, looking at the doorway. Tevi stepped aside as the drumming of running feet grew louder. Anvil charged in and skidded to a stop before the Queen, gasping for breath.

A cacophony of questions greeted the sentry. "What have you seen?"

"Is it Rathshorn?"

"What's wrong?"

The Queen waved her hands for silence. "Let her catch her breath."

The questions stopped, although the noise did not. Feeling strangely detached, Tevi leaned against the doorpost and surveyed the hall, taking in the fear on the faces of the old and the excitement of the young. Laff looked happy, as if she had received a gift. Tevi watched with something between irritation and sorrow. *Maybe not a gift, but a prize*, the thought came to Tevi. *Just one more game for Laff to win.*

Anvil had a hand pressed to her side, but the heaving of her shoulders had eased enough for speech. "There's a boat...it must have... come close...during the night."

"Just one?" the Queen asked.

"That's all I could see. There might be more around the headland."

"Anything else?"

"There's a green pennant on the mast." Anvil's words drew a sigh of relief from some corners. The green flag was a sign of parley.

"They want to talk," the Queen said thoughtfully.

"They've got shields on display."

"They want to talk while reminding us what they back their words with." The Queen's face twisted in irony as she amended her words. "Did you recognise the shields?"

"It's Rathshorn." Anvil confirmed everyone's guess.

"It might be a diversion while they attack elsewhere," Red said from her position at the Queen's shoulder.

"True," the Queen agreed. "Send scouts to Hanken Ridge and the Skregin to see if any other boats are lurking. And for this parley, we can play their game. Muster the war band on the beach."

"The whole band?" Red questioned.

"Oh, yes. It never hurts to bargain from a position of strength."

Laff was at the weapon rack even before the Queen finished speaking. The family broke into groups. Men herded children to the back of the hall, old women stood in the centre talking in low voices, councillors gathered around the Queen, and the young women of the war band assembled by the weapons.

Tevi joined them, her heart thumping. All her life, there had been relative peace—only a few minor raids, such as the one in which her mother had been hurt. However, word was that the new Queen of Rathshorn was looking for trouble.

Swords hung in scabbards under the shields. Tevi slipped the strap over her head and evened out a kink in the leather so it would not dig into her neck. The weight of the sword against her leg was familiar, but not at all reassuring. Around her, women were putting on helmets and greaves. It was all so serious, deadly serious, yet the mood was like children playing on the beach.

"Tevi, what do you think? Is it war?"

Tevi glanced over her shoulder. In the enthusiasm, Laff's hostility was forgotten. It was the first time in months she had addressed Tevi without a sneer.

"Hopefully not," Tevi said quietly.

"*Not*?"

"I don't want to see women killed for no good reason."

"You're frightened." Laff's voice returned to its usual contempt.

Tevi cursed herself; she should have held her tongue. "It isn't that—"

Her words were cut off. "I'm sure it is. And in your place, I'd be frightened. It's only because the handle sticks out of the scabbard that you know which end of your sword to grab hold of. And you're supposed to lead the war band. It's going to be embarrassing following you. You're the worst fighter we have. You'll be dead within minutes."

"Then you won't have the embarrassment of following me for long," Tevi snapped back. She rammed the helmet onto her head and left the hall.

Of course, Laff was right. If it was war, then Tevi knew she would be dead within days. Her incompetence at fighting was a running joke. The sight of Abrak's chapel made Tevi remember her prayer. *Give me the chance to prove myself, so people will speak of me with respect.* Another bad joke. No one would talk ill of a woman who died in battle, no matter how quickly or incompetently.

The Queen's retinue marched towards the beach, gathering the war band from their family halls as they went. The women were in high spirits and laughing, but only Brec had a smile for Tevi.

"I hear we have visitors," Brec said as she joined the line.

"Just one boatload, from Rathshorn."

"So we're all going to pose prettily on the beach for them." Brec's laughter rang out.

"I think that's about it." Despite her bleak mood, Tevi found herself smiling.

Unfailing good humour was possibly Brec's most valuable trait—that and the simple, uncritical friendship she offered. Tevi was aware that her own feelings for Brec were far more complicated. Everyone liked Brec. She was witty and good looking, skilled with both sword and fishing net, easygoing but not weak willed. *So why is she eager to be my friend, when anyone in Holric would welcome her company?* The thought sprang from Tevi's bitter mood.

The war band formed an untidy phalanx on the dunes. Tevi, her mother, and the matriarchs of the families stood detached from the warriors, behind the Queen. They had barely reached position when the boat rounded the Stormfast Cliffs. The figures of several women were visible, taking in the sail as the small craft cut across the blue waters of the bay.

Behind her, Tevi heard the excited exchanges between members of the war band.

"What do you think they want?"

"Might be some sort of ultimatum."

"As a pretext for war?"

"Could be."

"Perhaps Queen Fearful wants her brother back."

"I say we should let her take him. He's useless."

"You've had him?"

"Only once." The exaggerated exasperation in the woman's voice brought yelps of laughter that were quickly stifled by glares from the matriarchs.

The boat ran aground in the shallows. Seven women jumped out, up to their thighs in the waves. Together, they hauled the boat up beyond reach of the tide. An older woman then disembarked and splashed through ankle-high water. The green pennant from the boat was tied to a long spear in her hand. A dozen yards from the Queen, she stopped and planted the butt of her spear in the sand.

The two groups studied each other in silence. Tevi looked at the leader, taking in her spiky white hair and the twin scars across her left cheek. Seeing a face you could not recognise was so strange; months, even years, could pass without it happening. When it did, the temptation was always to try mentally forcing the features into familiar contours.

At last, the stranger spoke. "I am First-in-battle, cousin and envoy to Queen Fearless-warrior of Rathshorn." Her clear voice was loud over the waves.

"I am Fists-of-thunder, Queen of Storenseg," Tevi's grandmother replied, at her most austere.

The envoy's gaze raked over the Queen. "My companions and I have travelled far to speak with you. We bring an offer that will aid both our islands."

"Then we will be pleased to hear to it." Despite the conciliatory words, there was an icy edge in the Queen's voice.

The envoy was unflustered. "May I introduce my companions? This is Raging-shark, foremost in victories, whose courage is famed in song throughout the isles." A tall, redheaded woman nodded. "This is Steadfast-shield-wall, the despair of all who stand against her, fearless and invincible. This is..."

Tevi stopped listening to the meaningless formality. Custom demanded that the women be identified before the parley could commence, but the ascribed feats were fictitious and the warlike birth names were always abandoned in favour of abbreviations, puns, or (as in Tevi's case) acquired nicknames.

Once the envoy finished, the Queen continued the ritual, naming the small group between her and the war band. Brec's grandmother, Lizard, was introduced as Dragon-heart; Miam, ancient, half blind and deaf, as Mighty-sword-arm. All were credited with feats of valour. Tevi would have found it funny if she had not been dreading her own introduction.

The Queen was nearing the end, with only Red and Tevi to go. "This is my daughter, Blood-of-my-foes, a warrior whose name is spoken with awe, who has triumphed in countless battles." For once, the acclamation was completely true. The envoy looked with interest, but her attention was fixed on the crutch under Red's arm. "And this is my granddaughter, Strikes-like-lightning, who boldly leads the war band."

Tevi tried not to wince. It was decidedly weak praise, but anything stronger might have drawn sniggers from the women behind her. Now, at last, they could return to the royal hall in Holric and learn the nature of the envoy's mission.

❖

Thick brown wax sealed the stopper of the terra-cotta flask. Tevi's hands shook as she picked at it with her knife, aware that everyone was watching. Not that there were crowds; in fact, Tevi had never seen the royal hall so empty. Apart from herself and the Queen, the only ones present were the women from Rathshorn, the matriarchs, and three veteran captains of Storenseg's war band, including Red. Everyone else had been ejected. Guards outside the doorway were keeping the curious at a distance, but undeterred, folk had gathered around the square and were peering in as best they could. Shouts drifted on the morning air, but no one inside was yet talking.

The Queen was the only one seated. Tevi stood before her, struggling with the stubborn cork. She could feel eyes burning into her back, imagining the shame should it be said that the leader of the Storenseg war band could not fight her way into a wine flask, but soon the sealing wax was gone, and the stopper was loose enough to be pulled.

Tevi balanced the flask in the crook of her arm and poured the yellow wine into a drinking bowl. The sweet, sickly smell seemed too heavy for the early hour, yet custom had to be observed. She offered the drink to the Queen, who accepted with a nod and took the smallest possible taste. No one with her grandmother's experience would risk negotiating when drunk. Tevi moved to the envoy and again offered the bowl. The woman from Rathshorn also swallowed a sip, barely wetting her lips, but enough. The tension in Tevi's neck eased. Whatever else the envoy might say, by all rules of honour, she had shared their hospitality and could not declare war.

Brec's grandmother, Lizard, was the next to be offered the wine. Thereafter, it passed in order of seniority. Some accepted with exaggerated formality; others knocked back the wine as if throwing down a challenge. Last of all, Tevi herself took a draft. The sweet liquid rolled over her tongue like waves over sand. She had not realised how dry her mouth was.

With the wine ritual over, benches were pulled from the sides and arranged about the hearth. The drinking bowl was refilled and commenced a second, less formal circuit. Tevi found herself seated at the end of a bench next to her mother. Her eyes flicked from person to person. The older women sat in postures of rigid authority, their backs as straight as swords. The younger ones were more blatantly aggressive, with bodies tensed as if ready to leap up and hit someone, and with fierce expressions as if watching for an excuse to do so. Tevi tried to imitate the pose, but she felt ridiculous, a poor burlesque of her sister. She prayed the women from Rathshorn did not realise.

It was hard not to flinch as she met Blaze's eyes. Blaze had been the one charged with the impossible task of training Tevi in the arts of war—impossible not because Tevi lacked strength or enthusiasm, but rather due to her inability to put what she knew into effect. The set exercises were easy—the feint, parry, thrust, and advance. But as soon as she was pitted against a living opponent, Tevi's defence crumbled so completely that she might as well have been blindfolded. "Watch her feet out of the corner of your eye. Don't just follow her sword!" Blaze had screamed over the years until even she had given up in disgust. Her caustic remarks about Tevi's incompetence were common knowledge. Blaze swore that Tevi was the worst excuse for a warrior she had ever attempted to train.

The voice of the Queen broke the silence, pulling Tevi back from her brooding. "And now, may we ask the reason for your visit?"

The envoy got to her feet. Her gaze travelled over the assembled women. "I speak on behalf of Queen Fearless-warrior, head of the families of Rathshorn, rightful ruler of all the Western Isles—" She got no further.

"You must be aware I would also claim that last title." The Queen's voice was firm.

"As would several others."

"Not all have history or law on their side."

"True. However, the rival claims of Rathshorn and Storenseg are not the subject I wish to discuss."

"Then perhaps you should leave the titles until such time as you do." Steel underlay the Queen's voice.

After long seconds of silence, the envoy continued. "I have come to speak concerning the island of Argenseg. This island is subject to the crown of Rathshorn. But as you know, twenty years ago, traitors overthrew their lawful rulers. They have not honoured the oaths of their mothers. They have not sent tribute; instead they have sent bands of pirates to harry our villages. The insult can go unpunished no longer. Our Queen intends to reclaim her rightful property."

"Why do you come to tell us? Surely she is not seeking our assistance."

"We do not ask you to fight beside us. But Storenseg is blessed with mines that yield ores of the highest quality. Your swords are the envy of the islands. It sometimes happens that these blades find their way into rebel hands. Queen Fearless-warrior would take it as a sign of goodwill if you would stop this trade."

"Swords may get from Storenseg to Argenseg by many routes. What benefit do I get from interfering in the concerns of traders?"

The envoy paused, as if weighing her next words. "There are some who say Storenseg has given aid to the rebels. Some, no doubt misguided, even say Storenseg first encouraged the treasonous revolt. A friendly gesture would silence the calls for retaliation. Otherwise, Queen Fearless-warrior might be hard put to ignore the council of war."

"Thank you. I think you have made yourself clear. Is this all you wish to say?" By her tone, the Queen might have been bored.

"It is."

"An interesting offer, and one I must consider further. While I prepare my answer, you will be our guests."

"My crew and I are willing to camp on the beach."

"Lodgings will be found for you. And so that none of your misguided councillors may say I slighted the envoy of Queen Fearless-warrior, tonight we will hold a feast in your honour."

The Queen stood, signalling the end of the debate. The meeting broke into small groups. The matriarchs huddled together, clearly waiting for the envoy to go before expressing their opinions. However, the envoy had other business before she was led from the hall. She made her way around the hearth and intercepted Red.

"Blood-of-my-foes, it has been some years since we met, and the last time I saw you was over the rim of a shield. I'm sorry we did not have time to talk on that day."

"It was a brief visit to Rathshorn." Red spoke so calmly that it took Tevi a second to realise they were talking about her mother's last, ill-fated raid.

The envoy went on. "But you went away with such valuable souvenirs. The Queen greatly misses her brother, not to mention the fine jewellery and weapons."

"And no doubt she complains I scorched the roof of her hall."

"She was none too pleased." The envoy's tone was also light-hearted. "But I heard you were wounded returning to your boat. Now I see you with a crutch. Has your leg not healed?" There was no mistaking her interest in the state of Red's health.

"One souvenir of Rathshorn I would rather not have taken."

"It has been a bad time for Storenseg, losing both you and Abrak's chalice."

"Neither loss is unbearable."

"Of course." The envoy's eyes shifted abruptly to Tevi. "Now your daughter leads the war band. She must be a great comfort to you."

The urge to shuffle out of view swamped Tevi, but somehow, she managed to meet the envoy's gaze. Before anything else could be said, they were joined by Blaze, who addressed the envoy.

"My name is Blazing-sword. If you are ready, I have been appointed to lead you to your lodgings."

"Ah, yes. Thank you. I was just commending Strikes-like-lightning.

Although young, the child of such an illustrious mother must surely be a warrior to be reckoned with. Doubtless the defence of Storenseg rests safe on her shoulders."

"Her skill with a sword is the talk of all the island. I've trained many warriors, but never before have I met her like," Blaze said, deadpan.

The crowd outside moved apart as Blaze led the women from Rathshorn to a hall with sleeping space to spare. After a short discussion, two of the visitors trotted to the beach to collect their things. Several young girls tagged along, whooping in excitement. The rest of the population, eager to learn what had happened, surrounded the matriarchs as they emerged from the royal hall.

Tevi stood by the doorway, watching until the envoy disappeared. As quietly as possible, she slipped around the edge of the square. Few would choose her as a source of information, but she had no wish to get involved in the overblown and facile arguments that she knew would take place.

Brec jogged over. Her habitual grin was replaced by an anxious frown.

"Tevi, what's happening? What did they say?"

"They're playing some sort of game; the goddess knows what the point is. Our grandmothers will have a better idea than me."

"Someone said they've given an ultimatum about selling swords to Argenseg."

"I'm sure there's more to it. Come on, let's get away from all this, and I'll tell you everything they said." Tevi gestured for Brec to follow.

The pair started down a narrow passage between two halls, leaving the noise of the square behind, but before they had taken a dozen steps, another voice assailed them.

"Tell me, did the women of Rathshorn tremble in their boots at the sight of our mighty war leader?"

Tevi turned around. Laff stood at the end of the passage with her arms crossed and a sour expression on her face.

"I'm sure you won't be surprised to learn they hardly noticed me."

"What? You managed to avoid drawing attention by walking into a bench? You must be having a good day." Laff moved closer until she was less than an arm's length away.

The two sisters glared at each other until Tevi sighed in exasperation and dropped her head. She was not in the mood to deal with her sister's hostility. "Look, I know you're angry that I was at the meeting and you weren't. Honestly, I'd much rather you'd been there instead of me, but I wasn't given the option."

"I couldn't care less about the meeting." Judging by her tone, Laff's words were blatantly untrue.

"Then what are you so wound up about?"

"You, and the way you're going to bring shame upon our family." Laff spat out the words.

"I'll try my best not to."

"Your best is pathetic. Strikes-like-lightning. They named you well. You couldn't hit the same spot twice for trying." Laff rephrased one of Blaze's jokes.

"And you could do so much better?"

"Of course I could! I should lead the war band, not you."

"Then perhaps you should go to Mother and suggest she reschedule our births." Over Laff's shoulder, Tevi saw women gathering at the passage entrance, attracted by the raised voices. It was time to cut the argument short, but Laff was not about to let it drop.

"How do you have the nerve to bring Mother into this? She was a great warrior. She must be so ashamed to have you as a daughter."

"Oh, she is. She makes that quite clear." Tevi spun about and began to walk away.

"You aren't fit to follow her. You should have been a boy. You go out of your way to act like one. How far do you take the act?"

Tevi knew she should have kept walking, but there was an edge to Laff's voice that could not be ignored. She turned back and snarled, "At least I don't act like a girl who has to think with her sword since she keeps her brain between her legs."

Laff grinned in satisfaction at provoking a reaction. She looked her sister slowly up and down before saying, "Oh, no. No one would ever accuse you of that. I don't know about being a real warrior; you're not even a real woman."

Tevi could feel herself shaking. Getting into a game of trading insults with Laff had been a bad move, but she could not back off now, not with the audience. "I'm enough of a woman to ram that stupid remark back down your throat."

"You think you want to try?" Laff was getting louder. "Where were you and Brec going? Off to hold hands and stare into each other's eyes? But I'm being unfair to Brec. She probably doesn't realise you'd like to play the man for her—on your back, with your pants down."

Laff had gone much too far. Tevi leapt forward, fist swinging for her sister's face. The sudden attack took Laff by surprise, but she managed to raise an arm to parry. Even so, the punch clipped the side of her head and knocked her back against the wall. Tevi moved in for a second blow, but her sister kicked at her legs, causing her to stumble and miss.

The fight was short and predictable. Tevi attempted to take the offensive, knowing that she was better in attack than defence. Unfortunately, Laff was equally well aware of this. They traded a few easily blocked punches. Then Laff connected with a hard kick to the knee. Tevi did not see the unexpected low strike coming. She never did. The first she knew was pain exploding in her leg. She crumpled forward, straight into another vicious punch to the stomach that sent her crashing to the ground.

Laff stood over her fallen sister. "You should have been a man. Even our brothers can fight better. You're—"

"What do you think you're doing?" Blaze pushed her way through the spectators.

"Tevi and I had a disagreement."

"This isn't the time to pick fights with her."

"Tevi started it."

"Then she's a bigger fool than I thought. And you're no better." Blaze's voice was low but biting. "Supposing the women from Rathshorn had seen this."

"So what if they had?"

Blaze pulled Laff around and glared into her eyes. "We all know Tevi is as much use to the war band as a straw dummy—in fact, slightly less. We could burn the dummy to cook our dinner over. But she's your mother's eldest daughter, and she has to lead us. How would they react in Rathshorn if they learnt the truth? Have you considered the boost it would give them? Because when you're as old as me, you'll know how confidence can win a battle against the odds." Blaze paused while the defiance faded from Laff's face. "Try to act like adults, at least until the envoy leaves."

Blaze stalked away. Laff gave a last angry glare at her sister and followed. The crowd dispersed. Tevi managed to haul herself to her feet, flexing her knee.

"You should have let me tackle Laff. I was only half a second behind you," Brec said.

"I lost my temper."

"I don't blame you. I don't know what gets into Laff sometimes. She can have a nasty mind. What made her say that?"

Tevi kept her eyes fixed on her knee. Brec was a good friend, but Tevi wondered how she could be so naive. Not that Tevi would complain. Of all the women on Storenseg, Brec was the only one Tevi could rely on for support, the only one she could talk to. But even so, there was no way she could admit to Brec that Laff's accusation was true.

❖

The Queen's sleeping area had its own hearth, though the fire was unlit on the warm spring morning. A bed of straw took up a third of the space. Two low stools were the only furniture. The Queen sat on one; her chief adviser, Lizard, on the other. Their heads were close as they spoke in low voices, discussing the envoy's message.

War had taken both of the Queen's sisters long ago, depriving her of close family support. Lizard had filled the gap. Together, the two women had dominated island politics for decades. The current situation was the latest in a series of crises they had averted or overcome.

Lizard was scathing in her appraisal of the Queen of Rathshorn. "Silly young fool."

"She'll learn—if she lives long enough."

"Do you think she'll attack Storenseg?"

"I think she'd like to. Control of the two biggest islands is a logical first step in conquering all the Western Isles." The Queen sighed. "She won't be able to take Storenseg, but a lot of women will die while she finds that out."

"The traditional claims to rule all the islands create a lot of wild dreams."

"I know. I'd drop my own claim if I could do it without losing face. I worry about Red trying once I'm gone."

"She won't," Lizard said confidently.

"Can you be sure?"

"I agree she lacks political sense, but she knows enough about war to spot a lost cause."

"And Fearless doesn't," the Queen said firmly. "We need her to learn, and quickly. If I read things right, she's heading for war but can't make her mind up on the target. We need Fearless to go for Argenseg. She'll take it—it's a lot smaller than Storenseg, but she'll still lose a fifth of her war band in the fighting. It'll give her a better grasp of the practicalities of war, and she certainly won't be in a fit state to bother us afterwards."

"I'm worried about this nonsense over the swords. It sounds as if she's trying to create a pretext for war with us. There was nothing subtle about the threat at the end."

"I noticed. But I don't think it's reached that point. This parley is just an excuse to scout things out. You saw the envoy's eyes light up at the sight of Red limping."

Lizard pursed her lips. "So what will you do about selling swords to Argenseg?"

"That's a hard one. To agree might be taken as a sign of weakness. To refuse would give an excuse to attack. But if I'm right, she's not serious about the swords, and she can always find another excuse." The Queen looked thoughtful. "Perhaps I could send Fearless's brother back as a meaningless gesture."

"That won't please Hilo. She's taken rather a liking to him."

"There's no shortage of men."

"We can't afford bickering among our families."

The two women sat in silence for a while with identical frowns on their faces.

Lizard was the first to speak. "We might be able to manoeuvre Argenseg into provoking Fearless—suggest to some of their hotheads that it might be funny to take another of her brothers captive."

The Queen nodded. "That would be good if it worked, and I think I know the right hothead to suggest it to. We could also send Red to visit folk on Varseg."

"With what purpose?"

"We'd say she merely wants to see the site of her greatest victory again."

"Who's going to believe that?"

"No one, probably."

"So what's the real reason?"

"To make Fearless wonder why I sent Red to Varseg."

Lizard froze for a second and then yelped with laughter. "Her spies and councillors will tie themselves in knots looking for a reason that doesn't exist. With your reputation for being a conniving old fox, they'll end up convincing themselves that you're hatching a plot so clever it's beyond them."

"And if Red goes to Varseg, it will remind people of all her victories with the invincible Storenseg war band. A good reputation can be the best weapon of all. My family has a lot of prestige, and I'll use it to bluff a way through this. I want to make sure everyone remembers that the royal family of Storenseg is a very dangerous enemy."

"I do see one potential problem," Lizard said after a moment's pause.

The Queen's face was grim. "I know...Tevi."

Chapter Two—In The Hay Barn

By midafternoon, although her knee was still sending darts of fire up her leg, Tevi was able to climb to the fortified stockade high on the hillside. If war came, the enclosure would keep livestock safe from raids. Tevi had volunteered to inspect the defences as a way to get time alone to think. However, Brec had tagged along, and there was no way to refuse her company without pointing out the interpretation Laff might put on their going off together.

The timber stockade was surrounded by a deep ditch that made use of natural contours wherever possible. From the embankment, Tevi looked down on the village nestling among fields far below. Holric looked like a toy made by a child in the sand. Tevi felt as if she had only to reach out her hand and she would be able to knock it flat. The image was appealing.

"The ditch and bank are sound, but the palisade needs a bit of work in places." Brec's voice interrupted her brooding.

"Umm, I'll tell Grandmother to send some women up here with axes. What do you reckon...about a day's work for three women?" Tevi suggested.

"That'll do it easily."

Tevi nodded but said nothing more.

"Come on. Let's go back and see how preparations are going. We could check out the cooking—sample a few bits to make sure they're doing it properly," Brec said in her brightest tones.

"You could. I might go and see my boat."

"Surely it can wait?"

"We've missed out on fishing today. We'll have to set off early tomorrow. I want to be sure everything is ready."

"I'll come with you."

"You don't have to," Tevi said quietly.

"Yes, I do. But I warn you, if you don't cheer up, I'm going to start singing happy little songs."

Brec was irrepressible; at last, Tevi smiled. "That's quite a threat."

"I know. That's why I reserve it for dire emergencies."

The path to the beach took them through the jumble of barns and workshops on the outskirts of Holric. Decades of trampling feet had worn hollows in the dark soil. Drystone walls lined either side of the path, overhung by steep thatch roofs reaching nearly to the ground.

The area was deserted; even the fires in the smithy were dampened. The envoy from Rathshorn and the coming feast had disrupted the daily schedule. Little real work was being done. The men still cleaned and cooked, but older women gathered to discuss the prospect of war while younger ones practised swordplay and archery with even more zeal than usual.

Outside one storeroom, three men were struggling with a large cider barrel. Brec marched over and put out a restraining hand. The men—Brec's brother, Sparrow, and two of Tevi's cousins—immediately stood back.

"Is this for the feast?" Brec asked.

"Grandmother told us to get it," Sparrow answered defensively.

"You were shaking up all the dregs."

"We were trying to keep it steady."

Brec relented and smiled. "Tevi and I will carry it."

"We'll cope."

"I'd rather not take the chance. I'm hoping to drink some tonight."

"They'll be all right without us." Tevi said, hoping to spare her knee.

"We can't leave the boys to lug this around. It must weigh twice as much as them," Brec argued.

Tevi gave in. The full barrel was clearly too heavy for the men, but thanks to Abrak's potion, it presented no problem for Brec and Tevi, apart from Tevi's knee complaining with each step. They wove their way to the main square while Brec directed a stream of banter at the men.

"You don't want to pull a muscle, else you'll be no fun at the feast and even less fun afterwards. Although the fun thing to pull then doesn't have a muscle in it."

Tevi's cousins giggled and blushed above their beards.

Sparrow walked beside Tevi, smiling at her shyly. He was barely an inch taller than her, with long hair and large brown eyes. As children, they had played together, collecting crabs on the beach and acting out games of make-believe. As adults, they led lives divided by the roles allocated to them, but he still seemed to like her company.

"It's kind of you to help us," Sparrow said.

"Brec was right. It's too heavy for men to carry."

"I guess Grandmother didn't think."

"She must have a lot on her mind."

"Do you think Rathshorn is going to declare war on us?" Sparrow asked seriously.

Brec overheard the question. "Don't worry. We'll look after you. We'll cut the Rathshorn war band into pieces to use as fish bait."

The men smiled, and Brec returned to her flow of innuendo, clearly feeling she had said all they wanted to hear, but Tevi was not so certain. Every woman in Holric was arguing strategy and politics; were men so different? Sparrow was not stupid. Surely he could not be content with Brec's trite boasting. Yet he asked no more questions.

The barrel was deposited in the busy village square. Tevi was anxious to leave, but Brec prolonged the conversation, her attention fastened on one of Tevi's cousins, who appeared flustered but not displeased. While waiting for Brec to finish flirting, Tevi observed the people in the square. She was getting more than her usual share of critical looks, but it was impossible to say whether it was due to the prospect of her leading the war band or to Laff's accusation. *In fact*, she told herself, *it could be that I'm looking for signs of contempt rather than trying to ignore them*. It was easy to be oversensitive.

Finally, Brec was ready to continue. They walked in silence. Tevi assumed that her friend's thoughts were on the young man, but as they reached the boat, Brec said, "Do you mind if I say something?"

"Would saying no stop you?" Tevi placed both hands flat on the hull and felt its solid reassurance flow into her. Silence made her look back. Brec was staring at her own feet, and her jaw was set. She had clearly built herself up to say something and was not going to be deflected. A nasty premonition kicked at Tevi's stomach.

Brec swallowed and said, "You like Sparrow, don't you?"

"Yes. He's a nice lad. Easy to talk to."

"I don't mean like that."

"What do you mean?"

Brec hesitated, biting her lip. "I mean...like...as a man."

Tevi fixed her eyes back on the boat. *Laff has got even Brec wondering. What must the rest of the village be thinking?* Aloud, she said, "Well, yes. He's good-looking, and he..." Tevi's words died.

Brec was also not at her most fluent. "Because...well, what Laff said...before you hit her..."

"She was just being spiteful."

"Oh, I know that. But I think I know what made her think it."

Tevi's mouth went dry.

Brec's words came in a rush. "Tevi, I can tell you're nervous with men. I know that doesn't mean anything...lots of women are; they just hide it. That's what the stupid bragging is about. I do it myself, like with your cousin just now." Brec raised her eyes, her expression worried but sincere. "But you've got no need to be nervous. Lots of the men like you, I can tell. Sparrow likes you. You must have noticed how he's started hanging around you. And...I think he's just waiting for you to... say something. You have to be more..."

For a moment, the truth hung on Tevi's lips. *Actually, Laff was on the right track. I'm attracted to women, not men.* They were words that could not be said. Tevi mumbled, "I don't know."

"You can't let rumours get out of hand just because you're not like Laff, chasing after every man like a bitch in heat."

Even if she was naive, Brec was right, but Tevi did not want to discuss it. "Er...I'll...um...think about it."

"If you want, I'll speak to Sparrow for you."

"No," Tevi said quickly, but then gave a weak smile. "I'll sort it out myself. But thanks."

"All right." Brec looked relieved, clearly feeling enough had been said and happy to move on. "Why does Laff hate you so much?"

The shift in topic was not the direction Tevi would have chosen, but she tried to give an honest answer. "I don't think she does. She just puts on a show to distance herself from me."

"Why?"

Because she's too astute to get linked to a loser. The words would have been too blunt and too simplistic. As a child, Tevi could remember Laff running after her, adoration in her eyes, but at some stage, Laff had learned that her big sister was not someone to be proud of. Tevi suspected that most of the venom behind her sister's attacks was revenge for that first disillusionment.

Brec answered her own question. "She's jealous because you'll be Queen one day."

"No, that's not fair. Laff would be happy with the role of loyal sister to a respected Queen, but she feels I won't be able to play my part when the time comes."

"You'll do fine."

"Laff may be right," Tevi said quietly.

"Don't be stupid."

"I'm hopeless at fighting."

"From what I've heard, so was your grandmother. It's why she wasn't so keen to go into battle with her sisters—and why she's still alive. Yet she's been a great Queen. You must have more faith in yourself. Why are you so worried?"

The conversation was getting worse. The scrunch of footsteps on sand was, at first, a welcome distraction.

Red appeared behind the stern of the boat. Her eyes skipped over Tevi. "Brec, I was looking for you. Lizard wants to see you right away."

If Red was acting as messenger, it had to be something serious. Brec trotted off immediately, saying, "I'd better go and see what Grandmother wants."

Alone on the beach, Red looked at her daughter with distaste. "I don't suppose you know where Laff is?"

"She was practising her swordplay by the river."

Red grunted and turned away.

"Mother." Red stopped at Tevi's call, but did not look back. "If there's something you need? Can't I help?"

"I doubt it." Red limped away.

"Right. Fine. I'm sure Laff will be more use to you." Tevi spoke to her mother's retreating back in a tone pitched too low to be heard.

Red vanished behind the dunes. The black sands held a ragged cover of sea grass, and the first blooms of sand pinks were showing a flush of colour. Nobody was in sight. Tevi turned and leaned her shoulders against the hull of the boat, staring bleakly at the sea.

"You want to know why I'll be no good as Queen?" Tevi addressed to the waves the words she could not say to Brec. "I don't like shouting and arguing. I don't like swaggering around all the time as if I'm looking for a fight. I don't like pretending the only strong emotions I feel are anger or lust. I'm no good at the act anyway."

Of the children Red had borne before Tevi, only three sons survived infancy. Tevi had been a desperately longed-for heir. By her third birthday, her mother was planning the victory feast for Tevi's first triumphant return from battle. Tevi was supposed to become a great warrior and leader. Watching her dreams crumble had made Red bitter.

Tevi's head sagged. If only one of her brothers had been a girl. She envied them. They went about their work, unheeded and unchallenged. *Men don't have to pretend to be something they're not*, she thought. *If I'd been a boy, it wouldn't matter how I feel about women. Brec might even want to be my lover, and...* Tevi squashed the thought.

The islands had a strict set of laws. For cowardice in battle, a woman's family would disown her. A range of punishments were specified for stealing, from a fine to enslavement. Treason or murder warranted the harshest penalty: death by stoning. For one woman to take another as a lover was not so clearly defined. You might be executed, exiled, flogged, or merely ridiculed—at least, for a first offence. It would depend on circumstance, the mood the Queen was in that day and possibly the direction the wind was blowing.

A memory came to Tevi, sharp and vivid. Eight years before, a prisoner had been brought before her grandmother. The woman had killed another in cold blood. The Queen had passed judgement. Tevi had gone with the rest of the village to see justice done. The crowd had been overawed, watching the Queen ceremonially throw the first stone. Others had joined in. The first forty or so hits had resulted in torn and bleeding skin, a broken shoulder joint, and fractured ribs. The woman had screamed for forgiveness. The next large stone had smashed her skull and killed her.

Tevi groaned and looked at the boat. Everything was in perfect order. There was no reason to stay away from the village any longer, except she could not face it—not just yet. Turning away, she walked along the beach and up the cliff path. Brec's words kept running through her head, especially about the risks of rumours. Her status in Holric was low enough. She did not need further scandal.

Everyone else Tevi's age had been sexually active for years. The tally Laff was notching up gave rise to jokes and envy in equal parts. Women's sexual exploits formed a major part of their conversation, with imagination used where necessary to embellish the facts. Tevi had known that her own lack of enthusiasm for men would be noticed eventually.

For a long time, Tevi stood on the cliff top watching the seagulls while listening to the crash of surf below. A line of clouds hung over the horizon, but the sky above was clear. Sunlight glittered off the waves. The brisk wind, heavy with salt, snapped at her hair. It eased her tension, but the decision could not be put off. She had to take steps to silence the gossip, and one particular course of action was unavoidable.

Brec had spoken of Sparrow. Presumably, Brec knew her own brother. Would he really be willing if she made a play for him? A rueful smile crossed Tevi's face. Actually, his response was unimportant for her purpose. A more useful effect on gossip would probably be had if he ran from her screaming, "No, no, you beast, leave me alone!" But if he agreed...? Tevi pursed her lips. It probably would not be so bad. After all, she liked Sparrow. He was a friend.

Tevi hung her head. She had to do it, but the coming evening would be a trial. The rest of her life would be a trial. She remembered her childish disappointment when she realised that being the Queen's granddaughter did not automatically make her the best at everything.

Tevi turned around. The sun was sinking to the horizon. It was time to go to the feast, but all things considered, maybe death in battle might not be so bad.

❖

The smell of roast boar greeted Tevi on her return to the main square. The air was thick with ribbons of sweet smoke. Every child in Holric seemed to be gathered by the fire pits to watch the cooking. Many stood with eyes and mouths wide open, while others laughed and squabbled.

Women had begun passing around flagons of wine and beer. There was no sign of the envoy and her comrades. Presumably, they were in the Queen's hall. The mood in the square was cheerful, and for once, Tevi did not feel that she was the subject of hostile scrutiny. A gang of young women were sprawled to one side. Tevi was tempted to join them, but she had an objective to achieve that night. She turned in search of Sparrow.

The interior of Lizard's family hall was dark and noisy. Once her eyes had adjusted to the light, Tevi spotted Sparrow sitting surrounded by a group of small boys, helping to braid their hair. Tevi made her way to within a few feet, then came to a standstill, suddenly very nervous and uncertain. A boy tapped Sparrow's shoulder and pointed in her direction.

Sparrow looked up and smiled. "Are you looking for Brec? She's only just gone."

"No...I was looking for you."

"Me?"

"Well, I thought...you might like to come with me...if you're finished here. And...we could see if the cider has settled. It might be nice if you and I, er"—Tevi knew she was flustered. She prayed she was not blushing as well—"spent some time together."

To her relief, and slight surprise, Sparrow's smile broadened. "I'd like that. But I thought you were due to meet Brec. She was looking everywhere for you."

"We had no plans."

"I think it was important."

"I don't know..." Tevi hesitated.

"It's not a problem. I'm going to be a bit longer with the children. When I'm finished, I'll look for you. I promise." Now it was Sparrow's turn to be shy. He fiddled with the comb in his hand.

"Right. I'll go and find her. We'll meet later." Tevi shifted from foot to foot, wondering if she should hug him, but it felt false. Besides, all he had agreed to was meeting her at the feast. There would be time to say more later, and the cider would help.

Once outside, Tevi raised her face to the sky and let out a deep sigh. Sparrow had seemed happy. Maybe Brec was right about him liking her. Tevi did not know whether to feel pleased or frightened.

Remembering Brec, Tevi scanned the village square without success. "Have you seen Brec recently?" she asked a nearby woman.

"I saw her head off to the beach a while back."

"Thanks."

Tevi jostled through the crowded square with as much speed as possible. The sun had not yet set, but already, some people were drunk.

One almost fell in her path. Running bands of children collided with her at waist height. Several minutes were needed before she cleared the press of people lining the square and left the noise behind.

Tevi spotted a lone figure returning from the beach. "Hey! Brec!"

The figure raced towards her. "Where've you been? I've searched everywhere for you."

"What's up?"

"We need to talk. Come with me." Brec was clearly agitated, now that she was close enough for Tevi to see her face.

"What about? What's wrong?"

"We can't talk here. Come on."

Brec could not be drawn to say more. Anxiously, Tevi followed her friend past the empty workshops. At last, Brec led the way into one of the barns at the edge of the village. A mound of hay filled the back, and a row of small barrels lined one side. Apart from these objects, the building was empty.

"Right. So what is this about?" Tevi asked.

Brec held up one hand. She clambered onto the hay and peered over at the rear wall. Tevi stared in astonishment.

"I have to check if we're alone."

"What...why?"

"You'll understand."

Brec jumped down and pushed the door shut. The last of the sun's rays fell squarely on the timber planks. Light squeezed through the cracks. Tevi selected one of the barrels and sat on it, waiting for an explanation.

Brec had her hands clasped behind the back of her head, staring at the ceiling. Judging her expression was hard in the dimness. Only the faint sounds from the distant square broke the silence.

"Brec?" Tevi prompted.

"I've been thinking...about what we were saying beside the boat. At least...I've been doing a bit more thinking," Brec said unsteadily.

"So have I. I've talked to Sparrow, and I think you're right. He does like me."

"You're not really keen on him."

"Of course I am."

"But not as a man." Brec's voice was quiet. "Your sister was right, wasn't she?"

"Brec!"

"It's all right. You don't have to deny it."

Tevi's mouth went dry. For the space of a dozen heartbeats, she could not force out any words, while fighting the temptation to give in to panic and run. Eventually, she found her voice. "Has someone been getting at you? Was it Laff? You shouldn't bother about her." Tevi stood. "Come on, let's go back to the feast."

The other woman made no attempt to move.

"Brec?"

Brec's face dropped into her hands. Her voice came in a strangled whisper through her fingers. "I love you, Tevi."

The words hit like a physical blow. Blood pounded in Tevi's ears. Her legs turned to jelly. Stunned, she sank back onto the barrel.

"Tevi?" Brec's voice was tense, devoid of emotion.

Tevi did not answer. In her mind's eye, she saw the body of the executed murderer, broken and blood-soaked.

"Tevi. Did you hear me? I said I love you."

"It's dangerous."

"But do you love me?"

"You must know that I do," Tevi said in a monotone whisper.

"Will you meet me here tonight?" Brec spoke urgently.

Things were going too far, too fast. The solid world was wrenched out of joint, and Tevi felt stunned, yet the request struck through the fog. She stared at her friend in alarm. "Have you gone mad? Do you know what'll happen if we're caught?"

"I don't care."

"We could be exiled or executed."

"Are you frightened?"

"Yes. Aren't you?" Tevi's head was spinning.

"But it's just the fear of being caught? If it was safe, you'd want to be my lover?" Brec's voice was harsh in its insistence.

Tevi fought for control of her voice, but now she could be honest. "More than anything in the world. I've loved you hopelessly for years."

"Then please meet me here tonight. No one will miss us with the feast."

It was insane, but Tevi could not say no. "All right, I'll be here."

"And we'll be lovers?" Brec's question sounded like a challenge.

"Yes."

"I think we've heard enough." The Queen's voice rang out. Tevi's head jerked in its direction, also hearing movement at the rear of the barn, behind the hay. Bewildered, Tevi turned back just in time to see Brec's fist. The blow knocked her sprawling on the floor. A foot swung into her stomach, driving the air from her lungs.

"Stop that," the Queen said sharply.

Gasping for breath, Tevi was vaguely aware of the presence of more people in the barn—walking around, standing over her.

Brec's voice sounded over the others. "Goddess! Did you hear her? I don't know how I managed to—"

The Queen interrupted. "We heard her. You played your part well. Don't overplay it. Now bring her over here."

Still fighting to suck air into her lungs, Tevi was hauled to her knees. The sound of striking flint was followed by the gentle light of a lantern springing into life. Tevi's head cleared as her breath returned.

She found herself kneeling in the centre of the floor. Both arms were twisted behind her, sufficient to hurt and prevent her from moving but not enough to cause injury. Tevi twisted her neck. Brec was holding one arm; Laff, the other. In front of her, Lizard and the Queen sat on barrels. Red adjusted the lantern before limping over and joining the two older women. A cold fist clenched Tevi's stomach: three judges and herself as prisoner. The hay barn was empty apart from the six of them.

The Queen spoke. "I take it you accept the authority of this court. Or would you prefer a public hearing?"

Tevi shook her head, not trusting herself to speak.

"I thought as much." Her grandmother leaned forward. "So what are we going to do with you? You really do present quite a problem."

"She always has. I blame myself for bearing her," Red interjected.

"Blame isn't the issue. As I said, Tevi presents us with a problem. We have to decide what to do about it."

Tevi was swamped with the bitter knowledge that her mother would be unmoved to see her provide the village with an afternoon's entertainment in the quarry. "You're going to have me executed." She found her voice.

The Queen shook her head. "That's an option, but not a very

good one. I'd have to tell people why, and I'm afraid it would have a damaging effect on our family's reputation. With war imminent, we cannot afford that sort of scandal."

"So why have you engineered this?"

"Because you were all set to cause a scandal whether I acted or not. Knowing you, you'd set it off at the worst possible moment. That's why I pre-empted things. Always meet trouble halfway. It lets you pick the battleground. I learnt that years ago. Right now, we're in an awkward situation. Executing you will only make it worse." The Queen paused while she brushed loose straw from her knees. "So I'm going to give you a choice."

Tevi raised her chin. A pulse leapt erratically in her throat. "You want me to kill myself." It would spare her the humiliation of public execution, but before she could weigh up the option, her grandmother shook her head.

"That would be a better way out, but not the best. If you commit suicide, people will talk. The gossip might even make things worse than they actually are. You can bet Queen Fearless-warrior will encourage the rumours. Even if you make your death look like an accident, it will be seen as bad luck. Coming on top of your mother's injury and losing the chalice, we'd be seen as a very unlucky family. People would say the Goddess had turned her back on us, which won't help in gaining allies."

"What do you want me to do?"

"I want you to go," the Queen said firmly.

"Where?"

"Anywhere. The farther, the better."

"You're exiling me."

"In effect, yes. To do it officially would give free rein to the rumourmongers, so I want you to appear to go of your own accord. The feast tonight will provide a suitable audience. I want you to put on an act, like Brec did just now. Make a scene. Say the theft of the chalice is an insult to our family, and you can no longer sit back and do nothing. Swear that you're going in search of Abrak's chalice and won't return until you find it."

"But nobody knows were the chalice is."

"So nobody will be surprised when you don't come back."

"And if I refuse?"

"I'll have to think of something else. Maybe frame one of the women from Rathshorn for your murder. It might work in our favour, but it would be a very high-risk plan. Much better for you to disappear on a heroic quest. It's romantic and will make for some good songs. But one way or another, I'll make sure you don't disgrace the family." Steel had crept into the Queen's voice.

Tevi raised her eyes to the roof. Shouts and laughter carried from the square. Someone was beating out a drum rhythm, displaying more enthusiasm than skill. Both Brec and Laff were shaking, even more than herself. A trap had closed around her. "It's not a real choice, is it? All right, I'll give you what you want. I'll go." The gasp of relief from her sister surprised Tevi.

The Queen nodded. "Let her stand."

Tevi's arms were released. A dazed numbness settled on her. She got to her feet, rubbing her shoulders, hardly conscious of the room. She did not look at Brec.

The Queen also stood. "Now I think we should leave as discreetly as possible, not all at once."

Laff beat everyone to the door, wrenching it open and rushing out. Brec would have followed, but the Queen snapped, "I said, not all at once."

Brec stopped dead. She leaned against the doorpost, her eyes fixed on the Queen. After a while, the elderly woman nodded. Brec marched off in the direction Laff had taken.

Tevi made no attempt to move until a gentle push sent her tottering through the doorway. She stumbled away like a sleepwalker, blind and deaf to her surroundings.

Lizard left next, after a brief exchange of regrets.

Alone with the Queen, Red ran her hands through her hair and scowled. "It's the big disadvantage of being a woman; you can't dispute who your children are. If I were a man, I could've questioned whether she really was mine."

"Nor can I deny that I'm her grandmother, but unlike you, I'll confess I'm saddened to lose her, particularly in this fashion," the Queen said quietly.

"You can't mean that."

"But I do. And I also think somewhere deep inside, you're grieving, too. Though I know you'll never admit it."

Red stuck out her chin. "That's because I'm not. If I'd been in your place, I'd have gone for framing one of the Rathshorn women for her murder."

"How can you say that? It's your flesh and blood we're talking about—mine, too."

"Supposing she doesn't leave the islands? Supposing she joins with Fearless-warrior?"

"She won't."

"How can you be so sure?" Red demanded.

"That's what this whole charade was about. I could have spoken to her in private, explained my suspicions about her preference in lovers, and asked her to go. Then she might have fled to Rathshorn. I had to drive it home that she had no future on any of the islands. There'd always be the risk of rumours catching up. On top of that, my guess is she'll want to get as far from Brec as possible. If she sails to the opposite end of the earth, she won't feel it's far enough."

"Well, it's my bet that she comes to a miserable end, no matter where she meets it."

"Hopefully not. Anyway, she should do better than she would here. If only she knew it, I've done her a favour. She wouldn't last five minutes in battle or five days as Queen. But if I thought she had a chance, I'd back her to the hilt."

"You've always had a soft spot for Tevi."

"While you've long preferred Laff. But let me tell you, Tevi would make a much better Queen. Leastwise, I'd feel happier passing Storenseg on to her care."

Red laughed in disbelief.

"I'm being serious."

"With respect, Mother, I think you are being blinkered."

"Tevi is neither a fool nor a coward."

"Nor is Laff," Red retorted.

"Laff doesn't think she can lose, and that's a good starting point for disaster."

"At least I can trust her."

"You can trust Tevi. She'd never betray a friend. Unlike Brec." Contempt was clear in the Queen's voice.

"Lizard will tell you it took a lot of argument and downright threats to get Brec to go along with this. Come to that, it took me enough time to talk Laff into assisting."

"She clearly wasn't happy."

"I'd have thought she'd be more eager for her chance to lead the war band."

"I've always suspected she taunted Tevi more to persuade herself of her dislike than anyone else—as do you."

Red scowled. "Anyway, it's over now."

"Oh, yes, for us." The Queen looked at her daughter with clear disapproval. "We'd better get to the celebrations before our absence becomes too marked." She stalked out.

Red collected the lamp and followed slowly, addressing her last comment to the empty barn. "I still think we're well rid of her."

❖

The rush of waves over sand sounded soft on the night air. Stars peeked between shreds of clouds. Tevi lay in the lee of her boat, wrapped in an old wool blanket. She was warm and sheltered but could not sleep. The scene she had made kept running through her head. It had gone much easier than expected. Carried by the pain of her betrayal, her vehemence surprised even those expecting the speech. People had sat stunned, some with jaws hanging open. The Goddess alone knew what the women from Rathshorn had made of it.

Throughout it all, her mother had stared at the ground, lips compressed in a tight line. Laff's eyes had darted nervously, not resting on anything, but particularly avoiding Tevi. No doubt some had added Laff's guilty expression to the fresh bruise on Tevi's face and drawn the wrong conclusions. Brec had been nowhere in sight. Only the Queen dared meet Tevi's glare, but that ancient face, schooled by decades of intrigue, had given no indication of her thoughts.

The surge of emotion had carried Tevi on. She had gone further than required, swearing by earth, wind, and water not to eat another mouthful or sleep another night under her family's roof until she returned with the stolen chalice. Now it was over, her rage had faded, and she was alone with her boat on the beach.

She placed a hand on the wooden hull, a small fishing boat barely fifteen feet in length. Normally, it held a crew of four, but without the need to handle nets, Tevi would have no trouble sailing it alone. Her grandmother had not said she could take it, but she could hardly be expected to leave Storenseg on foot. A day would suffice to stock the boat and gather her few belongings. Then she would be gone—forever.

Sounds from the feast were dying down. Only the occasional barked laugh or chorus of song disturbed the peace. The revellers were going to their beds. The poorest—the slaves and outcasts—would sleep crowded in rough shacks. The more fortunate would enter their family halls. In the Queen's house, the members of her family, cousins, aunts and nieces, would settle around the fire. At the edges, men of the household who were not claimed by a woman would sleep with the young children snuggled to them for warmth.

In that hall, Tevi had slept virtually every night since she was born. She could imagine the scene. Many, overcome by drink, would already be snoring loudly. Young girls, too excited to sleep, would be whispering jokes and gossip. And then there would be the quiet noises of women amusing themselves with their choice of man for the night, the only privacy coming from darkness and custom. It would be appalling rudeness to watch or make comment, but of course, everyone knew who every woman's lover was. Tevi realised she had been beguiled by the etiquette. It must have been so obvious that she always slept alone.

Even Great-Aunt Wirry, toothless and deaf, had taken a man four or five times a year right up to the month of her death. It had strained convention to the limit, only her great age sparing her. Like most deaf people, she underestimated the volume of her own voice. Tevi recalled once, when Wirry had snapped out, "What do you think you're doing now?" Back in the days before hostility had grown between Laff and her, the two sisters had shared a blanket. Laff had cupped a hand to Tevi's ear and suggested an answer so outrageous that she had been forced to bite on her arm to stop from laughing aloud.

The memory cut Tevi to the heart. Never again would she sleep in her family hall. She rolled onto her back and lay staring up. By now, Holric was silent. Tevi could hear the sea grass whispering in the breeze and then the sound of uncertain footsteps approaching.

She slipped from her blanket and crouched in the shadow of the boat. In the faint light, she could see a silhouette standing a few yards away. Tevi fumbled for her knife, worried that her grandmother might be putting another plan into effect.

"Tevi?" It was a quiet male voice.

"Who is it?"

At that moment, the moon drifted clear, illuminating the beach. Sparrow leapt forward and dived into her arms. Tevi was surprised to realise that he was crying.

"They say you're going," Sparrow said between sobs.

"That's true."

"Please don't."

"I've sworn an oath; I can't break my word."

Sparrow pulled back and sat upright. He turned his face from her. In the moonlight, his half-grown beard was invisible, and Tevi could see Brec's nose and Brec's high cheekbone. She had always known the source of the faint shadow of attraction she felt for Sparrow.

"You're going to get Abrak's chalice."

"That's what I said."

"How will you find it? I was in the square the day it was stolen. This big black bird just picked it up and flew straight out to sea. They say it was heading back to a sorcerer on the mainland. The chalice could be anywhere. How will you know where to look?"

There was no sensible answer. In the end, Tevi mumbled, "I'll talk to people on the mainland when I get there. Find someone who knows."

"Take me with you."

"Don't be silly."

"I mean it," Sparrow said earnestly.

"I'm leaving the islands. It's no place for a man." Tevi looked at him curiously. "Why do you want to go?"

"I like you. You're not the same as all the other women."

Tevi groaned inwardly.

Sparrow dug holes in the sand with his fingers as he continued. "All the men like you. You talk to us as if you're interested. The other women pester us. Some won't leave us alone, but you're the only one who acts as if you actually like men—as people, as if you want to be our friend."

Tevi tried to cover her surprise. "I've got to leave Storenseg, and I can't take you with me. The other women, they like men really. You'll be safe here with them."

"I'd rather be with you."

"You can't come with me."

"I'll miss you." Sparrow was crying again.

Tevi put her arm around his shoulder. "I'll miss you, too."

Sparrow continued pushing the sand back and forth while he built up courage for his next sentence. "Can I spend the night here with you? To remember you." Tentatively, he reached for her hand.

This time, Tevi groaned aloud and raised her eyes to the sky. Somewhere there was a goddess with a very poor sense of humour.

Sparrow drew back, hurt by her response. "You do like me, don't you?"

"Yes, I do, but...look, if things hadn't turned out how they did, I would have—" Tevi bit her tongue. She searched desperately for something to say. "I've got to go, and I don't know when I'll be back. It would be best if you tried to forget me, and sleeping with me tonight won't help. Also, I don't know what's ahead of me, but I'd rather face it without the chance of being pregnant."

Sparrow still wanted to argue, but Tevi did not give him the chance. "I think you should go back to your grandmother's. I'll escort you."

Nothing was said as they walked to the village. At the entrance to Lizard's family hall, they stopped. The square was deserted. Tevi was tall for a woman, her face level with Sparrow's. Tears were forming in his eyes. On a sudden impulse, she took hold of his shoulders and pulled him to her. They kissed while his arms tightened around her, exploring each other's mouths. For a moment, Tevi was tempted to change her decision just because Sparrow was the only person who wanted her. Yet finally, she pushed them apart. Sparrow stepped back, looking as if he was about to speak, but instead turned and disappeared into the hall.

Tevi walked back slowly. The moon lit familiar landmarks in harsh tones of black and white. She was overwhelmed by an unbearable sense of loss. This was the only world she had ever known; the fact that she did not like it hardly mattered.

Chapter Three—The Market Porter

Half a head taller than most of those about him, the middle-aged man wove between the jumble of stalls in the Torhafn market square. The first fanning of white hair at his temples accentuated his sharp features. Laugh lines around his mouth spoke of an active sense of humour, but he was not currently smiling.

The man, Verron, was aware that the quality of his clothing was attracting attention. The eyes of stall holders lit up as he approached. To his mind, the traders of Torhafn were no more honest than the pickpockets who were also sizing him up. Both groups were anticipating a well-filled purse, but Verron was far too experienced to fall prey to the cheap tricks of market thieves. He had seen it all before many times, although this did not mean he felt comfortable with his surroundings.

During his career as a Protectorate trader, Verron had been to many of the less attractive spots the world had to offer, yet Torhafn never ceased to impress him with its corrupt squalor. If a more sordid town existed anywhere in the world, Verron had no desire to see it, and particularly not after nightfall.

Centuries ago, Torhafn had been an elegant capital, the centre of a sorcerer's empire. The sorcerer and empire were now long gone. Only the ruins remained. The town huddled around its harbour, squatting amidst the ruined masonry. Timber and mud shacks encrusted the ancient walls. In the middle of the shabby marketplace, with its potholes and stench of rotting fish, two rows of broken columns raised themselves above a field of dirty cotton awnings, like the clean white rib bones of an ox protruding from the earth at the spot where the animal had met its end. Filth smeared the ground.

A stall holder held a length of material across Verron's path, flapping it to attract his attention. Verron neatly dodged both the vendor and his goods. There was nothing in the market he needed, and he did not have time to waste.

Numerous roads and alleys led from the square. Most were narrow, dark, and dangerous to walk down. Verron left the market on one of the wider streets, avoiding the tightly packed slums. Fortunately, he did not have to go far before he found what he wanted.

A group of mercenary warriors stood at a crossroad. The backs of their hands were tattooed with the red and gold swords of the Protectorate Guild, and their leather jerkins bore the badge of the recently formed Torhafn militia. The eldest was a granite-faced man whose hands were never far from his sword. As he approached, Verron made sure his own hands were clearly visible and away from any potential hidden weapon.

"Well met, fellow citizens. I'm Verron of Cottersford, a member of the Merchants' Guild."

The mercenaries assessed him for a few seconds before the eldest replied. "Well met, fellow citizen. Can we assist you?" The man's tone was polite but guarded.

"I hope so. I see you've all taken contract with the local militia, but I wonder if you know where I can find some of your comrades who're still available for hire."

"No chance of that, I'm afraid."

"Surely there must be some?"

"Not with how things stand."

Verron raised his eyebrows, inviting the speaker to continue.

"The local bosses have hired every able-bodied warrior who can tell one end of a sword from the other." The mercenary shrugged as he spoke.

"And a few who can't," another chipped in, contempt evident in her voice.

Verron pursed his lips. "So what is the situation at the moment?"

"What was the last you heard?"

"Before we left the Protectorate, we heard that the town council had created a proper militia to police the area. Has something changed?"

"*Town council* is an awfully grand name to give the bunch of thieves who run this place."

"You don't sound very fond of them." Verron spoke ironically. The councillors were not his idea of pleasant company either.

"I wish I'd never come here. I just want to serve out my contract and leave with the same number of arms and legs I started with." Several other mercenaries nodded their agreement. "As for the current situation, I don't know whether it started with good intentions, but half a dozen gangsters have taken control of the so-called council. It's my guess they're going to use us to thin out the competition. Now everyone is hiring bodyguards. I've never minded a good brawl, but when the blood starts flowing, it's going to be knives in the back down dark alleys." The man's jaw clenched in anger. "I'm a warrior, not a murderer."

Verron pinched the bridge of his nose, feeling like a fool. He had enough experience to know better. He should have guessed.

"Considering that the town has so much contact with the Protectorate, you'd have thought some of the civilisation would have rubbed off," someone muttered.

Verron shook his head. "Hardly. Torhafn just soaks up the worst the Protectorate has to offer. A large section of the population got here by fleeing justice in the Protectorate. Once they're over the Aldrak Mountains, they tend to stick around. The rest of Walderim is reasonably law-abiding and wouldn't put up with their nasty habits."

"You sound as if you're familiar with the town." The eldest mercenary spoke again.

"Only too well. We've been through every spring for the last five years, and we're always pleased to get away. Normally, we contract guild mercenaries before leaving the Protectorate, but when we heard a militia had been formed, we decided to wait until we got here before hiring guards. In hindsight, it was incredibly stupid of us." Verron sighed. "Do you know if there've been any robberies on the road south?"

The mercenary shook his head. "There's been no trouble that we've heard of. If it's any comfort, all the bandits have come into Torhafn to join the militia. The town is set to explode. The hills are probably deserted. Are you in a large group?"

"Just my partner and two of our children."

"Are your kids old enough to be much use in a fight?"

"No. They're just ten and fourteen. Last year, we had our eldest with us. She's handy with a crossbow, but she's joined the Ostlers' Guild and stayed behind in the Protectorate. We've got the youngster along in her place." Verron could not restrain his grimace. The presence of his youngest child made it so much harder to risk the road south without an adequate escort.

"You could go back to the Protectorate."

"We can't afford to abandon this year's trade cycle."

"One of our captains is in town. Given the circumstances, he might sell you a dispensation to hire non-guild guards," the mercenary suggested.

"I wouldn't trust any non-guild warrior that I picked up here. I'm afraid we're going to have to just take a chance."

"Oh, well, we mercenaries know all about that."

"I guess so, but thank you anyway for your time."

"I'm sorry we couldn't be more help. I wish you a safe journey." The faces of the mercenaries looked genuinely sympathetic as they parted.

On his way back, Verron's eyes frequently strayed to the fortified mansions on the hills overlooking the town, the homes of the gang leaders who ruled Torhafn. On previous visits, Verron had met some of the bosses. The elegance of their homes gave them a veneer of respectability, but hard-eyed henchmen always stood by, ready to follow any order.

The rest of Walderim, sandwiched between the Aldraks and the sea, was as civilised a land as could be found outside the Protectorate, but Torhafn was an ugly blemish on the country. It would, no doubt, stay that way until Walderim became part of the Protectorate, which was only a question of time. One day, a threat would come out of the Western Ocean sufficient to frighten the inhabitants into giving up their independence, swearing allegiance to the Coven at Lyremouth, and paying taxes to its sorcerers. Verron sighed. It could not happen too soon for his liking.

The two wagons with their cargo of merchandise still stood where he had left them, at the richer end of the market outside a warehouse. From their alert posture, it was obvious that his two sons, Derry and Kimal, were taking their guard duties seriously. Yet Verron knew the cargo's safety lay with the protection money the warehouse owner was paying to one of the local gangs—at least, the money he hoped the owner was paying. The boys smiled at the sight of their father.

"How's the haggling going?" Verron asked as he drew close.

"Last time I looked in, the merchant had tears in her eyes. I think it was something to do with her starving children. But I expect Mama will get the best of it in the end," fourteen-year-old Kimal answered with a grin.

"I expect so, too. She usually does."

Verron refrained from sticking his head through the doorway to witness the bargaining for himself. Over the years, he and his partner had reached a good working relationship, which involved the verbal side of business being handled by Marith. When money was involved, his partner could release a flow of rhetoric that would reduce Verron to giggles if he listened. Marith was a trader to the core of her being, and haggling was her favourite pastime. She would argue up the price of their goods as if her life depended on it. Not that she was tight-fisted—more that she took professional pride in never parting with a penny more than needed. It had been mainly at Marith's urging they had delayed hiring the guards.

Verron leaned against the wall and tried to ease the frown from his face. It was unfair to blame Marith for their present situation, and they would most likely reach Scathberg without meeting any criminal more menacing than an innkeeper who watered down the beer. More immediate was the danger that, caught in the passion of bargaining, Marith would lose track of time. Nightfall was less than an hour away. For the sake of a few small coppers, they should not risk reaching their lodgings after sunset.

Already, the shadows in the miserable alleys were hardening. The market was closing down for the day. Stall holders shouted frantically; the perishable goods that were not sold would be wasted. Even in Torhafn, it was hard to make a profit from rotten fish. Last-minute bargain hunters moved between stalls, but their numbers were dwindling.

The remaining people were poorer, more wretched and, if not more villainous, probably more desperate. Around the edge stood groups of vagrants and casual labourers, still hopeful of a little more work. Most looked like deserters from a zombie army; the rest looked drunk. As the carts got ready for departure, the vagrants moved in, searching the rubbish for anything of value.

Verron was just reaching the decision to join Marith and speed the negotiations when he heard movement. The hanging over the doorway was pulled aside.

"Your partner drives a hard bargain," the warehouse owner said in rueful tones.

"Oh, I know," Verron agreed.

Marith smiled as she passed, taking his words as a compliment, which in truth they were. Verron knew he would not succeed in trade half so well without her. Marith's light brown hair fell around her face in childlike curls; her body bordered on the plump; but her sweet-tempered, motherly exterior housed the keenest business mind Verron had ever met.

As he joined her by the wagons, she asked, "Did you find some guards?"

Verron shook his head. "There are local difficulties. We need to talk things over, but there isn't time now. Let's get the crates into the warehouse."

Marith accepted his words and turned to the warehouse owner. "We'll need to hire four labourers to unload the wagons."

"Let's make it eight. It's not long till dusk," Verron said.

From her expression, Marith was not convinced. However, the warehouse owner prevented any further debate by announcing, "Well, if she's free, you'll only need one porter." The woman scanned the clusters of people standing around the market, then raised her voice to a shout. "TEVI!"

A young woman detached herself from a nearby group and jogged towards them. In the evening light, her hair was dark, almost black. It lay in a spiky fringe, uncombed and hacked short. Her face and hands were grimy. She was dressed in rough, homespun material. However, the clothes were less ragged than those of the other porters. Rather than being barefoot, she had sandals on her feet. Even more unusual, her brown eyes met Verron's with honest candour as she came to a halt.

The warehouse owner gestured at the wagons. "These folk want their goods unloaded before the watch calls seven. Do you reckon you can do it?"

The porter looked at the sky, evaluating the time. "Sure," she said confidently. "Standard rate for the job?"

Marith looked confused but nodded. However, Verron could not stop from protesting, "Those crates are heavy. It took two men just to lift them."

"I can probably handle it," the porter said.

The warehouse owner winked and drew Verron out of the way. "Just watch."

The porter went to the first wagon and pulled on one crate gently, testing the weight. Then, in one fluid movement, she swung it off the wagon and walked towards the doorway, carrying the load with little sign of effort. Verron felt his jaw sag open.

One by one, the crates disappeared into the warehouse as the porter went on to empty both wagons well within the allotted time. Verron watched in astonishment. The woman was tall and sturdily built but certainly not muscle-bound. There was nothing to indicate the source of her strength. Once the last crate was safely stored, the porter walked back to the traders. Only the faintest sheen of sweat dotted her forehead.

"I think that's three copper bits you owe me." The porter held out her hand, although she seemed uncomfortable.

Marith pulled out the coins. Before the porter closed her hand, Verron added another three from his own purse. "For the entertainment value."

"Oh. That comes free of charge," the porter said, smiling.

"I'm sure you could use the extra," Verron insisted.

"I offered to work for the standard rate."

"You're still a lot cheaper than hiring another seven of your fellows."

The porter looked unhappy but then shrugged. "All right. I'll find a good home for the money." Her voice was a soft, lilting drawl, an accent Verron could not place, for all his years of travelling. She gave a respectful nod to the adults and a broad grin to Kimal and Derry, then strolled back across the square.

Verron turned to the warehouse owner. "Who is she?"

"Some youngster out to seek fame and fortune. She arrived by boat just over a month ago. I can't see her staying around long. She's too naive. I mean, when did you last have to offer money to a porter twice?" The warehouse owner's voice held something like astonishment.

"That won't last in Torhafn," Marith said pointedly.

"True enough. And she's far too honest. Not that there's anything wrong with honesty, of course," the warehouse owner added quickly, remembering her audience.

"But how is she so strong? It must be magic," Verron persisted.

The warehouse owner nodded. “Someone said she comes from an island way off to the west. They brew a magic potion that does it.”

That bit of information caught Marith’s attention immediately. “Do you think they’d be interested in trading for it?”

❖

The coins jingled in Tevi’s hand as she walked across the square. They felt hard, cold, and alien—rather like Torhafn itself. Money was not unknown on the islands, but she was not at ease with its general use. In Torhafn, it bought food and clothes, a mooring site on the quay, even the use of someone’s body for the night if you were so minded. With money, you could get whatever you wanted; without it, you could starve. Nothing mattered to the townsfolk except how much of it you had. To Tevi, money had come to mark the absence of trust, of honour, of family. She was tempted simply to open her hand and let the coins join the other debris of the market square.

The onset of dusk had sent most other porters to their homes. One ragged group remained, squatting on the steps of the tax office. They watched Tevi, hostility marked on their faces. One spat into the dust after she passed, not hiding his resentment. Tevi had earned more on the last job than they had made all day. Her strength and sobriety made her the merchants’ first choice. It also meant there was little the others dared do to object. In her first days, a few porters had tried, unwisely, to intimidate her. Now she received nothing worse than scowls and muttered comments.

Not everyone was unfriendly. An elderly voice called out, “Hey, Tevi!”

Tevi smiled and sauntered over to where old Aigur sat on a low wall with two of her grandsons in attendance. The elderly woman headed an enormous family with members scattered through all spheres of Torhafn life—few of them legal. Aigur had taken unconcealed pleasure in the rout of the market bullies. Realising that the young islander was unversed in the workings of the world, she had taken Tevi under her wing, giving freely of her lifetime’s store of advice. Despite her sharp tongue and questionable civic morality, Aigur was easily Tevi’s favourite person in Torhafn.

Aigur gave a toothless grin as Tevi stopped before her. A heavy blanket shielded her joints from the evening's chill. Her hair was white, her face deeply etched, but her eyes were as sharp as those of her teenaged grandsons.

"So how have you fared today?" she asked.

"Not bad." On impulse, Tevi held out the coins. "Here, I've got a present for you."

Aigur looked exasperated. "Don't be a fool. You can't go around giving money away."

"Why not? I've more than I need, and you've got more mouths to feed than me."

"That's not the point,"

"Yes, it is. It will help me sleep easier tonight."

"If you give money away, people will think you're a fool."

"So?"

"Fools make good targets."

"Then what do I do with money I don't want?" Tevi asked, not entirely in jest.

The elderly woman sighed and gestured to her grandsons. "If you're hell-bent on generosity, why don't you take these two layabouts to an inn and treat them? That way, you'll save me the expense of feeding them tonight, and I can still feel free to get ratty when they come home singing."

Tevi was about to argue when she saw the hopeful expressions on the young men's faces. "All right. Have it your way."

The two grandsons, Derag and Joran, eagerly leapt to Tevi's side. With an amused snort, Aigur rose and tottered off towards her crowded home on the edge of town. Her stooped figure disappeared around a bend.

Tevi looked at the two youths. "Well, boys, where would you like to go?"

Joran answered for the pair. "How about the Silver Mermaid?"

❖

A battered tankard was dumped in front of Tevi. Beer slopped over the top and rolled down onto the stained boards of the table. Tevi sat staring at it, making no attempt to touch the tankard. The metal was dull grey and pockmarked. It caught the light with the remembered sheen of Abrak's chalice, taunting Tevi in a fleeting vision of finding the heirloom and returning home.

She clenched her teeth, biting back the homesickness. The chalice was irrelevant; with or without it, there was no going back. The barman cleared his throat impatiently, reminding her of the need to pay. Tevi offered one of her coins, accepted a smaller one in change and then picked up her beer. The barman slouched away. Derag and Joran grabbed their drinks enthusiastically.

While surveying the tavern, Tevi sipped her beer, pacing herself carefully. She did not want to be wandering around Torhafn at night, alone and drunk—one of Aigur's many gems of advice. The bar had a low ceiling with smoke-blackened rafters. The tables were sturdy but well worn. The stone floor was sticky from spilt beer. The clientele was a cross section of the lower ranks of Torhafn society, except that the atmosphere was jovial and friendly, which was unusual, in Tevi's experience. After a few unpleasant encounters, she had avoided social contact with the townsfolk, Aigur's family excluded. However, leaning her elbows on the table, Tevi decided that the inn was a pleasant enough place to spend a few hours.

On the bench beside her, Derag and Joran were debating the merits of different ales. They were happy, giving voice to their opinions with a forthright vigour that, on the islands, would have been considered unseemly for men. Tevi watched with amusement. She was trying hard to come to terms with the men of the mainland. In her first days in Torhafn, she had formed the opinion that by shaving their faces, the men were trying to imitate the opposite sex. They certainly seemed to act like women. She now recognised that this conclusion was far too simplistic, especially as nobody seemed bothered when women acted in a manner the islanders would have considered masculine.

It was also received poorly if she treated Torhafn men with the patronising gallantry that was considered good manners on the islands. Tevi soon learned it was best to deal with each clean-shaven face as if it belonged to a woman—a trick that did not require the same mental gymnastics as it would on Storenseg. Without beards and distinctive styles of dress, Tevi found it very hard to tell men and women apart. She was often uncertain of a person's gender, even after lengthy conversation. On other occasions, she had formed an opinion one way, only to have subsequent events prove her wrong. The mainlander's flexible use of pronouns and other gender-specific words made her job harder, although it helped her hide her confusion.

"That old gut rot! It's awful." Tevi's thoughts were interrupted as Joran dug her with his elbow. "What do you say, Tevi? Have you ever drunk the cat's piss they serve in the Red Dragon?"

Tevi tried not to wince at the crude phrase coming from a male mouth. "I don't think so."

"You're lucky. I can guarantee it'd be the worst thing you've ever tasted."

Tevi smiled. "That's quite a claim. I doubt anything could outdo the potion they give girls back home."

"Is that the one that makes you so strong?" Derag asked.

"Came close to making me throw up as well."

"Even so, I'd happily down a bucketful." The young man sighed wistfully. "What do you reckon? If we sailed out there, do you think your family would sell us some?"

"Absolutely no chance." Tevi shook her head. "And it wouldn't do you any good. You have to take it regularly when you're a child. It doesn't work so well for boys even then."

Derag's shoulders slumped. "It would be great, though. Do you remember how you dealt with fat Barbo? Grandma smiles whenever she remembers it."

"I tried not to hurt him."

"I know. That's what made it so insulting for Barbo."

Joran joined in. "Why should you worry about hurting him? In your place, I'd have flattened the bastard."

"It's the way I was brought up. Women are so much stronger than men, it's seen as cowardly to hit them. But Barbo gave me no option. He had me cornered and wouldn't let me apologise. I hadn't meant to offend him."

"So you picked him up like a sack of flour and tossed him into the harbour." Joran's words were almost lost in his grin.

"What else could I do?"

"And what really amused Grandma was when you realised he couldn't swim—the way you dived in, dragged him out, and then offered to escort him home to his parents to explain how he'd got so wet." Both men dissolved in laughter.

Once he calmed down, Derag said, "You know, you're getting quite a name. People are—"

Whatever he might have been about to say was swallowed by a burst of noise from the far corner. All heads turned towards the disturbance. A crew of dock workers were cheering on one of their comrades who had left their table. From his size, Tevi was sure it was a man. His shoulders and arms were knotted with muscle; his head brushed the rafters, towering over the seated patrons. He did not look angry, but to Tevi's dismay, his eyes were fixed on her. The noise fell to a murmur. Tevi placed her hands on the table and pushed her bench back, readying herself for action. However, when the man reached her, he squeezed onto the opposite bench and smiled in a friendly fashion. Tevi took little reassurance from this.

"Good evening." The man's voice was a bass rumble.

"Good evening."

"I've heard that you reckon you're the strongest person in town."

"I make no claims."

"Then others do it for you."

"I can't help what people say."

"That's true." He watched Tevi from under bushy eyebrows. "Well, there's this game we play. It's called arm wrestling—"

His sentence was cut off as Derag whooped and slammed his palms on the table. "You'll slaughter him, Tevi."

One of the man's friends shouted back, "Three tin halves says she doesn't."

"You're on."

Tevi interrupted the betting. "I'm not going to fight you."

"It's just arm wrestling."

"And that isn't fighting?"

"Oh, no. It's just a test of strength."

Over the background commotion, it took the stranger and Joran some minutes to explain the rules. At last, Tevi understood what was involved. She studied the man. His arm would have served most people as a leg. She could not have joined the fingers of both hands around his biceps. In an assured manner, he rested his elbow on the table. Around the room, people stood on benches to get a better view.

"Are you on?" he asked.

She frowned. "It's no contest."

"You concede defeat?"

Joran nudged her. "Go on, Tevi."

Tevi sighed. "All right." She positioned her elbow on the table, stretching to grasp his hand. "Now I just push?"

The stranger nodded and started to apply pressure. Tevi considered her opponent thoughtfully. He really was very strong for a man; his bulk was evidently muscle rather than fat. Veins stood like rope on his arms and forehead. His breath came in raw, hissing gasps. Apart from this, the room was silent.

It was possibly the absence of sound from Tevi that finally alerted her opponent. His gaze shifted to her face. The man's expression fell in disbelief as he realised she was not even exerting herself. Tevi shook her head slowly, and a smile twitched at the corner of her mouth. In a jerk, she cracked his hand down on the table and released her grip. The audience exploded in uproar.

"I didn't hurt you, did I?" Tevi asked, suddenly contrite that she had overdone the force.

The man held out his hand to examine his knuckles. The skin was unbroken but showing red. His expression was one of utter bewilderment. His friends muttered among themselves. For a moment, Tevi wondered if he would make trouble, but then he threw back his head and roared with laughter.

With a beaming smile, he pointed at her tankard and asked, "What do you want to drink?"

Chapter Four—Torhafn by Night

By the time she left the Silver Mermaid, it was far later than Tevi had intended, and as her feet stumbled on uneven cobbles, she realised she had drunk slightly more than was wise.

Night had fallen, and doors were locked and shuttered, but the narrow, rubbish-filled streets were not deserted. Surly individuals posed aggressively at intersections, faces lost in shadow. Drunken gangs of youths jostled in the torchlight, their voices erupting in shouts as they spotted friends or rivals. One fight broke out as Tevi passed, but no one attempted to waylay her.

Derag was right to say she was acquiring a name in Torhafn. She had been pleased about it—trouble left her alone. However, as that night's challenge had shown, notoriety could also attract attention. So far, her reputation had not gone beyond the circle of quay and market, but if the gang bosses heard, there might well be attempts at recruitment or elimination. Worrying though it was, that danger could be dealt with when it happened. Right now, Tevi had to get safely back to her boat. She straightened her shoulders and walked purposefully through the darkened town.

The east wharf, with its houseboats, was one of the more depressing parts of a generally depressing town. The poverty, both material and spiritual, was sharply visible. Few of the boats were seaworthy. Many were little more than lashed-together rafts with flimsy shacks tacked precariously on top. The area swarmed with rats and other vermin, some of it two-legged. Rubbish floated in what little scum-covered water could be seen between the jostling boats. Everywhere were wide-eyed children, ragged and hungry.

The inhabitants formed a tightly knit community, spending the whole day in and out of one another's boats. Tevi had given up trying to make sense of their family structure, deciding that it was either nonexistent or so complex as to be incomprehensible to the outsider.

Throughout the day, the air was filled with shouting. People seemed to need to conduct their lives at high volume to compensate for the other deficiencies. At night, Tevi would lie in her boat, listening to the sounds of cold water slopping against the hull, creaking timber and the dull knock of wood on wood as boats rolled together. The only human sounds would be a baby crying or the distant shrieking of domestic strife. She desperately wished she were somewhere else, but in Torhafn, she had a mooring and an income, for the summer at least. Perhaps autumn would be a good time to move on.

Tevi paused and looked back along the squalid, filthy street. There was little she would miss about the town. Eventually, she emerged from the smothering crush of houses onto the open dockside. The usual assortment of people was visible in the pools of light from oil-soaked torches. Guards patrolled the warehouses; vagrants curled in corners; and a few drunk sailors staggered by the whores trying to attract their attention. Farther down the quay, dockers were loading a ship, working into the night so the vessel could depart on the dawn tide.

Tevi passed a lamp that smoked and guttered in the offshore wind. She stood on the pockmarked flagstones and breathed in deeply. The rising moon reflected off bands of luminous surf. The sound of the waves was gentle, calming, and somehow honest.

Tevi resumed her march along the dock. She jumped over a coiled rope and rounded the last warehouse. Her boat was moored less than twenty yards along the quay, although it was hidden between the larger houseboats. For once, the east wharf was peaceful—enough for her to hear the desperate sobbing from the depths of a rubbish pile. The sound of crying was not uncommon. Tevi intended to give only the briefest glance in passing. She had no wish to be drawn into the petty feuds between the inhabitants of the houseboats.

The source of the noise was a child of ten or so, huddled between two broken crates, head sunk on knees. The image of pitiful misery brought Tevi to a halt. All Aigur's advice told her to keep on walking, but her sense of caution was dulled by the beer.

She went over and knelt. "It's not that bad, surely?"

A tear-streaked face was raised to hers. The first thing Tevi realised was that the boy was not from the boats. He was too clean and well dressed. He gulped for air, but "Lost" was all he said.

"And how did you get lost?" Tevi asked gently.

"Don't know." The downturn of his eyes suggested that this was not the entire truth.

Tevi sat back on her heels and considered the boy. The townsfolk were always ready to leap to the worst conclusions. Tevi could expect few thanks and even a charge of kidnapping if she were found with the child, yet her thoughts drew her back to the islands, where everyone was known and recognised. A stray boy would be quickly taken back to his family hall. Tears came to Tevi's eyes as she wished she could be a child again—that somebody would come and take her home.

Tevi stared at the dark, menacing bulk of the town spread before her, full of locked doors and strangers. She took a deep breath and held out her hand, saying, "Come on. Let's go and find your parents."

❖

All along the wharf, decayed jetties projected over the polluted waterway. These were joined by lashed-together catwalks that formed a web of pathways between the decrepit assortment of boats. The rough-cut planks were covered with a slippery film of algae that made them treacherous to walk on—doubly so by night.

After instructing the boy to wait on the dockside, Tevi sidled out along the rotten timbers. Her small boat was moored on the seaward side of the swaying mass, between two derelict river barges that each housed several families of dock workers. The jetty swayed beneath her feet as the larger boats were pulled by the surge of the waves, drawing tortured groans from the piles driven into the seabed. Tevi reached the point where her boat was tethered. The tide was ebbing, and her boat was rocking gently several feet below the level of the jetty. She gripped hold of the mooring rope in one hand, then swung over the edge and dropped into the open end of the hull.

The boat was now her home. The mast had been lowered, and a waterproof tarpaulin sheet was draped over it as a roof, protecting the rear two-thirds from the elements. There was just enough space to crawl under the canvas, but it was adequate for her needs, particularly when judged by the standards of her neighbours.

At the rear was a heap of blankets and spare clothes, under which Tevi hid her weapons. Her hand closed around the scabbard of her sword, but she hesitated. Aigur had given lurid warnings of the dangers one could find roaming Torhafn by night. Tempting though it was to take the sword, it would be better to avoid confrontation. A visible weapon might attract more attention than it deterred. The best defence lay in her coarse-spun clothes, soiled by work in the market. She hardly presented the appearance to attract the attention of the professional thief and should not need a weapon to deal with any amateur opportunist.

Other considerations came to mind. Tevi peered from under the tarpaulin. Through the piles of the jetty, she could see silhouettes moving against the night sky. In what little honour they showed, the residents of the wharf did not steal from one another, but Tevi placed no trust in this honesty. She suspected it was only because the boat people owned nothing worth stealing. Since she could not guard her boat by day, she avoided displaying the few valuables she possessed. Tevi returned the sword to its hiding place and took instead a long knife, which she slipped inside her jerkin, out of sight.

She rejoined the boy, and the pair of them walked back along the quay, leaving tightly packed houseboats behind. To their left, the black ocean stretched out into the night. The cold wind carried the sound of unseen waves crashing against the crumbling harbour wall. They passed two figures arguing in a doorway and another staring bleakly out to sea.

On the western wharf, there was a scrum of activity beside the berth of a seagoing merchant vessel. Relays of dockers were manhandling bales and crates into the ship's hold. Another group stood nearby, awaiting fresh instructions while warming themselves around a fire and shouting humorous but impractical advice to their fellows. The flames snapped, sending a stream of sparks into the night sky. Hunched at one side, an old woman was stirring a large pot of stew. She was filthy, wrapped in layers of rags, but the smell of the food was tempting. Before going any farther, Tevi thought it might be wise to soak up the beer she had drunk.

Tevi stopped at the woman's side. "Is the stew for sale?"

"It's for the loaders...counts as part of their pay." The old woman glanced at Tevi. Her voice dropped. "Why? Did you want to buy some?"

"That would be nice."

"Well, as a favour, I can let you have a couple of portions for a tin half."

"I don't want you to get into trouble."

"I made the stew. I can sell it, but don't let everyone see. I don't want the whole dockside bothering me."

Tevi passed over the coin without comment. With the two bowls in her hands, she nonchalantly strolled to a spot behind a mound of cargo, obscured from the view of anyone aboard ship. Of course, the woman was planning on pocketing the money, and the term 'whole dockside' referred specifically to the work overseers, who would be angry if they knew—not because the woman was selling what was, technically, their employer's property, but because they did not get their cut of the profit. It was the way things worked in Torhafn.

Tevi and the boy sat on an empty crate and sipped the hot stew, using crusts of stale bread as scoops. The stew was highly spiced—probably to disguise its contents. Despite this, the food was welcome, and its warmth offset the night's chill. The boy's spirits had improved, bolstered by the upturn in his fortune. His eyes fixed on Tevi.

"I know you. You're the strong porter from the market who unloaded our wagons. My name's Derrion, but everyone calls me Derry," he said happily.

"And everyone calls me Tevi."

"Is that your full name?"

"More or less." Her birth name was something Tevi was happy to have left behind on Storenseg.

In the light of the fire, Tevi also recognised the boy, despite the dirt and the streaked lines of tears that now adorned his face. His parents had been wealthy foreign traders and, to judge from the extra payment, more generous than the local townsfolk. They might even be grateful for the return of their son.

"Do you have any idea where your mother and father might be?" Tevi asked.

"Probably at the inn."

"Which inn? Can you remember its name?"

The boy considered the question gravely. "No." After a moment's thought, he added brightly, "There was a sign hanging outside, though."

"What was on the sign?"

"It was a barrel."

"I think you'll find every inn in Torhafn has a barrel outside as its symbol," Tevi said dryly.

"Really?"

"Yes."

Derry took a mouthful of stew and grinned. "I'm not being much help, am I?"

Tevi tried a different approach. "After leaving the market, did you cross over the river?"

"Yes. And we climbed up the hill beyond, but not quite to the top."

This was only as Tevi expected. The west side of the river Tor was the richer part of town, where the better class of inn was found. It was the place one would expect wealthy traders to stay, but the confirmation of her guess gave her somewhere to start the search.

"Do you think you'd recognise the inn if you saw it again?" Tevi asked.

"Probably."

"Well, then, if you've finished your stew, we might as well be off."

Instead of moving, Derry became unaccountably dejected. "Do you think Mama and Papa will be angry with me?" he mumbled.

"You know your parents better than me."

"I'm going to be in big trouble."

Tevi was about to assure him that no one would be too hard on a boy, but stopped. Maybe on the mainland, a misbehaving boy might be punished no less severely than a girl. Her face softened, and she tousled his hair. "Even if they are angry, you can't stay here forever," Tevi said sympathetically, reaching for his hand. "Come on, let's go."

Tevi led the way into the maze of houses behind the docks. The sinking moon lit the wider roads but did not penetrate the small alleys. Fewer street gangs were about than earlier, although they were more blatantly ill willed. They watched the pair with hostile eyes but made no move to intercept them. Angry shouts told of fighting a few streets away; then a scream cut above the clamour. Tevi was glad to be heading away from the brawl.

The marketplace was deserted as they skirted its edge on their way to the main bridge. The shop fronts and warehouses were blank and lightless. Even the gangs seemed to have melted into the dark, leaving only a threatening silence. Derry was jittery.

Tevi put her arm around the boy's shoulder. "It will be better once we cross over the bridge."

However, they did not get that far. The narrow passageway from the market opened onto a riverside wharf for unloading barges. The open area was about ten yards wide and five times as long. The moon lit the water's edge, but the shadows of warehouses covered the other side in darkness.

Derry suddenly grabbed her arm and pointed. "There they are." Despite his excitement, the oppressive, darkened town had affected him, and his voice was barely a whisper.

Tevi followed the direction of Derry's outstretched arm and saw his parents at the far end of the wharf. That was not all she saw. The well-cut clothes and obvious wealth of Derry's parents had not gone unnoticed. Silently emerging from a dark passage, halfway down the wharf, were two stocky figures. The thugs crept furtively through the shadows, cudgels in hand.

Tevi propelled the boy into a darkened doorway. "Stay here, and don't make a sound," she whispered.

The knife felt reassuring as Tevi pulled it from her jerkin and slipped it into her belt. Then she, too, began to edge around the walls, keeping to shadows.

The traders were deep in conversation and obviously unaware of the danger until a third figure stepped into the moonlight.

"Well, well, well. What have we here?" A woman's light voice delivered the mocking phrase with real menace.

Derry's parents jerked around and then backed away, unknowingly retreating towards the two thugs. The other footpad stood her ground, hand on hip in jaunty belligerence, then snapped her fingers. At the signal, the two accomplices stepped from the shadows, swinging their clubs. The sound of footsteps behind them rooted the pair of traders to the ground as they realised they were trapped. The leader of the gang began a slow advance towards her victims, clearly enjoying the game.

"Now why don't you behave yourselves, and hand over all your money and anything else that you think I might like?"

The gang's attention was fixed on the traders. No one noticed Tevi's stealthy approach. As the leader got within a few steps of Derry's parents, Tevi made her move. The nearest thug was hoisted into the air and hurled against the other, sending the pair of them smashing into a brick wall. They collapsed to the ground in a mound of arms and legs.

Tevi did not wait to see if the thugs would offer further resistance. Maybe Derry's parents would have the presence of mind to claim the dropped cudgels for themselves. She charged past the traders, bearing down on the third thief, only to be confronted by a drawn sword.

The years of training took over. Before Tevi realised it, her knife was in her hand and outstretched before her. She dropped to a defensive stance and met the gang leader's angry eyes. The pair of them glared at each other.

Tevi broke the silence. "Why don't you go and find someone else to play with?"

"Why don't you get out of my way?" The woman sounded rattled by the unexpected interruption, but she was not ready to back down. The two adversaries began to circle, watching for an opening.

In icy calm, Tevi reviewed Blaze's advice on how to fight when your weapon was outmatched. *Let your opponent make the moves. She'll be overconfident. Take no risks. Watch what she does. Wait for the mistake*. It was the style of combat in which Tevi was at her worst. The memory of countless defeats in practice assailed her, but this time, her life was at stake.

The thief's sword flicked out in a few feints to test Tevi's defence; amateurish efforts, easily blocked, and the sureness of Tevi's response drew a frown. Clearly, Tevi was not an untrained novice making free with someone's kitchen utensil.

For her part, Tevi was surprised at how easy it was. It was as if she could hear Blaze's voice, offering advice.

"*She's going for your throat!*" Blaze screamed, even as the woman made a more ambitious high thrust. In reflex, Tevi ducked and knocked the blade aside. She swung across sharply in riposte and felt the knife make contact. The footpad gasped and lurched a few steps backwards. They both knew it was merely a flesh wound, but the woman was unnerved, and her eyes flicked anxiously around the square.

The traders had been frozen in paralysis, but now they began to shout loudly.

"Help!"

"Call the watch!"

Tevi grimaced. Like all Torhafn residents, she knew the town watch were unlikely to come to anyone's aid. However, the sound further alarmed her opponent.

"Shut them up," the gang leader snapped to her accomplices, but a glance showed that she could expect no support. The thugs had barely managed to clamber to their feet. One appeared to have a broken arm. The other, with a blood-smeared face, was still braced against the wall. The cudgels lay where they had fallen. The leader's bravado had completely gone when the new sound of running feet reverberated around the walls.

The circling meant Tevi's opponent now had her back to the square. Over the woman's shoulder, Tevi could see that the approaching footsteps belonged to Derry. He was running down the wharf, wildly swinging a wooden stake. Fortunately, the thief did not want to hang around. She jabbed with her sword. Tevi parried easily but was forced to step aside. This was what the gang leader had intended—clearing her escape route. After one last swipe, she rushed past Tevi and disappeared down the dark alley.

Tevi watched her go and then turned to the two thugs. She gestured with her knife. "You can clear off as well."

No second bidding was needed. The pair hobbled in pursuit of their leader with what speed they could manage. The sound of their uneven footsteps faded away.

Tevi's gaze was caught by the dark smearing of blood on her knife. She looked at it thoughtfully before wiping the blade clean. Over by the water's edge, Marith had caught hold of Derry and was simultaneously hugging him while wresting the stake from his hand. Verron's face was pale in the moonlight, and his upper lip was beaded with sweat, but a relieved smile was spreading over his features.

Tevi slipped her knife into her belt and walked towards him. Suddenly, into her head came Blaze's voice, hammering out her favourite lesson: "*No matter how defeated she seems, never, never, never turn your back on an enemy.*"

Tevi spun around just in time to see a dark figure swinging its arm down in an arc. Without time to think, Tevi pitched backward, deliberately colliding with Verron and knocking him down. The knife flew overhead, passing through the space Verron had been occupying and went on to skitter harmlessly across the cobbles. Tevi let her momentum roll her over her shoulder and up onto her feet in a fluid motion, but the figure was already gone.

Tevi took a long step back to steady herself, only for her heel to hit a mooring ring anchored into the flagstones. The evasive roll had taken her a lot closer to the river than she intended or realised. The ring wedged between her sandal and foot, twisting her ankle. Her arms flailed in a desperate bid for balance, but no paving was beneath her second foot as it came down. Helplessly, Tevi tumbled backwards into the river.

The traders rushed to the embankment and threw a line to help her climb onto the quay, where she knelt, wiping water from her eyes and trying desperately not to think about how filthy the river looked in daylight. In response to the barrage of concerned questions, Tevi simply shook her head. It was exactly the sort of ending her mother would have predicted for her first serious duel.

❖

The traders' lodgings were small but comfortable, easily the most luxurious place Tevi had ever seen. She stretched her feet towards the fire and sank into the cushions on her chair. The room was currently empty apart from her. Her clothes were hanging on a rack by the fire and appeared to be drying nicely in the warm air. Amber light from the burning logs danced cheerfully over an array of tapestries and furniture. Tevi's toes dug into the thick sheepskin rug. A fresh awareness struck her of how austere life on the islands was; even the Queen's hall could not match the display of wealth about her. Yet she knew that, by the standards of the mainland, Verron and Marith were well off but not rich.

The door to the boys' bedroom opened and Verron emerged. He sank into a chair with a sigh.

"Are they asleep?" Tevi asked.

"Pretending to be. I think they just wanted me to go so they could talk."

"Have you sorted out how Derry got lost?"

Verron shook his head. "I doubt we'll ever get the full story. I don't think he's too certain himself. I'm just so relieved to have him back safe." Contrary to fears about his parents' anger, Derry's only ordeal had lain in being smothered by repeated hugs.

"You'll be wanting to sleep soon as well. Once my things are dry, I'll leave. You can have these back." Tevi indicated the borrowed clothes she had on.

"Please, you're welcome to keep them. They're only some old garments we had lying around. They were due to be thrown away."

"They may be cast-offs to you, but if I walk around Torhafn wearing these, I'll attract the same sort of attention you did."

Tevi suspected she would attract attention anyway. By the time she had escorted the family to their lodgings, she had been shaking from the twin effects of the cold dunking and ebbing adrenaline. On the other hand, the traders had regained their self-assurance. They insisted that she come inside and had badgered the innkeeper into providing food, drink, and a hot bath. The last of these had been a new experience for Tevi and she was still trying to evaluate whether she liked it. Whatever her final decision, it was certain that the effect would make her stand out from the other market workers for at least a week.

From the corridor outside, Marith's voice called indistinctly; then the handle turned and she entered, bringing a bottle of sweet brandy and three round glasses.

"Is the innkeeper calm now?" Verron asked.

"Reasonably," Marith said while pouring three generous measures of the brandy.

"And you didn't pay him double for the late meal?"

"Of course not." Marith pouted at the idea. She distributed the drinks and sat down.

"I could have warned him that separating you and money is like getting a limpet off a rock,"

"That's not true. For example, I'm going to try again to get Tevi to accept a reward."

Marith's indignant tone made Tevi grin. However, she still shook her head. "I don't want paying."

"But I insist."

"I don't particularly like money."

The answer left Marith nonplussed. In the resulting silence, Verron asked, "We were told that the people on your home island make a potion that gives you your strength. Do you think they might trade for it?"

"Never." Tevi had no doubt of her answer.

"We'd pay well. You might mention it when you return. Do you have any idea when that might be?"

"Never."

At first, Verron must have assumed that Tevi was merely repeating her previous assertion. His surprise showed when he realised what she meant. "But surely your family will miss you, and..."

Tevi fought to keep the pain from her face. From the way Verron's voicc trailed off, she knew she had failed.

After an awkward silence, Marith took up the conversation. "So you're planning on staying in Torhafn?"

"For the summer. Maybe I'll move on after that."

"Then you must accept a reward to see you through winter, when work dries up. We can really never thank you enough for finding Derry and rescuing us."

"It was nothing. I only regret leaving my sword behind."

"You've got a sword!" Marith said in surprise.

"And a shield, a short spear, and a hunting bow."

Marith swirled the brandy around in her glass thoughtfully. "I guess you have to be well armed in a town like this."

Tevi's composure had recovered enough for her to smile. "Oh, I wouldn't dream of walking around the streets with all that on me. But is Torhafn so much worse than anywhere else?"

"Definitely. You've picked the nastiest town I know."

"Where else would you recommend going?"

"Anywhere. It would have to be an improvement."

"Except the Halvia peninsular," Verron chipped in.

"What's wrong with Halvia?" Tevi asked.

"A family of dragons."

"Oh."

"But there's lots of other places you could make a decent living, and there are so many things you should see." Little encouragement was needed for the traders to launch into an enthusiastic account of their travels, which rapidly turned into a nostalgic review, their audience forgotten.

"You remember the first time we met?" Verron asked his partner.

"You won't let me forget it."

"There you were, hanging over the rail on the aft deck. I don't know about the ship, but you were certainly eight sheets to the wind."

"I was seasick, not drunk!" Marith said indignantly.

"So you said, but I've never seen you have trouble sailing since."

Tevi settled into the chair and closed her eyes. She had been working at the market from first light. The voices faded to a background hum as the warmth and the brandy overpowered her in a softly enveloping cocoon of sleep.

❖

Tevi awoke with a start. The fire had burned down to a dull glow, and the pale colour of her clothes indicated that they were dry. While she had slept, Marith and Verron had shifted away and were talking quietly, their heads close together.

Tevi hauled herself upright and said, "I must be off."

At Tevi's words, the two traders exchanged small nods as if a decision had been reached.

Marith spoke. "Actually, we've got a proposition to put to you. Tonight has brought home to us that we're very vulnerable. Normally, we'd have hired a couple of mercenary guards, but due to local difficulties, they're in short supply. We desperately need extra protection."

"You want to employ me as a bodyguard?"

"Ah...well..." Marith hesitated. "It's not quite that simple. We're members of the Protectorate Guild of Traders and Merchant Adventurers. Our guild has a negotiated agreement with the Guild of Mercenary Warriors so that we're only allowed to hire their members to guard us or our property. In return, we get discount rates. If we were caught breaking the rules, we'd be flung out of our guild, and all our loans would be revoked."

"Then what is your proposition?" Tevi asked, confused. A month before, Marith's words would have been complete gobbledegook to her. Now, she could just about draw some sense from them.

"Well, there's nothing to stop you coming with us as a friend. We could even pay you a reward, as long as we make it very clear that it's purely for finding our son."

"But of course, if we were attacked by bandits, we'd be very pleased if you were to defend yourself," Verron added brightly.

Tevi frowned as she considered what the traders had said and what they probably meant. "Isn't that what they call 'bending the rules'?"

Marith shrugged. "Oh, no. Just being a little imaginative in interpreting them."

While she turned the idea over, Tevi watched the embers twinkling on the burning logs. She did not know the identity of the thieves she had clashed with, but it was certain she had made enemies that night. Leaving Torhafn might be a very good idea—and sooner rather than later.

She nodded "It sounds better to me than staying here. When do you leave?"

"Tomorrow. Will that be all right?"

"I've got a boat in the harbour. I'm not sure what to do with it."

Verron smiled. "Well, if you like, Marith will help you sell it."

Chapter Five—The Trade Route

The watch were calling midday and Torhafn market was awash with its usual chaotic activity as the last bale was loaded onto the wagon. Tevi heaved it into place and then helped Verron and Kimal secure the tarpaulin cover. Nearby, Marith was finalising payment to a fur trader from northern Walderim, who appeared to be wearing half his stock across his own broad back.

"I hear you're leaving town."

Tevi glanced around at the voice. Aigur stood behind her. "Yes."

"Derag said you came looking for me this morning."

"I wanted to say goodbye. These folk have asked me to go with them, and it's not safe for me to stay in Torhafn."

"Yes. Derag told me about that as well." Aigur nodded in the trader's direction. "They're from the Protectorate?"

"Yes."

"You'll be going there with them?"

"Is that not wise?"

"You could do a lot worse." Aigur looked wistful. "I'm tempted to go back myself."

"You came from the Protectorate?" Tevi asked in surprise.

"Long ago. And if I hadn't been a fool, I'd never have been forced to leave. It's a good place for the honest. You should do well."

"Well...maybe." Tevi shrugged self-consciously.

"Oh, go on with you." Aigur nudged her in the ribs. "Promise me something?"

"Of course."

"There's a town called Longford Ash. You won't find anyone there who remembers me, or if they do, they won't speak well of me, but if ever you pass through, go to the Blue Boar Inn. Buy a tankard of their best ale, and toast the old place for me."

"I will. I promise."

Aigur gave a toothless smile and patted Tevi's arm. "Good luck. May your gods watch over you."

"And may your gods watch over you."

"I think they gave up on me long ago."

The wagon rocked as Verron climbed onto the driver's seat. Aigur met Tevi's eyes. "I think your friends are ready to go. Farewell, Tevi."

"Farewell, Aigur."

A lump rose to Tevi's throat. Life in the islands had given her little experience at goodbyes—until recently. Her purse was heavy with coin from the sale of her boat. She was tempted to give it to the old woman, but she knew the offer would be refused. All Tevi could do was smile and take her place by Verron. When she looked back, there was no sign of Aigur among the market crowd.

Marith, with Derry beside her, steered the leading wagon. Kimal rode on a saddle pony that was dwarfed by the huge carthorses. The wagons crawled through the busy streets, rumbling over uneven cobbles. Tevi watched the stream of mean faces flow past. She was not sorry to be leaving. The weather was at its most dismal for their departure, a grey overcast morning holding the promise of rain. Colours were muted in the sullen light. To the east, the Aldrak Mountains were lost in cloud.

A ruined gatehouse marked the remains of the old city walls. Thereafter, the dwellings became even more squalid, and the road turned into a rutted dirt track. Soon, they left the last miserable hovels behind and began the steep ascent into the hills south of Torhafn. As the gradient sharpened, the horses strained against the load, their harness creaking alarmingly. A niche cut into the rock held a small shrine. Tevi stared at the statue to take her mind off the sheer drop on the other side of the road. The nearer horse snorted.

"Is this road safe?" Tevi asked.

"There won't be any bandits this close to town,"

"I was thinking more about falling."

Verron smiled. "The horses will manage fine."

After more hairpin bends, the road levelled out. Verron leaned back and relaxed his grip on the reins. "I'm always glad to get out of Torhafn. It's the worst town I know, and I've seen some rough spots. Marith and I used to work the eastern seas, out past Ekranos and the straits of Perithia. We even travelled north to Tirakhalod a few times."

"You don't go there anymore?"

"They can be dangerous places. We risked it because there's a fortune to be made. But now we're getting older, we prefer a quieter life. For the last few seasons, we've done the southern trade route. It's a lot safer, apart from Torhafn. There's not as much profit, but we've built enough capital to trade in luxuries."

"I'd heard that in the Protectorate, the sorcerers take everyone's money."

"Not all of it. We pay our tithes to the Guild, who pass some on to the Coven as taxes."

"You don't mind paying taxes?"

Verron laughed. "I admit I'd rather not, but there isn't any option. Sorcerers have controlled every civilisation since time began. The Coven of Lyremouth leads the Protectorate, but they let the guilds manage their own internal affairs. It's benign and, best of all, stable. The Protectorate has been going for over four hundred years, which makes it unique."

"What happened to the other civilisations?"

"They collapsed when the sorcerer who built them died. But when the head of the Coven dies, they just elect another Guardian."

Tevi frowned. "Aigur said the Protectorate was a good place to live."

"It is, but you'll have to wait to see it—not until we reach Serac in the autumn."

The wagons reached the crest of the hill. Ahead of them, the road dipped across a swathe of rolling moor. Tevi twisted in her seat and looked back. Seen from a distance, Torhafn was not so bad. If you did not know better, you could imagine the docks were quaint. Tevi's gaze shifted to the horizon, a grey blur of rain and mist. Far out to sea was Storenseg. Then the wagons rolled forward, and both town and sea were lost over the brow of the hill.

❖

Despite Verron's fears, the journey to Scathberg went without incident. The only people on the road were fellow traders and couriers. To pass the time, Verron gave Tevi lessons in steering the wagon, and Kimal taught her riding.

The mountainous islands had not favoured land travel; the sea was the main highway and the original settlers had not taken horses with them. As a girl, Tevi had sat on the wiry donkeys that were used to pull carts, but that had been a game for children, not a method of transport. However, Tevi soon acquired a degree of competence on horseback.

They entered Scathberg eighteen days after leaving Torhafn. The sun was high as they rode down the main street, lined with shops and houses. The architecture bore a strong resemblance to the richer parts of Torhafn, with grey stone buildings and slate roofs, but there was no way Tevi could confuse the two towns.

"It feels friendlier," she said to Verron.

"True. You don't have to sit with your back to the wall in the taverns."

The distinctive sound of a market was growing louder, a hubbub overlaid with the shouts of peddlers. Just before they reached it, the wagons turned into a courtyard and came to a halt. A thin young man of twenty or so stepped out of a doorway. Although it was midday, his bleary eyes and dishevelled clothing revealed that he had not long been awake. The dark shadow of stubble on his jaw allowed Tevi to be sure of his gender.

Marith jumped down. "Well met, Yarle."

"Well met, Marith, Verron." He gave a half-hearted nod.

"Is your mother available?"

"She died last autumn. I'm running the business now," Yarle said, looking at his feet.

Marith floundered for a suitable response. "I'm sorry to hear that. I enjoyed doing business with her."

"She got a fever."

"That's tragic. She wasn't old."

Yarle shrugged. He clearly did not want to discuss it. "You're here to trade?"

"Of course. I'll show you our goods." Marith took her lead from the young man.

A tap on her knee made Tevi look down. Verron had wandered around the wagon. "We'll leave Marith to it. She works best on her own." He raised his voice. "I'm going to show Tevi around the market. You can meet us at the Three Barrels when you're finished. I'll reserve a couple of rooms."

"That'll be fine," Marith called back, preoccupied with the business of barter. She spared no more attention as Tevi and Verron left the courtyard, accompanied by the two boys.

❖

Marith joined them an hour later, sitting on benches outside the inn, overlooking a small square. Around the central fountain, children were playing and a few servants stood gossiping. Porters trundled across pushing handcarts or balancing baskets on their heads. In the distance, the Aldrak Mountains raised their snow-covered peaks against a clear blue sky.

"How did it go with Yarle?" Verron asked.

"Like a lamb to the slaughter. I almost felt sorry taking the money. He'll never be in business by next year. He's got as much talent for bargaining as I have for flying."

"Did you get the shirt off his back?" Verron teased.

"You could have given him an easy deal," Kimal added mischievously.

"We're not in business for charity. If I don't get his money, someone else will. But it's a shame. I respected his mother." Marith shook her head. "Are you ready to see to the wagons?"

Verron answered by standing and linking arms. Tevi and the two boys followed. While she walked, Tevi considered Yarle's situation. Her island-born morality was appalled at the thought of a young man, helpless and alone, being cheated—not that Marith was dishonest, but the experienced trader had an unfair advantage.

Tevi turned to Kimal. "Is there no one to help Yarle? Doesn't he belong to a guild or something?"

"You don't get guilds here—not the same as in the Protectorate. Anyway, from what Mama said, I can't see a guild lending him money."

"He wouldn't need to borrow money; he's got his mother's."

"But in the Protectorate, he wouldn't have inherited the money."

"Why not?"

"Because, strictly speaking, it wouldn't have been hers in the first place."

"Who would it belong to? The Coven?"

"No, the guild, of course." Kimal's tone implied that the answer was obvious.

"Your parents have got money...haven't they?"

"Not really. When they finished their apprenticeship, the guild licensed them and gave them their advance to set up in business. They could do what they liked with the money, within reason, though they have to pay tithes. But when they die, the guild will take everything back."

"You and Derry won't get to share it?"

"No."

The prospect clearly did not bother Kimal in the slightest, but Tevi was confused, not so much about the thought of losing money as the complete disregard for family and inheritance. She remembered being told that there were no hereditary leaders in the Protectorate.

Kimal carried on. "Hopefully, we'll be in guilds for ourselves long before our parents die. I mean, it must be awful, having to wait until your parents peg it before you can start your own career."

"Don't your parents want you to take over their business?"

"Why should they?" Kimal seemed as confused as Tevi. "We might not want to be traders."

"You told me that you did."

"I want to be a mercenary," Derry cut in loudly.

Kimal ignored his brother. "True, but when I'm ready I can get my own advance, if the guild think I'm good enough."

"And if you're not good enough?"

"Then there'd be no point in my parents giving me their business, would there?" Kimal said reasonably. "It makes sense. Protectorate traders always come out best, 'cause we don't let fools make a mess of things just because of who their parents were."

Tevi did not answer. It seemed a strange way to organise things, but how much simpler it would have been if her family had simply accepted that she was not cut out to be queen and had chosen someone more suited for the job, such as Laff. The corners of Tevi's mouth turned down as she realised that this was exactly what they had done.

The wagons were waiting in the courtyard. Yarle watched sullenly as Tevi unloaded the cargo. The others helped with lighter items and soon the party was ready to depart. Yarle had counted the load into his storeroom but seemed unsure what to do next. He still had not shaved. To Tevi's eyes, it made him even more pathetically vulnerable.

"Is everything all right?" She had to try to help him.

"Why shouldn't it be?"

"It's a lot of responsibility, running a business."

Yarle looked her up and down. "I can cope."

"Isn't there someone who can help you? A cousin or an aunt? People might take advantage of a young man."

"I don't need help." A surly note entered Yarle's voice.

"But it's not fair to expect you to run your own finances."

"I'm not an idiot."

"I wasn't saying you were. I just think you could do with a woman to look after you. It's too much to expect a boy to take care of himself."

"What are you going on about?" Yarle's voice rose. "I'm not a child. I'm probably older than you."

"Yes, but..." Tevi stopped herself before she finished the sentence; *it's not the same for a woman*. It was the island's way of thinking and, rightly or wrongly, would not be understood on the mainland. She drew a deep breath and tried to forget she was talking to a man. "It's just... losing your mother must have been a shock and...I thought you might need advice, or..."

"I don't need anyone's advice," Yarle snarled. He marched into his storeroom, slamming the door behind him. Tevi glanced over her shoulder at the others.

"I didn't mean to insult him."

Verron's face held a perplexed frown. "If you don't mind me saying so, you sometimes have a problem taking men seriously."

Tevi sighed and raised her eyes to the sky. "I know, but I'm working on it. Believe me, I'm working on it."

❖

The line of wagons rolled out of Scathberg, accompanied by the crunch of stones, the shouts of riders and the crack of whips. Hired guards flanked the caravan as outriders. Tevi was halfway down the line with the reins in her hands and Verron beside her.

Hills rose on either side, striped with rows of grapevines—the source of the famed red Scathberg wine. Between the neat lines, the ground was dry and bare except for tufts of yellow grass. Greystone farmhouses dotted the vineyards. High above, the sun shone through wisps of cirrus cloud. A light morning breeze carried dust, stirred up by the horses ahead.

"How far will we go with these people?" Tevi asked.

"Through the desert to Kradja," Verron replied. "Then we'll join another caravan for the journey to Limori."

"Do you travel with groups for protection?"

"Partly. It's also a way to share resources. The desert is unpredictable; landmarks shift. If we were on our own and we missed a water hole, it could be fatal. The nomads are friendly, but you can't rely on them coming to your rescue."

"How long till we get to Kradja?"

"Twenty-three days, twenty-five at most," Verron estimated.

"Kimal said there's an enormous temple there."

"There certainly is."

"We had a shrine in the middle of our village. I've been trying to imagine it scaled up, but I guess the temple won't be quite like that."

"I doubt it. Unless your people confuse brooding with meditation and have a liking for cryptic images and overblown dramatics."

Tevi grinned and flicked the reins to encourage the horses to keep up. Behind them, the walls of Scathberg shrank into the distance and soon were lost among the farmlands.

❖

As they moved southwards, the landscape became ever more arid. Trees gave way to waxy-leafed shrubs. On the nineteenth day out of Scathberg, they reached the edge of a plateau. An eroded escarpment overlooked a plain of dust and rock beneath a turquoise sky. Isolated cacti were the only things growing on the parched landscape.

That night, they pitched camp in a gully where clumps of greenery indicated underground water. This was confirmed once they swept windblown sand from the well cover. A guide told Tevi that during the autumn rains, the gully was a riverbed. It was strange to think of water flowing through this dry land. The sun sank low, and after the heat of the day, the wind was chill as it whispered across the desert.

When the evening meal was over, Tevi took a thick cloak and

left the fireside. From the top of the gully, she watched the sunset turn the sky to fire. The heavens flamed gold first, then blazed with fierce red that smouldered to purple and finally blackness, strewn with white sparks of stars. Tevi stared across the barren land in awe at the harsh, inhuman beauty. She returned to the camp with tears in her eyes. She had not wanted to leave Storenseg and wished with all her heart that she could return, yet to have lived her life without ever seeing a desert sunset would have been an unbearable loss.

Five days later, they reached the oasis town of Kradja, a sprawling mass of mud-brick houses, the same colour as the ground, so that the town seemed to be growing from the desert. Without transition, the rough trail became a dusty street crowded with workers, children, merchants, and servants. The air was filled with shouts and the jingle of horses' harnesses. Robed nomads led strings of improbable gangling beasts with sinuous necks and a wobbling lump on their backs.

"Camels," Verron told her, seeing Tevi's eyes follow the animals in amazement.

Closer to the town centre, the walls became higher, blank except for wide gateways guarded by sentries with barbed pikes. Through them, Tevi caught glimpses of gardens rich in lavish blooms. The scent of flowers mixed with the dust and sweat of the street. Tevi raised her eyes. The soaring crowns of palms pierced the blue sky, and towering over all was the green copper dome of the temple.

Later that afternoon, she stood in the cavernous interior. The echoing void was filled with murmuring. Through a haze of incense, light filtered down on groups of chanting priests, wild-eyed prophets, and praying supplicants. Alcoves held grotesque statues. Some idols were bedecked with garlands of flowers. Before the more warlike were bloodstained altars.

"Impressive, isn't it?" Kimal observed.

"I should say so. Is this a very holy place?" Tevi whispered in reply.

"There's a legend among the locals that this is an auspicious spot to make money out of visitors. For a price, they'll tell your future or bless anything you feel needs blessing."

"Are the prophecies accurate?"

"If you've got money to waste, you could find out."

The question rose in Tevi's mind, *Will I ever return to Storenseg?* But it required no oracle to know the answer.

A fresh burst of chanting began nearby; voices rose and fell in wavering cadences. Tevi watched a robed priest throw fistfuls of incense into a crucible while an entranced seer swayed and shuddered. The oracle's eyes were glazed, but then they seemed to fasten on Tevi, and the head wobbled up and down as if nodding in answer.

Tevi's breath caught in her throat. Then she sighed and dismissed the taunting fantasy. The oracle twitched into a shuffling circular dance. Coughing from the incense, Tevi and Kimal moved on. It was time to go. They squeezed through the crowds blocking the main entrance. The open air was refreshing after the scented darkness, although the heat hit them like a blow.

The temple was set in gardens. Fountains splashed into geometrically shaped pools of dark green water. Birds sang from rooftops, the sound floating lazily on the hot air.

"What gods do the people in the Protectorate worship?" Tevi asked.

"It varies. A lot of places have their own local deities."

"Are there no temples like this?"

Kimal shook his head. "Oh, no. It's all very unorganised and informal."

"Who do the sorcerers worship?"

"No one in particular, although some of them have very elaborate ideas about the meaning of life and how we all came to be here."

"On the islands we worship Rangir, goddess of the sea."

"I shouldn't think anyone would mind if you want to keep practising your faith. But your goddess is almost certainly the folk memory of an ancient sorcerer. That's what most turn out to be."

"You sound as if you don't believe in any of them." Tevi was not sure if she did, either.

"The sorcerers can't find any proof, and they're the experts in unseen powers. So it's a bit silly for any ordinary mortal, like the priests in there, to claim they know the gods' names, what songs they'd like sung, or which style of headdress they normally wear."

Tevi smiled at his irreverent tone. "Still, it's a very impressive temple."

"Oh, yes, and their religion is as good as anyone else's."

Verron, Marith, and Derry were waiting at the appointed rendezvous. Together, they left the temple garden and wandered through the marketplace, full of noise and the tang of strange spices. The sight of a row of camels caught Tevi's attention.

The rubbery mouths moved in continuous chewing, and to judge from the peeling fur, they were all in the middle of a major moult. Tevi reached out to touch a shaggy haunch, but stopped as a nomad spotted her and jabbered harshly. She frowned. The nomad repeated a string of similar incomprehensible syllables.

"Pardon, I didn't catch that," Tevi said politely.

"I only know a few words of their language, but I think it's a warning that the camels bite," Marith said at her shoulder.

"Their language?"

"Not everyone speaks the same language as us."

"There's more than one language?" Tevi was dumbfounded. The idea had never occurred to her before. It felt as if it should be impossible.

Verron smiled at her surprise. "There are dozens of languages, maybe hundreds. The lands around the Middle Seas have a common tongue due to a sorcerer's experiment six hundred years ago. I think he had some naive idea that if everyone understood each other, there'd be no conflict. Of course, all that happened was everyone could argue much more effectively."

"How do people with different languages communicate?"

"With great difficulty. Although I think Marith can haggle in every language in existence."

"It's not me; it's money that can talk any language," Marith asserted.

Kimal joined in. "Even where languages start out the same, they drift apart. The Coven keeps the Protectorate constant, but you hear some strange accents from time to time—like yours. Another few centuries of isolation, and no one will be able to understand a word you islanders say." He spoke the last sentence in a fair imitation of Tevi's soft drawl, and then he elbowed her in the ribs.

The playful scuffle that followed ended quickly when Tevi caught Kimal around the waist, flipped him over, and effortlessly held him upside-down by his ankles. Kimal yelped, his arms flailing and hair brushing the ground.

"I think, my son, the moral is that if ever you meet a woman with an accent like Tevi's, you should treat her with respect," Marith said, laughing.

Tevi returned the boy to his feet, and they continued strolling through the streets. Yet she could not help thinking that there was little chance of Kimal's meeting anyone else with her accent. She alone was exiled forever.

❖

The traders' route went from town to town, with the value of their merchandise growing steadily. Autumn was approaching as they returned north. A last caravan took them to the city of Villenes, within sight of where the Aldraks trailed away into the Merlieu hills. On the other side were Serac and the Protectorate.

Over the months, a genuine affection had grown between Tevi and the traders, as if she were a favourite niece. She felt more accepted than had ever been the case with her own family, although there were things about herself she dared not reveal. Tevi was also aware she could not stay with them forever. She would have to find a way to make her own living.

While Verron and Marith completed arrangements for the next stage, Tevi wandered through the market with the two boys. The shops were piled high with clothes and rolls of material. Villenes was famous for its textiles. At one stall, the beaming owner extracted a crimson shirt from the nearest pile and held it against Tevi. She shook her head, abashed. On the islands, bright colours, particularly red, were reserved for men. Women wore neutral tones. It took little to imagine her family's comments if they saw her wearing anything the colour of the shirt—but there was no chance of them seeing her again, and trying to fit in had never stopped them talking. In a mood of defiance, Tevi commenced bartering and shortly walked away carrying the shirt. She felt like a naughty child.

The traders were lodging with an old friend. Tevi was assured that the woman had been a little wild in her youth, although she was now a highly respectable merchant. Her home was a rambling building set among gardens by the river. At the door, Tevi and the boys were greeted by servants who took their parcels and offered the traditional soft slippers. They found Marith in the central courtyard, surrounded by potted ferns and talking to two unfamiliar men.

One was about thirty, strongly muscled, with a bull-like neck and a round, good-natured face. His older, taller, and leaner companion had weathered skin and close-cropped grey hair. Both men wore mail-reinforced jackets. Swords hung at their sides and on their hands were tattooed red and gold crossed swords—the mark of the Protectorate Guild of Mercenary Warriors.

The men glanced around as Tevi and the two boys approached. Marith performed the introductions. "These are my sons, Kimal and Derry, and this is a friend of ours, Tevi." She gestured to the mercenaries. "This is Cade." The younger nodded. "And this is Alentris. They'll be escorting us to Serac."

Both men's eyes fastened on the sword hanging by Tevi's side.

"Do you know how to use that?" the mercenary called Alentris asked.

"A little," Tevi said diffidently.

Derry piped in, "We met Tevi in Torhafn when she rescued Mama and Papa from a gang of footpads."

The mercenaries looked satisfied. Evidently, their concern was solely with assessing the party's defensive capability. Only Tevi caught the relief that flitted across Marith's face.

"It never hurts to have—" Alentris was interrupted by Derry tugging his jerkin.

"I'm going to be a mercenary when I'm older." Derry's defiant tone made the adults laugh.

Cade grinned at Marith. "Don't worry. They grow out of it—most of them."

❖

The road to Serac led over a dusty plain of low-lying shrubs and windblown yellow grass. After travelling so long in large caravans, it was strange for them to be on their own again. The monotony of the landscape also subdued the traders. Only the two mercenaries were unaffected. They rode ahead of the wagons, swapping anecdotes and laughing.

On the third day, they left the plain. That night, they pitched camp beside a weathered rocky outcrop crowning a low hill. The ground was dotted with the same coarse bushes as the lowlands, but at the bottom of the hill were a small stream and the first greenery they had seen since leaving the irrigated fields around Villenes.

While the others arranged the campsite, Tevi and Cade went down to replenish their water supply. In the wet mud was a single row of footsteps. The pair examined the track.

Cade spoke first. "We're on a reasonably well-used route."

"We haven't seen anyone all day, and they're very fresh."

Cade shrugged and knelt to fill the water container. "It's probably a fur trapper or goatherd. And it should help sharpen the concentration of whoever's on watch tonight."

After the evening meal, Derry was put to bed inside one of the wagons, and Alentris sat first watch on top of the rocks. Leaving the lowlands had lifted the traders' spirits. The lighter mood kept the group talking around the campfire, well past the time they normally went to sleep.

Marith was affecting a comic burlesque of indignation. She tapped the ground with a forefinger. "Right. Who's pinched the last of the cinnamon biscuits?"

"Would I do a thing like that?" Cade asked, pretending to sound hurt.

"From the way you wolfed down the rest of them, I'd say it's more than likely."

"But the guild guarantees my honesty."

"So we'll put in a claim."

Verron laughed. "I can just imagine the response if I submit a claim for one cinnamon biscuit."

"Three!" Marith corrected, mock-righteously.

"The honour of the guild demands that I confess." Alentris's voice drifted down from above their heads as he joined in the performance. "It was I who took the biscuits, but if you forbear to submit your claim, I will make good the loss when we get to Serac."

"You see, Marith? It pays to hire mercenaries with two swords," Verron said. He caught sight of Tevi's puzzled expression. "Their tattoos. Junior mercenaries only have a single sword. It's not until they've proved trustworthy that the guild gives them the second sword. After that, the guild guarantees to refund any losses if they prove dishonest."

"Which is why they feel they can charge such an exorbitant fee," Marith concluded.

"We're excellent value for money." Cade spoke with heavy irony.

"What stops thieves from tattooing their hands to pass themselves off?" Tevi asked.

"We do," Alentris said. "If ever you're in Dresinton, you can see the remains of a couple that tried it."

Cade grinned up at his colleague. "Are the skulls still there, then?"

"Oh, yes, they're wedged in. They'll never—" Alentris's voice stopped. Something about the arrested speech instantly drew all eyes to him. His attention was fixed on the bottom of the hill. Cade scuttled to the side of the wagons and stared down the slope.

"By the bushes."

"I see them." The two mercenaries spoke in taut whispers.

Without a word, Marith leaned forward and doused the fire. Water hissed furiously for a second, then suddenly, it was very dark. The moon was low, lighting the hillside but not touching the campsite in the shadow of the rocks. Alentris scrambled down. The scuffing of his feet was the only sound.

The traders slipped into a wagon. Verron reappeared immediately, carrying two crossbows. Tevi's mouth was dry as she drew her sword and joined the mercenaries, shielded by the wagons but with a clear view down the hillside. Her eyes ached from staring into the dark. Nothing was moving.

Marith was whispering quietly to Derry. She emerged and took the second crossbow from Verron. A tap on her shoulder made Tevi look back. Kimal held up her hunting bow with an unspoken request on his face. She nodded her consent; Kimal strung the bow and then stood by his parents in the shelter of the wagons.

Alentris and Cade were conferring quietly. "About a dozen of them, do you think?"

"Maybe less."

Tevi bit her lip. "So what now?"

Alentris spoke grimly. "If they've got any sense, they'll realise we've spotted them, and they'll give up and go away." At that instant, there was a shout from the bottom of the hill and nine figures burst from the undergrowth. "Damn. They're idiots."

Cade caught Tevi's arm and hissed urgently. "There may be more in the bushes with bows. Stay back until this lot are close enough to shield you."

Tevi nodded to show she had understood.

The bandits continued their charge. To Tevi, it seemed as if they were running in slow motion. A succession of twangs erupted as the traders started shooting. One of the figures fell with hands clasped against a thigh. As the attackers got within twenty yards of the wagons, Alentris shouted, "Right!" and leapt forward with Cade close behind. Tevi took a deep breath and followed.

The nearest bandit took a defensive stance, planting both feet on the ground. With no attempt at subtlety, Tevi swung her sword down hard. Her opponent's blade rose, but the bandit was completely unprepared for the force. The attempted block was knocked aside, barely deflecting Tevi's sword, and the sharp edge sliced into flesh. With a cry, the bandit staggered backwards, then slipped and stumbled down the slope.

Her momentum carried Tevi some way after her foe until she regained her footing. Before she had time to turn, Tevi heard footsteps behind her. In her head, Blaze's voice screamed, "*Duck!*" By instinct, she obeyed, and a blade whistled harmlessly over her head. Tevi spun around on her knees. Directly in front of her face was a pair of legs. Tevi's hand tightened on the hilt as she drove her sword up into her assailant's body.

Only then did she raise her eyes. It was a young man. Surprise on his face turned slowly to horror. His sword slipped from his grasp. His hands twitched towards his chest and then stopped. Slowly, he keeled over and hit the ground with a soft, dull thump.

Tevi wrenched her sword free and looked around. Ten yards away, Cade was hard pressed by three attackers. The nearest did not even turn as Tevi ran towards them. Again, her sword swung in an arc, hitting the joint between shoulder and neck with enough force almost to sever the bandit's head. The body collapsed with a sharp, guttural sigh—a sound that froze the other outlaws. Cade lashed out, severing the sword, and possibly a few fingers, from one of the stunned bandits. Suddenly, the battle was over. The two turned and fled, followed by their surviving allies.

"Quick! Back to cover!" Cade cried.

They raced up the hillside and skidded to a stop behind the wagons. In a second, Alentris joined them. The older mercenary ran his hand through his cropped hair and then slumped, hands on his knees, breathing deeply.

"Are you all right?" Cade asked.

"Not a scratch. They were amateurs. But I'm getting too old for this game," Alentris said between gasps.

"How about you, Tevi?"

"Oh, I'm fine." Yet she was aware that the right side of her face felt wet and sticky.

Cade also noticed and reached over to wipe her cheek gently. He rubbed his fingers together. "That's a lot of blood."

Alentris looked up. "Is it yours?"

Tevi saw again the young man crumpling above her, blood gushing from his chest. "No. It's not."

Alentris nodded. "Good. That's the important thing."

❖

The crescent moon had climbed high. Tevi sat on the rocks and stared at it. She had volunteered for watch, knowing she could not sleep. Every time she closed her eyes, she saw the young bandit's expression, his eyes wide open with astonishment and fear. Each time she relived the sight, he looked more like Sparrow.

She heard scrabbling and then Cade's head appeared. He climbed to sit beside her and offered a mug of hot soup. Tevi took it with a mumble of thanks and sipped in silence. Cade shuffled back, leaning against a rock.

Cade let her finish the soup before he spoke. "Was that the first time you've killed someone?"

Tevi nodded, not trusting her voice.

"You know you had no choice?"

Again, Tevi nodded.

"No. I suppose it doesn't help much." Cade's nose wrinkled. "Didn't help a great deal when someone said it to me."

"But it didn't put you off becoming a mercenary?" Tevi's voice cracked.

"It made me think long and hard for about a month. Still does, sometimes."

"Will tonight give you much to think about?"

"No. I guess it gets easier after a while. And tonight was simple—it was us or them."

Tevi put down the empty mug and wrapped her arms around her knees. "I keep wondering what he was like, what his name was."

"That's a bad game to start playing," Cade said softly.

"I keep thinking someone must have cared for him. Someone said goodbye to him as he went out tonight. They'll never see him again. For the rest of their life, that person will hate me for what I did." Tears were rolling down Tevi's face. "He'll have parents who fed him, washed him, watched him grow, dreamed of grandchildren, and now all that's gone."

"Then they shouldn't have raised him to be a thief and a murderer. Believe me, you can't tear yourself up like this. At least tonight makes some sort of sense. You were saving the lives of your friends. As a hired sword, I've been in some nasty brawls." Cade's voice grew bitter. "At the end, you don't know what it was about or what was gained or where the right and wrong of it lay. You just wake up in the morning, spare a thought for those who can't and thank whatever god watches over you."

Tevi's head sank onto her folded arms.

Cade slid over and put his arm around her shoulder. "Go on. Get some sleep. I'll sit watch."

"I can't sleep."

"You probably can. I put a spoonful of Marith's best sleeping draught in your soup."

Even as Cade spoke, the effects of the drug hit Tevi. The stars spun in a wave of drowsiness. Without another word, she slithered to the edge of the rock and accepted Cade's hand to help her down. She stumbled over to her blanket and was asleep before her head touched the ground.

❖

In the morning light, the wreckage of the fight littered the slope. Apart from blood and dropped weapons, four attackers lay dead on the ground. As well as the two Tevi had slain, there were a woman with a crossbow bolt in her throat and a man cut open by Alentris. Their silent presences unsettled the travellers. People moved quietly about their tasks, preparing to depart as soon as possible. Even Derry was subdued.

After breakfast, Tevi walked down to the young man she had killed. In daylight, he looked nothing like Sparrow. She stared at him for a long while until a call roused her.

"Hey, Tevi. We're ready to go."

"Aren't we going to bury them or something?"

"Haven't got the time or the inclination. If their friends are concerned, they can get them once we've gone," Alentris shouted back.

"And if not?"

"Then they'll make some little furry animals very happy."

Tevi took a last long look around the scene, as if trying to impress it on her memory, then she turned and trotted up the hill to the wagons.

Chapter Six—The Mark of the Guild

Serac was a busy port, with wide streets full of traffic. The town was obviously prosperous and well ordered, but nothing about it seemed noteworthy—although Tevi was not quite sure what she had been expecting from her first sight of the Protectorate. Most of her time was spent sitting on the harbour wall, watching boats bobbing on the water and smelling the heavy, salt-laden sea air.

The mercenaries were paid off. Alentris bid the group farewell, taking contract as a guard on an outgoing caravan. Cade, however, wanted to visit Lyremouth and would still travel with them, although no longer as an employee. At Serac, the traders also parted company with the horses.

Marith explained, "You can always find a buyer for wagons among the people who've just arrived by boat. You don't make much profit, but we'll earn a fortune from the spice in Lyremouth, and the sea is the quickest way there."

"Couldn't we take the horses with us?"

"It would be too expensive."

Tevi was unhappy about saying goodbye to the animals. "Will they be all right?"

"Oh, yes," Marith assured her. "They're too valuable for anyone to abuse."

The party boarded their ship a few days later. Like all islanders, Tevi was a born sailor and felt at home with the pitching deck beneath her feet. However, she had never been on a ship the size of the *Aspen Rover*. It dwarfed the boats of the Western Isles. Tevi realised her experience of fishing would not qualify her for a career as a Protectorate sailor, and the time to plan her future was getting close.

❖

Nine days out of Serac, the northern shore hove into sight. In the warm afternoon, Tevi leant on the starboard rail, dividing her attention between the distant shoreline and the seagulls fighting over the pickings churned up in the boat's wake. Kimal and Cade were beside her.

"I was born in Lyremouth. It'll be nice to see the old place again, and it's about time I called in on my parents. They worry about me." Cade sniffed reflectively. "Can't say I blame them."

"What's Lyremouth like?" Tevi asked.

"Big," Kimal said quickly.

"Isn't the Coven there? Do you see many sorcerers?"

"A few."

"What do they do?"

"Walk around, looking important." Kimal was dismissive.

"We don't get sorcerers on the islands, just stories. I guess I'm hoping to see something spectacular."

"Then you'll be disappointed. Sorcerers don't do shows for people's amusement." Cade laughed.

"So how can you tell them apart from anyone else?"

"The amulets on their wrists. Witches' are various colours, depending on rank. They're all engraved with an oak leaf pattern. Sorcerers have a black amulet, and the Guardian's is white, but there's little chance you'll see it. She rarely leaves the Coven buildings except for festivals."

"I'd still like to see some real magic." Tevi's voice was wistful.

Kimal whooped. "You walk around with the strength of five and complain you don't see any magic!"

"I grew up with the potion on Storenseg, so it isn't anything unusual for me."

"Don't you have any other magic?" Cade asked.

"No, and we only got the strength potion from a shipwrecked sorcerer ages ago."

"How about dragons or werewolves?"

"No. A dead sea monster washed onto the beach when I was a child, but it was half eaten and not very impressive."

"And no magic users at all?"

"None."

Cade's eyes travelled to the horizon. "It would be nice to be rid of them all."

"Don't you like sorcerers?" Tevi asked with surprise.

"I don't like thunderstorms, but they're unavoidable. It's the same with sorcerers. You have to put up with them. But given the chance, I'd happily ditch the lot."

"What's wrong with them?"

"They're not like us. They're too bloody powerful, and they give me the creeps. Though don't get me wrong—as things stand, I'd die supporting the Coven. It's still a damn sight better than any of the alternatives." Cade's tone was resigned rather than bitter.

"You sound like Papa," Kimal said. "He says folk complain about the Coven and the taxes, but if it disappeared, they'd soon change their tune."

"The places we've seen get on okay without it," Tevi pointed out.

"Only because we haven't been too far from the Protectorate, and the Coven won't tolerate trouble on its borders. The non-Coven sorcerers with evil plans move farther away so they'll have a free hand to do whatever they want."

"Evil plans?"

"Building empires. Enslaving people. Using them for experiments," Cade spoke angrily. "Throughout history, they've destroyed millions of ordinary folk who wanted nothing more than to get on with their own lives in peace—farming or hunting or whatever."

"Couldn't people resist?"

"A sorcerer is so powerful compared to ungifted folk like us. The only person who can do anything to stop one is another sorcerer, and the gods alone know how many have died in wars between them. They make the nastiest brawl I've ever seen look like a lover's tiff. And all for nothing. Once the sorcerers die, their empires collapse into anarchy."

"Couldn't their children take over?" Tevi asked.

"They don't have the ability. Maybe one person in a hundred has limited magical gifts, but only one in a hundred thousand has enough to be a sorcerer. I don't think anyone knows what makes a sorcerer, but it's not inherited. A sorcerer's children are no more likely to be gifted with magic than a labourer's."

"The empires all rise and fall in the space of a lifetime," Kimal added.

"Verron told me the Protectorate has lasted for hundreds of years," Tevi said.

"The Protectorate is different. It's not dependent on any one sorcerer." From his tone, Kimal was more sympathetic to the Coven than Cade. "The Coven also leaves us alone as long as we pay our taxes. They even do useful things, like training healers and weather witches. We don't—"

Any thoughts about the other advantages to the Coven were lost as a bucketful of water landed on Kimal's back, followed by a giggle. Tevi looked around in time to spot Derry disappearing into the hold. Kimal had also identified the culprit. He shouted and chased after his brother, but there was a smile on his face.

"They're nice lads," Tevi said, putting aside the conversation about sorcerers.

"True," Cade agreed. "Will you be staying with the family for long?"

"Marith and Verron have invited me to spend the winter with them."

"Any plans for what you're going to do after?"

"Not really."

"You should join a guild."

Tevi shrugged. "I'm a bit old to start an apprenticeship."

"You wouldn't need to if you already had the skills for the trade."

"I'm not sure I have any worthwhile skills."

Cade chewed his lip for a while. "Would you be interested in joining the mercenaries?"

Tevi gave a humourless laugh. "My old weapons trainer would be dumbstruck to hear you ask that. Back home, I was considered to be the worst warrior of all time."

Cade looked surprised. "There's a gang of bandits outside Villenes who'd disagree."

"I guess being three times as strong as anyone else here gives me an unfair advantage."

"You don't worry about fairness in battles. Use every advantage you've got. Anyway, I know the guild would be pleased to have you."

"Can anyone just ask to join?"

"No. You need to be nominated by a guild member. Normally, it's the warrior you've been apprenticed to, but it doesn't have to be. And you weren't born in the Protectorate, so you'd need two other citizens to vouch for you. But I can't see Marith and Verron refusing you that."

Cade patted Tevi's shoulder. "Think about it. If you like, I'll nominate you. You did all right with the bandits—certainly saved my neck."

He walked away, humming softly. Tevi looked out to sea, deep in thought.

❖

The *Aspen Rover* reached Lyremouth harbour late the following evening. Sunset turned the rooftops of the city dull pink. Overhead, stars were starting to show. The ship dropped anchor out in the bay. It would not dock until high tide next morning. Tevi and Marith leant against the railing and watched dusk claim the city. Against the darkening sky was a forest of tall masts. Light from numerous torches shimmered off the still water. Farther inland, other lanterns speckled the hills rising behind the harbour.

Marith pointed out the major landmarks.

"Which is the Coven?" Tevi asked.

"Over there. It's the group of buildings on the southeast of town."

"The Guardian lives there?"

"Yes."

"Have you ever met her?"

Marith snorted at the idea. "She doesn't mix with the likes of us. I saw her predecessor once, but that was in the days before he was elected Guardian."

"A man can be Guardian?"

"Of course. Why not?"

Tevi tried to explain her surprise. "Well...it's just, coming from the islands, I don't think of men being in positions of power."

"The only thing that affects someone's ability to wield power is whether or not they're a sorcerer. It's the most important difference between people, and the only one that really counts."

"On the islands, we'd say the most important difference is between men and women," Tevi said thoughtfully.

"That's silly. There are a few minor physical differences, but none amount to anything significant. Slightly more women than men are witches, but then men are generally stronger, so there are more of them in the mercenaries. But either way, the odds aren't good enough to gamble your life on—and if you insult a female mercenary assassin, muscles won't save you."

Tevi stared down at the dark waters lapping against the hull. She could think of one area where the differences were very significant but did not want to raise the subject. The traders had never commented on her lack of interest in the young men they had met, nor asked why she had left the islands, and Tevi was not about to risk their friendship by telling them.

"My people would say that men are naturally inferior to women," Tevi said at last.

This time, Marith laughed aloud. "And that's even sillier. You can only get away with it because you don't have sorcerers, so everyone is in the same state. On the mainland, any baby in any family, male or female, might grow up to be a sorcerer. It's hard trying to act superior to someone who can incinerate you with a single word."

"I'm not trying to justify my people's beliefs, just explaining why I have problems sometimes."

"I understand. You're doing all right." Marith squeezed Tevi's shoulder affectionately.

"I can see that sorcerers create problems for hereditary rulers," Tevi said, although she had a gut feeling that her grandmother would do fine, regardless of the political system.

"The setup on your islands only works because there are no real differences between people to get in the way of the imaginary ones you invent."

"But men and women..." Tevi let her sentence trail away, no longer certain quite what she believed.

"It doesn't count for anything," Marith stated confidently. "If ever you meet a sorcerer, you'll see what I mean."

Tevi decided it was wiser not to push the point. The two women remained on deck, talking quietly until the light faded.

❖

The traders found lodgings at a comfortable inn not far from the docks. They took a light lunch in the main room, seated with the other guests at a long oak table. Sun streamed through the thick glass windows, casting bands of green light over the floor. From outside came the sounds of the city.

With the meal over, Marith pushed back her chair. “I’ll go and finalise the sale of the spice.”

“I suppose you want me to see the guild auditor,” Verron said with a heavy sigh.

“Oh, go on. You love presenting the accounts.” Marith grinned mischievously as she headed for the door.

Derry leapt eagerly from his chair. “Can I come, too?”

“If you want.” The pair departed, bound for the spice market.

“Do you want me to come with you?” Kimal asked his father cautiously.

“It wouldn’t be a bad idea for you to see how the accounting goes.” Kimal’s face fell, and his father took pity on him. “But I know you’ll have more fun showing Tevi around the city.”

They went together as far as the traders’ guildhall. It was an imposing structure with a gabled roof and half-timbered walls. Fanciful beasts were carved over the windows. The three parted company at the arched gateway and the younger pair spent the afternoon strolling around the wide tree-lined avenues, narrow alleys, and open squares of the city.

Shops sold a bewildering array of goods. Many items, Tevi had never seen before and she had no idea what they were. The size and wealth of Lyremouth overwhelmed her. All the guilds had halls and there appeared to be some form of competition to determine which profession could outdo all the rest. She was also surprised to find there were no city walls, as if Lyremouth, or the Coven, was boasting of its impregnability.

On one wide thoroughfare, they were passed by an open carriage, complete with uniformed footmen. Sunlight sparkled off the inlaid gilt and polished wood. Tevi pointed at the passenger. “Who’s she?”

“It’s ‘he.’ And he’s the head of the Potters’ Guild,” Kimal replied. “You can tell from the crest on the door.”

Tevi frowned, uncertain whether the symbol related to the passenger’s occupation or gender. Before she could ask for clarification, Kimal disappeared into a shop. Tevi leant against a tree and waited his return. After a little thought, she was sure the crest would be the mark of the Potters’ Guild, like the crossed swords were for mercenaries. Tevi smiled ruefully; it would not be such a bad idea if Protectorate citizens wore badges proclaiming their gender. She still had great difficulty telling the sexes apart. On the other side of the street, two young lovers ambled along, arms around waists. For the life of her, Tevi could not tell which one was the woman.

Kimal reappeared, carrying a parcel, which he opened to display a tiny jade figure of a horse—a midwinter's gift for his sister. He talked of her as they continued their stroll.

"Arnet's been working up north, but she'll be home for midwinter. I can't wait to see her again. I've missed her."

"Your parents have as well." Tevi had heard the ache in Marith's voice when she spoke of her daughter. Tevi was sure there would be no similar distress in Red's voice when speaking of her.

"Oh, I know, but Arnet was never interested in trading. Her only love is horses. Doesn't care about its shape or size. As long as it's got four legs and neighs, she's happy."

"Didn't your parents mind her not becoming a trader?"

"Why should they?"

"Where I come from, you had to follow in your mother's footsteps."

"Like having kings and queens and things?"

Tevi was about to correct the mention of kings, but it did not matter. "Yes."

"It wouldn't make sense on the mainland. Power is dependent solely on ability. I guess the guilds mimic the Coven. All our leaders are elected by their members."

"It's fair."

"And it makes sense. Anything else would be very chancy. I mean, just because your mother or your grandmother was good at something doesn't mean you will be as well, does it? You might be absolutely hopeless."

That was altogether too close to home. Tevi decided to change the topic. "Do you have any other brothers or sisters?"

"Mama and Papa had two other children, but Uncle Ged and his partner are their parents now. We'll be seeing them when we get home."

"He adopted them even though their true parents were alive? Isn't that unusual?" Tevi was surprised.

"No. Happens all the time in the Protectorate. Obviously, a lot of people won't produce their own children, so they adopt any spare ones their siblings or cousins have."

The 'obviously' did not follow in Tevi's experience, but much of what she was told about the Protectorate baffled her and Kimal had a knack for throwing her off balance. She was saved any further confusion by their arrival at the open parkland surrounding the buildings of the Coven.

Once upon a time, when Lyremouth was still a village, the Coven had been located some way from the dwellings of ordinary folk. With the passage of years, Lyremouth had grown into a great capital, yet none of the new buildings encroached on the land around the Coven. Tevi guessed it was due to nobody wanting the sorcerers as close neighbours rather than to a sense of aesthetics. The buildings were nothing to look at and the open panorama only served to emphasise it.

The tower of the Guardian stood proudly in the centre, but the remaining structures were an unplanned jumble. The walls were old and plain compared to the guildhalls, even dilapidated. The few touches of grandeur appeared to have been tacked on as afterthoughts.

"It's not as impressive as I expected. The temple at Kradja was more to look at." Tevi's disappointment showed in her voice.

Kimal grinned. "When you're as important as the Coven, you don't have to resort to fancy brickwork to impress people."

To bear this out, many groups of travellers were gathered, looking at the buildings with expressions ranging from apprehension to reverence. The onlookers even included a party of dwarves, who babbled among themselves in their clipped, guttural language. Judging by their actions, they were having an intense debate about the architectural virtues of the flying buttress.

In the middle of the grass was a low granite outcrop. Its highest point barely reached shoulder level and it was dominated by an ancient oak. There seemed nothing noteworthy about the rock, yet it was getting considerable attention.

"What's that?" Tevi asked.

"The Heart of the Protectorate. The spot where Keovan sat and looked out on the world."

"Who was Keovan?" Tevi had heard the name before.

"A sorcerer. He died four hundred and forty-seven years ago. He lived in a hut on the site of the Coven and sat on that rock every day, talking to anyone who would listen."

"He founded the Protectorate?"

"No. All Keovan did was bewail the state of the world and the futility of life."

"Then why is he famous?"

"He was the strongest sorcerer of his day. His reputation kept trouble at bay, so the land around here had peace, and a group of followers built up—other witches and sorcerers who wanted to learn from him. After he died, none of his students was up to taking his place. Everyone assumed the region would be swallowed up by another sorcerer's empire. But his students agreed to work together and swore a pact with the townsfolk. Other sorcerers joined them, and that was the beginning of the Coven."

"And they kept the rock."

"Oh, yes. It's used every year for a ceremony on the anniversary of Keovan's death. They all troop out here, and the guild masters swear allegiance to the Coven on behalf of their members. Then the Guardian swears on behalf of the Coven to defend the Protectorate. After that, all the new sorcerers are introduced to the people. And then they stand on the rock and repeat the Guardian's oath and are given their black amulets."

Tevi frowned. "I don't see what the sorcerers get out of it. If they're as powerful as you say, why don't they just take what they want?"

Kimal looked thoughtful. "Not all sorcerers are power-mad maniacs, but before the Coven, the ones who just wanted a quiet life used to sit back and let the empire builders get on with it. Then the Coven came along and gave the peaceful sorcerers a chance to chat to each other and write books and things. I think the Coven gave the thinkers and talkers something to fight for—fortunately. If the Coven falls, the Protectorate goes with it."

Tevi and Kimal stood surveying the buildings. The walls did not seem in danger of collapse despite the dwarves' concern. Eventually, they headed back through the winding streets of Lyremouth.

❖

Verron and Marith were busy totalling up the money and making plans for the final stage of their journey. Their work was interrupted by

Tevi, who hesitantly entered the room and slipped into a seat at the end of the table. Her serious expression caused Marith to roll up the map she had been studying and Verron to put down his pen.

"Is something wrong?" Marith asked.

"No...not really."

"But?"

"I've been thinking." Tevi took a deep breath, then continued in a rush. "I appreciate the offer to spend winter with you, but...did Cade say anything to you about me joining the mercenaries?"

Neither of the traders looked happy. Marith was the first to speak. "He mentioned it, since we'd have to vouch for you. Of course, we're willing to do that."

Verron stared at the table, picking at some spilt wax. "If it's what you want...not that there's anything wrong with the mercenaries' guild, but its members don't tend to reach old age."

"If I don't join a guild, I'm stuck as an unskilled labourer. And the mercenaries are the only guild I'm trained for."

"We'd be sorry to part company with you."

"Once I'm a member, there's nothing to stop you hiring me officially. If you want."

Marith brightened up. "That's an idea. There are so few mercenaries who know how to take care of a wagon team."

"Then we'd have the Waggoners' Guild down our necks." Verron glared at his partner.

"There's nothing to say a mercenary can't—"

Tevi stepped in before the discussion could get waylaid. "So if it's all right with you, I'll go and visit Cade tomorrow and tell him I want to join."

The traders hesitated before answering.

"Yes, of course."

"We'll come with you."

❖

Two mornings later, Tevi stood on a riverside wharf. Autumn was advanced, and her breath formed white clouds in the dawn air. The traders solemnly hugged her in turn before boarding the river barge. The boat would take them home on the last step of the trade route. Once everyone was aboard, the crew loosened the mooring rope and pushed the barge away from the dock.

Verron called out, "You won't forget how to get to Cottersford, will you? We're always at home for two months either side of midwinter."

"I hope we meet again soon, but if not, farewell, Tevi," Marith added.

"Farewell, Marith, Verron, and you, too, Kimal and Derry," Tevi called back. The words sounded awfully final, but it was too late to change her mind.

The barge reached open water and the oarsmen set to work. Tevi watched until the craft was lost from sight amidst other traffic on the busy river Lyre; then she turned and retraced her steps through the city. The working day was just beginning. Shopkeepers were removing shutters and setting out their goods, peddlers shouted their wares, rowdy gangs of dockers headed for the harbour, and children on errands raced by.

Tevi headed to the largest square, in the heart of the city. The grandest civic buildings were there—the law courts and mayor's palace. Standing proudly beside them was the most imposing guildhall of all, displaying the prestige of its members. Without hesitation, Tevi walked up to the main entrance and entered under the sign of two crossed swords in red and gold.

❖

The point of the man's sword came straight for Tevi's heart. She pulled her own weapon across to parry while pivoting on one heel. The sword missed by a hair's breadth, but her desperate defence left her unbalanced. A long step back stopped her from falling; however, her opponent pressed on with his attack before she had time to recover.

The rear of the hall was getting close. Tevi was running out of room. In a bid to gain space, she launched her own series of sharp jabs. Her opponent evaded them easily and immediately shifted back into attack. With lightning speed, the edge of his sword flicked upwards. Tevi blocked at the cost of yet another retreat, and her heel touched the wall. Her opponent smiled and took six paces backwards, generously allowing her more space. Tevi took a deep breath. The man was good, easily the best warrior she had ever fought. Hardly surprising—he was senior sword master to the Guild of Mercenary Warriors.

Their eyes met. The sword master raised his wooden sword and gestured with his free hand, inviting her to attack. Tevi clenched her teeth. She could not defeat the sword master by skill. He was quicker and vastly more experienced than she was. Strength was her only advantage. Dropping her left hand on the hilt, she leapt forward, swinging her whole body into a double-fisted stroke that caught her opponent by surprise. Still he managed to block and the two swords met with a resounding crack, striking close by the cross-guards. As ever, the sword master's timing was perfect, but he was unable to withstand the force of the impact. The blow sent the wooden sword spinning from his hand. It bounced off the wall and skidded across the floor, finally coming to rest some thirty feet away. The sword master treated it to a rueful stare while shaking his jarred wrist.

From the edge of the hall came a burst of assorted noises indicative of both support and good humour. The sword master scowled in feigned belligerence at the three other nominees sitting at the side. The sounds ceased, only to be replaced by broad grins. Everyone knew the sword master was an amiable character, indulgent of high spirits. Consequently, he was well liked by all.

Once order had been re-established, the sword master turned back to Tevi. "Crude, but effective," he granted. "You'll do."

"Thank you, sir."

"But it's risky to rely solely on strength. You must pay closer attention. I got you with some very simple traps. You can't afford to let things like that through."

"Would you be surprised to learn that I've been told that before?"

"No. So why haven't you taken more notice of the advice?"

"I try, sir."

"Not hard enough. Your sword teacher should have made more effort to help you work out the problem. Generally speaking, you've been well trained from an early age."

"I started when I was three."

"Quite right, too. You'd be surprised at the number of wide-eyed hopefuls who think they can pick up a sword and become a hero overnight." He turned to include the other nominees. "Remember—swords are like some musical instruments. If you don't start young enough, you'll never develop the right muscles and reflexes. If a child hasn't started training by the age of seven, they'll never be anything other than a very poor average. So if ever you get an untrained teenager pleading with you to take them on as apprentice, don't. You're not doing any favours, just raising false hopes."

The other nominees glanced towards Cayell. It was no secret that she was the worst swordsman among them. However, Cayell was unconcerned; her skills lay in other directions.

The sword master resumed his appraisal of Tevi. "You know, I'm loath to suggest it, but do you have any experience with a battle-axe?"

"Some. It was—" The rest of Tevi's reply was drowned out.

"Tell him you're a warrior, not a lumberjack."

"Forget it."

Cayell's voice came loudest of all. "Axes are for warriors too stupid to work out which end of a sword to take hold of."

"Ignore the hecklers." The sword master waved his hand dismissively. "It's true axes are unsubtle. They come down to how much force you can put behind them—which in your case is a lot. It was a classic axe stroke you used to disarm me. You're not bad with a sword, but you can't structure your defence. With an axe, you wouldn't need to bother."

Cayell was shaking her head vigorously. Tevi decided to talk to her later and gave a noncommittal response. "I'll think about it."

At that moment, the gong signalling the end of the morning session rang out. The sword master collected the practise weapons and dismissed the nominees, saying, "I'm going to pass you, Tevi. You can report to the assessor after lunch. But I want to see the rest of you back here."

The four nominees left the practice hall and filed through the maze of buildings. Long ago, the mercenary guildhall had been laid out to an elegant plan, which had been modified and added to over the intervening centuries so that very little of the original design remained. It resulted in a bewildering network of passages and doorways sandwiched between the old and the new. Even after a month, Tevi had great difficulty finding her way around. In contrast, Cayell seemed to have the entire guildhall mapped out in her head. She was never lost for direction—or for something to say. Her body was lightly built but had an acrobat's agility. Her footsteps were silent, but her personality was loud.

"Down here. It's a shortcut," Cayell called as she disappeared between two buildings.

"Are you sure?" asked Perrin, an affable young man with the general proportions, and appetite, of an ox. His six foot six inches of solid muscle made him the strongest of the nominees, apart from Tevi.

"Of course. Don't you trust me?" Cayell sounded hurt.

"Well, yes, but dinner's important. I want to be sure I'm in time for seconds."

"And maybe thirds," added Rymar as he pushed Perrin down the alleyway.

In the rear was Tevi. She studied her comrades' backs as they walked in single file. Cayell was lost beyond Perrin's bulk, though the sound of her laughter drowned out his bass rumble. Rymar was a head shorter than Perrin, yet broad-shouldered and athletic. They were a good bunch, Tevi thought, although Rymar looked to be a little too fond of beer and mayhem when let loose. He was on his best behaviour while being assessed, but the wildness showed through.

The air inside the guild refectory was thick with the smell of food and the hubbub of conversation. The tables held large pots of stew and trenchers of bread to use as plates. Tevi and the others wove their way to the table reserved for nominees. Referred to as "the babies' table," it left them in no doubt of their status. There were currently eight nominees for assessment. Apart from Cayell and Tevi, only one other was a woman—a fact that, as Tevi had discovered, fairly represented the male-to-female ratio of the guild.

Once they had sat down, Tevi addressed the table in general. "What's so bad about a battle-axe?"

"Poor image." Perrin was squeezed directly opposite.

Cayell joined in, a grin on her face. "Don't worry, Tevi. You're great with a sword. There are precious few nominees who've been able to disarm the sword master."

"She didn't!" someone else said in disbelief.

"She did," Perrin affirmed.

"He might be right. An axe might suit me better," Tevi said.

Cayell shook her head. "Women warriors with axes are a joke. Axe men tend to be warriors who are poorly endowed with brains—"

Perrin butted in. "Women are outnumbered in the guild, particularly as warriors. They usually specialise in a field that requires less strength—"

Cayell cut back in. "—and more intelligence. Like scouting. Me, for example." She threw out her hands in an extroverted gesture that was met with jeers from the nominees and frowns from the other tables.

"I've got the strength for an axe," Tevi pointed out.

"You've also got brains, and you'll get work easier if you let people know it," Cayell said.

"How does that follow?"

"Girls know they can't count on developing the strength necessary for fighting. Boys can't, either, but they're more likely to. Most girls who want to be mercenaries try to specialise. Being a scout is ideal. Women are often smaller and lighter, so we make less noise. We can go farther on less food and can withstand harsher weather. Women warriors tend to be girls who lacked the brains to do anything clever but turned out lucky with the physique. Axe-wielding just compounds the effect."

"Which could all work to Tevi's advantage," Dale, another of the nominees, said thoughtfully. He was a lanky lad whose serious face masked a mischievous sense of humour. People looked with surprise as he continued. "Just think. In a battle, someone would see Tevi with an axe and think, 'Oh, yes, axe woman—not going to be too bright.' Then Tevi could say something really clever and hit them while they were still stunned with astonishment." Laughter and a few flicked peas greeted this idea.

"Someone told me that in the Protectorate, you don't make assumptions about people based on their sex," Tevi said.

Cayell looked blank, then shrugged and said, "I suppose it depends on what assumptions. Sometimes, you have to play the odds."

"Like you don't expect people from over the Spur to be particularly alert," Perrin said—a playful dig at Rymar, whose accent marked him from that region. Tevi frowned. The indolence of people from the east of the Protectorate was an item of folklore she had already encountered, yet Rymar was one of the quicker nominees and astute enough not to rise to the bait.

Cayell laughed. "Or sorcerers who specialise in prophesy. For some reason, they tend to be..." She paused. "Now, what's the word?"

Suggestions came from around the table.

"Neurotic."

"Highly strung."

"Unbalanced."

Cayell waved a piece of carrot. "No, no. Sensitive. That's the word

I wanted." She pointed the carrot at Tevi. "Now, remember, if ever you meet a Coven seer, the word is 'sensitive,' unless you have a desire to experience life as a toad."

Tevi chewed thoughtfully. "I guess nobody dares to call axe men many names to their faces, either."

"As long as the word has more than three syllables, you're quite safe."

The banter continued with a bawdy story about the mad axe woman of Rizen. Many of the jokes were lost on Tevi. She had not come to grips with the necessary slang use, but she got the general idea of the perception of axes and their users.

❖

Once the meal was over, Tevi left the others and found her way to the assessor's quarters, needing to ask directions only twice. When she got there, the clerk in the anteroom informed her that the assessor was busy with somebody else. Tevi wandered back outside and stood on the veranda at the front of the building, watching people pass through the courtyard. It was a mellow autumn afternoon. The sun shone on ornate stonework surrounding the open grass.

Directly opposite the assessor's rooms was the infirmary. Many of the occupants had been placed in the open, to get what benefit they could from the sun and fresh air. The invalids sat on a bench, tightly wrapped in warm blankets. Some laughed and joked, swapping stories of their exploits. Some sat in silence. Tevi studied a gaunt young man, no more than a year older than herself. Both his legs ended in stumps just above the knees. Next to him sat a middle-aged woman, one side of her face a scarred wreck, undoubtedly blind in that eye.

Tevi was certain that the location of the assessor's rooms, next to the infirmary, was no accident. All hopeful applicants had to walk past the grim reminder of what might await them. She suspected that the warning had little effect. Most mercenaries were overconfident, sure that the worst could never happen to them. Many were blind to everything they did not want to see. They would not know or care where the infirmary was until they were carried into it. They would begrudge the share of their income the guild took, unaware of where the money went, until they became the beneficiaries.

Ten minutes later, the door opened behind her, and a tall mercenary strode out, followed by a young woman. Neither paid any attention to the people sitting opposite. Tevi wondered if that did not hurt more than all the scars—to no longer be worthy of notice.

After a last look at the invalids, Tevi turned and entered. The clerk pointed her to a small room, where she found the assessor, a stout, elderly woman sitting in a high-backed chair beside a fireplace. Despite the warm day, logs burned vigorously in the grate.

"The sword master told me to report to you, ma'am," Tevi said hesitantly.

"Ah, yes. Please." The assessor gestured to a second chair and waited until Tevi was seated before continuing. "I'm happy to say we've decided to accept your nomination."

It was the announcement Tevi was expecting, but instead of replying, she stared at the fire. Only the crackling of the flames broke the silence.

"You're not looking overjoyed. Have you had second thoughts?" the assessor asked.

"No, ma'am. I'm pleased you've accepted me. It's what I came here for. But I was watching the invalids opposite and I was thinking about them." Tevi looked directly at the assessor. "That's what we're supposed to do, isn't it?"

"It's true that we prefer our members join with as few illusions as possible. We get too many young idiots dreaming of glory."

"I don't think I have any unrealistic hopes."

"No, I don't think you have." The assessor watched Tevi thoughtfully before continuing in a brisker tone. "You realise, of course, that the assessment is not just about fighting skill. We could have evaluated that taking considerably less time than the month you've been here. If you join the guild, you'll receive its mark—a single sword tattooed on each hand. With that mark, the guild is declaring that it believes you to be competent, honest, and reliable. Although we're not yet backing our judgement with money. It will be some years before we're likely to guarantee you and add the second sword."

"I understand that."

"It's important that the mark of the guild mean something. Our livelihood depends on people trusting our integrity. The time a nominee spends here constitutes part of a general appraisal, which has been all the more important in your case, as you haven't served a formal apprenticeship. But we're quite satisfied. In our judgement, you will not do anything to bring the guild into disrepute, and we're willing to accept you. The final decision lies with you. We don't allow people to desert the guild once they've accepted its mark. Those we expel leave their tattoos, and their hands, behind."

The assessor stood and walked to the door. "I'm going to suggest you think about it for this afternoon; then come and see me first thing tomorrow. If you decide to join, we'll move you to the junior members' quarters. You'll need to be instructed in the first level of guild passwords, which shouldn't take you too long to learn." The assessor rolled her eyes to the ceiling with a sigh. "Unlike some other nominees. And we'll make an appointment for you with the tattooist. So...unless you have any questions?"

"No, thank you, ma'am. I think I know all I need in order to make my mind up."

"Whatever you decide, I wish you well."

The assessor held the door open. Tevi gave a respectful nod and walked back into the autumn sunlight. Her aimless steps took her out of the guildhall and into the streets of Lyremouth. She spent the afternoon wandering and thinking, although in truth she had little choice. As a mercenary, she could earn a good living. Without a guild, she could be nothing more than a poorly paid labourer.

Standing by the main docks, she watched the ships sail across the harbour. If she closed her eyes, from the sounds and smell of the sea she could imagine herself back on Storenseg. Guild membership would be one further, irrevocable step away from the islands. Tevi shook her head at the folly of her thoughts and left the quay, heading into the busy streets of the city. There was no going back.

Chapter Seven—Dishonourable Conduct

By the time Tevi returned to the guildhall, the evening meal was in progress. Luckily, Perrin had not yet embarked on his third helping, so there was still food left. The others shifted along to make room for Tevi. Even before she sat down, it was obvious Cayell was in high spirits.

"They've decided I'm more help than hindrance in a fight. Now they're going to see what I can do as a scout." Cayell was bouncing up and down with excitement.

"What tests do you get now?" Tevi asked.

"Oh, dreadful, awful things that would make you shudder just to hear about." Despite her words, Cayell was grinning. "I'll be dumped in the middle of nowhere and have to survive off the land while hunters try to catch me."

"You'll have to eat spiders," Perrin said, taking a large bite of his food.

"Big, juicy, tasty spiders?" Dale asked innocently.

The young woman Tevi had seen leaving the assessor's rooms was sitting at the table. She now joined in. "There's no such thing as a tasty spider. Believe me. I speak from experience."

"Are you a scout as well?" Perrin asked eagerly.

"Er...yes. My name's Aroche."

"Right. Well, while Cay's away, do you mind making it your job to find shortcuts to the refectory?"

Aroche smiled. "I'll do my best, if you think it's important."

"We're talking about Perrin's stomach. Of course it's important," Rymar said.

When the table had quieted, Tevi asked Cayell, "How long will you be gone?"

"About ten days. You can take my bed, if you want." Predictably, Cayell had wangled the best position in the dormitory.

"I won't need it. I've been accepted into the guild. I'm moving to the members' quarters tomorrow."

Cayell cheered and punched the air, drawing stern looks from other tables. She pointed at Tevi. "Promise you'll save the celebration until I get back. There's not time to do it justice tonight, and with luck, we can celebrate my acceptance as well."

Confronted with such exuberance, Tevi could do nothing but agree. As she got ready for her last night in the nominees' dormitory, lighthearted banter was flying around—as were pillows and items of clothing. Tevi joined in, mainly by ducking at the appropriate points. For the first time since childhood, she felt like an accepted member of a group. The camaraderie of the guild enveloped its members. Although she had been fond of Marith and Verron, they had been more like an aunt and uncle. Cayell and the other nominees were her friends.

❖

Eleven days later, Tevi was wandering along a colonnaded walkway that she hoped would lead her back to the junior members' quarters, when she was startled by a loud whoop. Running towards her was a figure—presumably Cayell, on account of the size and shape, though the exterior was so covered in mud that almost anything could have lurked beneath.

"I passed," the figure screamed, confirming its identity.

Cayell would have flung herself onto her friend, but Tevi held the mud-covered scout at arm's length.

"Cay! Look at the state of you!"

"I've only just got back," Cayell said, as if it were an explanation.

"I hadn't realised mud fights formed part of your appraisal."

"It's camouflage. I had to blend into the countryside."

"You've been somewhere where walking cow pats are commonplace?"

"Um...actually, most of it is due to an accident just outside town." Cayell grinned mischievously

"Why don't you tell me about it on the way to the bathhouse?"

"I've got to see the assessor." Cayell paused and inspected herself. "Or do you think I should get cleaned up first?"

"I've seen more presentable scarecrows thrown out as scrap."

"You're probably right." Cayell grabbed Tevi's hands. Holding them palm down, she inspected the tattooed red and gold swords. Her eyes met Tevi's. "Very pretty. We've got to celebrate. Get some of the others to meet up tonight."

"Dale and Rymar will be keen, and probably Perrin as well."

"That'll be great." Cayell walked away backwards.

"You can tell us all about the accident."

"Only if you promise not to laugh. It was a touch unfortunate." Cayell raised one hand to her head in a melodramatic fashion and then grinned before disappearing in the direction of the bathhouse.

❖

The Golden Swan was a noisy tavern with splintered tables and lanterns burning foul-smelling oil. The straw on the floor looked as if it had not been changed since the founding of the Protectorate. The only heating came from the largely unwashed bodies of the customers. However, the beer was cheap, and the staff kept selling it long after more respectable establishments had closed.

In a poorly lit rear corner, the five young mercenaries were studiously trying to get drunk and meeting with considerable success. A succession of toasts was made to the new guild members. These included Rymar, who was also sporting tattoos, only two days old and still itchy.

Putting down his tankard, Perrin leaned across to Tevi. "Do you remember us talking about women with axes? As a good example, have you seen that Big Bron is back in the guildhall?"

Tevi shook her head.

"You must have seen her," Dale chipped in. "You know the one, six foot two, square, long blond hair and wears a copper torque that could double as a wagon wheel. She always scowls like she's just sat on something uncomfortable."

Tevi groaned; she had been mistaken yet again. "I thought that was a man."

"Now that's unusual," Cayell said seriously. "Most people mistake her for some sort of architectural support structure."

Rymar nudged Tevi's shoulder. "You wouldn't make that mistake if you'd seen her naked."

"You what!" Cayell was the only one not stunned speechless.

"Oh, no, no. Nothing like that." Rymar held up his hands in denial. "She was in the baths, and someone swiped her clothes as a joke. It wasn't me. I'm not suicidal. But I was there when she stormed out, looking for blood."

"That could have been a cute beginning to a beautiful relationship," Dale said.

"The words 'cute' and 'Bron' do not belong in the same sentence."

"You did it just then."

"Don't be a fool. She eats boys like me for breakfast." Rymar ran a finger around his collar.

"And you wouldn't like that?"

"Look...just take it from me, romance was not in the air. Murder, yes. Romance, no."

"Probably just as well. They say Bron doesn't have much in the way of a sense of humour," Cayell said.

"And...?" Rymar prompted.

"From what I've heard, she'd need it with you." Cayell grinned.

Rymar acted hurt. "That's a nasty, malicious rumour. I am a lover of great sophistication and skill, as I'll demonstrate to anyone here." His expression changed to an idiotic leer. "Come on, any takers?"

"I would, but..." Perrin clasped a hand to his breast in a flamboyant gesture. "I am sworn to another."

Dale put his arm around Perrin's shoulder. His voice oozed sincere concern. "Look. You've got to be adult about this. One night of passion with a mange-ridden sheep does not constitute a binding commitment. For either of you," he finished, as everyone gave way to yelps of laughter.

Tevi wiped her eyes. Sometimes, she was unable to tell whether people were being serious. Even when she had that sorted out, she was often unsure what the point of the joke was, but this she realised, was an invented leg pull.

Summoning her self-control, she looked at Perrin. "Take no notice. They're just being silly. I'm sure she didn't have mange, and even if she did, there are medical treatments. There's no reason why the two of you can't be very happy together."

At the sight of Perrin's expression, Cayell curled forward, holding her sides. Perrin rose to his full height and looked down sternly. "If you're all going to act the fool, I'm going to buy another round of drinks." His features broke into a grin.

Dale hugged him round the waist. "Your logic's flawed, but I'll love you forever." And then he fell backwards off his stool.

❖

By the time they left the tavern, they were incapable of walking in a straight line. They formed a row, five abreast, with arms wrapped around each others' shoulders to provide mutual support, and marched back to the guildhall to a song about a mercenary called Mighty Marrick. The lyrics told of the hero's encounters with, among others, a ship full of pirates, a family of hill trolls, and one very surprised dragon. Tevi had trouble understanding the slang phases and euphemisms, but she made enough sense to know that the tale was both obscene and biologically impossible.

Cayell took three attempts to get up the steps to the side entrance. Tevi stayed to help. In the end, Cayell literally crawled up and then collapsed at the top, giggling. Tevi dragged her to her feet and propelled her forward. Some distance ahead, the three men were embarking on a spirited repetition of the fourth verse.

The singers were crossing a courtyard when a door was flung open. A large shape blocked the light, filling the entrance. Tevi was about to step into the open, but Cayell pulled her back behind a pillar. "It's her. Big Bron."

While the two young women hid, biting their knuckles to stop from laughing, Bron loudly extolled the virtues of peace and quiet. She proceeded to give an unflattering account of the men and, by implication, their parents. Bron seemed to know only one adjective, but used it to great effect.

When they heard the door slam, Tevi and Cayell peered cautiously around the pillar. The courtyard lay deserted in the moonlight. With exaggerated care, they tiptoed across, then rushed all the way to the junior members' quarters, where Tevi had her room. They stumbled to a halt outside.

"I've got to see the assessor again first thing tomorrow," Cayell gasped. "Then I can move my things down here. Is there a spare room near yours?"

Tevi nodded. "I'll meet you in the dormitory and give you a hand."

By way of acceptance, Cayell flung her arms around Tevi, which threatened to send the pair of them sprawling. They regained their balance, and Cayell stepped back. "Right, then. Tomorrow, midmorning. See you there." She staggered away, heading towards the nominees' dormitory, while humming the chorus of "Mighty Marrick" under her breath.

❖

The dormitory was deserted the next morning, when Tevi and her hangover entered. A muted grey light fell over pale blankets on the row of empty beds. To Tevi's bloodshot eyes, the effect was dazzling, forcing her to squint. The pulse throbbed at her temples with hammer blows, and waves of nausea threatened her hold on her stomach contents—or would, had there been any.

She groped her way to Cayell's bed, fell down, rather than sat; and then wrapped her hands about her head as if her skull might split. The only sound was of her sucking air into her lungs through clenched teeth.

The door swung open with a crash. "Oh, dear, oh, dear. Look what the cat's dragged in." Cayell's voice boomed mercilessly.

"Go away. I hate you," Tevi mumbled, drawing a peal of laughter.

"I can see you're going to be a bundle of fun."

Tevi only groaned.

"Don't worry. Sit still. I haven't got much to pack."

When Tevi still made no reply, Cayell sat on the bed opposite and studied her. "Feeling rough? I wondered how you were when you didn't show up for breakfast."

"Don't mention food."

"Best thing for you. Come on."

Cayell thrust a hand under Tevi's armpit and yanked her to her feet. She pushed and coaxed Tevi all the way to the refectory. The smell from the kitchens made Tevi's stomach heave, but her protests were ignored. She collapsed at the table where she was dumped and listened with half an ear as Cayell browbeat the staff into providing breakfast and a mug of the "chef's special." The food and drink arrived shortly. Tevi could only stare in horror.

"I can't eat."

"Yes, you can," Cayell said firmly.

"I feel ill."

"That's obvious. Look, take this. It's the chef's special remedy. Mercenaries swear by it." Cayell thrust a mug into Tevi's hand.

"By it or at it?"

"Down it in one. It will make you feel better."

Resisting was too much hard work. Tevi drank the potion and started gingerly on the food. She hated to admit it, but Cayell was right. Her stomach settled, and the pounding in her head eased.

"That's better. You're getting some colour back in your face."

"Hmmph."

"You're supposed to say, 'Thank you, Cay.'" Cayell's tone was cheerful but hardly sympathetic.

"You can't expect gratitude from the dead."

"Oh, you'll survive."

"I'm not certain if I want to."

"It's amazing the philosophical insights alcohol can bring. It took Keovan forty years of meditation to question whether life was worth living. One night and twelve pints of beer, and you've matched him."

Tevi managed her first real smile since waking. "Was that how much we drank?"

"I lost count. If it's any consolation, Dale and Perrin both looked green this morning, and they were due at the archery butts after breakfast."

"You're looking all right."

"Practice," Cayell said primly.

Tevi finished off the bread. The blinding headache had shifted to a throb at the base of her skull. Tevi massaged it with one hand, then grinned ruefully. "I guess we can collect your things now."

"If you're ready."

"Sure...and thanks, Cay," Tevi said softly.

"Any time."

Dark clouds hung low over the guildhall; rain was not far off.

The wind was cold and damp. People scurried along with heads down and collars up. Seagulls sat despondently on the roofs. As they walked through the gloomy maze of pathways, Cayell slipped her arm through Tevi's. Despite the beneficial effects of breakfast, Tevi was grateful for the additional support.

Back in the dormitory, Cayell began to assemble her belongings, not that she, or any nominees, had much. A chest at the foot of her bed held everything she owned. There was little need of Tevi's help—fortunately. Although she was feeling better, her overall condition remained decidedly fragile.

Tevi wandered to a window and stared out. The first splats of rain struck the glass. "You had no doubts about joining the guild?" she asked over her shoulder.

"No. It's what I've always wanted."

"Don't your parents mind? Or were they mercenaries as well?" Even as the words left her mouth, Tevi bit her tongue. It seemed an unspoken rule that nominees did not mention their families.

Cayell paused and her face grew sombre. "Little Papa is worried sick. But he won't stand in my way."

"I'm sorry. I didn't mean to pry."

"It's all right." Cayell shook her head, as if trying to clear her thoughts, and returned to packing. "Little Papa is a forester. He taught me how to live in the wild. He hoped I'd follow him. When he realised I wasn't interested in trees, he wanted me to be apprenticed to a fur trapper. Big Papa helped me talk him round. I want to pit myself against an enemy who's my equal, not an animal. I think all scouts feel like that."

"Does Aroche?"

"She's no scout."

"She said she was."

"She may have said it. Doesn't make it true. My guess is she's an assassin."

"Assassin!"

"There are politer names, like 'personal security guard.'"

"Why did she lie?"

"Force of habit. It can become a way of life with those people. Or perhaps creating a false identity is part of her assessment. I don't know if anyone else has twigged, but she can't fool a real scout."

"I know the guild has assassins, but I thought—"

"That we're always good guys?" Cayell suggested. "Don't worry, 'security guard' isn't such a euphemism. Most guild assassins are hired by Protectorate traders who are going to places where murder is part of everyday business practice. Her training is all about poisons, traps, and breaking into places. The knowledge works both ways—doing or preventing. In general, guild members go for the latter. I'm sure she'll spend most of her working life stopping people from bumping off her employer."

"But not all of it?"

"Maybe not. But in theory, there's nothing to stop thieves hiring you or me. However, the guild masters don't like members fighting each other and we provide most of the guards. They've also decided that theft doesn't contribute to long-term economic growth, and the more money honest citizens make, the more they can afford to pay us. So traders are in and bandits are out." Cayell's things were folded neatly in two piles. She looked at Tevi and asked, "Are you all right to help carry?"

"I'll survive."

Outside, the rain had arrived in full force. Large drops pounded the flagstones. Water washed down the walls and dripped from the doorway. The distance was lost to the grey falling sheets.

Cayell grinned. "We're going to have to run. Last one there gets wettest."

The two women raced between buildings, hurdling puddles and rivulets pouring from downpipes. Cayell charged through the entrance to the junior quarters at full pelt. Tevi was close behind. Their shoulders were soaked, and hair stuck to their foreheads. Laughing and wiping water from their eyes, they walked down the narrow corridor.

The quarters had originally been one large open dormitory. During an expansion of the guildhall facilities some years before, it had been divided into individual small rooms by thin wooden partitions. Tevi halted outside one door and pushed it open. "This one's empty, and you're just three along from me."

The furniture consisted of a narrow bunk and a chest. A wide shelf ran the length of the wall above the bed. There was not much in the way of floor space. Light came from half a window, which the partition had divided in two.

"It's small enough. They're certainly not splashing out on us lesser mortals," Cayell stepped into the room.

Tevi deposited the pile she was carrying on the chest. "It's pure luxury. In the village I came from, only the Queen had her own room, and she still slept on the ground. I hadn't seen a proper bed before I reached the mainland. At first, I used to lie awake at night, frightened I'd roll over in my sleep."

Cayell laughed and turned to face her. The scout's expression changed to concern. "You've gone very pale. I don't think the run helped you."

"It'll ease." However, the sick pounding had returned. Specks of light danced before Tevi's eyes.

"Why don't you lie down while I put my things away? You'll only get under my feet if you stay standing."

With relief, Tevi dropped onto the bed and scrunched her eyes shut. The pressure built in waves, as if her skull was about to crack open.

"Do you want me to get some water for you?" There was an uncharacteristic gentleness in Cayell's voice.

"I'll be all right."

At the touch of something soft on her face, Tevi opened her eyes. Cayell had knelt beside the bed and was using a shirt off the pile as a towel. Tevi was surprised. Her friend's face was serious, even tentative, both rare emotions for the exuberant extrovert.

"You don't need to worry. I'm only hung over."

"I don't want you passing out on me. Or throwing up. There's not enough room for me to get out of your way."

"I won't."

Cayell's mouth opened, as if she was building up to say something important. She squeezed Tevi's shoulder. "You know, I think I...er...You have..." Cayell's mumbling ground to a halt.

Tevi was confused. It was not like Cayell to be tongue-tied.

Abruptly, the scout stood and busied herself about the room, unpacking her clothes. She started talking quickly. "I suppose we're lucky to get rooms to ourselves. If more people wanted accommodation, they'd shift us juniors into a dormitory quickly enough. It's only because winter's a slack time. Not much happening, so folk take the chance to visit their families." She looked at Tevi stretched out on the bed. "I guess you won't be going home much."

"I'm not planning on it." Even with the headache, Tevi could hear the bitterness in her own voice.

Cayell hurried on. "It will be great here in Lyremouth. The midwinter festival is one big party."

"Perrin told me about it."

"Big Papa brought me here one year. I'm really looking forward to it. Since there's no work to be had, we can have fun without being accused of shirking."

Although lodging at the guildhall was nominally free, Tevi was familiar with the guild rules requiring its members to take whatever work was offered. Tevi frowned, not at the thought of work, but at the feeling Cayell was using the festival as a diversion and that her friend had been about to say something else. But with the state she was in, it was easy to get confused.

"I'm not sure how much fun I can stand," Tevi said with feeling.

"You could stick to drinking milk. Though I'm not sure what it'll do to the reputation of mercenaries."

"I could threaten to thump anyone who laughed."

"Now that would be more like the way a warrior is supposed to behave."

"How long do you think the guild will let us stay here without working?" Tevi asked after a while.

"Probably till early spring, when things start moving again."

Cayell shut the chest and sat on the edge of the bed by Tevi. "What do you say that we try and get on the same contract? Some large caravan going north, maybe. They can be pretty rough. It would be nice to have at least one good-looking face around. I'd be doing you a favour."

Tevi punched her friend gently. "You flatter yourself."

"It's good for my ego. But you'd be pleased if we were together?"

"Of course."

"I'd like...having you around." Cayell's voice was quieter, the joking tone gone.

"Even when I'm hung over?"

"Maybe you're not at your best right now, but..." Cayell paused, as if bracing herself. "I like you...a lot." Cayell carefully raised her hand to stroke the side of Tevi's face, pushing the wet hair back from her cheek.

"What do you mean?" Alarm flared in Tevi's gut.

Cayell's lips twisted in a nervous half smile. "I mean that I think you're really nice, and I'm hoping that you feel the same about me. And you're great to have as a friend, but I'd like to be more. And I know you probably won't feel like it at the moment...with your hangover, but I'm desperately hoping that I can talk you into keeping me company tonight."

The memory of the hay barn on Storenseg surged into Tevi's head. Again, she could smell the stale odours of the barn and hear Brec's treacherous voice. Wild panic stopped the breath in her lungs as she sat up and shoved Cayell away. The onslaught of old nightmares sent searing bolts ripping through her skull. Tevi glared around, eyes screwed in agony, searching for hiding places. There were none, but the partitions were thin. Anyone might be standing next door. She lurched to her feet, stumbling in her haste.

Tevi raised her voice, loud enough for any eavesdropper to hear. "If I want that sort of company, I'll find a man."

Cayell had landed on the floor. Looking dazed, she stared wordlessly and had still made no attempt to move by the time that Tevi had wrenched the door open and raced away down the corridor.

❖

Tevi ran wildly through the guildhall, paying no attention to where her footsteps led her. She finally stumbled to a halt in the covered walkway surrounding a quadrangle. Several stone benches were set between the pillars. Tevi picked one at random, sat down, and watched the rain. The surface of a small pond in the middle was laced with ripples.

Tevi pulled her heels onto the seat and rested her forehead on her knees. Her skull was about to explode. Ideas scrambled through her head, fighting between the stabs of pain. The words of the assessor came back to her: "*In our judgement, you will not do anything to bring the guild into disrepute.*" Tevi's face contorted as she tried to remember all the guild rules. Nothing specifically had been said, but she guessed it was covered by the catchall clause of "dishonourable conduct."

Why had Cayell done it? Or had she? Tevi groaned. In her current state, she could not be certain of anything. Perhaps she had misunderstood and should find Cayell and apologise, although there was no explanation that was not in itself a confession of guilt. Then Tevi remembered the look on Cayell's face. She was sure she had not been wrong.

Was Cayell's overture genuine or a trap? The latter option made no sense. The guild should have made their tests before accepting her, not after. Yet surely Cayell would not be so reckless in risking their futures. What if they had been overheard? Tevi settled her chin onto her knees. Her chaotic thoughts would not settle into any sensible order. The hangover made thinking as easy as fighting with fog. The pain and nausea rendered her incapable of tackling anything else.

The rain fell in sheets, drowning out all other sounds, including that of footsteps approaching.

"Ah, Tevi. I was looking for you." An elderly voice spoke.

Tevi jerked around so violently that she almost fell. One of the guild masters was standing at her shoulder.

"Sir?" Her heart thumped in her breast. Her mouth was dry.

"I've been told you have experience of driving a wagon. Is that true?"

The question was so unexpected, Tevi could only stare back blankly.

He tried again. "You know, a wagon? Wheels underneath and some horses in front to pull it. You know how to drive one?"

"Er...yes. A wagon. Yes."

The guild master chuckled. "I'd heard you had a good time last night." He smiled indulgently. "We've had a request from someone who wants to hire a mercenary. He intends to go north, to spend winter with his daughter at Treviston. The route is straight through the heart of the Protectorate, and all he needs is a wagon driver. Which is what we told him. However, he seems convinced that everyone outside Lyremouth is a psychopathic barbarian, and he wants protection. I said we'd try and find someone." The guild master paused. "Normally, the guild insists junior members accept any contract they're qualified for, but this is not how we expect our warriors to be employed, and I imagine that you would much rather stay here. So we will let you refuse the contract this time—as a one-off concession."

"I'll go."

The speed of Tevi's reply clearly surprised the guild master. "You're sure?"

"Yes, sir."

"Well...it's good to see such enthusiasm."

"When does he want to leave?"

"I told him if we found someone, we'd send them over tomorrow morning. If you're certain you want the job, I'd recommend you spend the afternoon buying yourself warm clothes. Treviston is some way north and in the mountains. Don't worry about the cost; your new employer is paying well. After you've bought what you need, you can call at the pursers' and pick up the contract. I'll arrange to have it ready."

After a final puzzled look at Tevi, the guild master left. Tevi followed his departure with her eyes, then swivelled back and sat for a long while watching the rain fall.

Chapter Eight—Difficult Company

Early the next morning, Tevi arrived at the address she had been given, a substantial townhouse in one of the richer areas of Lyremouth. A scattering of tradesmen were about, but the street was quieter than most. Tevi suspected it would remain so throughout the day. Nothing would be permitted to disturb the genteel tranquillity. While waiting for the door to open she shuffled from foot to foot, examining the half-timbered frontage of the house in a futile attempt to distract herself from feeling exposed and vulnerable.

She had risen before the bell and grabbed food from the kitchens, not wanting to take her breakfast with the others. The previous evening had been a strain. She and Cayell had ignored each other, although once or twice, Tevi had caught the other woman glaring at her in undisguised confusion and anger. Perrin and the others had clearly been surprised by the broken friendship but had wisely refrained from interfering. Tevi wondered what they had been told.

Eventually the door opened and an elderly servant studied her with cursory disdain. "You are the mercenary guard?"

"Yes. I've got the contract with me." Tevi held out the paper.

"Master Sarryle is expecting you. Follow me."

She was led into a small parlour. Her new employer was sitting by the fire, blankets draped over his knees. To a first glance, he looked far older than he actually was—an effect he seemed to be cultivating deliberately, by his outmoded dress and frail mannerisms. His head was bald on top, with a frill of white hair hanging over his ears. Sunken eyes blinked irritably in Tevi's direction as if she was an unpleasant distraction. A partly eaten breakfast lay to one side. His lips pulled into a sour pout.

"You're very young. I was expecting somebody more experienced."

The caustic tone was disconcerting. However, Tevi stepped forward, presenting the contract. "I have experience with wagons, sir. And I am a trained warrior."

"You're early. The horses aren't harnessed yet. Eli will have to do it after finding my willow bark ointment. I always wake with this terrible pain in my joints. I don't know how I'm going to cope with the journey. The town councils never maintain the roads as they should."

Tevi latched onto a break in the tirade. "I could harness the horses, sir."

"If you think you're able." Sarryle's tone made his doubt evident. "Though I'm not sure how far we'll get today. The weather witch said it will be fine, but you can't trust them. My knees ache—that's always a sign of rain. We'll be up to our necks in mud by midmorning. I don't know why my daughter had to move so far away. Typical of her."

"The horses, sir?"

"Oh, yes, yes. Eli, show her to the stables. And these eggs are overdone. You'll have to do some more. You must—"

Tevi and Eli escaped. As they walked to the stables, Tevi tried to catch Eli's eye, wondering how seriously she should take Master Sarryle's behaviour.

"Will you be coming with us to Treviston?" Tevi asked.

"I am to stay and look after the house."

"There'll be other servants?" Tevi was not too sure about being alone with the old man.

"The cook and the valet have recently left Master Sarryle's employ and have not yet been replaced."

Tevi assumed that meant no. Eli's voice was so deliberately neutral, it was obvious there was a lot that was not being said. Unsurprising—Tevi had already worked out that her new employer was not easy to deal with first thing in the morning.

❖

It soon emerged, however, that Tevi was mistaken in her judgement. Master Sarryle was never easy to deal with, regardless of the time of day. Before the journey was halfway complete, Tevi had formed the opinion that the protection of a guild mercenary was not an extravagance on her employer's part. Without her presence, Tevi was convinced that someone would have strangled the old man. She was not sure if she could withstand the temptation herself.

The journey limped from town to town. Before leaving Lyremouth, Tevi had established that the distance could be travelled in fifteen days, twenty at the most. Yet thirty days did not see them to their destination. Master Sarryle would not start early, nor would he travel after nightfall. He complained about potholes if she raised the speed above a walk. In Lower Deaford, he developed a chill and would not move for three days. Tevi was approaching the end of her patience.

On the thirty-second day of the journey, they lodged at a farm less than nine miles from Treviston. The weather had been mild for the time of year—a sharp frost most nights, but the skies had remained clear. However, that night, winter struck. They awoke to a world cloaked in white. Huge flakes danced in the light wind and drifted into deep banks. Tevi was astonished. Snow was rare on Storenseg, never more than a dusting on the mountains.

The snow continued to fall all morning. Just before lunchtime, it slackened and finally ceased. Tevi stood in the doorway with Master Sarryle scowling at her shoulder.

"If you'd made better time, we'd be safely in Treviston by now. I thought you were supposed to be competent at driving a wagon," he snapped before stalking off.

"I'll throttle him," Tevi mouthed silently to herself.

His place was taken by the farm owner. Tevi continued to look out across the hills. Only the stark blackness of trees broke the soft contours of white. The wind blew across the threshold with an icy bite. The farmer studied the ominous grey clouds before offering her opinion.

"It will hold off for a while, but when it gets going, we'll be snowed in. It's always the same when winter comes late. It hits quick and hard and won't let up till spring."

"Do you think it will hold long enough for us to get to Treviston?"

The farmer pursed her lips. "Chancy."

At that moment, they heard Sarryle's voice. "You, boy. Don't screech. It hurts my ears."

"Lee put an icicle down my neck," a young voice wailed.

"I don't know what your parents are thinking of, letting you run wild."

"I was only playing," protested a second child, presumably Lee.

"You think this weather's a game. If you had my knees..."

Tevi met the farmer's eyes. She could tell that the same thought was going through the other woman's head. Freezing to death would be fun compared to months cooped up with Master Sarryle.

"I'll risk it."

From the dazzling smile, Tevi thought the farmer was about to kiss her.

While Tevi and Sarryle dressed in their warmest clothes, the entire farm workforce was called on to make ready the wagon. Even one ancient great-grandparent hobbled out to offer advice.

Sarryle was not grateful for the help. He stopped in the yard and looked at the snow settling over the tops of his boots. "I'm not sure if we should travel today."

"Nonsense, sir. It will be quite all right," Tevi said briskly.

Sarryle's mouth started to open. Tevi did not give him a chance. She swept her elderly employer off his feet and hoisted him into the wagon; then she fastened the awning and leapt onto the driver's seat. The wagon rolled into the snowy landscape, accompanied by a barrage of accusations emanating from the covered section. When Tevi looked back, she could see the farmer's whole family standing by the gates, waving an enthusiastic goodbye.

The deep drifts made it hard to tell the line of the road. Only the gap between stunted upland trees showed the route. Twice, the wheels ran into the drainage ditch and were pulled free with much coaxing of the carthorses. By the time they had travelled three miles, Tevi was obliged to get out and lead the horses while feeling for the road with her feet. Her toes were frozen, but at least she could no longer hear what Master Sarryle was saying.

As afternoon advanced, the snow began to fall again. White flakes swirled ghostlike in the half-light. The horses fought their way over the last hill, their hooves sliding on the ice. Faint lights shone in the valley below. Treviston at last. Snow lay less thick on this side of the hill, and the road was again visible. Tevi climbed back onto the wagon with relief. She set the horses off at a good pace, ignoring the complaints from behind.

Two miles outside town, they reached a side road. Lights from a large farmhouse shone at the end of a short track. Tevi knew this was the approximate location of the daughter's farm. She raised the awning. Master Sarryle was wedged sullenly in a corner under a mound of blankets.

"Do you know exactly where your daughter's farm is, sir?"

"Do you mean to tell me you're lost?"

"No. There's a farm over there. I wondered if it was your daughter's."

"Didn't you pay attention to your instructions?"

"I was told your daughter lives two miles south of town."

"Well, you obviously—"

Tevi dropped the flap, her patience snapped. She did not care whose house it was. They could take the old man; she was not going a step farther with him.

Fortunately, it was the right farm, and Sarryle was welcomed inside. The affectionate greeting impressed Tevi. She could not believe it was genuine. Tevi stood, slightly dazed in the knowledge that her contract was completed, while Sarryle was led to the room prepared for him and the wagon was taken to the stables.

The daughter beckoned Tevi aside. "Do you wish to stay here tonight?"

"It's taken longer to get here than planned. I think I should report straight to the guild master in town."

The excuse was weak. One night's delay would make no difference, even if her arrival were expected. In truth, Tevi would rather have slept in the snow than spend another night under the same roof as Sarryle. The daughter smiled sympathetically. Using a wax candle, she put her father's seal on the contract and passed it back with the money. As an afterthought, she handed Tevi a few more coins. "I'm sure you've deserved it."

In a mood of euphoria, Tevi shouted goodbye to everyone within earshot. Night was descending rapidly. The freezing wind had picked up, and the snow was falling hard, but Tevi felt so happy to be rid of her charge that she practically skipped all the way into town.

❖

"So she came over to me, and she looked me straight in the eye, and she said, 'Lad,' she said, 'I need a volunteer. But it's a tough one, and I can't guarantee you'll come back.' So I looked at her, and I said, 'I'm your man.' Then she took me by the hand, and she said, 'Good lad. I knew I could rely on you.' 'So what's the score?' I said. 'Well,' she said, 'We need someone to get behind enemy lines and set fire to their stores.' So I said, 'Consider it done.' And when she'd gone, I went straight to the captain, and I told him what she'd said, and do you know what he said to me?" The narrator paused dramatically.

Tevi was not sure how much more she could stand. It would not be so bad if the old warrior did not expect audience participation. "No. What did he say?"

Ricard rested his hands on his knees importantly. "He clapped me on my shoulder, and he said, 'Ric,' he said, 'the honour of the guild rests on your shoulders.' That's what he said."

A month had passed since Tevi had arrived at the Treviston guildhall and it was the third time that Ricard had told of his part in the Troll Wars, three decades before. The story was not improving with retelling. Tevi's eyes wandered around the dining room, but no escape was in sight.

The guildhall was a modest building, busiest during the summer months, when the town was the stopping point for people crossing the Langhope Pass. The harsh winter had blocked not only the pass, but also all other access to the town. Only three mercenaries other than herself were lodging in the guildhall. They were elderly officials, retired from armed service, who managed the guild affairs. Ricard was running out of people he could recount his life story to.

The tale rambled on. "I could see the rabbits everywhere. We called them 'rabbits' because they were always popping out of holes. I remember old Chalky, the cook. Do you know what he said? He said, 'If ever I catch one, we'll have rabbit stew all month.'" Ricard's face broke into a smile, which grew to chuckles, his shoulders shaking. Tevi assumed that the joke had lost something with the passage of time.

The tedium was plumbing new, mind-numbing depths when a door opened and Nevin, the Treviston guild master, limped in. A mace had shattered her knee several years before, making a mockery of Nevin's otherwise athletic body. She was younger than the other residents and marginally more entertaining to be with. Tevi suspected that Nevin would have been good company, except that the constant pain made her short-tempered and cynical. Sandy hair hung in a fringe over shadowed eyes. Her lips were permanently turned down at the corners.

Ricard halted his story. "I was telling young Tevi here about the old wars, up north."

"You can give it a rest. I've heard it all before," Nevin said bluntly.

Tevi leapt at the excuse to flee. "Ricard can finish the story some other time." Then she smiled at the old man. He meant well.

"We could go to the kitchen," Ricard offered.

"Well, actually, I'd planned to go into town tonight." It was not strictly true, and Tevi could feel herself blushing.

Fortunately, Nevin spoke up. "Ric, get the chessboard out, and give me a game. That should keep you quiet."

"Oh yes...yes, of course." Ricard's confusion showed as he adjusted to the change in plans. He shuffled across the room to collect the board and pieces.

Seizing her chance, Tevi slipped from her seat. At the door, she paused and glanced back. Ricard was fussing over the playing pieces, swapping them back and forth as he tried to remember their positions. Nevin was slumped, her head sagging, as she rubbed her maimed leg with the heel of one hand. It was the same gesture Tevi remembered her mother making—the easing of tendons in a wounded knee. Yet the setting was so very different from the family hall on Storenseg.

Instead of drystone, the wood-panelled walls were hung with tapestries. A log fire blazed in the chimney. Rather than bare earth, there were flagstones, scrubbed clean. Suddenly, it all seemed very alien to Tevi. Swamped by homesickness, she closed the door and retreated to her room.

❖

The private quarters did not have fires, and the air was freezing. Tevi's breath formed white steam. Her room was austere, clearly intended to be functional rather than homelike. The bed was piled high with blankets and furs, though it was too early for sleep. Tevi's few possessions were neatly arranged. Nothing needed cleaning or mending; the previous month had taken care of that. Tevi sat on the edge of her bed and stared at the four bare walls. They seemed to close in around her with the weight of the deserted guild house.

A door below slammed. The sound reverberated through empty corridors. Listening to the fading echoes, Tevi became aware of voices through the thick green glass of the window. Drawn by the sound, she wandered over and stared out on the town. A panorama of snow-covered roofs filled the skyline. On the narrow street below, well-wrapped figures made what haste they could on the slippery pavements. The scene reminded Tevi of her fabricated excuse to escape Ricard. On impulse, she decided to make good her words.

She grabbed her thick woollen cloak from the rack in the entrance hall and changed into the boots she had bought with money from Sarryle's contract. One-quarter had gone to Nevin as the guild's share, but that still left plenty. Coins filled the purse at Tevi's belt. Fleece-lined gloves and hat completed her attire.

Dusk was settling as Tevi walked down the steps of the guildhall. It was a crisp, clear evening; the first stars already showing overhead. The street was filled with snow, brilliant white close to the walls, turning to brown slush in the ruts where traffic passed. The snow lay on every horizontal surface and clung to details in the brickwork. The road was busy with people going home after a day's work.

With no clear destination in mind, Tevi wandered from street to street until she reached Treviston's market square. The stalls and peddlers were gone. Tevi stopped in the middle and inspected each side in turn. The buildings were timber framed, with cream-coloured plaster and steep slate roofs. Tevi finally halted, facing east. Mountains loomed above the chimneys, vertical rock faces stark against the darkening blue sky. The last rays from the sun glinted off the icy peaks and washed them with pink. With each passing minute, more stars appeared.

Tevi watched until the white snow on the mountains was lost in darkness. She lowered her gaze and continued her restless wandering. By now, most townsfolk were home. Doors and window shutters were closed. Yellow light gleamed through joins in the wood.

Tevi passed a group of children indulging in one last snowball fight and ignoring the calls to come in for as long as they dared, until a more emphatic parental shout ended the game. A knot of townsfolk caught her attention, laughing boisterously with one another as they trudged home. Tevi's eyes followed them enviously until they were out of sight. She knew that she was desperately lonely. Pools of lamplight glittered off the white ground and sparkled on the plumes of powdery snow her boots kicked up. Her thoughts drifted aimlessly, like the dancing flakes.

She was caught completely unaware when a figure cannoned into her, careering wildly out of a steep side street. The collision knocked Tevi skidding sideways on the icy paving. Her arms flailed but caught only on the new arrival, who was even less steady than herself. The two of them crashed to the ground.

Once her shock had passed, Tevi was able to squirm from under her involuntary assailant. "I'm very sorry," Tevi apologised on reflex, offering a hand to assist the other person to rise.

"Oh, no. It was my fault. I was going too fast, and these shoes are useless. Can't get a decent grip on the snow."

"You haven't hurt yourself, have you?" Sir? Ma'am? Tevi could not tell. The accent was local, but the speaker was so muffled that it was impossible to guess the gender. The person was shorter than Tevi by several inches, yet the voice seemed low for a woman. Not for the first time, Tevi wished mainland men would grow beards. One of these days, she was going to make an embarrassing mistake. It was just as well that gender was of so little consequence in the Protectorate.

"I'm fine, apart from my dignity. Are you all right?" the stranger asked.

"Yes. The snow's soft to land on."

"Though I guess I wasn't quite so soft, landing on top of you."

Tevi grinned. "It was a bit like being hit by a sack of potatoes... meaning no offence."

The other person let out a peal of laughter. "None taken. If someone tells me I look like a sack of potatoes, then I'm offended."

"I'm sure that isn't likely to happen."

"I don't know. I'm a greengrocer. They say traders end up looking like their wares."

Tevi joined the laughter. The pair exchanged pleasantries while brushing the powdery snow from their clothing. Before long, all traces of the accident had been erased.

"I must be off. Good evening to you, and once again, my apologies." The greengrocer headed off with cautious steps, one hand braced against the wall.

"Excuse me! Before you go. I'm a stranger in town. I wonder

if you could recommend a good tavern." Tevi spoke, hoping her new acquaintance would offer to join her for a drink.

The face inside the fur-lined hood turned back, smiling broadly. "The ale in the Bees and Bonnet on Mickle Street is very good. My new lover's one of the bar staff. He won't be there tonight, but it's always friendly."

With arms held out for balance, the unsteady figure tottered away. Tevi stared at the empty street. In disappointment, she continued her aimless roaming.

She would have willingly bought as much ale as the greengrocer could drink, just to have someone to talk to. Tevi was wondering if even Ricard's stories would be better than nothing when she noticed a painted sign above a tavern door. Several garish yellow and black bees swarmed around a frilly object that was, just conceivably, an item of headgear. This must be the Bees and Bonnet.

The greengrocer had said it was friendly. While Tevi watched, three townsfolk approached, pushed the door open, and went inside. She caught a glimpse of busy tables and scrubbed floor, the sound of people talking, even the faint smell of beer and wood smoke. Without making a conscious decision, Tevi found herself following the three townsfolk into the tavern.

Sweat prickled at her sides as the heat and noise of the alehouse swept over her. The sensation was like wading into treacle. All around, benches were filled with animated customers, though a scattering of empty seats remained. Tables lined the walls, with more arranged in the middle. A huge stone fireplace dominated one end of the room. The flickering light played over the low rafters and added to the cheerful glow from a dozen lanterns. An L-shaped counter was squeezed into the corner facing the door, with a row of barrels stacked behind.

Tevi tugged off her gloves, hat, and cloak. The bar was busy, but she was able to find a spot to rest her elbows and wait her turn to be served. It did not take long. A barman rushed to attend to her, ignoring other customers. From the uneasy glance at her hands, Tevi realised it was the tattoos that gained her prompt service. Tevi recognised the three townsfolk she had followed in. She gestured to the waiting group. "They were here before me."

"Oh, no. You first," one spoke quickly and then looked away.

Most ordinary citizens treated mercenaries with caution.

Remembering Big Bron, Tevi could understand why. There was no point explaining that she was happy to wait her turn. It would only waste time and fail to reassure anyone.

"I'll have a pint of ale, please."

"Yes, ma'am."

The other customers did not act overly nervous, yet Tevi got the impression that they wished she were not there. Hope of finding companionship faded.

During her journey with Sarryle, she had become aware that the red and gold tattoos served to distance her from the general population. Young children would gape at her with hero worship, but their older relatives gave her a wide berth. Traders and others used to employing her guild comrades were less apprehensive, but mercenaries were generally left to their own company.

She fared no better once she got her drink and took a seat close to the fire. As soon as they noticed the tattoos, people sitting either side shifted ever so slightly away and buried themselves in conversation, mainly about the weather, from what Tevi overheard,

Farther away, some stared in her direction, although they looked away sharply if she caught their eye. Tevi's lips tightened in annoyance, and then a thought struck her. *Am I being too sensitive? On the islands, we would always stare at strangers*. But on Storenseg, you could go from one year to the next without seeing an unfamiliar face. She remembered how odd outsiders looked to her then. *And I've changed, to sit here surrounded by dozens of strange faces and find them no more noteworthy than the bricks in the walls*. It was a sudden, unsettling realisation. Somewhere on her travels, the islander's mentality had slipped its hold on her.

The mellow ale washed the tightness from her throat. In the hearth, flames leapt over the burning logs. Looking at them, you could see demons and castles, swords and flowers, if you chose. The fire was a glowing well of fantasies that drew her thoughts in. A wry smile touched Tevi's lips as she remembered the family hearth of her childhood and sitting by it, playing games of make-believe. She had dreamed of growing up to be a warrior queen who would conquer all the known world—or at least the nearest couple of islands. *Things never work out the way you expect*.

But what next? Precise plans were hard, although a job would not be a problem. In spring, the pass would reopen, and traffic would flow through the town again. Traders would be heading off to the wildlands beyond the Protectorate, in need of guards. The world was wide and diverse, beyond the dreams of her childhood, beyond the imagination of the island women. Visions of the sights she had seen with Verron and Marith danced among the flames.

❖

Her tankard was empty. Tevi considered returning to the guildhall, but she was warm and comfy, and the other customers had long ceased paying her any attention. The tavern noise had become a background rumble in her ears, letting her think in peace, and the ale really was very good—enough to tempt her to a second tankard.

She had scarcely returned to her seat when the door opened. The drop in noise warned Tevi that the new arrival was not just another customer seeking cheer on the frosty night. A tall, middle-aged woman stood just inside the entrance with an expression of bored arrogance on her face. The hem of her blue cloak fluttered in the last of the icy draft that had followed her into the tavern. The cut of her clothes indicated wealth, but that alone would not explain the way the innkeeper rushed to escort her to a table by the fire, unceremoniously displacing its original occupants.

Obviously everyone recognised the woman. Folk returned to their gossip, but the atmosphere was strained. Then Tevi caught sight of a black amulet on the woman's wrist, engraved with oak leaves. It explained all—the town sorcerer. By now, a bottle of wine had arrived at the table, accompanied by much bowing. As the bar staff retreated, the bottle floated into the air and poured itself. Oblivious to the disturbance she had created, the sorcerer picked up the glass and sipped, while her eyes stared vacantly into the air.

The floating bottle was the first piece of magic Tevi had seen on the mainland, but it did not appear to be the precursor to anything more dramatic. Soon, Tevi's attention drifted back to the fire and her plans for the future. Taking work as a caravan guard would bring money and the chance to see more of the world. It would also bring new friends and new risks. Tevi frowned at the memory of Cayell that had dogged her all the way from Lyremouth and the questions it raised. *Why did she try to tempt me like that? How did she know I would be open to the approach?* On the islands, with hindsight, it was obvious. *I stood out like a sheep in a pigpen. Too soft and masculine. Even the way I walked and talked must have had them guessing.* But on the mainland, the same codes of conduct did not apply. Or did they? *How did Cayell know about me?* Until she could answer that question, Tevi knew she dared not let anyone get close. She bit her lip, heartsick at the prospect of loneliness. *But I want friends.*

Tevi's eyes fell on the woman sitting alone. The sorcerer was someone who must have even greater problems finding company. The people kicked off their table had shown no sign of objecting, but it was hardly a way to make people like you. *Do sorcerers enjoy the way they're treated?* Tevi wondered. *Might they prefer a bit less deference?*

It was no surprise that normal folk had mixed feelings about the Coven, although if it did not exist, there would be nothing to stop sorcerers from taking whatever they wanted. At least the Coven ensured that its members gave something in return. The town sorcerer was responsible for supervising healers and other witches in the area. She was oath-bound to protect the people from attack, magical or otherwise. She was the final arbiter of all inter-guild disputes and the chief civic judge. Her word, quite literally, was law. On top of that, she could be called on for advice in any situation.

And what advice could the sorcerer give me? Tevi sighed. The situation was hopeless. She had learnt to treat the mainland men as if they were female, but it was only a mental game that she was playing with herself. Tevi knew she would only ever want a woman as a lover.

Her tankard was empty. Tevi was again served without delay, but a clump of people blocked the route back to her seat, forcing her to detour by the sorcerer's table. Tevi glanced at the woman's face as she passed. Seen close up, she was older than Tevi had first thought. Wavy grey hair framed a deeply lined face, and brown liver spots marked both hands. *What advice could she give me?* The words repeated in Tevi's head. Before she had the chance to think it through, her feet had stopped.

Immediately, Tevi knew it was a mistake. Heads twisted in her direction, only to turn away as folk decided that true wisdom lay in minding their own business. The sorcerer looked up, yet her eyes were focused on a point far beyond the room.

"May I talk to you, ma'am?" Tevi asked politely.

By way of consent, the sorcerer indicated an empty chair. She waited until Tevi was seated. "And what do you want to talk about?"

"I'd like some advice."

"Eat three meals a day, sleep well, and avoid sharp objects when they're poked in your direction." The sorcerer rested her head on one hand. "Or was there something slightly more specific bothering you?"

"Er...yes. I wanted...if, er..." The unfocused gaze was disconcerting. Tevi's eyes dropped to the tabletop as she floundered for words. The mocking tone made it even harder to speak.

"I'm afraid you'll have to be a little more precise with your question. Very few sorcerers can use telepathy to any useful extent, and I'm not one of them."

"My problem is...I need to know what to do..."

Again, Tevi's words ran into a brick wall. However, instead of taunting her, the sorcerer's expression became puzzled.

"What to do?" For the first time, her eyes focused on Tevi. "Well, unlikely as it may seem, you should ask those two men to give you a job." She pointed to the people she meant, sitting at one side of the room.

"I...? Pardon?" Tevi's surprise jolted her out of her awkwardness.

"You should ask them for a job. Do you know why you should do that?"

"No."

"Neither do I. Isn't it intriguing?" The mocking tone returned. "Perhaps they pay well."

"That wasn't the question I wanted to ask, ma'am," Tevi said with slightly more determination.

"Maybe not, but it's the question you should have asked."

Tevi opened her mouth to speak and then closed it as she considered the implications of the sorcerer's words. "You mean it's a prophecy?"

"In a way."

"I thought oracles were supposed to be cryptic."

"If it makes you happier, I could tell you that you're about to go on a difficult journey and to expect health problems towards the middle of next month, possibly with your eyes. But I think my original advice was better. It's certainly easier to act on, wouldn't you say?" The sorcerer drained her glass and stood. "Before I go, do you want to try again and see if you can ask me your original question?"

"Er, no. Thank you, ma'am. You've been most helpful."

"True. I have."

The woman swept out of the tavern. The door swung closed behind her. In the hush that followed, Tevi looked around. The two men identified by the sorcerer appeared extremely uneasy. Judging by the looks they were receiving, it was obvious that everyone knew they had been pointed out.

Tevi picked up her drink and walked towards them, hoping it was not just the sorcerer's idea of a joke. Both men were in their early twenties. The taller of the two had a round face and unruly fair hair that fell over his forehead. His companion was dark, with angular, boyish features. Their eyes, edgy and distrusting, fastened on the tattoos on the backs of Tevi's hands as she sat down.

"Well met, fellow citizens."

"Well met," they replied in disjointed uncertainty.

"The sorcerer thought you might be able to offer me a job. My name's Tevi, by the way."

The fair-haired one answered cautiously. "My name's Harrick, and this is my partner, Rorg. We're traders from Rizen." His companion nodded sharply.

"Are you looking to hire people?" Tevi asked.

"Um...yes. But we're mainly after guides and mule drivers. Though I suppose a scout might be useful—if that's what you are."

"No. I'm just an ordinary warrior."

Harrick's wariness was fading into confusion. "Then I can't see we'd have much need of you. Bandits are rare in the mountains, even in good weather. They aren't going to be about in conditions like these."

"We'll be lucky to get anyone," Rorg interjected. Like his companion, he spoke in the clipped accent of the eastern Protectorate.

"Look, I keep telling you, it will be all right," Harrick shot at his partner with unconcealed anger.

"You've said that before." Rorg scowled.

Tevi realised she had stepped into an ongoing argument. "You have a problem?"

Rorg merely shrugged, retreating into a mood of sullen despair.

Harrick turned to Tevi. "We're planning on going over the old pass, but Rorg has some doubts."

"The old pass? Is that different from the current one?"

"Oh, yes. The new Langhope Pass was made sixty years back. Three sorcerers and a couple hundred dwarves did the work. Before that, the old route ran farther to the north—an old pack trail, twisting all over the place. The new pass just blasted its way straight up one side and down the other. They even knocked a couple of tunnels through bits that got in the way. You can drive two wagons abreast the whole way."

"Except when it's neck-deep in snow."

The interruption from Rorg was met by an angry glare. Eventually, Harrick went on. "We were held up on our way to Treviston. By the time we got here, the Langhope Pass was closed, and it may not reopen for months. We're on a tight schedule and low budget, and can't afford to wait 'til spring. We only got our loan from the guild last year."

Tevi remembered Verron's remarks about young traders overreaching themselves. "You think the older route may be passable?"

"Yes. On foot. It always was, according to Rorg's grandmothers. They used to cover this route in the days before the new pass."

"If you can believe the old fools," Rorg mumbled.

"And why not? The old pass isn't so high, and it's sheltered from the northwest wind all the way," Harrick snapped angrily.

"So that's your plan?" Tevi tried to ease the tension.

"Yes. We're going to sell the wagons and transfer the load to mules. Not right now, but according to the weather witch, there should be a clear patch in another twenty days. If we can get a team together we'll be setting off then." He frowned at Tevi. "We're looking for guides and muleteers. The only unskilled labour we're going to need is the brute strength to dig our way out of snowdrifts, and that's not going to be your field."

Tevi looked at the table. It was about ten feet long, made from solid timber, probably weighing more than she did. She raised her eyes to meet Harrick's and placed one hand on the underside of the table. With a smile, she lifted it a foot into the air. People sitting at either end called out in surprise.

"When you discuss the contract with the guild master, it would be better not to use the word 'unskilled.' You could say you wanted me to fight off starving wolf packs and the like. The mercenaries are very keen to be seen as professionals."

The two young traders stared at Tevi in astonishment. Even Rorg was shaken from his bitter cynicism. He peered at her hand under the table and then sat upright again.

"I don't suppose you've got a couple of friends? We could forget the mules."

Chapter Nine—Nightmares

Either Rorg's scepticism of his grandmothers was well founded, or the old women had been tougher in their youth than they'd been given credit for. The journey over the old pass was a nightmare.

On the day they left Treviston, Tevi began to have second thoughts at the sight of ice-scoured crags overhanging the trail, but she brushed away the doubts. Ahead of her went the others in the team, mounted on hill ponies. Apart from Harrick and Rorg, there were two muleteers, a local guide, and nineteen very unhappy mules.

It was not long before Tevi was wishing that she had turned around and headed straight back to the comforts of the Treviston guildhall. For the first two days, the route wove its way into the mountains. The track hugged the southern side of a long winding valley that was comparatively sheltered and free from snowdrifts. However, the temperature was bitterly cold, firewood was scarce, and the damp found its way into everything. The track then rose along a steep-sided ravine that acted like a wind tunnel, hurling walls of sleet in their faces. At the top, they were met by a trackless expanse of moor under a leaden sky.

This was when Tevi fully came to realise that Harrick had been obliged to employ anybody he could get. The guide, Lerwill, had less idea of direction than anyone else in the party. After two hours of his dithering, Tevi was left wondering how he normally found his way home from the tavern.

The wind whipped them with freezing blasts as Lerwill looked around in confusion. "It wasn't like this last time I was here," he muttered.

Tevi shouted to be heard over the wind. "Let me guess. There wasn't any of this white fluffy stuff about."

Lerwill pouted sullenly and pointed to a long ridge cresting in a triple peak. "That's Langhope Rigg. The new pass goes to the south of it, which means..." His hand shifted to gesture in a vague northeasterly direction. "We need to go that way." He scowled at Tevi as if daring her to dispute his words.

They set off across the snow-covered upland. The mules were miserable and made no attempt to hide it. The same could be said for the muleteers. Tevi pulled her hood forward to shield her face from the wind and wished she could place more confidence in the guide. Listening to Ricard's stories by the fire suddenly seemed like an extremely enjoyable way of spending time.

❖

Over the following days Tevi learnt a lot about mules. She also learnt that although adversity often brings people closer together, this was not necessarily the case. Harrick cursed the weather, the muleteers cursed the mules, Rorg cursed his grandmothers, and Lerwill fell into a sulk and cursed everyone. It was mainly due to Tevi that they found their way across the moor and back onto the trail. Thereafter, the route got worse as it passed through the heart of the mountains.

The muleteers, Jansk and Orpin, were a couple barely out of their teens whose relationship fluctuated between vicious argument and passionate reconciliation. Orpin had the same wiry build and stubbornness as his mules. Jansk was a solid young woman with a short temper. Neither appeared overly endowed with brains. Throughout the early part of the journey, the pair quarrelled incessantly. For some reason, both chose to confide in Tevi. She heard more intimate details about their relationship than she had any wish to know and soon ran out of sympathy for the tales of jealousy, selfishness, and spite, but neither muleteer picked up on hints that she did not want to listen.

As far as she could judge, Tevi spent her twentieth birthday carrying the cargo over a rock fall while Jansk and Orpin took the mules around a detour judged too dangerous for the animals when laden. The voices of the muleteers were audible long after they had disappeared from sight.

"Why are you wearing that old hat again?"

"It keeps my ears warm."

"It makes you look stupid."

"You're only saying that 'cause Lonny gave it to me."

"I didn't know who gave it to you."

"Yes, you did. You were there."

To Tevi's relief, the voices faded, leaving her to work in peace—apart from the unhelpful advice from Harrick, Rorg's sarcastic interjections, and Lerwill's muttering. That night, she crawled into her bedding cold and exhausted. Her fingers were chafed, and a wrenched ankle was throbbing.

Jansk crept over. "Do you know what he said to me?" Her voice was a whine.

Tevi peered from under her blanket. Tears were in Jansk's eyes. Knowing the woman, they were more likely due to frustration than grief.

"Who?" A silly question, Tevi realised, even as she spoke.

"Orpin. The dog sucker."

Tevi had heard Jansk use the phrase on several occasions. She had not tried to find out its derivation, though several possibilities occurred to her. From Jansk's tone, it was not a term of endearment.

Go away. I can't be bothered. The words were on Tevi's lips, but instead she asked, "What's wrong?"

"I told you...Orpin."

"What's he done?"

"He won't let us name our first child after my father. He said Pa's an evil old toad."

"Are you pregnant?"

"Not yet. But after all my Pa's done for us...can you believe it?"

Tevi buried her head under the blanket. She could not believe any of it.

By the next night, the mule drivers had got over their quarrel. Ignoring the rest of the team, they sat by the fire, staring into each other's eyes. Kisses grew ever more passionate, and hands disappeared under the layers of clothing, accompanied by giggles. Tevi found the display acutely embarrassing. On the islands, people used the cover of darkness and did not make love brazenly in the firelight. She tried to distract herself by talking to Lerwill, but his eyes were glazed and his speech slurred. What words she could distinguish carried little sense. Harrick gestured for her to leave the guide. She slid across to where the traders were sitting.

"What's wrong with Lerwill?"

"Opium," Harrick whispered.

"He's an addict?" Tevi had heard of the drug during her travels with Verron and Marith—even seen users sprawled blank-eyed outside taverns and brothels—but had never made the connection with the guide's erratic behaviour.

"Sort of. He promised not to take any on the journey, but he can't seem to function without it. I let him have a little to see if it helps."

"Bloody stupid idea to try this route without a decent guide," Rorg muttered.

"It's all due to your grandmothers' stories," Harrick snapped back.

"I told you not to believe the senile old liars."

"And it was your fault we were late getting to Treviston."

"Oh, not that one again!"

The two traders swung into their bitterest argument to date. Both were soon trying to get Tevi to side with them.

"Tevi, can you believe the crap we're hearing?"

"He's the one talking out of his arse, isn't he, Tevi?"

Tevi had no intention of being drawn in. With an excuse, she left the fireside and went to where the ponies were hobbled. Her own mount snorted in the darkness and nuzzled against her. She hugged the pony's neck, burying her face in the mane. "You and me. We're the only sane ones here," Tevi whispered, although she wondered if confiding in an animal might prejudice her own case.

The next day, the trail rounded a sheer-sided mountain before dropping into a thickly wooded valley. They were now on the eastern side of Whitfell Spur, and the air was noticeably warmer. That night, they camped under pine trees. For the first time since entering the mountains, firewood was not in short supply.

The trail continued its steady descent for another two days. On the morning of the sixteenth day after leaving Treviston, they reached the head of a wide valley. Fields, roads and villages were spread out below. The party made their way eagerly down the hillside, encouraged by the thought of a dry bed and food other than trail rations.

At midday, they passed beneath the remains of an old castle perched on a spur of rock. Heavy ramparts linked two towers, one tall, one short. All were built of dark grey granite and dotted with black arrow slits. Tevi looked up.

She turned to Rorg. "Who lives in the castle?"

"Nobody, as far as I know."

"Why is it here?"

"It goes back to when this was the main route over the Spur. A small garrison was stationed here. Since the new pass was built, this valley has become a backwater, and the soldiers have gone. They now patrol the new pass."

"The castle seems in good shape."

"Perhaps the locals are keeping up the maintenance, just in case."

The road took them on through the bare winter farmlands until, with enormous relief, the party entered the largest village, a mile and a half below the castle. The difficult part was over. Three days' easy travel would get them to Rizen. Harrick was as keen as anyone to rest and arranged accommodation with the local reeve, a thin middle-aged woman who led the handful of surprised villagers that came out to greet them.

❖

The villagers used their arrival as an excuse for an impromptu party. Visitors from outside were cause for excitement, especially during the winter isolation. Everyone from miles around squeezed into the hall in the centre of the village. However, their curiosity was confined to the local area, and the main interest was Harrick, Rorg, and their news from Rizen. Once it was learnt that Tevi came from "far distant lands" she was ignored, apart from the customary band of children entranced by her mercenary tattoos.

A barrel of beer was opened, and someone played a fiddle, although the space was too cramped for dancing. From what Tevi could see, the hall doubled as a hay barn and shearing shed. It would also be their accommodation that night. Tevi lifted her eyes to the rafters and smiled. The thought of sleeping on dry hay with a roof over her head was bliss.

As the evening progressed, the children were sent to bed, and the crowd began to disperse. The reeve, Sergo, was one of the few villagers with any interest in the wider world. She had just engaged Tevi in talk about Lyremouth when the door opened and a grim-faced man stepped in. He made straight for the reeve, who stopped mid-sentence at the sight of the newcomer's face.

"You've found more victims?" Sergo sounded frightened.

"Two sheep. Up by the north falls." The man jerked his head.

"Spring's on the way. It won't stay around much longer, surely?"

"So you say, but I reckon it depends on who called it here, and why." The man crossed his arms on his chest belligerently while a circle of villagers formed. Voices in the rest of the barn were muted.

"Nobody has called it." Sergo's tone did not match her confident words. "It's just that the bad winter has forced the thing down the Spur from the high Barrodens."

"Or her, up at the castle, has called on another pet."

Sergo looked at him in dismay.

In the resulting silence, Tevi asked, "What's been called here?"

"A basilisk." The man snapped the answer.

"What's a basilisk?"

"A monster from the wildlands. It's got this third eye in the centre of its forehead. It locks eyes with its prey and drains the life out. Turns the body to stone and the eyes become like jewels."

"Has it killed anyone?"

"Not yet. So far, it's just taken a dozen sheep," Sergo said weakly.

"But it's going to get someone soon. Mark my words, we've got to do something." The man glared at the reeve.

"Nobody here can deal with it. You need magic. But it will go soon. I know it will." Yet Sergo sounded as if she did not truly believe her own words.

"Can't you call in a sorcerer to help you?" Tevi asked, remembering the one in Treviston. After the journey she'd had, Tevi would happily have directed a hundred basilisks in the woman's direction.

"There's one too many in these parts as it is," someone in the crowd muttered.

"Most likely her behind it," a second voice added.

Others agreed.

The angry man faced Tevi. "We've got a Coven sorcerer, black amulet and everything. We never used to have one. We got by with a simple witch, a healer who could turn her hand to a bit of rain calling. Nothing much happens around here; we don't need anyone fancy. But when old Colly died, we got a sorcerer sent here. If I could, I'd slit her throat." His face twisted in hatred. "She's evil, and I tell you, the basilisk is her doing." The last sentence was spat at the reeve. Then the man spun on his heel and stalked towards the door.

Sergo called after the departing figure. "The Coven know what they're doing. They wouldn't send her here if she was corrupt or dangerous."

"If you believed that, you'd go and ask her to help." The man tossed the words over his shoulder and left.

Nobody else challenged the reeve's assertion to her face, but there was plenty of muttering. A short while later, Tevi found herself seated on a rickety bench next to a plump elderly woman who was noisily sipping a mug of beer.

"What's so bad about the sorcerer?" Tevi asked to open the conversation.

The woman glanced around the room, then whispered theatrically, "She's up to no good." The woman nodded to reinforce her words. "When she arrived, she wouldn't stay in the village. We offered her Colly's old house, but she moved up to the castle. Said if we wanted her help, we could go up there. But I won't. Not after what happened to Gerry's daughter. It's a mercy everyone's been so healthy, hardly as much as a cold since last summer, 'cause there's no one who'd go up to the castle if they were sick. Gerry was the one who came in just now with the news about the sheep. The sorcerer's put charms up on the hilltops. I dread to think what they're for. Gerry's been hunting them down. He reckons he's destroyed about five, but how many more are there? And what are they for? That's what I want to know. That sorcerer's up to mischief. Gives me the creeps."

"Perhaps she just wanted space to practice her magic. The charms might be totally harmless."

The woman grunted sceptically. "She's hiding something. She's got a room she won't let anyone in—she talks to evil spirits in there. We know, because Dorin went up to help out at first, but he wouldn't stay. He wasn't too clear in his wits to start with, but he's been worse since he came back. And you should hear the stories he has to tell." In her enthusiasm, the woman's voice had risen. "Then Shiral went to work up there. Now, she was a bright girl. But something happened. After a month, the sorcerer brought her back. The girl was out cold for three days, and when she woke up, she just screamed for hours on end. Her parents say she still has nightmares, and we've never got a clear story out of her. She was frightened senseless. Now the sorcerer has '*things*' running loose at the castle. Sergo says they're bears, but I've never seen bears act like that. And there's other creatures. She has a magpie that talks to her. It spies on folk."

The woman stopped and glanced fearfully over her shoulder as if expecting to see the malevolent bird behind her. Her voice dropped to a whisper. "But Gerry's daughter was the worst. The girl had cut her leg, and it was turning bad. When he saw there was nothing for it, Gerry took her to the castle. The sorcerer took the child and sent him away—forced him out of the castle. The next day, she brought the child back down." The speaker glanced fearfully in the direction of the castle, then leant forward. "The girl was dead."

"But if she's a Coven sorcerer hasn't she sworn an oath to protect people?"

"Oaths can get broken. Anyway, I don't reckon that it is the real sorcerer. I reckon that it is some fiend that has taken her shape and is just pretending to be her. The Coven don't go round killing children 'cause they want them to grow up so they can pay taxes." The elderly woman nodded at her own, inescapable logic.

Tevi left her and wandered around the room. She was not convinced of the sorcerer's wickedness. The villager had clearly enjoyed her own story too much to take it all on trust. The death of a seriously ill child was not proof of murder, and as for the rest, the Treviston sorcerer clearly had a peculiar sense of humour; perhaps this one did as well. The basilisk was a more urgent, and probably unrelated, problem. Tevi was considering the villagers' plight when she was disturbed by Orpin's whining.

"Tevi, I need your help."

"What with?" Tevi said impatiently.

"Jansk is ignoring me."

"What do you expect me to do about it?"

"Well...I thought...perhaps if you were to pretend that you were, you know, getting keen on me..." Orpin shuffled his feet. "She'd get jealous and stop acting funny."

The suggestion did not deserve a reply, and three more days with the muleteers did not bear thinking about. On the far side of the barn, Harrick was talking to Sergo. Tevi headed in their direction.

She spoke in a rush. "Harrick, I don't know if you've heard, but the villagers have a problem with a basilisk. Now we're over the pass, you won't need me. I wondered if you'd consider paying me off so I can stay here and help out."

Immediately, an overjoyed Sergo made her own appeal. "Please. You don't know what this could mean to us."

Harrick hesitated, shamefaced. "I don't mind you staying, but I don't have enough coin on me. I was counting on selling the merchandise first."

The traders were certainly running to a tight budget, but it was not Tevi's concern. She shrugged. "You can pay my salary into the Rizen guildhall. I'll collect my share when I get there and the guild can keep its quarter."

She could trust Harrick to do that; no trader would dare cheat the Guild of Mercenaries. In the end, Harrick let her keep her pony as collateral against her wages. Everyone was happy with the arrangements—except Orpin.

❖

The following morning, Tevi stood and waved goodbye to Harrick's team. She spent the rest of the day learning as much as she could about her quarry and getting a feel for the countryside. This involved a lot of travelling and being introduced to folk, all very keen to talk, yet with very little information to give. Only one ancient woman, huddled by her great-grandson's fire, could remember the last time a basilisk had troubled the valley, but her wits were going, and her speech rambled. Tevi left after lengthy questioning, unsure whether the woman's advice was for killing basilisks or peeling potatoes. The reference to eyes could have applied to either.

In the late afternoon, a shepherd took her to see the most recent victims. High on pastures above the main village stood two stone sheep with eyes like polished glass. Tevi ran her hand over one. It was not proper stone. It felt soft, like powdery grey chalk. Dust clung to Tevi's fingers, and already, much of the fine detail on the wool was gone, blown away by the wind.

The snow was pockmarked with the sharp round hoofprints of sheep and the larger, softer paw marks of the basilisk, like those of a great cat stalking its prey. Estimates of the size of the beast had varied wildly. Tevi tried measuring the prints with her fingers. Reaching any definite conclusion was not easy, apart from casting doubt on the more sensational claims.

The paw marks ran off in an undulating line across the fields. Tevi and her guide followed them until the trail reached a rocky ford across a stream, fringed with ice. The shepherd's two dogs ran sweeps, excitedly sniffing the snow, although probably more interested in rabbits than basilisks. On the other side of the stream, the paw marks continued towards a wooded area high on the hillside.

"That's where it's hiding out. Its tracks always lead there." The shepherd pointed to the trees.

"Has no one tried putting snares out?"

"One or two, but no one's dared go back to see if they've caught anything."

"Since the beast struck yesterday, they obviously haven't."

"True."

"Have you seen it?"

"No. But my sister did at dusk, drinking at the pool on Matte's farm. That's when it comes out most—dawn and dusk."

Tevi studied the distant wood, shading her eyes against the setting sun—a reminder that dusk was not far away on that day. The trees gave no clues to their unwelcome occupant. Tevi's survey followed the hillside down to the valley floor. Three villages and a dozen isolated farmhouses dotted the fields. Sheep, goats, and cattle grazed the lower slopes of the valley. Above them, directly opposite where Tevi was standing, the castle hunched on its outcrop of rock, a sombre presence in the valley. The fortifications were fading into the shadows of evening. The shepherd followed the direction of Tevi's eyes and spat into the snow but said nothing, only whistled in the dogs and led the way down to the welcoming lights of the village.

That night, Tevi lodged in the reeve's home. Sergo lived with a woman relative and a young son. Tevi could not work out whose son he was, but the three were so close, it did not seem to matter. The family lived in a room at one end of the cottage, while the rest of the building was given over to a cow barn, dairy and all-purpose workroom.

The cottage was cramped and noisy, particularly when a group of villagers squeezed in and stayed up late to recount all they knew of the basilisk. Their advice did not amount to much, apart from a general agreement that looking into the third eye was the thing to avoid. However, the cottage was warmer than the hall and homely, smelling of cows, cheese, and wood smoke. And the bed, when Tevi finally got to it, was soft.

❖

Dawn was cloudless, though the sun held little warmth. The mountains of the Spur cut a sharp line against the winter sky. In the reeve's cottage, Tevi awoke before first light. While Sergo and her relatives began their daily tasks, she sat by the fire with a bowl of porridge and completed her preparations. A knock announced the arrival of the village blacksmith. In addition to the promised small iron shield, he brought an old two-handed battle-axe, scavenged from the castle decades ago and since used for chopping wood. Now it had been sharpened to a keen edge. Tevi accepted it with a wry smile, remembering Cayell's remarks concerning axe-women.

On the previous afternoon, in a display of bravado, two local youths had volunteered to accompany Tevi. They joined her outside the shearing barn. The three left the village to a chorus of good wishes. The young men were putting a brave face on for their friends, although Tevi wondered if they were regretting their rashness. She was wondering the same thing about herself.

The wood was silent as they approached. All that they could hear was the whisper of wind in the branches, the bleating of sheep, and the distant clatter of a cowbell. A clear trail of paw marks, less than a day old, disappeared into the trees. The basilisk was using a path made by wild deer. Tevi peered along it. The summer undergrowth had died back, but there were still enough evergreen leaves and coils of bramble to prevent her seeing more than a few yards.

"Do you want to wait out here for me?" Tevi asked.

"We'll follow you a little way." One of the youths managed a sickly smile. "After all, you've got the weapons if the thing shows up."

Progress was slow and uncomfortable, watching each footfall while crouched double under low branches. They had covered about one hundred yards when they heard the unmistakable sound of a large animal nosing through the undergrowth ahead. The noise was too loud to be a bird, although it might be a lost sheep. The rustling ceased briefly and then began again. The sound played among the trees, making it difficult to assess direction or speed. Tevi's hands tightened on her spear. Her heart thudded against her ribs. Behind her, the villagers froze as if already turned to stone. Even their breathing stopped.

"Wait here. If it's safe, I'll call to you," Tevi whispered.

"Right."

"And if anything goes wrong..."

"We run."

Tevi smiled grimly. "Right."

Twenty yards farther on, Tevi reached the edge of a small clearing. She hid behind a tree with her back braced against its trunk and then cautiously peered around the side. The rising sun had cleared the treetops. Light glinted dazzling white off the ground, while in the shadows, the snow was palest blue. Bushes and trees on the far side made a dark, knotted, unbroken barrier. At first, nothing stirred. Then a bush twitched, and another, and then stillness. Tevi's eyes were locked on the spot where the last sign of movement had been. Abruptly, the branches dipped and the basilisk broke through the undergrowth.

The beast was smaller than Tevi had expected, the size of a large dog, with a long, sinuous neck and a head that would have been otter-like if not for the bulging third eye in its forehead. The basilisk was dark brown, covered in a thick pelt that told of its home in the high northern mountains. It stood poised ready to spring with its nose pointed into the air, casting about for scent.

Tevi loosened her sword in its scabbard and tugged the strap of the axe over her shoulder. One hand grasped the spear firmly. The other hand raised the shield in front of her face, guarding her eyes. All she could see of the creature was its shadow. She stepped around the tree into the open. The basilisk gave a soft whine and padded towards her.

Under the rim of her shield, Tevi watched the basilisk's shadow approach. She noted the swinging of its head and its graceful catlike gait. *And will it also pounce like a cat?* she wondered. *Or charge like a boar?* The villagers had been able to give no advice.

The basilisk halted a few feet away, wary. It appeared to rise up and then drop back on all fours. Its head swung low and wide. Tevi prayed that she was interpreting the shadow correctly. For a split second, she almost gave in to the temptation to lift her shield and see what the basilisk was doing. She clenched her teeth. A second's lapse in concentration—that was all it would take.

Without warning, the beast sprung, a high, lunging attack. The claws of one paw caught the edge of Tevi's shield, but already she was moving, ducking with her eyes closed and thrusting upwards with the spear. She felt the point make contact and lodge in the animal's chest. The basilisk's howl filled the clearing. It flung itself back, dragging the spear from Tevi's hand. Still with her eyes shut, Tevi shrugged the axe off her shoulder and grasped the handle. She risked one glimpse of her quarry. Scarcely an arm's length away, the basilisk's head was thrown back in a second long howl. Its front paws scraped at the shaft of the spear while its body writhed backwards. The axe felt solid in Tevi's hands. She swung as hard as she could and, with a single stroke, decapitated the beast.

Suddenly, it was very quiet. The headless carcass collapsed, gushing red blood into the snow. There was the twitch of a back leg, and then the beast was still. Tevi was surprised to realise she was shaking violently. She sank to her knees, breathing deeply, and waited for the pounding of her heart to ease. Unexpectedly, she felt a childish grin spread across her face. Fighting back giggles, she scooped up a handful of snow and rubbed it over her cheeks, and then took another deep breath.

"It's all right. It's dead." She shouted to the young men. Despite her assurance, they advanced cautiously, with hesitant steps and hushed voices, until they reached the clearing and saw the scene.

"Hey, you did it!"

"Swiped its head clean off!" They gave vent to twin exclamations of delight.

"It was pretty straightforward. The thing didn't..." Tevi stopped; too much modesty might seem arrogant.

Feeling detached, Tevi stood back and watched the men approach, prodding the body with their feet and making silly jokes. Her gaze shifted to the basilisk's head. It had bounced, rolled, and ended up in a small hollow a dozen paces away. Tevi walked over and grabbed it by the fur between the ears. "Who gets to keep the trophy?"

One of the villagers laughed. "You do, if you want it."

"It could go on the wall of the shearing shed," the other suggested.

Tevi held the basilisk's head level with her own. The jaw hung open, revealing a row of peg-like teeth. The basilisk could never deliver a serious bite, and its body was ill adapted for a fight. Tevi had already noted that its claws were weak and blunt. The creature had only one weapon: the strange protrusion on its forehead. Tevi examined the thick lids. Close up, the organ looked more like a mouth than an eye. With her free hand, she tried to prise it open to see what lay beneath. The lips were just starting to part when Tevi felt the twitch of muscle under her fingers. The central eye snapped open.

❖

The young men did not realise that anything was wrong until Tevi screamed. Both heads jerked in her direction, in time to see her crash to her knees, the echo of her scream still ringing in the air. Tevi's hands were pressed against her eyes.

The men froze, caught on the brink of flight, but no new danger was apparent. Slowly, one crept to Tevi's side.

"What's wrong, Tevi?"

She did not answer.

He took hold of her wrists, trying to pull her hands away. The attempt was futile. Whatever the problem, her strength was unaffected. Tevi's shoulders shook with gasps, sounding like they were ripped from her throat. The man looked to his friend, unsure of what to do. The other could only shrug.

"What's happened?"

Again, there was no answer. Instead, Tevi threw back her head and screamed again. Her hands clenched into fists.

"Tevi?"

At last, she turned her face towards his voice and the young man found himself staring into two blind eyes of polished glass.

❖

A small group huddled in one corner of the reeve's house, arguing among themselves. Tevi lay on a bunk, within earshot but incapable of paying attention to what was said. Her eyes felt as if they had been replaced by red-hot coals. The pain ran like liquid fire across her face and down her neck, surging with each throb of her pulse. Nothing existed except the pain. For what little good it did, a crude ice pack was tied over her eyes. Despite her efforts at silence, Tevi knew she was whimpering like a whipped child.

Sergo's voice was the clearest. "It's her only hope."

"Better to give her a knife, like she asked, and let her put an end to it."

"The pain will probably ease in a day or two," said a third voice.

"But she'll still be blind," Sergo spoke again. "We owe her a better chance."

"She won't get that at the castle."

"We could send her to Rizen."

"Is she fit to travel?"

"It's easy to give advice you wouldn't take yourself."

"Enough!" Sergo raised her voice and put a stop to the disagreements. "She can choose."

Footsteps approached, and Tevi felt a hand on her shoulder. "Tevi, do you hear me?"

Tevi managed a nod to show she was listening.

"We can do nothing for you here. I think you should go to the sorcerer. She might be able to help you."

"Is that likely?" Tevi had to fight to form each word.

"There's a lot of silly rumours, and I admit I'm disturbed by her. But I don't think you have any other options."

After a long pause, Tevi whispered, "Yes." She would have agreed to anything.

❖

Tevi was vaguely aware of being bundled out of the cottage and onto her pony. There were voices, but she could not be bothered to make out the words. The only detail that registered was that her weapons were still on the saddle pack. Presumably, nobody had taken the time to unload her belongings. Tevi certainly had no use for them.

The journey to the castle seemed unending. At last, hands helped her dismount, patted her on the shoulder, and guided her to the pony's reins. She wrapped them around her wrist and leaned against the flank, fighting the twin urges to pass out and throw up. Without the support of the pony, Tevi knew she would have fallen. A bell clanged loudly. One of the people who had brought her must have rung it, or maybe it was the sorcerer's magic. Whatever the cause, the bell was followed by the sound of her guides running away as fast as their legs could carry them. In a better state, she might have been apprehensive, to be left abandoned at the sorcerer's door. However, Tevi was completely beyond caring.

The silence was broken only by the whisper of wind and the call of wild birds. Then came soft, furtive shuffling from within the castle. Hinges groaned as the gate swung open. Knowing what was expected, the pony trotted forward a dozen yards or so, dragging Tevi with it. She felt the loss of warmth as she went from sunshine into shadow. Underfoot, the ground changed from earth to cobblestones. The echoes indicated that she was in a large, enclosed courtyard. The gate closed behind them—not a loud crash, but a solid, decisive thud.

Rapid chattering broke out just above Tevi's head. Small things rushed past her feet. Claws touched her knee. Then the shambling steps came in her direction, accompanied by wet, guttural breathing. It was surely not the sorcerer or anything human. Whatever it was frightened the pony. It skittered away, nearly jerking Tevi to her knees. She yanked on the reins. There was no point running from anything in the castle; it could do its worst; she only hoped it would do it quickly.

Again, the pony tried to flee. Lacking the will to fight, Tevi released the reins and let it go. She was alone, surrounded by the unseen creatures of the castle. The ground seemed to sway beneath Tevi's feet. Her teeth clenched shut. The approaching thing grew near. Something warm and wet touched her hand, and despite her resolve, Tevi flinched away.

A new sound caught Tevi's ear—the unmistakable rhythm of human footsteps. The sorcerer was coming, walking confidently and descending stairs. Abruptly, the soft shuffling stilled and retreated. The small things around Tevi's feet fled. Tevi twisted her head, following the sound of heel and toe, first on stone and then over a hollow, wooden platform. The feet descended more steps and stopped. In the sudden silence, a harsh, inhuman screech rang out, echoing off stone walls. The cry seemed to reverberate from beyond the limits of the known world, cold and desolate.

For the space of two dozen heartbeats, nothing stirred. Then the human footsteps resumed, walking towards her, getting closer. With the last of her courage, Tevi turned towards the sound, waiting until it was no more than ten paces away before she spoke.

"Please. I need your help."

"I know. I've been expecting you."

Part Two

The Sorcerer

CHAPTER TEN—A STUDENT OF MAGIC

The wind blew in gusts over the castle walls, sending flurries of snow to swirl and chase around the battlements. Stars burned cold in the night sky and stark moonlight glittered on frost coating the trees growing in the enclosed courtyard. A warmer yellow light spilled from the icicle-encrusted windows of the great hall and lay in bars across the trampled snow covering the cobblestones.

Inside, it was warm and still. The steady light from small floating spheres was supplemented by red flickering from the stone fireplace. In front of the hearth lay a brown bear, sleeping peacefully on a rug, like a huge dog. Faint snores and the crackling of flames were the only sounds.

The hall was a workroom. Charts and shelves lined the walls, holding collections of books, herbs, bones, stones, and arcane instruments. Dozens of multicoloured bottles reflected back the firelight from every corner of the room. The flagstones of the floor, although stained, were swept clean. A wooden staircase rose at one end of the hall. It gave access to two doorways: the lower one was halfway up the wall, the higher level with the blackened rafters. The opposite end of the hall had a raised dais. An ancient table stood there, its scorched and battered top bare apart from an open book, an ink bottle, and a pen.

A floating sphere hung over the table, but this one was very different from the lamps. It was nearly two feet in diameter. A green tincture rippled over it, and the surface quivered in the soft currents of air like a soap bubble. It was semitransparent, but the indistinct outlines seen through it did not look like the far side of the room. It did not move, but it still gave the unmistakable impression of searching—or hunting.

The sphere's creator, Jemeryl, oath-bound sorcerer of the Coven, sat back to view her handiwork, supporting her chin in her cupped hand. Her free arm was draped along the back of the chair. One leg was hitched over the armrest. Her clothes were loose fitting and clearly chosen for comfort rather than to reflect her status. They looked not so much as if she had slept in them, but rather that it would be hard to tell if she did. Her face was composed of angles—narrow chin, pinched nose, chiselled cheekbones. Her hazel eyes studied the green sphere intently. Then, slowly, the serious expression gave way to an impish grin. She ran a hand through her curly auburn hair and then punched the air in triumph.

"Well, what do you think?"

On a nearby bookcase, Klara, the magpie, stopped preening her wing and glanced in the sphere's direction. "I can't see why you're so excited."

"It will create a lot of interest in the Coven."

"Why? Is there a serious shortage of hideous green blobs?"

Jemeryl grinned at the magpie before swinging her leg down and bouncing to her feet. She paced around the table, appraising the globe from all sides. "It's the theory behind it that's important. By all accepted rules of magic, it ought to be utterly impossible."

"Well, personally, I think it's a bit of a shame that it isn't." Klara glided over and considered the object with distaste. The sphere emitted a faint whine like a hundred trapped mosquitoes. The air around it was unpleasantly chill. Klara fluffed up her feathers. "I suppose I should be grateful it doesn't smell. Or is that likely to come next?"

Jemeryl brushed the sarcastic magpie off the table, ignoring the indignant squawk, and hooked a stool from under the table with her foot. Klara returned to her perch on the bookshelf. For several minutes, Jemeryl riffled back through her notes; then she picked up a pen and began writing. All was silent except for the faint scratching of quill on paper. On the other side of the room, Klara tucked her head under her wing and fell asleep.

❖

The logs were burning low by the time Jemeryl put down the pen and stood up. She stretched her arms and rolled her head to loosen stiffened muscles. It was far later than she had intended. Jemeryl gave a mental shrug. One advantage of her current situation was that she could set her own schedule, taking a late supper and having a lie-in the next morning—especially as there was one more thing she wanted to do.

"Now what I need is..." She spoke aloud, awakening Klara.

Jemeryl's staff was leaning in a nearby corner, six feet of polished oak, unadorned apart from the iron end caps, and looking better suited for use in a street brawl than as a magical aid. From her observation point atop the bookcase, Klara watched with increasing alarm as the sorcerer grabbed the staff and returned to the sphere. After five years as Jemeryl's familiar, the magpie knew an ill omen when she saw one. She launched herself from her perch and landed on the head of the sleeping bear.

"Quick, Ruff! Get up and hide. Jem is going to do something silly," Klara said.

The bear awoke with a jolt and snorted, a loud, surprised, "Wuff."

At the magpie's insistence, he scrabbled to his feet and lumbered down the hall as fast as his four legs would carry him, vanishing behind a heavy cupboard in a far corner. After a few seconds, his head reappeared cautiously around the corner, with Klara still in place between his ears.

"Cowards!" Jemeryl called, grinning. She gestured at the three squirrels on a high shelf that were peering down with inquisitive eyes. "Look. They aren't frightened."

"They haven't got the sense." Klara and Ruff again disappeared from view.

Jemeryl spoke to the squirrels, using tones normally reserved for babies. "Don't worry your fluffy little heads. Auntie Jemi knows what she's doing."

"Rubbish!" came the derisory squawk from behind the cupboard.

Jemeryl's smile faded as her attention returned to the sphere, and a look of intense concentration took its place. Her eyes stared at the shimmering globe. However, her perception was not limited to sight. Her extra-dimensional senses let her see far beyond the boundaries of the ordinary world. Long seconds slipped past. Then she raised the staff horizontally, holding it firmly in both hands. The time had come to put theory to the test.

The sphere heaved and began to swell. From deep inside its core, a glow appeared, pulsing and surging like a heartbeat. Forms started to congeal, twisting like imprisoned phantoms. Jemeryl's breath came in strained gasps, and sweat beaded her forehead, while the intertwined shapes grew ever more chaotic. They filled the entire sphere, flowing around the inner surface until, without warning, the globe exploded in a blast of acrid yellow smoke.

The boom resonated in the stone walls. Glassware on the shelves rattled, and dust rained down from the rafters. Then the echoes faded into silence, leaving only the sound of squirrel claws frantically scrabbling as the animals dashed for the exit. Hand held over her mouth and nose, Jemeryl followed as quickly as she could, bumping into furniture in her haste and swearing when she cracked her ankle on an unseen obstacle, before making it through the doorway and out to the covered porch. She leaned against the wall, coughing spasmodically. Wisps of luminous smoke trailed away from her hair and clothes into the night.

Klara arrived in a blur of black and white. "Did you mean to do that, Jem?" The innocent tone was utterly unconvincing.

A fresh bout of coughing prevented Jemeryl from answering. Once it subsided, she rested her head on the stonework and took in gulps of the cold air. Her eyes stung; her throat would be sore tomorrow; and her ears were still ringing, though she had taken no serious harm. The aegis of the staff had shielded her and the animals—at least, she hoped so. There was no sign of Ruff. Even as Jemeryl realised this, the bear ambled from the door at the foot of the adjacent small tower, trailing a plume of smoke and carrying a thick cloak in his mouth. She took it gratefully and pulled it around her shoulders. The bear sneezed, and more yellow smoke snaked away from his fur.

Through the open doorway, the sickly yellow haze had swallowed the lights. There was no point trying to clear up; it could wait until morning. Jemeryl sighed and stepped out from the porch. All the castle buildings opened onto the snow-covered courtyard, surrounded by battlements. To her left were kitchens where she could find supper and the small tower where she had her bedroom. But her stomach was queasy from the smoke, and to reach her bedroom meant using the stairs in the hall. Waiting for the air to clear would definitely be a good idea. So instead, she headed for the keep.

The tall stone tower that dominated the site served no real purpose. She need not have bothered including it in the reconstruction, except that it completed the aesthetic feel of the castle and provided a wonderful lookout.

Jemeryl climbed the stairs to the drawbridge and entered under the old portcullis. The spiral staircase led up past the armoury and barrack room and onto the roof. She emerged under stars. Dawn's freezing mists had coated the stonework in a sparkling rime that had not melted during the short winter's day. It crunched under her hand as she leaned against the battlement and looked down.

The castle courtyard was laid out below, with its circle of buildings. Five beech trees grew in the enclosure. They did not belong in the reconstruction, having sprouted after the garrison left, but Jemeryl had let them stay for the squirrels. Ruff was padding around the trunks, sniffing at anything that caught his notice. The other bear, Tumble, came out of the kitchens, and while Jemeryl watched, the two began to play, skidding on the ice and sending up plumes of snow as they chased each other. Squirrels scattered before them, chattering in indignation—or maybe it was excitement. Even a sorcerer could be hard put to know exactly what a squirrel was feeling.

Jemeryl wandered to the other side of the tower and looked down on a winter landscape of bare fields. White snow, brilliant in the moonlight, was cut by inky shadows under the firs. Small silhouettes of cattle and sheep clustered near their barns. The houses of the village were grouped in picturesque disorder around the shearing shed. The wind had dropped, and the far side of the valley was lost in blue-grey mist through which twinkled the lights from distant farmsteads. It was starkly beautiful, but as Jemeryl looked out, troubling thoughts marred her appreciation of the scene. Klara landed on the parapet beside her.

From the village came the faint sound of music and voices, the noise carrying cleanly on the cold air. A party seemed to be underway, presumably to entertain the small group of travellers who had passed below the castle earlier that day, leading a train of mules. Visitors from the outside world were rare at any time of year. It was unsurprising if folk were making an event of their arrival. Jemeryl considered the high mountains above the valley. Even with her magic, she did not like the thought of crossing Whitfell Spur in midwinter. She wondered what desperate circumstances had prompted the travellers to risk the journey. Perhaps she should go and find out.

A sudden desire to meet people and talk struck Jemeryl. Her eyes fixed bleakly on the village hall as she imagined the reception she would get. Jemeryl could not remember the last cheerful face she had seen, but she certainly would not find any if she entered the village.

"They don't like you, you know," Klara volunteered.

"I know." Jemeryl sighed deeply. "I just wish I knew why."

As a child, in the village of her birth, Jemeryl had inspired fear and resentment. The other children would not have her as a playmate, although they soon learned it was unwise to throw stones at her. When she was four, her family had persuaded the local witch to adopt her, purely to rid their house of Jemeryl's disturbing presence. She had felt no regret to go. It had been a home without love. At eleven, she had gone to study at Lyremouth, still holding a child's contempt for the ungifted. Her education at the Coven had done much to increase her tolerance—for all the good it had done with the villagers.

True, she had not wanted to come to the valley, had not wanted to leave Lyremouth. She loved the esoteric study of magic and would happily devote her life to it. However, Coven rules insisted that new sorcerers spend time out in the world, to learn firsthand the needs of the ungifted. Her application for assignment to the valley had been a long shot; she was ridiculously overqualified. To her astonishment, the authorities had agreed.

At the time, Jemeryl had assumed that they saw things the same way she did; the rule was a waste of talent. All her responsibilities in the valley would take no more than a few days each month, leaving her free to concentrate on her studies. Jemeryl had a high opinion of her own talents and would not have been at all surprised to learn that many of her teachers secretly agreed with her.

Two years had passed since she had arrived in the valley. The research had gone well, but her relationship with the villagers had not proceeded totally to plan. Over the months, contact with them had dwindled to the point of non-existence. On the rare occasions when they crossed her path, many displayed blatant hostility or fear.

"I've tried to be nice," she said defensively.

"That was a waste of effort."

"I know. I just couldn't seem to talk to them."

Klara's head swivelled towards her. "If you want my opinion, the lessons about getting on with the ungifted took the wrong approach. Instead of going on about citizenship and equality, they should have taught you a few amusing anecdotes about sheep. That would have helped you fit in. It's all the locals ever talk about."

"I think they now talk about me quite a lot."

"In a year's time, you can apply to return to Lyremouth; then they'll have to go back to the sheep."

The dream of returning to Lyremouth was what sustained Jemeryl through the hard work and isolation, but standing on the battlements, she was hit by unusual self-doubts. "Am I deluding myself, thinking my research is important? That they'll want me back? Perhaps the Coven let me take this assignment because it's all they think I'm fit for."

"Nonsense. The office is trivial. It wouldn't strain the powers of a third-rate witch."

"Even so, I'm not fulfilling its requirements."

"Only because the locals don't want you to. It's not your fault, Jem. You can't force them to ask you for help."

Jemeryl was not convinced. "It shouldn't come down to what they will or won't let me do. I'm supposed to be looking after them."

"You've done your best. You've set up so many charms to keep out enemies and illness, a belligerent hamster couldn't enter the valley, especially if it were feeling a bit poorly."

"I'm not sure. I might have gone too far."

"In what way?"

"Overprotecting people is bad for them. It has side effects. They can lose all common sense and start acting like children."

"In which case it might be nasty. Some of them didn't have far to go to start with."

"Perhaps I should go and talk to Sergo."

"You *are* in a dismal mood. Look, if I say I'm sorry your sphere blew up, will it make you happy? You can invoke another one tomorrow." Klara hopped onto Jemeryl's hand.

"There's a strange emanation in the air tonight."

"A premonition, or are we downwind of the village dung heap?"

"Probably just me worrying." Jemeryl studied the distant houses before asking softly, "If something was seriously wrong, they'd come to me, wouldn't they?"

"Of course they would. They'd race up here like scared rabbits."

Jemeryl stroked the magpie's head and dismissed all thought of going to the village. If she admitted the truth, she was nervous of the villagers and unwilling to face their hostility. It brought back painful childhood memories.

She forced a smile to her lips. "Perhaps things aren't so bad. I've got time to study, and if the villagers aren't happy and healthy, they've only got themselves to blame. Still, I wouldn't object to someone to talk to."

"Don't I count?" Klara sounded indignant.

"You know you don't."

Music from the village drifted on the wind. Jemeryl turned her back on the sound and retraced her steps down through the courtyard, in search of supper and then bed. She waited at the kitchen door, holding it open until the bears galloped in; then she pushed it shut, leaving the courtyard once more deserted under the stars.

Two mornings later, Jemeryl sat in her study. A large book lay open before her, but her concentration kept drifting. Something was pricking the edges of her mind, all the more irritating since she did not have a clue what that something was. For the third time, she started reading at the beginning of a long paragraph. Before she got halfway through, her attention slipped, and she lost the thread of the argument.

"I don't know what's wrong with me today."

"You mean in addition to what's wrong with you generally?" Klara asked.

The gibe from her familiar softened Jemeryl's frown. With a yawn, the sorcerer flipped the covers shut and stretched back. The book could wait.

"Maybe I've been overdoing things. A break might help. I could take the bears for a walk."

The suggestion found favour with Tumble, who had been sitting in a corner. The bear lumbered to her feet and trotted over to the desk, stubby tail wagging. The big, hopeful eyes made Jemeryl's smile broaden. She scratched Tumble's head, causing the bear to growl with pleasure. However, now that she had abandoned all attempt to read, Jemeryl's sense of foreboding shuffled to the front of her mind. Something was about to go very seriously wrong.

Jemeryl left her chair and went to a window. Everything appeared normal in the valley below. Snow lay on the ground, though less thick than of late. Sheep dawdled across the fields, tended by shepherds wrapped in layers of clothes. Smoke rose from distant chimneys. Jemeryl leaned her head against the glass and tried to call on all her training and talents to identify the threat.

"What do you think it is, Jem?" For once, Klara was devoid of sarcasm.

"I don't know."

"Are you going to see Sergo?"

"She might know nothing. Perhaps an oracle would..." Jemeryl shook her head indecisively.

"You hate oracles."

"True."

Jemeryl stood, biting her lip and trying to pinpoint the core of her anxiety. The harder she concentrated, the less substantial her fears seemed, until there was nothing but a vague feeling of unease. "Perhaps I'm mistaken. I might just be picking up leakage from one of the crystal reservoirs in the hall."

"So what are you going to do?"

Jemeryl took a deep breath and straightened her shoulders. "I'm going to visit Sergo. Even if I'm imagining things, it's about time I had a word with her."

Jemeryl hoped that making the decision would ease her tension, but, if anything, her agitation intensified as she left her study and stepped onto the high platform at the top of the stairs in the great hall.

The small tower had been the captain's quarters in the days when soldiers were stationed at the castle. The top floor was now divided between Jemeryl's study and her bedroom. The floor below held a larger room that had been the captain's audience chamber. Jemeryl had intended to use it for the same purpose. However, since nobody ever came to see her, it had become her private parlour and was now cluttered with personal belongings, including the outdoor clothes she would need for the ride.

Jemeryl descended the stairs in the great hall. She had reached the lower landing and was about to open the parlour door when a noise made her jump. Echoing around the great hall was the sound of a gong, beating softly—a summons, and one Jemeryl recognised instantly. It set her leaping down the remaining steps and skidding to a stop in the centre of the hall. An image was intensifying before her, accompanied by hissing and rumbling. The figure was just identifiable as Iralin, Jemeryl's mentor in Lyremouth.

Klara landed on Jemeryl's shoulder. "It's a sending from the Coven."

Jemeryl nodded anxiously. It meant trouble. A full sending of sound and vision over the many miles between them was an enormous undertaking, undoubtedly requiring the energies of several sorcerers. In practice, it would require less effort for Iralin to walk from Lyremouth on foot. It implied a desperate urgency that confirmed her sense of grim foreboding.

Iralin's image was becoming firmer by the second. She was sitting in familiar surroundings, her study in the Coven, with Lyremouth harbour visible through the window behind. The charts lining the walls were unchanged since Jemeryl had last seen them, two years before.

Apparently, Iralin's view of Jemeryl was also improving. The senior sorcerer glared sternly. "What have you been doing?"

The last thing Jemeryl expected was for the conversation to start with her own activities. The angry tone also threw her. "Ma'am?"

"I said, what have you been doing?"

"With regard to anything in particular?"

"Don't be flippant. We've had reports about you, passed on by sorcerer Chenoweth in Rizen. They haven't been amusing."

Jemeryl was bewildered. "Are you sure there hasn't been some mistake, ma'am?"

"What have the villagers said to you recently?"

"I, um...haven't spoken to any of them for months."

"Why not?"

Jemeryl could think of no suitable words to say aloud, although dozens of unsuitable ones came to mind. She cursed herself for not paying more attention to the locals. Somewhere, something had got completely out of hand.

"You're supposed to be looking after the inhabitants. How do you do that without talking to them?" Iralin persisted.

"I assumed they'd come to me if they had any problems."

"You don't consider it your job to go to them?"

"They said they didn't want me to." Only as the sentence left her mouth did Jemeryl consider how it might sound.

A long silence followed, during which Jemeryl could hear her heart pounding.

At last, Iralin leaned back and steepled her fingers. "Why don't you tell me, in your own words, from the beginning, just how this situation has arisen between you and the people entrusted to your care?"

The emphasis on the last four words made Jemeryl flinch. "I'm not quite sure."

"Make some intelligent guesses." It was an order.

Jemeryl took a couple of deep breaths to clear her thoughts—not that they helped. "Um...when I first came to the valley, they offered me a cottage in the village. I think it belonged to the previous witch. But I wanted to work on my research, and it wouldn't be safe with lots of people around. There was this abandoned castle, so I moved here instead...just me and Dorin."

Jemeryl's face brightened. "Yes, of course. Dorin. He'd be the source of anything you've heard. The villagers insisted I had someone to wait on me. It wasn't necessary, but I think Dorin was the village simpleton, and they wanted an excuse to get him off their hands. It was ridiculous. He couldn't cope. The mere sound of Klara talking would terrify him. He only stayed a month. He spread some daft rumours back in the village. It's understandable. For the first time in his life, people wanted to listen to what he had to say. I know he made up things. Stories about me calling up the dead, turning people into frogs, even sacrificing babies to the full moon, for all I know."

"Do you think we'd pay any attention to stories like that?" Iralin said curtly.

I can't imagine what else you've got the arse-ache about. The words nearly escaped Jemeryl's lips. Fortunately, she managed to phrase it more diplomatically. "Then I'm afraid I don't know what stories you have heard, ma'am."

"How about stories concerning two children lured to your castle? The lucky one left in a coma; the other was dead."

"They weren't my fault, ma'am, neither of them," Jemeryl said quickly.

"So why don't you tell me what happened?"

Jemeryl frowned. What had people been saying? But at least she now knew what Iralin was after. "The coma...that would be a girl called Shiral. She came here after Dorin left, and I think she had some of his stupid stories stuck in her head. One day when I was out, she went poking through my things. I'd told her not to. Perhaps that was the attraction. She found an old shadow mirror. I'm not sure what she saw in it, but we both know the visions can be nasty. The fright sent her into shock. It wasn't a coma. I took Shiral back to her parents. I thought a home atmosphere would do her good while I helped her recover, but her parents wouldn't let me near her. There was nothing else I could do."

"And the child who died?"

Jemeryl would rather not recall the incident that had caused her anguish at the time and still intruded into nightmares, but there was no avoiding the question. "About a year ago, a man brought his daughter to the castle. She was only a toddler. She'd had an accident. Gangrene had set in, but they'd left it too long before coming to me. I fought to save her life; I really did. A day earlier, and I might have done it. I know her parents were upset and blamed me, but it was their fault. They should have brought her here sooner."

"Has it occurred to you, that if you'd performed your duties properly and talked to your citizens, you might have heard about the child's injury in time?"

"They wouldn't talk to me. Even when I made the effort to see them, they hid things from me."

"They were frightened of you."

"I suppose so," Jemeryl conceded.

"Why?"

"I don't know."

"So if you haven't been performing your duties, what have you been doing?" Iralin's voice could have cut through stone.

"I've been researching into overcharged ether currents, using them to induce field containers for elemental auras."

"That's a waste of time. It's been proved it can't work."

I've done it. Jemeryl was proud of her achievement, but now was not the time to boast.

Iralin's gaze shifted as she caught sight of something moving. "Is that a bear behind you?"

Jemeryl glanced over her shoulder. Tumble had followed her down. "Er...yes."

"You have bears in the castle?"

"Only two."

"Only!"

"They are both fully entranced and safe."

"You have bears roaming the castle and then wonder why the villagers are too scared to come and ask you for help."

"The bears are harmless. To be more frightened of them than of gangrene is stupid."

"Looking after stupid people is the job you asked to do."

"But—"

Iralin did not let her finish. "I was against your taking this appointment from the start. My objections were overruled, but I find I've been proved right. I doubted your motives, and I felt you lacked the necessary maturity. In dealing with ungifted folk, you have always been arrogant and inconsiderate. You see the villagers as unimportant—a distraction from your real interests, but it is their lives at stake. They are simple, honest folk, who are also loyal citizens of the Protectorate. If you were unable to feel responsible for them, you shouldn't have taken the job. You have failed to perform the duties of your post and failed due to lack of effort rather than inability. You have disgraced the Coven."

Jemeryl was stunned. Wilful failure to fulfil an appointment was one of the worst offences a sorcerer could commit. "I've tried my best to perform all my duties."

"Your duties consist of caring for these people. You have not cared for them. You made no attempt to work thought your difficulties with them; you were happy to give up. When you realised you were having problems, you should have asked the Coven for assistance. We have considerable experience of young sorcerers alienating their charges. Apart from that, you could have monitored them without their knowledge. You have the ability to aid the villagers without being asked. But you didn't care. You have not shown a shred of concern for their well-being."

Here was a charge Jemeryl could refute. "I haven't just forgotten them. I set wards. I'll detect disease or anything dangerous entering the valley. Nothing serious could harm the villagers without my knowledge."

Iralin regarded her solemnly. "Then I take it you would be surprised to learn that a basilisk has turned up?"

"It can't have. There must be a mistake."

"There is no mistake."

"I'll go and—"

"You needn't bother; the basilisk has been taken care of. Even as we speak, a passing warrior has done your job for you and killed the creature."

Jemeryl was speechless. Eventually, she found her voice. "I am indebted to him."

"Her," Iralin corrected. "However, she has paid for her bravery. She removed the head of the basilisk but neglected to treat it with due caution. The beast was able to transmute her eyes to a crystal bridge. You must rectify that."

"Yes, of course. I'll go and find her at once." Jemeryl spoke in a half-daze.

"There's no need. She will come to you."

"Yes, ma'am."

"There is only one more thing."

"Ma'am?" What more could there be? Jemeryl fought to keep her composure. As a student, she had been hauled up for her share of misdemeanours—juvenile pranks and the like—but never had she been in trouble like this.

"The judgement of the Coven is upon you." Iralin's voice had been harsh before; now it was cold and uncompromising. "Sorcerer Jemeryl, you are removed from your post, and it will be recorded that you failed to perform the appointment you accepted. The mark will stand against you until you prove yourself fit for some other work. Your new assignment is this. The aforementioned warrior is currently on a quest of some importance. You will accompany her and assist until the quest is completed or you die in the attempt."

"But my research? I have been achieving so much."

"Your so-called research is unendorsed and unapproved. There is nothing more to say. You will heal the warrior and leave the valley with her. You have twelve days to quit the castle. Is that clear? I would suggest you use the next few hours to get ready for your guest. This conversation is terminated. Next time we speak, I trust the circumstances will be more favourable."

With that, the image imploded on itself and vanished. Jemeryl stared in horror at the point where the figure had been. Her head was in turmoil as she fought to absorb the implications of what had just happened. The least of her worries was the curtailment of her studies.

The reprimand meant her reputation might be permanently sullied, blocking any hope of claiming a permanent post in Lyremouth. As the impact hit home, tears filled her eyes. Her mood shifted from shock to shame to anger. Jemeryl's hands clenched into fists, and she was overwhelmed by bitterness—at Iralin, at the villagers and at the unknown fool of a warrior she was now bound to follow.

❖

Many miles away, Iralin slumped back in her chair, exhausted by the effort of maintaining the link. She pinched the bridge of her nose between her forefingers. After a couple of deep breaths, her arm dropped, and she looked at the other two sorcerers, a man and a woman, who had monitored the conversation. Her eyebrows raised in a silent query.

"That was a bit heavy." The man's tone implied a statement of fact rather than criticism.

Iralin snorted. "Conceited young puppy. She needed something to shake her. Everything I said was quite true and I wanted to be certain that her behaviour was simply due to thoughtlessness."

"You surely didn't think Jemeryl had become a murderer?"

"Oh, no, but she can be arrogant enough to think the rules don't apply to her. I wanted to know how far over the line she'd been stepping, and there wasn't time for gently wheedling out the truth."

"I guess you know Jemeryl best, but I don't think I'd have been that hard on her. My own record with the ungifted isn't good."

"Jemeryl has to accompany this warrior, and it's vital she applies herself to the task wholeheartedly. Given her low opinion of prophecy, I doubt she'd do that if I gave her the candid truth on the matter."

The third sorcerer had been staring out through the open window, her thoughts clearly pursuing some other goal. She was older than the other two; sunlight etched deep lines on her face. Yet despite her frailty, she had an aura of authority that even Iralin could not match—a power that made it unnecessary to see the white amulet on her wrist to know that she was Gilliart, the Guardian and leader of the Coven.

Gilliart's lips twisted in an ironic grimace. "In Jemeryl's place, I wouldn't take it very well either. She has to drop everything to go...gods know where with some muscle-bound oaf, just because an extremely vague oracle said the future of the Coven probably depends on it."

The three sorcerers sat in dour reflection. Iralin shook her head slowly, as if combating her disbelief. "I guess we're just incredibly lucky to have got the warning at all. When I received the report from Chenoweth about the villager's complaints, I was torn between ignoring it completely and writing to Jemeryl for an explanation. I'm still not sure in my own mind why I put it to the oracle. It was just an odd whim, and that was the answer I got."

"The whims of sorcerers can be serious things."

"Don't I know it."

The Guardian waved her finger at Iralin. "Your awareness of the future is far better than you're prepared to admit, even to yourself. Something this momentous was bound to attract your attention. If it hadn't been Chenoweth's report, you'd have found yourself wanting to cast an oracle just to find out how Jemeryl was going to cook her eggs for breakfast. You only resisted the call because you're one of the few people who hate prophecy even more than Jemeryl."

Iralin pouted. "Because all you get is ambiguous hints that only make sense with hindsight. Like now—have we still got no real idea of what's involved?"

"No. Our best attempts have produced no more information than you gave Jemeryl: a blind warrior, a basilisk, and a quest. Make what you will of it." The Guardian shook her head. "We've even tried some active intervention, which is asking for trouble. We've caused as much temporal disruption as we dared and got nothing from it. We've had to give up and weave the neatest patch we could. Even so, Jemeryl will pick up the after-waves when she hits the critical moment."

"Jemeryl won't be pleased if she thinks we've been tampering with her fate," the man said.

Gilliart's expression hardened. "Which is why I was happy for Iralin to give her a good kick in the right direction. The future of the Protectorate is at stake, and the only useful thing we know is that our best hope of success is if Jemeryl goes on the quest. The Protectorate is my sworn responsibility, and I'm helpless. We don't know enough. The oracle was the next best thing to useless."

Iralin nodded and said dryly, "In fact, a quote from Jemeryl herself comes to mind: 'Foretelling is great as a party trick, but you can't rely on it to tell you tomorrow's date.'"

Chapter Eleven—The Web of Fate

The preparations took Jemeryl the rest of the morning. Even so, her expected patient had not arrived by the time she had finished. As the day stretched on, Jemeryl found herself checking and rechecking artefacts, pacing the hall, and snapping irritably at the squirrels, although they were the only things Iralin had not picked out for criticism—presumably, even the villagers were not frightened of them.

Her actions were becoming increasingly pointless. She swapped the positions of two talismans, considered the new arrangement, and then swapped them back. She was reaching out a third time when irritation took over. Her fist thumped on the tabletop.

Jemeryl marched out onto the porch. She glared at the castle gates, fighting the childish urge to blast them into flames. She was in enough trouble as it was and did not want to imagine what would happen if she actually did something to justify the villagers' fear of her.

And where was the blinded warrior?

Jemeryl raked the fingers of both hands through her hair in frustration. What could she do? If she tried to scry the entire valley magically, she would be exhausted before she even started reconstructing the eyes. If she went looking in a conventional manner, she would probably miss the woman on the way. Iralin had been confident that the warrior would come to the castle. Presumably, the senior sorcerer had a reason for thinking this.

"It would've been nice if she'd shared the information, rather than acting like a dragon with diarrhoea, and dumping me in it." Jemeryl gave vent to her feelings.

Ruff whined in sympathy. The bears had been avoiding her, clearly unsettled by her anger. Jemeryl glanced over her shoulder. Ruff was peering around the edge of the door with dark, pathetic eyes. The sight caused Jemeryl a twinge of guilt, and her expression softened, which emboldened Ruff to pad to her side and bat his head against her hand, wanting his head rubbed.

"It's all right. I'm not angry at you. You're both good bears. I don't care what Iralin thinks." Blaming the bears for her misfortune was unfair. There was no one to blame but herself.

Still the warrior did not come. Jemeryl left the bears happily digging into lunch and climbed to the old barrack room high in the keep. Once, a squad of soldiers had slept there; now it was an empty room with bare floorboards and unplastered walls. The windows were arrow slits set in wedge-shaped alcoves. The openings were a couple of feet above floor level, intended for kneeling, rather than standing, archers. They made good window seats— provided you used magic to warm them.

Jemeryl clambered into the one commanding the best view of the path down to the village and curled up inside, bracing her knees and shoulders against the slanting walls. There was no sign of anyone, blinded or otherwise, approaching the castle.

With nothing else to occupy her mind, Jemeryl's thoughts kept returning to Iralin's tirade. To call it a severe reprimand was an understatement. Iralin had verbally ripped her apart. Jemeryl's face twisted in a pained grimace. Tears stung the backs of her eyes. Whether they were due to anger, humiliation, or disappointment, Jemeryl could not say, and she did not want to poke around at her emotions to find out.

Her relationship with Iralin had never been warm, but Jemeryl had believed it to be marked by mutual respect. Several times, she had been tempted to request a change in mentor. However, Iralin was third in seniority in the Coven, and Jemeryl was keenly aware of the honour of being her apprentice. She knew Iralin had taught her more than anyone else could have done. Their talents and personalities were very similar, and therein lay the source of much of the friction between them.

In all honesty, Jemeryl had to admit that Iralin's words held some truth, but she could not see that she had been so wilfully negligent as to deserve all that was said or the final judgement. It felt as if Iralin had deliberately skewed the facts to justify an outcome that had been determined before the start.

Jemeryl was still brooding when Klara flew in and landed on her knee. There was no need for the magpie to report her findings aloud.

Jemeryl already knew what she had discovered on her circuit of the valley: six of the protective ward charms, broken and scattered.

"Someone's been deliberately wrecking them." Klara's beadlike eyes mirrored Jemeryl's anger.

"But who, and why?"

"Does it matter?"

"Yes, it does. Why break the wards and let the basilisk in? Was someone deliberately trying to harm the villagers? Or was it just a game by someone too stupid to see what they were?"

"I wouldn't bother trying to make sense of it. You can't hope to understand the ungifted. They've got less sense than the squirrels."

Jemeryl thumped the stone. "How could I have been so careless?"

"You couldn't have predicted it."

"I shouldn't have relied on the wards. It's the sort of mistake novice witches make. I should have gone down to the village every day and made certain I knew what was going on. I've walked into this like an idiot, and there's more to come. I can feel it."

Klara tilted her head. "I think you should try to calm down. Otherwise, you'll be in no state to heal the warrior when she finally decides to show up."

Jemeryl sighed and closed her eyes, then opened them again. A squirrel had left a small pile of broken nut shells. Jemeryl arranged them into a neat row, and then irritably swept them out the window. The thought of the warrior had brought a fresh set of worries.

"Who goes hunting basilisks without the most basic knowledge of the risks involved?"

"A fool?"

"She must be. I've got to go with her—and no idea for how long. It could be months, even years."

"Following a brainless, sword-swinging lout." Klara's words were not comforting.

"You're coming, too. Iralin didn't forbid it, and I'll need a friendly beak to turn to," Jemeryl said, although this was a trap in itself. The magpie was a fully locked familiar, giving only the appearance of independence. In a very real sense, Jemeryl was talking to herself.

The bell outside the gatehouse rang loudly. Jemeryl jumped. While talking to Klara, she had forgotten to watch the path. The intervening castle walls now prevented her from seeing whoever had rung the bell, but at the last peal, two villagers raced away and fled down the hillside.

"Have they left the warrior outside?"

"Either that or they've become totally infantile and are playing knock and run," Klara suggested.

Tumble lumbered across the courtyard below. With her teeth, she caught the rope hanging on the inside of the gate and pulled it open. Jemeryl heard the grinding of the hinges and the clatter of hooves, and then a pony trotted into view. The saddle was empty, although its pack bristled with assorted weaponry. Someone on foot was hidden on the far side. The sight of the weapons reminded Jemeryl that Iralin had said "warrior," not "scout" or even "assassin." It did not bode well for the woman's intelligence.

Jemeryl glanced at Klara. "I guess I'm going to need you to talk to after all. Her conversation skills might be very limited."

The pony came to a standstill. A two-handed battle-axe protruded prominently from behind the saddle. "An axe woman!" Without waiting to see more, Jemeryl scrambled from the alcove.

Klara fluttered onto Jemeryl's shoulder. "Limited conversation, my foot. She's probably still at the grunt-and-point stage."

Jemeryl braced herself for the worst. She cast a last muttered obscenity at Iralin and strode to the spiral staircase. With each step, her anxiety grew—not about healing the warrior's eyes, she had no doubt of her own ability, but at the sense that she was being pushed into something irrevocable. She was quite certain that far more was at stake than Iralin had implied.

The scene greeting Jemeryl in the courtyard was approaching chaos. The pony had fled in panic from Tumble, who was trying to make friends. The frightened pony was now threatening to kick over the water butt by the kitchen door, while Tumble was licking the warrior's hand, and even Jemeryl would accept that the gesture might be misunderstood. Squirrels were bouncing around the woman's feet, excited by the novelty; others sat on a branch, chattering a noisy welcome. And still, Jemeryl could not get a good look at her visitor. The woman had her back to the keep and was obscured behind a tree.

Re-establishing order was a good starting point. Jemeryl pulled all the animals under her control and commanded them to back off and keep quiet. Peace descended on the courtyard. In the resulting silence, Jemeryl crossed the drawbridge and descended the steps. At the bottom, she turned for her first clear view of the warrior.

The future crashed into the past. Time was ripped open. Jemeryl recoiled in shock, with no sense of when she was. A gaping hole opened in the web of fate, inviting her to see things she had no wish to know. She was sucked in, while forever spun around her. Klara screeched in terror, a cry more awful than anything Jemeryl had ever heard from her familiar.

The sound pulled Jemeryl back to the courtyard, to here and now. She hurled out every temporal barricade she knew and forced the future out of her head. For a space, fate rippled in the courtyard, distorting Jemeryl's time sense in the same way that heat above a fire distorts vision. Then, gradually, the seconds resumed their steady march, each one following the last.

Jemeryl stood with her eyes closed. This was the meeting that had overshadowed her all day, she realised, not the confrontation with Iralin. It was also a meeting that had not been allowed to run its own true course. Someone had been tampering with fate, and it took little to guess who that someone was. Iralin and the Coven were playing games.

Why couldn't they trust me? Jemeryl thought in fury. *Instead, they just left me to walk into that botched mess.* However, there was nothing she could do. She was going to have to bite back her anger and get on with the task before her.

Jemeryl opened her eyes and again looked at her visitor. This time, there was no upheaval, and she was able to evaluate the warrior. The results were unexpected. The woman was both younger and smaller than anticipated—scarcely older than Jemeryl and only a handbreadth taller. She was of medium build, with short dark hair. Over her eyes was a wet bandage. Her hands bore the mercenaries' red and gold tattoos. Her clothes were splattered with blood, which, judging from its colour and quantity, had belonged to the basilisk. She was clearly confused, frightened, and in pain, but making a desperate attempt to hide it all.

Jemeryl forced her feet to continue walking. The warrior turned to face the sound of approaching steps.

"Please. I need your help."

"I know. I've been expecting you."

While combating the aftereffects of time shock, Jemeryl continued to study the woman, aware that her emotions were lurching in a surprising direction. Jemeryl had anticipated feeling dislike, even contempt, for the warrior, partially blaming her for the turn of events. However, the young woman before her, vulnerable and suffering, could only inspire pity. She was even more of a victim than Jemeryl was, and in a far worse state. How much was her condition due to Iralin's tampering? Jemeryl directed a fresh blast of anger towards her mentor—this time, on behalf of the blinded warrior.

Jemeryl spoke, more gently than before. "Come with me, and I'll see what I can do."

The woman flinched at Jemeryl's touch. It seemed as if she might give way to panic and bolt—or would, if she could see where to run. But then she meekly allowed herself to be led towards the great hall.

Just before they entered, Jemeryl caused the harness on the pony to loosen. The pack slipped to the ground for the bears to take care of, and the pony was sent to the stables. Everything else could wait until the matter of the eyes was resolved.

The woman collapsed on the chair Jemeryl led her to. Her breath came in ragged gasps. She gripped the armrests so tightly that her knuckles were white.

Jemeryl put a hand on her shoulder. "Don't worry; you're going to be fine."

"Can you help me?"

"Yes, I can, and I will. My name's Jemeryl, and you've got nothing to be frightened of."

"My name's Tevi. A basilisk, it—"

"It's all right, I know." Jemeryl took a deep breath and released the warrior's shoulder. It was time to start work. "All right, Tevi, I'm going to remove the bandage and examine your eyes."

The clumsy knot took only a few seconds to untie. The material was wet and very cold—an attempted ice pack. Jemeryl swore under her breath. Everything was stacking against her. Were the villagers really so ignorant? The ice would have reduced blood flow to the eye socket and possibly cemented the crystallisation.

Despite her fresh worries, Jemeryl tried to make her voice reassuring. "Now, Tevi, I'm going to examine your eyes. I'm afraid you need to be conscious so I can test the reactions of the nerves. It will be unpleasant, but it won't take long. Do you understand?"

"Yes."

"Can you open your eyes?"

The prospects were poor if the twin effects of transmutation and ice had caused too much damage for Tevi to do this. To Jemeryl's relief, the eyelids quivered open. The glasslike orbs would have been unsettling enough for any ordinary ungifted person. It was far more shocking for Jemeryl, who could see the eyes for what they were—hideous twin drains in Tevi's aura, through which her life's energy could be sucked away.

Jemeryl placed her fingertips on Tevi's forehead, temples, and cheeks in a circle. With her extended senses she could feel the coursing of blood through veins, the electric messages in the nerves and the taunt elasticity of membrane. Unfortunately, it was impossible to numb Tevi to the pain without blocking the very responses she needed to examine. Jemeryl went as carefully as possible; yet still, she heard Tevi whimper.

Soon, Jemeryl let her hands drop and sat back, feeling very relieved. The sockets were undamaged, although it would have been less painful for Tevi had this not been the case. The active nerve ends must be causing her agony. Jemeryl looked at her patient with respect, surprised that she was even able to walk and talk. At least it was now possible to do something to help. A goblet with a sleeping draft was already prepared.

Tevi was slumped forward, gasping. The pulse in her neck beat rapidly. Jemeryl gently coaxed her upright and placed the goblet in her hands. "There's a lot of work to do, but I'm sure you'll be pleased to know you don't have to be aware of it. Drink this, and you'll sleep."

"Can you stop it hurting?" Tevi's voice was a raw whisper.

"I can do more than that. I can restore your eyesight. I can't guarantee it will be like before, but it should be good enough for you to remain a warrior."

At first, Tevi hesitated, with the goblet at her lips, but then she resolutely downed the contents.

"If you could come over here..." Jemeryl took Tevi's hand and guided her to the table. "You'll be asleep soon and won't know anything more until tomorrow morning. When I've finished, I'll put a bandage around your eyes. You mustn't remove it, even if you feel fine. Your eyes will be extremely sensitive to light. If you expose them before they've healed, you may cause fresh damage."

Tevi lay on the table with a cushion under her head. "I won't touch it." Her voice was already sounding drowsy.

"I'll try to be around when you wake up. If I'm not, you can say my name aloud anywhere in the castle, and I'll hear. My name is Jemeryl. Will you remember that?"

Tevi nodded and mumbled, "Jem'r."

Jemeryl moved to the few final preparations. Tevi was deeply asleep by the time she had finished. The expression of pain had faded. Without it, the warrior looked even younger than Jemeryl's first estimate. Her body was athletic but certainly not muscle-bound. *Where did she find the strength to use a battle-axe?* Jemeryl wondered. *And how did anyone so inexperienced kill a basilisk?* The questions would have to wait. Jemeryl had a long afternoon's work ahead of her.

"Oh, Keovan's knickers! I forgot to ask what colour eyes she wanted." Jemeryl paused. "I guess it's down to me." She studied Tevi's face for a few seconds and smiled. "Grey."

❖

Night had fallen by the time Jemeryl was finished. The job had presented more problems than expected, and she was exhausted. She hauled Tevi from the table and onto Ruff's back for the short, shuffled journey up through the parlour and into a small side chamber. This had been allocated as a sickroom in the days when Jemeryl had expected to be called on regularly to nurse sick villagers. Tevi would be only the second person to occupy it. As she rolled Tevi onto the bed, Jemeryl pushed away the memories of the other patient, the young girl dying of gangrene.

She tugged off Tevi's boots and outer clothing, then pulled up the blankets and stood back. Waves of tiredness swept over Jemeryl. Lank strands of hair stuck to the sweat on her forehead.

Klara perched on the bedstead. "Finished already?"

"Just about. I want you to stand watch. Call me if Tevi wakes. Otherwise, let me sleep."

"Why do I get the boring jobs?"

"Because I'm the one who can open the food cupboard."

Jemeryl paused at the door, intending only a last backward glance. Instead, she froze, overwhelmed by the changes the day had brought. What was so important about meeting this woman? She studied her patient. Tevi's face was relaxed and at peace. Dark hair fell over the clean white bandage around Tevi's eyes, and the tip of her nose stuck out below. Her lips were parted. Her cheeks were smooth and flushed in sleep.

An assortment of vague ideas scrambled through Jemeryl's mind. The only one clear enough to be identified was an awareness that she had been celibate for over two years.

Jemeryl laughed at herself and shook her head. "It's amazing, the funny ideas you get when you're tired."

"You never needed tiredness as an excuse before."

"Impudent bird." With that, Jemeryl shut the door and headed to her own bed.

❖

Tevi awoke from a series of troubled dreams. Her first thought was that it was still night, since it was too dark to see. Then memories disentangled themselves from the nightmares. Her hand shot to her face, and with the feel of the bandage came the realisation that her eyes no longer hurt. Tevi's hand fell back to the bedcovers, but her relief was short-lived. From the foot of her bed came a sound like leaves rustling in the wind—except the air in the room was still. Something was moving.

Tevi's memories continued to drop into place. She was in the sorcerer's castle, alone and sightless. There had been nonhuman things in the courtyard. The villagers' stories suddenly seemed far more credible. Tevi felt an urge to hide, an urge all the more inane since her only options were under either the bedcovers or the bed itself. Neither was likely to be effective if the sorcerer, or anything else, meant her harm. Tevi fought back her panic. What was it at the foot of the bed?

A new set of muffled sounds arose. Tevi's entire concentration focused on her ears. Someone was moving in an adjoining room and getting closer. The noises stopped; then a handle rattled, and what had to be the door to her room opened.

Tevi jerked onto one elbow, facing the sound. "Who's there?"

"It's me, Jemeryl. Are you all right?"

Tevi fell back, feeling simultaneously frightened and stupid. "Yes...yes, I think so."

"Do your eyes hurt?"

"No. They feel fine." Tevi took a grip on herself. The sorcerer had kept her word. She had taken away the unbearable pain. The very least Tevi owed her was the benefit of the doubt.

The bed moved. Presumably, Jemeryl had taken a seat on the edge. Tevi pulled herself into a sitting position.

"Any other aches and pains?" Jemeryl asked gently.

"I don't think so."

"Did you sleep well?"

"Er...I must have." Tevi did not feel completely certain about anything.

"Then can I interest you in breakfast?"

"Oh, yes." This was the easiest question so far. Tevi had not eaten since breakfast in Sergo's cottage the previous morning.

"The villagers leave supplies. I can offer bread and honey, slices of ham, cheese. How does that sound?"

"Fine."

"There's a bowl of water on the table beside your bed. I was too tired to clean you up last night, but if you want, I'll help now."

Tevi shook her head. "I can manage on my own."

"Right. I'll go and get breakfast."

With her fears easing, Tevi's body was able to attract her attention. Jemeryl must have noticed the resulting expression.

"There's something else you want?"

"Um...a latrine?" Tevi asked sheepishly.

"Oh, of course." Jemeryl took Tevi's hand and helped her out of bed. "There are privies built into the wall where the tower overhangs the cliff. One is in the corner of your room. I'll show you. It's primitive but functional. Just a seat with a hole over a sheer drop. If you suffer from vertigo, it would be a good idea not to look too closely once your bandage is removed." Jemeryl paused. "However, in spring and summer, the cliffs below are covered with nesting birds. I sometimes think the latrines were the architect's idea of revenge."

Tevi laughed out loud for the first time in ages. There were a few seagulls on Storenseg she had a score to settle with, although they were unlikely to be so far from home.

Jemeryl let go of Tevi's hand. "There's not much furniture in the room. If you go carefully, you shouldn't bang into anything. Your saddle pack is under the table. If you're all right, I'll see about breakfast."

"I'll manage," Tevi said confidently. Only after the door closed did she remember the thing she had heard moving. What was it? And was it still there?

Tevi took a deep breath. She was being stupid. Nothing bad had happened so far; the sorcerer seemed friendly, and even if she were not, acting like a coward would not help.

Working by touch, Tevi was able to take care of herself, including finding a clean shirt in her pack. By the time Jemeryl returned, she was back in her bed, feeling much better. Her newfound composure lasted less than a second. Something small leapt onto the bed, and a tiny, clawed hand touched hers.

"What is it?" Panic cracked Tevi's voice.

"It's just a squirrel."

"A squirrel!"

"Most likely after your breakfast. It won't like the honey or the ham, but squirrels are incurable optimists."

"A squirrel?" Given the circumstances, an imp or huge spider would have been far less surprising. While Tevi was coming to terms with the idea, a plate was pressed into her hands. The small creature was lifted from Tevi's lap and deposited by her feet—not that it stayed there.

"I'm afraid the castle is overrun with them." Jemeryl sounded rueful.

"Aren't they supposed to be hibernating?"

"They should be, but it's warm in the castle, and I feed them, so mostly they stay awake."

"They're tame?"

"Lightly entranced. I can make it go if you want."

"It's all right." Tevi cautiously put out a hand and stroked the squirrel. She could feel that it was perched on its back legs and peering about the room. "Was it squirrels I heard in the courtyard yesterday?"

"In part. Tumble was also contributing to your riotous welcome." Jemeryl hesitated, as if considering her words. "Ruff and Tumble are bears...quite large bears. I'll try to keep them away from you, but you needn't be frightened. They really are completely safe. Tumble just wanted to make friends."

Obviously, some of the villagers' stories were based in fact. Tevi concentrated on eating while she turned ideas over, hoping Jemeryl would put her silence down to hunger. Although the sorcerer had been pleasant, it might be part of a less altruistic plan. Subconsciously reflecting her doubts, Tevi's hand rose to the bandage, wondering if her eyes really were cured.

"Stop that," Jemeryl said sharply.

Tevi flinched. "Pardon?"

"I'm sorry. Not you; the squirrel. It's eyeing up your bread. It's realised you can't see."

"Oh, well...if it wants some, there's more here than I need."

"Best not encourage them, or they'll be stealing dinner from under our noses." Jemeryl sounded exasperated but amused. "Here. I have some acorns in my pocket. If I put a few on the floor, that ought to distract it while we finish eating—unless it decides to try its hand at making a nut sandwich."

Again, Tevi found herself laughing. Pockets full of squirrel bribes did not fit with the evil necromancer of the stories.

"The villagers...they told me a bit about you," Tevi began.

"I'm sure they did."

"You don't seem quite like I expected."

"You mean I haven't fed you to my pet dragon?"

"Er..." Tevi wondered if she should have kept quiet.

"There's a simple explanation. It's not hungry yet."

Tevi could tell Jemeryl was joking, but there was an edge to her voice. The sorcerer was very serious about something. Uncertainly, Tevi asked, "Do you have a dragon?"

"Of course not. But I've got a mentor who could give real dragons nightmares." The second part was muttered so quietly that Tevi was not sure if she had misheard.

"I'm sorry. I didn't mean to sound as if—"

"It's all right. I'm aware the villagers don't trust me. In part that has to be my fault, but half of what they say about me is distorted, and the other half is completely untrue."

From the undercurrents to Jemeryl's voice, a lot was being left unsaid, but there was also unmistakable sincerity. Tevi realised that she trusted the sorcerer far more than the villager's stories, or would until her own experience persuaded her otherwise.

Before she could think of a suitable response, a large yawn caught her by surprise. "I can't still be tired."

"You probably are. It's a side effect of the magic. Having your eyes turned to crystal and back can take a lot out of you. Sleep might be a good idea."

After a moment's deliberation, Tevi slid down under the blankets. The squirrel hopped onto the bed and snuggled into the curve of her arm. There was something very reassuring about the small warm, furry body. The last of Tevi's fears dissolved as a wave of sleepiness washed over her. She was only vaguely aware of the door closing as the sorcerer left the room.

It was not only Tevi who needed sleep; Jemeryl felt drained by the previous day. She spent the rest of the morning dozing by the parlour fire in a battered old armchair while keeping one eye on the door to Tevi's room.

The blazing fire was purely for effect. Jemeryl did not need it to warm the room, but its light played cheerfully on the furnishings and the eclectic range of books, presents, and curios littering every horizontal surface. Jemeryl was by nature tidy in everything except her personal appearance. Somehow, the room had gained a life of its own, mostly due to the squirrels, who hated leaving anything where they found it. Any pretence at a formal reception room had vanished. The parlour was now cluttered, comfortable, and far less imposing than most citizens would ever imagine for a sorcerer's home.

Jemeryl's gaze drifted over the treasured items scattered about the room. They held memories of the many nights she had spent there, reading in front of the fire and making plans. *So much for planning.* Even without Iralin's intervention, meeting Tevi would have been a life-changing event, a node in the web of fate. But why? Jemeryl's eyes fixed on the door to Tevi's room. Was it to do with the quest or the woman herself?

Jemeryl was aware that a soft grin was growing on her face as she thought of the warrior. She recalled the sight of Tevi snuggling down with the squirrel curled at her side. *And if I didn't know better, I'd swear I was envying that squirrel.* Jemeryl shook her head in self-mockery. *One step at a time, and remember, your career depends on this. You can't afford to make mistakes*. If she was to achieve her ambitions within the Coven, she was going to have to fit in with Iralin's schemes.

Klara had been asleep on the back of the chair, tired after her nightlong vigil. At this point, she awoke and hopped onto Jemeryl's wrist. "Have I missed anything exciting?"

"No."

"How's the patient?"

"Sleeping."

Klara looked towards Tevi's room. "She doesn't seem too bad. Far better house-trained than you expect for a woman warrior, and I'm sure I heard her attempt a few polysyllabic words."

"Oh, I don't think she's stupid."

"Except when it comes to basilisks."

"We all make mistakes." Jemeryl groaned. "I know I have."

"So how do you feel now about going on this quest with her?"

"I'd rather not."

"But you're quite happy with Tevi as company?" Klara's voice was deliberately innocent.

Jemeryl gave her familiar a long, cynical stare. She knew exactly what Klara was implying. "I don't have a problem with Tevi. It's Iralin and the rest of the Coven seniors I want to incinerate. They're playing silly games. If they want me to join in, I wish they'd explain the rules first, rather than treating me like a football."

"They're probably making them up as they go along."

Jemeryl's frown deepened. "The attack of foresight when I first saw Tevi is the worrying bit. The Coven seniors have been poking about with fate, not just casting oracles. You don't get a rupture in time like that from merely asking questions."

"What do you think they were after?"

"I'd say they were trying to affect the outcome of events triggered by my meeting Tevi. As for why..." Jemeryl finished her sentence with a shrug. "They certainly left an ugly patch job behind."

"I noticed."

Jemeryl stroked the magpie's head. "You saw something in there that really upset you."

Klara said nothing. Jemeryl did not want her to. She was determined to resist the temptation to probe the magpie's memory. Klara had screamed in terror at something seen when they blundered into the ragged temporal discontinuity. More than just Jemeryl's dislike of prophecy stopped her from trying to find out what.

There was a fable, probably apocryphal, told to all young sorcerers. It concerned two brothers who went to consult the oracle at Kradja. They had only one question to ask, "Where will we die?", intending never to visit the place named. The oracle had replied, "In Kradja." Both brothers immediately attempted to flee the town. In his panic, the brother in the lead slipped and fell on the temple steps, breaking his neck. The other saw the accident and stopped, realising the futility of escape. He settled in Kradja, took a partner, made his life there, and prospered. He died there decades later, after a long and successful life, surrounded by friends and family.

Even if it never happened, the moral was sound. No matter what fate might dictate, the greatest chance of tragedy lay in trying to evade it. Klara had seen something bad. If it was inevitable, it was best not to know. Jemeryl's expression was grim. Iralin was the one who had told her the fable many years ago, when Jemeryl was a fresh novice. If the senior sorcerers were trying to rewrite destiny, it meant something very important was involved.

"So why not tell me what it is? Do they think I'll work better if I don't know what I'm doing?" Jemeryl glared into the fire, feeling like a pawn. "I never did trust oracles. I bet they've had some vague prediction and are even more confused than me."

Klara bobbed her head in agreement and then tilted it to one side. "But it could be worse. As I said, Tevi doesn't seem to be too bad, does she?"

Jemeryl's anger faded as a slow smile crossed her face. "No, she doesn't seem too bad at all."

Chapter Twelve—Old Legends

It was definitely a day for being lazy. Midafternoon, Jemeryl was still sprawled in her chair, the bears asleep at her feet. Ruff's ribs were serving as a footstool and Klara was perched on the armrest, adding her contribution as Jemeryl indulged in idle speculation about the quest.

"She might have to kill a monster," Klara said.

"More likely has to find something."

"Such as?"

"It would have to be important."

"Obviously. Iralin's hardly likely to think Tevi needs you along if she's just popped out to get a couple of cabbages."

"It could be a person she's looking for."

The sound of a door opening interrupted the debate. Sorcerer and magpie simultaneously turned towards the source. Tevi stood in the entrance to her room. The low winter sun was falling square on the window behind her. Its rays streamed out around Tevi, lighting her in silhouette.

"Madam Jemeryl?" Tevi asked dubiously, as if afraid of what else might answer.

"I'm here."

Jemeryl studied her guest for a moment longer before rising to guide her to a chair by the fire. The young squirrel bounced onto the warrior's lap as soon as she was seated, evidently feeling that it had made a true friend. It never seemed to occur to any squirrel that it might not be wanted. Tevi, on the other hand, although looking much better for the sleep, was uneasy.

"I am very grateful for your help, ma'am. I hope I haven't..." Tevi had obviously taken time to reflect on the status of Coven sorcerers.

Jemeryl stopped her. "There's no need to thank me. In fact, you could argue that it's my fault you were hurt in the first place. And forget the ma'am bit. Jemeryl will be fine, or you can call me Jem. My friends do."

"While her enemies call her much more interesting things," Klara added.

At the inhuman sound of the magpie's voice, Tevi's hands tightened on the arms of the chair. "What's that?"

"Just an impertinent magpie."

"It talks?"

"As you just heard."

"I'm sorry." Tevi slumped. "It was a silly question."

"She's a silly magpie. And, although you can't see it, she's giving us a rather indignant look at the moment."

"I guess even magpies don't like being called silly."

"Especially magpies. Her name's Klara. She's quite safe, as long as you can cope with sarcasm."

Klara turned her back on the pair of humans in disgust.

"So you have squirrels, magpies...and bears?"

"Just the one magpie—one is more than enough. The bears are asleep in front of the fire. If you want, I'll send them away."

Tevi looked unsure, but in the end, she said, "It would be mean to kick them out in the cold when they're doing no harm."

"They aren't dangerous." Jemeryl stressed.

"I know. You said. I'm being childish. It's just..." Tevi hesitated. "I think it's not being able to see them. Things are always worse in your imagination. Would it be all right if I touched them?"

"They won't bite."

Jemeryl mentally roused Tumble from her sleep. The bear rose with a snort, then shuffled around and lay her chin on Tevi's knees. Tevi patted the furry head with growing confidence, while her expression changed to a grin. Ruff also awoke and went to claim his share of the fuss.

"They're like a pair of great soppy dogs," Tevi exclaimed as Tumble licked her hands.

"I know," Jemeryl agreed. "It wasn't the effect I was aiming for, but that's how it goes when you enchant animals. Their own nature skews the magic."

Jemeryl settled back and rested her chin on one hand. Only Tevi's head and shoulders were visible above the bears' shaggy rumps. Light from the fire played over her face, highlighting the line of her jaw and throwing soft shadows at her throat.

One advantage of Tevi's blindfold was that Jemeryl could study her guest without inhibition. She found it a very pleasant occupation. *Not bad at all*, she repeated to herself, but she could not sit and stare all afternoon. Jemeryl got to her feet. "Now you're awake, I'll see about a late lunch. Do you want me to take the bears with me?"

"I'll be fine. Or do you need them to help?"

"Oh no. Their paws aren't up to doing anything worthwhile in the kitchen. The squirrels would be more use, but they will insist on putting nuts in everything. It wouldn't be so bad if they shelled them first."

Jemeryl left the room to the sound of Tevi's laughter.

❖

Once the meal was over, Jemeryl gave Tevi a tour of the castle. They went slowly, to let Tevi feel her way and build a mental image of the layout. In particular, Jemeryl pointed out the location of stairs and similar hazards. They stayed a while in the stables and made sure Tevi's pony had everything it needed.

Back in the parlour, the two women reclaimed their seats by the fire. Tevi told the story of the hunt for the basilisk. As the account progressed, Jemeryl's horror grew. She was appalled at how little Tevi had known of her quarry.

"A small shield was all the protection you had? That was suicidal."

"I held it in front of my face so the basilisk couldn't see into my eyes."

"But the crystal bridge works in the sixth dimension. It can only have been pure luck it worked." Jemeryl frowned. "How big was it?"

"The shield or the basilisk?"

"The basilisk."

Tevi indicated with her hands.

"Well, that partly explains it. It was only a juvenile, probably inexperienced."

"I thought I'd done quite well. Except for the bit at the end, of course."

"You did. But you should have come to me. I'd have given you proper shields. In fact, I'd have dealt with the beast myself."

"The villagers were against telling you."

"Why?"

"Some thought the basilisk was yours, that you'd called it to the valley."

"They thought..." Jemeryl stared at her guest, lost for words. Small wonder that bad reports had reached Lyrcmouth.

"Wasn't that what you meant when you said it was your fault I got hurt?"

"No! I would never do anything to harm the villagers. I'm sworn to defend them, with my life, if need be. They must know that. What's got into their heads?"

"I'm not sure they think very clearly. They seemed a bit gullible."

Jemeryl groaned. "And that's my fault as well. It's a side effect of the wards."

"Wards?"

"I put wards around the valley to keep out danger. Someone destroyed them, and that's what let the basilisk in. When I said it was my fault, all I meant was that I should have talked to the villagers more and not relied on the wards. But I never dreamed someone would deliberately wreck them."

Tevi looked as if she might have said something but held her peace.

"The thing could have killed someone, but the villagers were more frightened of me than the basilisk." Jemeryl was speaking mainly to herself.

"Perhaps when the villagers hear that you've healed my eyes it will give them some faith in you...if you're sure I'll see again..."

"I promise. Your eyes will be fine."

"I didn't mean to imply..." Tevi's words tailed off awkwardly. "I just don't understand what happened to them and why I wasn't turned to stone."

Jemeryl sighed and then shook her head. Cursing yourself for past mistakes was pointless. She redirected her thoughts to finding an explanation for Tevi. "The basilisk feeds directly on energy. It doesn't really turn its victims to stone. It's like burning. It takes the energy out and leaves ash behind, fused into place. To extract the energy, it has to create a bridge in the sixth dimension, which is the easiest place to work with elemental forces. Its third eye is a receiver, which also changes the eyes of its prey to transmitters. I'm afraid it's hard to put it in simpler terms."

"I have a vague idea of what you mean. Very vague."

"Vague is probably good enough. The organs that extract the energy are where its stomach would be, if it had one. The receiver was able to transmute your eyes even after you cut its head off, but it couldn't complete the link to its stomach. Fortunately for you."

"The head can survive on its own?"

"Only for a very short time, a bit like a headless chicken."

"So everything is quite safe after a few minutes?"

"Not from the chicken's point of view," Klara said.

Tevi laughed and sank back in her chair.

Jemeryl studied her patient. Tevi's aura was clean and regular; all traces of the sickening crystal drains were gone. Jemeryl could still detect unfamiliar perturbations, but in her opinion, they were not dangerous. It was something she might look into later. After all, she was going to be spending quite some time with this woman.

"Changing your eyes back was a bit tricky. There were a few problems I hadn't expected, but it went all right in the end." Jemeryl's memory prodded her. "Oh, and um...I don't know if you were keen on your previous eye colour, but they're now grey."

"Grey?"

"Were you hoping for something else...green or blue?"

Tevi shrugged. "As long as they work, I'm not bothered." However, she was clearly disconcerted by the idea and raised a hand to her eyes. "When can you take this bandage off?"

"I'd like to leave it another day. If you don't have headaches or other problems, we can see how your eyes are after nightfall tomorrow. It would be best to remove the bandage when it's dark, as your eyes will be very sensitive to light for a few days."

Tevi looked happy with the answer.

They talked for a while longer before Jemeryl announced, "I think it's time for bed."

Although Tevi could have managed alone, Jemeryl took her hand and escorted her to the door of her room. The warmth of Tevi's fingers sent ripples through Jemeryl, spurring her to ask, "Are you sure you're all right in here? The bed's pretty small, and there's no fire. Won't you be cold?"

Before she could say more, Tevi interrupted, grinning. "Thanks, but I've just come over the old pass. I've been sleeping on snow and rock. This room is heaven by comparison, and if I get cold, there's a spare blanket in my pack." She slipped her hand from Jemeryl's and closed the door.

The sorcerer's face held a bemused smile as she made her way to her own bed. She spoke softly to the empty room, "It wasn't a blanket I was planning on offering."

Klara crowed with derision. "Oh, go on. Give the girl a chance to view the merchandise first."

❖

After breakfast the next morning, the two women went onto the battlements. The sun was rising in a clear blue sky. Jemeryl breathed in the sweet air and listened to the sound of water dripping from melting snow and trickling along gutters. With her extended senses, she could feel the presence of new life ready to burst forth.

"Spring is on the way," she announced, although this would hardly count as news, even to her blindfolded companion.

"Good. I've seem enough snow for this year."

"Your trek over the Spur can't have been fun."

"It wasn't."

"Why did you do it?"

"I was hired by traders who'd got stuck in Treviston. They didn't have time to wait until spring."

Jemeryl was confused. She had assumed that the dangerous journey was in some way connected with Tevi's quest and had been probing for information. "But you must have had your own reasons for crossing the Spur midwinter."

"No. Why?"

"Because I know that you're currently on a quest." Hearing her own words, Jemeryl frowned. It was a bad habit of sorcerers to use scraps of information they picked up to give the impression of infallibility.

Tevi, however, seemed more puzzled than impressed. "I don't think so."

"You've not sworn to catch someone or to find anything?" Jemeryl suggested, feeling a trifle foolish.

"Oh, well...yes. Abrak's chalice." Tevi's sudden downturn in mood was conspicuous.

"Has Abrak lost her chalice?"

"She's dead. Her chalice is a family heirloom."

"But you're looking for it?"

"Sort of. A bird stole it, so I said I'd get it back."

Jemeryl's eyebrows rose. Tevi's apathy certainly made a change from the self-important arrogance of most quest-bound warriors. In fact, from Tevi's expression, Jemeryl got the feeling that her guest would much rather talk of something else. On the other hand, Jemeryl was becoming very tired of not knowing what was going on. She wanted answers.

Once they were settled back in the parlour, she allowed Tevi no opportunity to evade the subject. "We've got all day. Why don't you tell me about this chalice?"

For a moment, it looked as if Tevi might refuse, but at last, she started. "Do you know anything about the Western Isles, out from the coast of Walderim?"

"Is that where you come from?" It would explain Tevi's unfamiliar accent.

"Yes."

Jemeryl searched her memory. "I didn't know there were any islands. I've never seen them marked on a map. I take it your people don't have much contact with the mainland?"

"No. Abrak was the last person to arrive. And I'm the first person to leave for..." Tevi's face contorted in distress.

Jemeryl sensed that Tevi was fighting with memories. The young islander must be missing her home and family very much.

Softly, Jemeryl asked, "Tevi?"

"I don't...it's..." Tevi took a couple of deep breaths. "I'm not sure what to tell you about Abrak. We have lots of songs and stories, but you won't want the full saga. It would take days." Tevi bit her lip. "I guess I should start with the old clans fleeing to the islands..."

❖

One hundred years after its founding, the Protectorate was expanding rapidly. At first, this worked to the advantage of the warrior clans of Walderim. Practitioners of magic withdrew from the strip of land between the Aldrak Mountains and the sea, either to join the Coven or to go places where their power would be unchallenged.

Their departure created an opportunity for the men who relied on strength of arms. They believed that their swords had freed the land from the tyranny of sorcerers. It was what they wanted to believe. Real men could put their faith in sharp steel and not submit to the whims of women and weaklings with their cowardly magic.

Yet the days of the warrior clans were short-lived. Within decades, the wealth of the Protectorate guilds, rather than the magic of its sorcerers, had undermined their dominion. A few warlords saw the inevitable coming and remembered the tales told by storm-blown sailors of uninhabited islands far out to sea. Magic could not cross water, so common knowledge had it. With their rule failing, the warlords took their families and fled, although in their stories, it was not retreat but regrouping. They saw themselves as heroes in exile who would one day return to burn every sorcerer and become kings of the known world. They called themselves the Sons of Freedom.

The men settled down to a life of fighting and fishing. They engaged in bloody feuds. They made sure that women kept in their place. They told stories, reinventing the history of the world they had left, and made prophecies of their glorious return. None dared admit that the islands were not a cradle of kings but a forgotten backwater. In time, all contact with the mainland ceased, while each year, the shoals of fish returned and the war bands fought their petty wars.

No one would have predicted any great change when Thurbold the Blood-Reaper became ruler of Storenseg. He was a strong and ambitious warrior who had murdered several relatives to become king while scarcely into his twenties. His schemes went further. He led his war band into battle, inspiring them with his berserker courage, in a bid to conquer all the islands.

Then Rathshorn, Varseg, and Tanenseg allied against him, forcing him back from every gain he had made, until Thurbold was on the point of surrender. On a bitter winter morning, he sat brooding in his hall when he learnt that a shipwreck survivor had been washed onto the beach.

The castaway was not an enemy sailor, as first assumed, but an elderly woman. She had no possessions except for a small leather bag containing a battered pewter chalice. Exposure had addled her wits. She cackled and talked to herself. Yet, between the nonsense, she said enough for Thurbold to realise that she was a sorcerer.

It should have been straightforward. In the clansmen's way of thinking, a burning was the only option, but Thurbold was desperate. (Although, as things worked out, he was quite secure. The coalition against him would soon break down, victim to the mistrust between islands.)

In his despair, Thurbold decided to bargain with the sorcerer. He offered her gold if she would cast a spell to make his warriors invincible; she giggled about seaweed. He offered her a boat off the islands; she sang about apple blossoms. He did unpleasant things to her and then offered to stop, and finally, she agreed.

The sorcerer was named Abrak. She was allowed to roam the island, muttering and babbling her nonsense. Thurbold's warriors muttered in turn—that he was a fool to trust the madwoman. Yet his reputation was such that none dared say it to his face.

Soon, Abrak returned to Thurbold's hall. She had found what she needed for a potion. She promised that Thurbold would conquer all the islands, and his name would be remembered there forever. Thurbold was elated; his decision to negotiate had been right.

Abrak offered to show the men how to make the potion, but even fear of Thurbold would not move his warriors to accept. They would take the potion if there was no other hope of victory, but they would not defile their hands by brewing the sorcery. It was woman's work. None thought anything of it when Abrak's screeched laughter shook the rafters of the hall. The sorcerer was mad.

Abrak instructed the women on harvesting plants and preparing the potion. She stood before Thurbold one last time to explain how the magic worked. A boy should be given a mouthful of the potion each day from the time he was weaned until his beard started to grow. Then, with the change to manhood, there would be a change in his body, and his strength would be increased twofold for the rest of his life.

Abrak swore by the gods of earth, sea and sky that she was telling the truth. However, it was not the spell Thurbold wanted. His fear was for the coming summer campaign, not for the wars of twenty years hence. This was his excuse—if he felt that one was needed—to order a pyre built and send Abrak to the flames. The brutality and double-dealing were typical of Thurbold, yet all accounts agree that Abrak's laughter was never louder than when she went to her death.

The decision to use the potion could not have been easy. In the end, Thurbold took the risk and gave it to his infant son and every other baby boy. However, the concoction was not poisonous, and time proved that Abrak had spoken the truth. The potion-enhanced warriors of Storenseg were unbeatable. Within twenty-five years, they had conquered all, and Thurbold was King of all the Western Isles, the first to claim the title—as his son was to be the last.

Thurbold's ancestors might have warned him—those who'd had dealing with magic users in the days before the flight to the islands. The vengeance of sorcerers may be slow and subtle, but it is as sure as the turn of the tides.

Abrak's vengeance began with the rebellion of the sons. The superhuman warriors would not long take second place to a rabble of weak, elderly men. Thurbold had less than one year as king, then spent the rest of his days as his son's slave, tending the sheep. Yet worse was in store for the men of the Western Isles.

The legends differ as to the reason, although all agree on the outcome. Some man was eager to push more work onto his daughters, or a nurse found it easier to give the potion to all babies in her charge, or a woman had been privy to Abrak's plans. Whatever the cause, even before Thurbold's son had grown, it became the custom to give the potion to girls as well as boys.

The men who ruled the islands had no regard for their daughters. Their lives revolved around men, swords, and the clan. Women were not worth consideration, except as vessels of sons or trophies to their virility. Which is how it escaped their notice that while the strength of men was increased twofold by the potion, the strength of women increased fivefold and more.

Maybe this oversight was not so remarkable. Most women failed to see what the potion would mean, unable to conceive of the social order standing on its head. But not all were so blind. One woman in particular foresaw a new future. She was a schemer and a fighter who engineered the second rebellion and became the first queen.

It was not easy to turn women, trained to cower, into warriors.

However, Abrak had put all the weapons into their hands. Even the facts of reproduction worked in their favour. They could kill ninety-nine men out of a hundred, but the men could not reciprocate without forgoing the next generation. By the fortieth anniversary of Abrak's death, the warlike patriarchy had been replaced with a mirror-image matriarchy.

The women settled down to a life of fighting and fishing in a society that revolved around women, swords, and the family. They called themselves the Daughters of Abrak's Revenge.

❖

"It sounds as if they got a bit carried away with the rhetoric," Klara observed at the end of the tale.

"I think they got a bit carried away with everything," Tevi said.

Jemeryl had mainly listened in silence. Now she asked, "So on your islands, the warriors are all women?"

"Yes."

"And the story of Abrak explains why," Jemeryl mused. "It's imaginative, but it must raise more questions than it answers."

"Such as?"

"For example, what excuse do people give to explain why the potion no longer works?"

Tevi looked puzzled. "They don't."

"Aren't you curious?"

"About what?"

"The..." Jemeryl stopped. The conversation had got out of step somewhere. She started again. "I know enough about herbalism to know the potion could never have worked the way the story said. Therefore, it—"

"But it did. It still does."

"It's impossi—" Jemeryl broke off mid-word. "Have you ever seen a woman with this supernatural strength?"

"Of course. I took the potion myself."

The announcement left Jemeryl dumbfounded. She stared open-mouthed at Tevi, recalling the strange perturbations in the islander's aura and the unexpected problems rebuilding her eyes. Still unsure of how seriously to take the claim, she asked, "So how strong are you?"

"In the mercenaries' guildhall, they use an iron ball to test applicants' strength. I think there are different weights for different groups. As a warrior, I had the heaviest. I was told to throw it as far as I could. I did ask the examiner if he was really sure he wanted me to. He said yes." Tevi shrugged. "The ball made a nasty dent in the wall at the other side of the yard. Apparently, no one has ever thrown it more than half the distance before."

"That's..." Jemeryl was lost for words.

"Is the potion really so unusual?"

"I've never even heard of anything like it. Do you mind if I do a few tests?" Jemeryl added hesitantly.

Tevi considered the request and then nodded. "It's forbidden to discuss the potion with strangers, but it was a gift from a mainland sorcerer to start with. And you'll be working out things for yourself, so it's not as if I'm telling you secrets."

Jemeryl led Tevi into the great hall. A few minutes were required to assemble the necessary equipment and then, at Jemeryl's request, Tevi removed her jerkin and shirt. Jemeryl studied her thoughtfully.

Tevi stood very still. Her top half was clad in a thin, close-fitting shift, leaving her arms and shoulders bare. It did not conceal much. Jemeryl was aware that her thoughts were drifting away from the line of pure scholarly interest. Out of the corner of her eye, she saw Klara watching. The magpie's head was tilted jauntily to one side. A faint blush rose to Jemeryl's cheeks and she concentrated her mind more firmly on the matter in hand.

Jemeryl stood behind Tevi, close enough to run her hands over the muscles in the islander's back and arms. She managed to keep her thoughts almost, but not completely, on the subtle irregularities she could detect.

To the perceptions of the ungifted, there would be nothing unusual. Tevi's body showed the effect of regular exercise but was in no way overdeveloped. Any young woman involved in manual labour would look much the same. However, now that Jemeryl's extended senses were alerted, it was apparent that the islander's body had been changed on a cellular level. It was definitely magic of the very highest order. Jemeryl reached for her notebook.

❖

Recounting the tale of Abrak had been a constant battle for Tevi. The story had launched an onslaught of memories—nights around the fire in her family hall, singing the old songs. Through the blindfold, she could see the familiar faces, hear their voices.

The migration to the hall came as a relief, a chance to regroup while Jemeryl's bubbling curiosity took over. Very little of what the sorcerer said made sense, but Tevi never felt she was being patronised or ridiculed—quite unlike her experience with the Treviston sorcerer.

Jemeryl talked excitedly. "You must go to Lyremouth and let them examine you fully. That is, if your laws allow it. The potion is astounding."

Tevi knew her family would not approve, but they had never approved of anything she had done. "Would the Coven be interested? Surely you've got similar potions. I haven't come across anybody who's taken one, but I assumed they were being kept secret for some reason."

"Oh, no. All attempts to make strength enhancers have had nasty consequences. If you're lucky, it's just people breaking bones when they try to lift things. Often, the heart goes wild and bursts a blood vessel in the brain—hearts are muscles, too. Your potion is different. It doesn't try to channel external forces through the body. It changes the way a child grows, so the muscles are more efficient. Your bones are stronger as well. That's the really clever bit. The hormones released at puberty spur everything into action. That's why it works differently for the sexes. Muscle structure is identical for men and women, but the hormones aren't."

Tevi was unsure of what hormones were, but the results were something she had thought about. "It's a shame the potion couldn't have made men and women equal, like they are on the mainland. When I was growing up, I never saw anything wrong in the way men were treated. If anything, it seemed they were having an easy time—always having women to look after them. But since I've been on the mainland, my attitude has changed. I don't think the men in my village could really have been happy."

"Having heard the whole story, it sounds like poetic justice to me," Klara said.

Jemeryl spoke thoughtfully. "It's actually the inequality of sorcery that makes for the balance of the sexes on the mainland. Without it, men's physical strength usually distorts things, and patriarchal warrior clans take control. I seem to recall from my history books that they flourished briefly in Walderim a few centuries back. Which would tie in with your story."

"It's a shame they were so violent and that they took the bloodshed with them." Tevi's musing was interrupted when something that felt like a glass pyramid was placed in her hands.

"Can you hold it above your head?"

Tevi did so.

"Presumably, once the women took over, things became a bit more peaceful." Jemeryl picked up the conversation.

"Not that you'd notice. The first queen was the only one ever to rule all the Western Isles. Straight after her death, a dispute broke out between her daughters. Before long, the islands were back in a state of permanent warfare, only with women doing the fighting instead of men."

"The first queen must have been a very strong personality."

"According to my family, she was. I'm her great-great-great-granddaughter." Tevi's head sank. She could hear again the taunts, naming her a pathetic product for such a famous lineage. At least living up to her ancestor's reputation was no longer a problem.

Fortunately, at that point, the glass pyramid must have revealed something unexpected, requiring Jemeryl's full concentration. The conversation was temporarily abandoned.

❖

Some hours later, after a break for lunch, Jemeryl had discovered all she could, given the limited resources available. She scribbled down the last of her observations and put the notebook away. The pair returned to the comfort of the parlour.

"I'm astounded, but you're right. The potion most definitely works," Jemeryl said.

"So do you think the story is true?"

Jemeryl chewed her lip. "It still has to be more fiction than fact. If I had to guess, I'd say Thurbold brought Abrak from the mainland on purpose and gave her far more help than the story implies. He could have invented the shipwreck story so it wouldn't appear that he'd gone looking for a sorcerer."

"What makes you think that?"

"Herbalism isn't my strongest discipline, but I can estimate how long it would take to develop a potion like yours. The sorcerer would have needed vast amounts of luck and inspiration, and decades rather than a few days. Which is why no one else has done it before. The disproportionate effect on the sexes has to be an accident. The subtlety to do it deliberately is way beyond anything a lone sorcerer could achieve."

Tevi looked thoughtful. "Would Abrak have been a Coven sorcerer?"

"Probably. Herbalism isn't well developed outside the Protectorate. It's only because the Coven is responsible for citizens' health that we spend so much time on it. Sorcerers elsewhere aren't too bothered about colds and sprained ankles." Jemeryl frowned. "But it's hard to see how a Coven sorcerer could have become mixed up with the island clans."

"I always wondered why someone as powerful as Abrak allowed herself to be burnt."

"I suppose that bit might be true," Jemeryl replied slowly. "The idea that magic can't cross water is an oversimplification. The elements affect magical forces in different ways. Water focuses the flow. Small islands are hard to predict until you reach them, especially if they have a high iron content. Some concentrate all the power for hundreds of miles around, and some are so dead you can't light a candle. Your islands must be the inert sort if magic users aren't found on them. Abrak might have been virtually powerless once she got there. When Thurbold realised it, he got rid of her to destroy the evidence of his complicity."

"But surely then the potion wouldn't work."

"Living things hold their power in a dimension that isn't affected by water. Herbalism is the most universal of all magical disciplines; not even iron disrupts it."

"Would you be surprised if I said I don't know what you mean by other dimensions?"

"I'd be more surprised if you did." Jemeryl's forehead creased as she tried to find an easy explanation. "Virtually everyone can perceive four dimensions, three spatial and one temporal. And most people have seven senses to perceive them: sight, touch, taste, smell, balance, hearing, and time. However, there are three further dimensions and at least six other senses, even sorcerers can't agree on the exact number. Everyone's body extends across all seven dimensions, but most people's paranormal senses don't work, in the same way a deaf person can't hear in the four ordinary dimensions. Objects exist in the paranormal dimensions. If you're aware of them, you can use them, and that's what's called magic. I know it seems strange to the ungifted, but if you have full use of your senses, it's very straightforward. When we sorcerers wave our hands about, all we're doing is moving things on other planes of existence."

"You touch them with your hands?"

"You use your limbs as they project in the other dimensions. The gestures the ungifted see are largely incidental."

Tevi's forehead creased as she thought it over. "I suppose if nearly everyone was blind, the few who could see would be able to do things—like use a bow and arrow. To the blind majority, it would be a powerful mystery. Is it something like that?"

"That's it precisely. Many people have limited awareness of their paranormal senses, though it results in nothing more than the sensation of icy fingers down the spine and things like that. Probably nobody has complete control of all their extra-dimensional senses, but the more you can perceive, the more powerful a magic user you are. A witch is someone who is aware of one or two of the paranormal dimensions. A sorcerer is competent in all three."

"So you can see me in these extra dimensions?"

"Yes."

"How do I look?"

Really nice, was Jemeryl's first thought, although she did not say it aloud. "Umm...it's hard to describe."

"And I suppose it wouldn't mean much to me." Tevi's wry grin faded into a sigh. She raised her hand to her blindfold. Jemeryl guessed that the talk of extra senses had made her more aware of her current blindness.

Jemeryl returned to the earlier conversation, partly to divert Tevi from worry about her eyes. "You said you were looking for Abrak's chalice. Finish your story. How did it go missing?"

The change in topic did not work as planned. If anything, Tevi looked even more miserable. "The island I come from is Storenseg, which is where Abrak landed. Her relics are still there. They don't amount to much—her satchel, her pewter chalice and some ashes."

"Her mortal remains?"

"They're supposed to be. They were kept in a shrine on the site where she was killed. One day nearly three years ago, a large black bird swooped in through the door, picked up the chalice and flew off with it. People say it went straight out to sea, heading for the mainland. Nobody knew what to do. So I said I'd go and get it back." Tevi finished in a rush.

"How were you going to find it? The mainland is a very big place."

Tevi shrugged.

Jemeryl leaned forward. It seemed a good time to gently introduce the idea of accompanying Tevi on the quest. "It's a good job that you came here. I can give you a lot of help and advice."

"To be honest, I've given up hope of achieving the quest."

Tevi was avoiding something she did not want to talk about. That much was obvious. Jemeryl eyed her guest, hoping it was nothing more than feeling foolish for taking on a task she could not perform. But watching the tight set of Tevi's lips, Jemeryl got the nasty feeling that a whole new set of pitfalls had lined up in front of her.

Tactfully, she decided not to push the point and allowed Tevi to change the subject again, to her travels through the mainland. Jemeryl settled back and listened with interest, watching the firelight play over Tevi's face. The afternoon was well advanced. Soon, it would be dark and time to remove the bandage. Once Tevi could see again, Jemeryl was sure that her enthusiasm could be revived. Plans for the quest could wait.

Chapter Thirteen—New Eyes

While the short winter's day drew to a close, the two women sat chatting in the parlour. The clear skies of the morning were gone. Clouds had blown over from the east and a stiff wind had sprung up. Tevi shivered, hearing bursts of sleet splattering against the windows, a reminder that winter was not over.

She lazed comfortably in her chair by the fireside with two squirrels asleep on her lap. Jemeryl was an attentive audience, and Master Sarryle was an amusing topic for conversation, now that he was far away. A simple description of him ordering a meal at an inn could be guaranteed to entertain anyone.

"I watched him do it. Then he called the waiter over and said, 'Young man, do you consider thirty-six peas to constitute an adequate portion?'" Tevi managed a fair impression of the old man.

"You mean he counted them?"

"Every time. Luckily, he was never given rice."

"What happened?"

"Well, it didn't help when the waiter offered to get a ruler so he could measure the length of the sausages."

"He hit the roof?"

"No. Irony was lost on the man. He said yes. In the end, he had the innkeeper, the chef, and half the staff around the table. They cooked him a fresh meal, with double potions of everything. Sarryle then said he wasn't hungry anymore and went to bed. I thought they were going to lynch him."

"In your place, I'd have offered to get them a rope," Jemeryl said, laughing.

Tevi grinned and continued with the tale of her travels. She was finding it increasingly difficult to reconcile the woman she was getting to know with the villagers' tales. She did not see how anyone could spend five minutes in Jemeryl's company without liking her, but she had noticed that the mainland people had a peculiar attitude towards sorcerers. Many spoke of them as if they were not properly human. Tevi had already learnt that Jemeryl had a lively sense of humour. Perhaps the villagers had taken her too literally, not ready to credit a sorcerer with being able to make jokes.

For her part, Tevi found Jemeryl very good company, a feeling that seemed to be reciprocated. Sitting and chatting by the fire had Tevi completely at ease. It was hard to remember when she had last felt so content. Jemeryl's voice was light and clear, with a rich nasal burr of an accent. Tevi was not familiar enough with the Protectorate to place it, but it sounded easy on her ear. She found herself wishing Jemeryl would say more so she could listen. It would be interesting, when the bandage was removed, to see her and match a face to the voice.

No doubt the villagers were already working on stories about the young mercenary who went into the castle and was never seen again. Tevi suspected some would be quite disappointed when she returned, whole and healthy.

❖

Tevi's story ended with her arrival in the valley. Harrick's team of misfits provoked their share of witticisms. She also made brief mention of the villagers. Jemeryl suspected that Tevi was being tactfully vague about their gossip.

Jemeryl stretched back and looked about the room. She was surprised to see how dark it had become. Beyond the firelight, thick shadow filled the corners. Even the squirrels were sleeping. At the snap of her fingers, the window shutters closed. The sound of wind over the battlements stopped abruptly.

"What's happened?" Tevi asked, sounding curious rather than alarmed.

"I've just fastened the shutters. It's night."

"Already?"

"I lost track of time as well. It's been an unusual day." Jemeryl took a deep breath. "I think we're ready to take off the bandage and examine your eyes."

Tevi's hands tensed. "All right."

Jemeryl leaned over and squeezed Tevi's shoulder. "Don't worry. I did a good job on your eyes."

"I'm sure you did. It's not that I don't trust you, but I don't know what will happen if my sight isn't restored. The mercenaries could refuse me a pension, as I got the injury in an unauthorised venture."

"You're not going to need the pension—not for a long time." Jemeryl stood and took Tevi's hand. "Come on. It will be better if we go to your room, where there's no firelight, while I do a few tests. Then we can come back in here."

In the small side room, Tevi sat on the edge of the bed. Jemeryl removed the bandage and lightly touched her fingertips to Tevi's eyelids. The faint electric currents of nerves at the back of her retina were directly perceptible to Jemeryl's extended senses. Everything seemed fine. Jemeryl sat beside Tevi and twisted sideways so that she faced her patient.

"I'm going to make three small balls of light: a red, a blue, and a green. They should all appear the same size and have sharply defined edges. Tell me if you see them." Jemeryl gently rippled the currents in the sixth dimension to create the effect she had described.

"Yes. I can see them. Just like you said." The joy in Tevi's voice was unmistakable.

"Right. I'm now going to merge the three coloured balls to make a white one. I'll move it to where it won't shine directly into your eyes."

The lights merged. Slowly, Jemeryl started to raise the level of illumination. Tevi's outline became faintly visible, then the bed and the floor, but just at the point when the light touched the far wall, Tevi gave a gasp and screwed her eyes tight with a look of panic.

Jemeryl doused the light immediately. "What's wrong, Tevi?"

"There's too much." Tevi's voice was raw and tight.

"Does it hurt?"

"No, but it looks all wrong."

Jemeryl matched Tevi in despair. She had been so sure the reconstruction had gone well. "What did you see?"

"Things were where they shouldn't be, all over the place."

Jemeryl thought furiously. "That sounds as if a nerve has been misconnected. Wait a few minutes and we'll try again. If you can give me a better idea of what you're seeing, I should be able to correct the fault. Let me know when you're ready."

Tevi's hand clasped Jemeryl's arm. "I'm all right. It wasn't painful, but it threw me. "

Once again, Jemeryl gradually increased the light. "Now. Tell me what you can see that's strange."

Tevi let go of Jemeryl and gripped the edge of the mattress, keeping her head very still. "I'm looking straight ahead, but I can see the floor and the ceiling, my knees, your shoulder, and there's too much wall." Again, her eyes squeezed shut.

Inspiration hit Jemeryl with a thump. She studied her patient in astonishment. The unexpected snags while reconstructing Tevi's eyes at last made sense. Abrak's potion had not been the cause, although the truth was just as surprising.

"Can you fix it? Do you know what's wrong?" Tevi's voice held an edge of panic.

"I know what *was* wrong."

"Was? But they still aren't right."

"No. Your eyes are fine now. The problem with them was in the past, and I'm not referring to the crystallisation."

"What...when?"

"It's known as tunnel vision. In rebuilding your eyes, I've inadvertently cured it."

"Cured?"

"Even before you fought the basilisk, you had defective vision. You only saw out of the centre of your eyes. The nerves to the outer segments were damaged. I guess you were born like it and never realised you weren't seeing properly."

"My eyes were fine."

"I don't think they were. While I was rebuilding them, I hit a few unexpected snags with your eyes. I put them down to something weird about the crystallisation, but they would tie in with tunnel vision. More to the point, what you just described seeing would be considered perfectly normal by anyone with healthy eyesight."

Tevi sat in silence while Jemeryl's words sank in. "You mean that everyone sees the world like this all the time? It's awful. How do they cope?"

Jemeryl laughed, mainly with relief. "It's just what you're used to. Once you get the hang of it, a wide peripheral vision is a useful thing to have—especially, I would have thought, for someone in your profession."

❖

Some time passed before Tevi was able to open her eyes without being overwhelmed by nausea. It took a conscious effort on her part not to try focusing on the entire room simultaneously. She needed Jemeryl's assistance to get back to the parlour, walking with her eyes closed. Jemeryl dimmed the fire to a dull red glow that illuminated without casting any harsh, bright light.

Tevi sat uneasily in her chair, taking quick peeks at her surroundings while trying to keep as still as possible. Every time she moved, the room whirled. Only by a very slow, cautious effort was she able to turn and examine the sorcerer. The subdued firelight showed a young, triangular face surrounded by unruly auburn curls. Dark amber shadows were cast in the hollows of Jemeryl's eyes and cheeks. A lopsided grin completed the impish effect.

"I'd wondered what you looked like."

"Well, don't say whether I'm better or worse than you imagined. It gives grounds for offence either way."

"Can I say you look a lot better than the villagers implied?"

"You mean I haven't got a hooked nose, fangs, and bloodshot eyes?"

Heedless of the dignity of her status, Jemeryl's appearance was highly informal. One leg was stretched out, while the other was pulled up on the seat. Her arm rested along the back of her chair, with a slender, long-fingered hand dangling loosely at the end. She was wearing a shapeless white shirt, several sizes too big, with sleeves rolled back to the elbows. Tevi thought that Jemeryl's looks, if not exactly as imagined, accorded very well with her easygoing manner.

"You're younger than I expected. I could tell by your voice you weren't old, but I still had a picture in my mind." Tevi studied the sorcerer. "Do you genuinely look like that, or have you altered your appearance?"

Jemeryl laughed. "I'm really, truly only twenty-two. Using magic to change the way you look is seen as very immature. I'll admit to combing my hair from time to time—not that it does much good."

"If she was going to muck about with magic, wouldn't you

expect better results than this?" Klara said, from her habitual perch on Jemeryl's chair.

"Oh, I would say she..." Tevi's mouth went dry; her stomach flipped over.

Jemeryl's face was not one of refined classical beauty. Such a face could not have taken the mischievous grin that lit her features. Yet as Tevi felt her heart pounding against her ribs, she knew that Jemeryl's appearance was altogether much too much to her liking. Almost against her will she found herself picking out the details: the belt pulling the shirt in around a slim waist, Jemeryl's finely formed hands, and the small dark hollow at the base of her throat.

"What?" Jemeryl asked.

"Pardon?"

"What would you say? You didn't finish your sentence."

"Oh...nothing."

"It's all right. You're allowed to have an opinion about me. After all, I've been watching you for the last couple of days, and I've formed some opinions of my own. If you like, I'll sit beside you and tell you what they are."

Tevi did not think about Jemeryl's words. Her only coherent idea was a desperate hope that mind reading was not one of the sorcerer's skills. She had no desire to discover Jemeryl's response to the uncontrolled emotions churning inside her.

She could feel Jemeryl's eyes as if they were deliberately trying to catch hers. Rather than risk that happening, Tevi twisted back to the fire and was swamped by nausea as the room leapt cartwheels around her. Her lips pulled back in a grimace and she scrunched her eyes shut.

After all her plans to avoid personal contact, she had allowed herself to become far too keen on Jemeryl and had not realised it until the moment she set eyes on her. *Just because you were blind to the world didn't mean you had to be blind to what was going on inside you.* Tevi cursed herself as a fool. She was in trouble. She was a heartbeat away from being in love—with someone it was far too dangerous to offend.

❖

At the other side of the room, Jemeryl was waiting for Tevi's response to her overture. Part of her was confident that Tevi would welcome the offer to sit beside her, and from there, things would progress in a predictable, and very enjoyable, direction. Part of her was gnawed by agonised apprehension. Butterflies in the stomach did not begin to describe it. Jemeryl found herself praying for a smile. Instead, she saw Tevi's expression switch to one of pain.

"Are you all right, Tevi?"

"I moved too fast. It upsets my stomach. Are you sure everyone sees like this?" Tevi said quickly.

"Everyone with normal vision."

"I guess I'll have to get used to it."

And I guess I'll have to improve my timing, Jemeryl commented to herself. *Try waiting until she's not feeling sick.* Aloud, she said, "I could block off your peripheral vision, but I'd be loath to do that. You should give it a good try before you make any decisions."

"It's strange to think that all my life, I just assumed everyone saw things the same way as me." Tevi's voice was strained.

"Didn't you notice that other people could see more of what was around them?"

"Not really. Although some things now make sense. My teachers were always telling me to watch my opponent's feet out of the corner of my eye. I never knew what they meant."

"It must have been quite a handicap."

Tevi's attempted smile was unconvincing. "It would be nice to think it's the reason I'm so incompetent at fighting."

"*Incompetent* is not a word normally applied to any warrior who kills a basilisk."

"I am by the standards of my village. Do you think I'll be better now?"

"It's hard to say. You may be able to make full use of your vision, or habits may be so ingrained you'll be unable to change. But your family can't have thought that badly of you if they entrusted you with the quest."

"I wasn't given the quest as a mark of honour." Tevi looked as if she was about to throw up.

"Are you sure you're all right?" Jemeryl was now very concerned.

"I'm just a bit queasy. Maybe some smoke from the fire..." The halfhearted words died away.

Jemeryl moved to a stool by Tevi's side but restrained the urge to touch the other woman. Adding everything together, things were making more sense. *She volunteered to find the chalice as an act of bravado to silence her critics.*

Tevi stared forlornly at the ground.

"I can't promise, but now that your eyes are fixed, if you find the chalice and go back..."

"There's not much chance of that."

"Yes, there is, with my help."

"Do you know where the chalice is?"

"No, but I know how to go about finding it."

"I suppose if you point me in the right direction..."

"Better than that, I'll come with you."

"You can't do that." Unlike her previous apathy, this time Tevi's response was immediate, horrified.

"Why not? The villagers will be relieved to see me go and I can help you enormously. Wouldn't you like my company?" Cautiously, Jemeryl reached out and took hold of Tevi's hand.

The effect on Tevi was instantaneous. She snatched her hand away and lurched to her feet. "I don't know about the chalice. But you can't come with me."

"Tevi?"

"I'm sorry. I don't mean to sound rude. Thank you for the offer. It's kind of you, but it's out of the question. I...I'm...I think I need to go to bed." Tevi fled.

Alone in the parlour, Jemeryl sat bewildered. How had things gone so wrong, so quickly? She looked at Klara. "Why was she so upset? What did I say?"

"I think it's more what you did. She doesn't want to hold your hand. Mumbling sweet nothings in her ear and strolling in the moonlight are probably out as well. You can forget the rest."

Jemeryl stood up. Her eyes fixed on the door to Tevi's room. She took a half step and then stopped, turned around, and threw herself down in her chair. She glared at the embers of the fire, confusion giving way to hurt. Somehow, she had taken it for granted that Tevi would return her affection, but it was impossible to miss the rebuff in Tevi's behaviour. And it did not take any sorcerer's arts to know the rejection had been largely personal.

"I thought she liked me."

"Ah, but that was before she saw you. Maybe you look an awful lot worse than she was expecting." Klara fluttered down to the arm of the chair. She tilted her head to one side. "And to be brutally honest, her expectations needn't have been that high."

With a forced attempt at a smile, Jemeryl pushed the magpie off her perch.

❖

Jemeryl left the shutters in place the next morning, since she knew that Tevi's eyes would be hypersensitive. Consequently, the parlour was still in dim half-light when Tevi finally made her appearance. Jemeryl watched with concern. It was apparent that the night's sleep had done nothing to improve Tevi's mood. Problems with vision had to be a contributing factor, but Jemeryl was gloomily certain there was more to it.

"Good morning, Tevi. How are you?"

"Not good," Tevi mumbled.

"Is it just your eyes?"

"More or less. I feel a bit nauseous as well."

"Breakfast might help. There's bread, honey, and milk on the table."

Tevi stumbled across the room and sat with a groan.

Jemeryl joined her at the table, though she kept a discreet distance. For a while, Tevi picked at her food, her whole manner subdued. The easy friendship of the previous day was gone, replaced by a strained reserve. This was not the time to press the issue of joining Tevi on the quest, but it would be several days before Tevi was able to travel. Jemeryl could only hope that things would improve by then.

Tevi ate slowly, her eyes glued to the tabletop. "I'm not sure if I'm ever going to be able to cope with this."

"It will get easier. Give it time."

"I...I'm sorry if I'm not seeming too grateful at the moment."

Tevi's voice had lost some of its sullen tone, which gave Jemeryl the confidence to quip, "That's all right. I can wait until tomorrow for you to tell me how wonderful I've been."

"I suppose, to be fair, I could concede that now." Tevi closed her eyes in a grimace. "But the light is very bright."

"The shutters are closed."

"I know. How long before my eyes will be better?"

"You should notice some improvement by tomorrow. In eight or nine days, you'll be able to cope with full daylight."

"I guess that's not too bad."

"It might be a bit boring for you. There's nothing exciting I can offer in the way of entertainment in the dark," Jemeryl said. *At least, nothing you've given me grounds to think you might be interested in.*

"I've had enough excitement in the past few days. But I don't want to stop you, if there's anything you need to do. I don't mind being left alone." Tevi's tone implied that she would even prefer solitude.

Jemeryl tried to prevent her disappointment from showing—an unnecessary precaution, given that Tevi had not once glanced in her direction. There seemed little hope of charming her way back into Tevi's favour. Investigating other options seemed the best hope. She was sure that part of Tevi's reticence was due to a belief that finding the chalice was impossible. Proving otherwise might not remove all objections, but it would be a start. Few resources were at hand in the castle, yet they were almost certainly sufficient to deduce Abrak's true identity. From there, other leads might come.

A little diplomacy was called for. Jemeryl tried not to sound too eager as she said, "There's nothing I have to do. However, your story of Abrak caught my interest, as a sorcerer. I thought while you're around to answer questions, I might try to find out more about her."

"What would you like to know?"

"I've got books in my study that will mention her, but I'd need to know her real name."

"Her real name? What's wrong with Abrak?"

"It's like a miller called Dusty or a carpenter called Chips. 'Abrak' is a joke name for a sorcerer, short for 'Abracadabra.' It's a piece of meaningless gibberish that for some reason is linked with magic in the minds of storytellers."

"Oh."

"Do you know any other name for her?"

Tevi shook her head and clearly regretted it instantly. She clasped her hands to her temples. "Idiot," she winced between clenched teeth.

Her arms dropped and she met Jemeryl's gaze with a faint smile for the first time that morning. "I meant me, not you. The room whirled when I did that."

"I realised." Jemeryl smiled back, happy that the tension had eased slightly. "Since you don't know her name, it might help if I had some dates to work with. Do you know when Abrak arrived on your islands?"

"We islanders don't go in for keeping written records of dates. We don't even have words for numbers over twelve. There's no need. If you see an enemy war band with more warriors than that, you don't hang about to count the rest. Sheep are added up on tally sticks. I've mainly learned about numbers since I've been on the mainland. Marith gave me lessons. She said I needed to keep track of money and things like that."

"Perhaps you can give some indirect dates. You said the leader in the rebellion was your..." Jemeryl's forehead creased. "Great-great-great-grandmother. Do you know how old your ancestors were when they gave birth?"

"My mother was quite old when she had me. She'd had three boys and several miscarriages, plus a couple who died in infancy. She was my grandmother's first child, but after that, it gets a bit vague. My grandmother had two elder sisters. I think there was also a brother. My grandmother was still a child when both her older sisters were killed in battle. Which was how she became queen."

A gesture from Jemeryl stopped Tevi. "Males don't become kings?"

"Never."

"And your grandmother was queen?"

"Yes. Didn't I say?"

"And you're the eldest daughter of her eldest daughter." Jemeryl frowned. "I admit I'm not over familiar with hereditary monarchies, but doesn't that mean you'll be queen one day?"

Tevi's expression became even less happy. "Probably not. I promised not to go back without the chalice, and I doubt I'll find it. But I've got a younger sister, and I'm sure she'll do a good job."

Despite her diffidence, Tevi was clearly fighting to keep her lower lip steady. Jemeryl was confused. From what she had put together, Tevi had not been held in high regard by her family and had volunteered to find the chalice to prove her worth. That Tevi had been willing to risk her place in the succession must have been a desperate gamble on her part. People from hereditary cultures attached immense importance to following their parents, or so Jemeryl had heard. Yet although Tevi was clearly distressed, she showed no sign of being driven to reclaim her inheritance. Tevi's character did not appear to lack determination, and the basilisk proved she was no coward. Why was she so ready to abandon all hope of returning home? Something else had to be involved. However, Jemeryl was sure it was unwise to probe the subject until some level of trust could be re-established.

"I'm sorry. I didn't mean to...er...interrupt. We were talking about dates. Do you know how old you are?"

"Twenty, I think."

"And your mother had been pregnant quite a few times before. So when you were born, she must have been...mid-thirties?" Jemeryl guessed.

"Yes, about that." Tevi's voice was steadier.

"Right. Then your grandmother..." Jemeryl grabbed a pen and began making notes.

A short while later, Tevi had passed on all the relevant information she possessed. Jemeryl added up the figures and chewed the end of the quill.

"I estimate Abrak was shipwrecked about one hundred and forty to one hundred and seventy-five years ago. It's something to work with."

"I'm sorry I can't be more help."

"That's all right. There can't have been too many sorcerers who disappeared without a trace in the vicinity of Walderim during that time."

"Is there anything else you want?"

Jemeryl sighed. She would have liked to bring her books down and sit in the parlour, but Tevi would clearly be happier on her own. "No. I'm going to see if I can find anything out. If you have any problems, call me."

"I'll be fine. The bears can keep me company."

Jemeryl tramped despondently up the stairs. She had hoped that Tevi's abrupt departure the night before had been due to a misunderstanding, but Tevi had been blatantly building barriers between them. Even allowing for problems with her sight, she had pointedly avoided looking in Jemeryl's direction. And it was too late for Jemeryl to wish she had kept a tighter rein on her own emotions.

A long row of books on herbalism lined one shelf in the study. Jemeryl groaned at the sight. None was quite what she needed. A directory of sorcerers would have been best, but all she had were the medical books she had brought, anticipating the needs of the villagers. Iralin's words of censure echoed in her ears. Most had not been off the shelf since she arrived. Jemeryl was not even sure what some of them contained, but there should be biographical notes for the creators of various potions, with cross-references for people who were interested in further details of their work.

Jemeryl called a book over to her. It was going to be a long, tedious search.

❖

By late afternoon, Jemeryl had gone through five books and learnt nothing. She closed the cover and sent the last one back to the shelf. The hours were taking a toll, and her concentration was suffering. The best course was probably to stop for the day and start again in the morning.

It was getting dark. When she looked at it, the window displayed only her reflection. Apart from a brief meeting at lunch, she had not spoken to Tevi. Maybe by now, the mercenary would be ready for company.

The parlour was much as she had left it. The bears were sleeping in front of the fire. Several squirrels had dragged a cloak over to make a nest. However, there was no sign of Tevi. The absence was surprising. On her way from the study, Jemeryl had seen that Tevi was not in the hall. Even at dusk, being outside would put a strain on Tevi's eyes, although it was possible that she was attending to her pony. Before checking the stables, Jemeryl tried knocking on the door to Tevi's room.

"Tevi?" There was no answer. Jemeryl pushed the door open and peered in.

Tevi was curled on the bed, her face knotted in agony.

"Tevi, what's wrong?" Jemeryl rushed to her side.

"My head hurts," Tevi hissed through clenched teeth.

"Why didn't you call me?"

"I'll be fine."

"No, you won't. When did this start?"

"I was practising walking. Things were starting to spin. I thought I could manage, but—"

"But you pushed it too far." Jemeryl finished the sentence for her. "You should have called me."

"I'm sorry."

Jemeryl's initial alarm gave way to anger. There was no need for Tevi to start acting like one of the stupid villagers. Why had the warrior not called when she started feeling unwell? Why hide in her room? It was unlikely that any damage had been done, although Tevi was clearly in pain. Her face was bloodless pale; her aura, distorted.

As she took in the details, Jemeryl's mood softened to exasperation. *Maybe it's my fault,* she told herself. *There's something about me that makes the ungifted act like frightened idiots when I'm around.* She just wished she knew what it was. In the meantime, Tevi needed her help.

"Roll over and lie face down," Jemeryl ordered. Once Tevi had obeyed, she sat beside her on the bed.

The muscles of Tevi's neck and shoulders were snarled like twisted rope. Deftly, Jemeryl began to massage away the tension. At the same time, she worked on Tevi's aura. As a sorcerer, Jemeryl could see the series of tiny vortexes littering Tevi's astral projection. They disrupted the flow of life energies. In time, they would fade of their own accord, but reversing the spin would speed the process. Relaxing the cramped muscles and raising the blood flow would prevent their return.

Within minutes, she could tell that the pain in Tevi's head was easing. The hard cords in Tevi's neck softened, although the tightness in her shoulders was proving more stubborn. It would be easier if Tevi removed her thick jerkin. Jemeryl was about to ask, but stopped. Suddenly, her hands were very aware of the touch of Tevi's skin—the texture and the warmth.

Jemeryl's gaze travelled the length of the body lying motionless on the bed. She finished staring at the back of Tevi's head. There was an overwhelming temptation to run her hands though Tevi's hair, to take hold of her shoulder, turn her over and look into her eyes. It was so easy for Jemeryl to fantasise the act of then kissing Tevi, slowly and very thoroughly, and imagine the feel of Tevi's arms tightening around her. Jemeryl's hands started to move before she had a chance to think, but then she mastered her emotions.

From Tevi's reaction the night before, it was easy to guess what the outcome would be. Jemeryl suppressed her groan of despair. Iralin had given her a job—one she had to succeed at. She dare not risk further alienating the woman she was obliged to accompany. After a second's pause, Jemeryl continued to massage Tevi's shoulders, but with her hands outside the jerkin, breaking the contact with Tevi's skin.

"How do you feel?" Jemeryl asked once the last of the vortexes had disappeared.

"Better. The pain has gone." Tevi's voice was muffled.

"Will you come and sit in the parlour?"

"I'd rather lie here a while."

"Do you want me to stay with you?"

"No."

The answer was faint but unmistakable. Jemeryl got off the bed and walked to the door. "All right. But in future, call me when you don't feel well."

"I'm sorry. I didn't want to disturb you."

Before leaving the room, Jemeryl stopped for one last look at her patient. Tevi had not moved. Her face was buried in the pillow, preventing any eye contact. Jemeryl shut the door and went to her seat by the fire. The faint noise she made woke Ruff briefly. The bear snorted and rolled over before falling back asleep.

The room was very quiet. With only the animals' slumbering presence for company, Jemeryl sat for a long time staring into the flames. Her heart was pounding. Her hands ached from the memory of touching Tevi. In despair, she thought, *Oh, gods, I've really fallen for her*. Her emotions were totally out of control.

And Tevi was not interested. She was making it very obvious, taking every chance to put literal as well as metaphorical distance between them. Jemeryl could guess why.

Many of the ungifted were uncomfortable around sorcerers. Few would be willing to have one as a friend, let alone as a lover. Tevi had shown no sign of being bothered by Jemeryl's status. *Until she saw me*, Jemeryl thought. *Or, rather, until she saw how I was looking at her.* Tevi's tolerance of sorcerers apparently did not extend that far. It was not merely that Tevi did not return the feelings. She was running scared. *Does she think sorcerers can't take no as an answer*?

Of course, there was one definite area where Jemeryl could not accept a no. Whether Tevi agreed or not, she had to go on the quest for the chalice. Tevi's agreement would make it less unpleasant, but either way, it was going to be unbearably miserable, spending months in Tevi's company with her close at hand but out of reach. *Did Iralin know what she was condemning me to?* Jemeryl's lips twisted into a bitter grimace. *Probably not. It's just one of those things.*

❖

When she heard the door close, Tevi rolled onto her back and flung an arm over her eyes, but she could not block out memories of the hay barn or the contemptuous voices. What would her mother say to see her now? Would Red be able to overcome her disgust long enough to laugh at the bad joke?

Tevi clenched her jaw. She should have called her grandmother's bluff back on Storenseg. Even if she had lost the gamble, it would have been honest. She could have been true to herself, but like a coward, she had accepted the option to run. She had been running ever since. She had fled from Cayell and now she wanted to escape again. However, Tevi knew in her heart that it was the most pointless form of flight. She was trying to run away from herself.

"What else can I do?"

She was not handling things well. Her behaviour had been nothing short of rude in rebuffing Jemeryl's friendship. She had snubbed the offer of help on the quest, but even if the search for the chalice had been in earnest, she could not have risked Jemeryl's company. She liked the sorcerer far more than was safe, far more than could be hidden. It could not be long before she did or said something to give herself away. She knew that she had annoyed Jemeryl. The knowledge hurt; she did not want Jemeryl to think badly of her.

The honourable course would be to face things squarely, to go to Jemeryl, tell her the whole sordid truth, and accept what might come of it. But what would Jemeryl do? As the Coven representative in the area, Jemeryl was responsible for maintaining law and order. Would she, in her official role, feel obliged to report to the mercenary guild masters? How would it feel to have Jemeryl look at her with loathing?

I can't do it. It was an admission of cowardice. Tevi hated herself.

Tevi got to her feet and walked to the window. The shutters had been in place all day. She shoved them open, venting her anger by using far more force than necessary. Night had fallen. The moon was rising in the eastern sky, floating above the mountains. To Tevi's newly rebuilt eyes, its gentle light burned like the blast of a furnace. Fumbling blindly, Tevi refastened the shutters and collapsed on the bed.

The only option was to get away as soon as possible, and keep moving, but there was no chance of doing it immediately. She must wait until her eyes were stronger. Until then, she would have to guard her words and actions. When she could withstand daylight, she would go. But she did not want to. The thought of staying with Jemeryl was appallingly tempting. Tevi could hardly believe how much she craved it. The memory of Jemeryl's hands touching her neck washed over her with painful intensity. Tevi's self-control deserted her. Hot tears escaped from under her eyelids as she sobbed.

Chapter Fourteen—A Cautionary Tale

The next day's research did not produce the name of even one candidate for Abrak. By evening, Jemeryl was becoming dejected. Tevi contrived to be both more sociable and less friendly. She would engage in conversation, but her words were cold and guarded. Tension permeated the castle. The bears were irritable, and even Klara's stream of sarcasm dried up; only the squirrels were unaffected.

Affairs improved slightly on the following day. Tevi's eyes were less sensitive, which improved her mood. Her greeting at breakfast was warmer. Jemeryl wondered if this was a cue to stay and chat, but as soon as the meal was finished, Tevi disappeared into her room. She returned after a few seconds, carrying her sword.

"I need to do some exercises."

"Promise you'll stop if you get a headache?"

Tevi nodded sheepishly and moved to the largest clear space in the parlour. Her sword began to trace swift patterns, moving in set routines of feint, parry, and riposte.

Clearly, Tevi was not ready to talk. Jemeryl was about to leave when an idea struck her.

"That doesn't look much fun," she said casually.

Tevi glanced over her shoulder. "It isn't, but it's the only way I have to keep the muscles in my sword arm in shape."

"If you want, I could conjure a phantom opponent."

"A phantom opponent?"

"An illusion to spar with."

"Um...thanks, but I wouldn't want to waste your time." Despite her words, Tevi was clearly intrigued.

"It's no trouble. It will only take a minute to set up. Everything I need is in the hall."

Tevi looked uncertain, but then nodded. "If you don't mind."

Jemeryl reduced the great hall to a soft twilight that would not hurt delicate eyes. While Tevi wandered around, bemused by the strange artefacts, Jemeryl drew a twisting chalk pattern on the floor. A grey humanoid shape formed above it, sword in hand. Once it was ready, she called Tevi over.

"I don't know enough weapon craft to make it a serious opponent, but it should be more fun than waving a sword at thin air."

"Oh, no, it's...er..." Tevi ground to a dumbfounded halt. "What do I do?"

"Just attack. It will stop when you move away."

Tevi tentatively jabbed at the phantom's midriff. The figure responded instantly, and a shower of sparks fell as the two blades clashed. Tevi swung her sword across in a more purposeful attack. The phantom dodged and then struck out with its own weapon, forcing Tevi to parry.

She stepped back and looked at Jemeryl quizzically. "Before I go on, how dangerous is it?"

Jemeryl grinned. "Don't worry. I'm not about to see my work fixing your eyes go to waste. The sword will tingle, but that's all."

Tevi returned to the attack. Tempting though it was to stay and watch, the phantom did not need Jemeryl's presence, and leaving might be wiser, but then something caught her attention. She focused in intently on the timing of the two swords.

After several minutes of sparring, Tevi stood back, breathing heavily, with a hand pressed against her forehead.

"Are you all right?"

"Just giddy. The room spins when I move, but it doesn't make me feel sick anymore."

"Good." Jemeryl paused, unsure how her discovery would be received. "You know, I don't think you're completely ungifted."

"Pardon?"

"You've got a trace of a paranormal ability."

"I've what?"

"Nothing too conspicuous. I'm sure that nobody else would have noticed. But it's my phantom, so I knew what it was going to do, and I could tell you were getting ready to parry its blow before it moved. I'd say your second-dimensional time sense warned you." The surprise on Tevi's face made Jemeryl laugh. "Time exists in two dimensions.

Nearly everyone can perceive the first, although a few can't—a bit like being blind or deaf. They appear mad to the rest of us. For them, everything happens without order, cause, or effect."

"And the second dimension?"

"It's used for fortune telling and the like. Fortunately, it isn't well developed in me."

"Why fortunately? It sounds like a good thing."

"It's more trouble than it's worth. If you see time in two dimensions, the future is as fixed as the past. Keovan was a rare sorcerer who was fully aware of two-dimensional time and still able to cope with other people."

"Wasn't he the one who founded the Coven?"

"No. His apprentices did after his death. Keovan couldn't have started the Protectorate. He was too overwhelmed by the ultimate futility of everything."

"The Protectorate doesn't seem futile to me."

"Nothing can last forever. One day, the Protectorate will fall. Four centuries of peace have produced a tenfold increase in the region's population. There are now over fifty million citizens. When the Protectorate goes, most will die, one way or another. And if I were permanently conscious that all the good I could achieve would only make for a bigger catastrophe at the end, I'd be as paralysed as Keovan."

"But you think I have this sense?"

"Nothing like enough to cause problems. I'd guess it's working a fraction of a second into the future and only giving you critical information, such as where your enemy is about to strike."

"How does it work?"

"You know what you were doing. How did it feel? How did you know where to move?"

Tevi looked thoughtful. "It sounded as if my old weapons instructor was giving advice in my head. I thought I was just remembering her lessons."

"That's the way your mind rationalised the information."

"I never got it on Storenseg."

"It's obviously a sort of magic that won't work on your islands."

"I'm not sure if I like the idea." Tevi frowned.

"I'd have thought it would be very useful to you. But if you want to block it out, wear iron or steel armour, particularly a helmet. Your sword will impair your precognition, although the wooden handle will insulate you to some extent. If, on the other hand, you want to make more use of it, you could get a rune sword that's been crafted to harmonise with temporal currents, but those swords are expensive."

"Supposing one day, the voice screams, 'You're going to die'?"

"Then it won't make any difference."

Tevi swung her sword back and forth pensively. "How rare is this extra sense?"

"Hard to tell. Many people have limited paranormal senses, but not enough to use. Just vague feelings. Sorcerers are rare; there are less than five hundred of us in the Coven. Witches are far more common—people with good use of one or two extra senses. For example, healers only need the sense we call aura empathy. They also make good farmers."

"That doesn't sound very magical."

"Plants have auras, too. Aura empathy is the most widespread of paranormal senses. It works virtually everywhere. Some people on your islands must have had it, though they probably weren't aware what it was. Senses are so personal. You assume that everyone sees the world the same way you can. Like your tunnel vision. But, think about it. Didn't you find some people were good at looking after plants...green-fingered?"

"Like my Aunt Han." Tevi's face brightened. "I remember her shouting, 'Any fool can see the peas need watering!' It may have been obvious to her; it wasn't to the rest of us."

Jemeryl nodded. "That's a typical remark from someone who can see the aura of plants."

For the first time in days, Tevi smiled directly at Jemeryl. The sorcerer felt her heart thump, but before she could speak, Tevi's face hardened. The warrior spun and attacked the phantom with a ferocious slash. Taking the hint, Jemeryl rose and went upstairs to her study.

❖

Four afternoons later, Jemeryl sat alone and disheartened. The search for Abrak was going badly. So far, she had come up with only two possible names, both of which were later discounted. It seemed as if sorcerers disappeared inexplicably even less often than might be imagined. She slammed the book shut and thumped her fist on the cover.

Klara looked on critically. "You could always throw it at the wall if you think it would help."

"I ought to have found something by now. Perhaps the Abrak story is a complete fantasy. Someone's idea of a joke."

"And the magic chalice was really just an old beer mug?"

Jemeryl sighed. "No, that wouldn't make sense either. The chalice must be genuine. Otherwise, someone wouldn't have bothered sending the bird to get it. And the strength potion is genuine as well. You can see the effect on Tevi."

"And I can see the effect of Tevi on you. You're really keen on her, aren't you?"

"She doesn't want to know." The pain showed on Jemeryl's face. "I can't make her out. Most of the time, she cold-shoulders me completely. Then her guard slips, and she acts like she wants..." Jemeryl's voice trailed off in despair.

Klara stood on one leg and examined the claw on the other foot. "And they have the nerve to call sorcerers temperamental. But I'm sure she'll make up her mind about you in the end."

"There isn't much time and I don't know what to do. Tevi will be ready to leave soon, and she's determined I can't go with her. I've got my future in the Coven to consider."

"She can't stop you following her."

"I don't want her to be frightened of me. I want her to like me."

"Like?"

"If she can't manage anything else." Jemeryl's thoughts churned in the state of chaos that Tevi normally inspired. She buried her face in her hands.

"Gods, you've got it bad."

Goaded into action, Jemeryl sprung up and marched to the bookcase. "I'm going to broaden my search. My grandfather's history of Walderim is here somewhere."

A smile touched Jemeryl's face at the memory of the old man, the only one of her blood kin who had not been frightened of her; the only one she had any fondness for. He had come from Walderim and had pretensions of being a scholar—hence, his history. The only good memories from her childhood were of him and her foster mother, the witch. The only items from her birthplace she still had with her were the copy of his book, given as a present on the day she left for Lyremouth, and a good luck charm from her foster mother. Jemeryl's own skill now far exceeded the elementary charm, and the book was not well written. Her grandfather's view of his own talents had been rather inflated, but both items were a source of comfort when she was feeling low.

Jemeryl pulled the volume from the shelf and hugged it tightly, eyes closed. She felt in desperate need of comfort right now. Then, with a resolute expression, she returned to the table and opened the cover.

❖

After sunset that evening, the two women wrapped themselves in thick cloaks and went for a walk around the battlements. Distant ice-capped mountains faded away into soft purple shadows. A few faint stars glinted in the dark blue overhead. It was the nearest thing to being out in daylight for Tevi since the bandage had been removed, and she looked happy. However, Jemeryl was having to hide her own anxiety. She was not looking forward to the coming conversation, especially since she still had no definite information to support her case.

"Do you think I'll be able to leave soon?" Tevi asked.

"In a day or two. You could probably go tomorrow, if it isn't sunny."

"Oh." Unaccountably, Tevi seemed deflated by the answer.

Jemeryl rested her arms on the parapet. The road passing under the castle walls was more mud than snow. Soon, Tevi would be riding along it, leaving the valley.

In her most decisive voice, she said, "I'm going with you."

"You can't."

"Why not?"

Tevi fiddled with the ties on her cloak in obvious distress. "Because the quest is a wild-goose chase. I haven't got a hope of finding the chalice, and there was never any expectation that I would. I told you I was an embarrassment to my family. The quest was just an excuse to go away and get lost."

The scenario painted was even sadder than the one Jemeryl had expected, and there was still something that did not tie in. "That was due to your tunnel vision. Now your eyes are fixed, surely it will be different."

"Maybe not. Anyway, I don't know how to find the chalice."

"Which is why you need me with you. I can guess why the chalice was stolen, and that gives me a start in knowing where to look to find it."

"How?"

"Abrak must have been a herbalist. Her chalice would have been made of crystalline silver—it's known as a memory chalice. It works like a magical notebook, letting you retrieve the formula for anything that has ever been made in it. That's why someone would have gone to the effort of tracking down the chalice and snatching it. They must want to reproduce some of her work. Once I work out who Abrak was and what her interests were, we can go to whoever's currently working in that area. Herbalists exchange information among themselves, so even if the sorcerer we select isn't the one who took the chalice, they'll have a good idea who was."

"But whoever it is won't just give the chalice back."

"No reason why not. They must have found out what they wanted to know by now, so they'll have no further need for the chalice."

"It's not that simple." Tevi's voice was raw with despair.

"Yes, it is, but you need me with you."

"Please believe me. I've got reasons I can't tell you. You can't come with me."

Jemeryl did not have the option to compromise. "I have to."

"I don't want you with me." Tevi turned to flee. "I'm going inside."

"I'm not such bad company, am I?" Jemeryl said softly.

Tevi froze, but did not turn back. "It's nothing to do with...it's not your fault, but you can't come with me. I'm sorry." She disappeared down the steps leading to the courtyard. Her footsteps faded away into the dusk.

"Tevi dashing off like that is getting a bit monotonous," Klara spoke from a perch on the battlements.

Jemeryl leaned against the wall and stared blankly at the stars. Somehow, she had managed to alienate Tevi. Jemeryl did not have the first idea what she had done wrong, but it was obvious that she had made mistakes as fundamental as those with the villagers.

The likely consequences if she returned to the Coven alone and explained that the warrior had refused her company did not make for pleasant contemplation.

"You'd be lucky to get off with spending the next five years cleaning the Coven latrines."

Jemeryl suspected that Klara's flippant comment was nothing short of the truth. "I have no choice. I've got to go with her, whether she wants me or not."

❖

Midafternoon on the following day found Tevi in the courtyard playing a fast-moving game of tag with the bears. The sky was overcast, easy on her eyes. The world still wobbled when she twisted quickly, but Tevi no longer found it disconcerting. She was confident that with practice, she could make full use of her new expanded vision, and she was already aware how much easier avoiding the bears was. Trees no longer threw themselves into her path as she dodged.

Tevi hurdled over Ruff's back. She charged through the kitchen door and collapsed, out of breath, in front of the massive fireplace. The bears lumbered in, also breathing heavily. Tumble flopped down at one side, while Ruff rolled onto his back, wanting his stomach scratched. He rumbled in pleasure when Tevi obliged.

Running her fingers through the thick fur was soothing. Tevi felt in need of something to calm her thoughts, now she was no longer occupied by the game. Her eyes were almost completely healed. The dull light had caused no discomfort; she could probably withstand sunshine. There was no reason to delay departure, yet the thought of saying goodbye was unbearable. Jemeryl's request to go with her was the final twist of the knife, but it was a risk Tevi dared not take.

Tevi's face knotted as she explained to Ruff. "It's not that I don't want her with me. It's that I want her too much, and in all the wrong ways. I've got to get away."

Ruff's stubby tail beat enthusiastically against the floor. He clearly had no idea what she had said.

Tevi got to her feet and walked to the door. Directly opposite, on the far side of the courtyard, were the castle gates.

"Where do I go?" Tevi whispered to herself.

In the first case, it was an easy question to answer: the Rizen guild house, where she could collect Harrick's pay and return the pony. From there, she could secure another contract, which might take her anywhere in the world. But to what purpose? How much longer was she willing to run?

Of course, it assumed that she would be allowed to leave the castle alone. Jemeryl's phrasing had shifted from an offer to a request. Should it become an order, Tevi could not legitimately refuse. The word of a Coven sorcerer was law in the Protectorate. So far, Jemeryl had not attempted to use her status. But she could.

Tevi's only hope would be if her guild masters made a direct appeal to the Guardian, which they were most unlikely to do. The fate of a sorcerer's magic chalice was clearly a valid Coven concern. If the assistance of one junior mercenary was required, the guild would not refuse.

But if she were to leave in secret, pack her things that night and be gone, what would Jemeryl do? Would she come looking for her ungrateful patient or go after the chalice herself? Tevi had no idea why anyone was interested in the thing, but obviously, it held significance for the sorcerer. If Jemeryl found the chalice, she was welcome to keep it. Tevi made no claim of ownership.

Tevi crossed the courtyard. Her footsteps echoed in the enclosed space. The gatehouse formed an arch over the entrance with its wooden gate. There were no locks or bolts that Tevi could see. However, she had no way to check for magic. Tevi caught hold of the hanging rope and pulled the gate open. If an alarm sounded, Tevi could not hear it.

Bracken-covered hillside rolled down to where trees breached the ruined outer wall. Snow lay in sheltered corners, but spring was on the way. A mild wind from the south had sprung up, bringing rolls of heavy cloud. There seemed to be nothing to stop her from going. Tevi took one hesitant step through the gateway, then another.

Without warning, Jemeryl's voice rang out. "Tevi. Come here."

A selection of excuses rushed through Tevi's head. Heart pounding, she returned to the courtyard. Jemeryl's head was poked through a window in the small tower.

"What is it?"

"Tevi. Come here. I've found her. I've found Abrak."

❖

Jemeryl waited on the landing at the top of the stairs in the great hall. "I've found her. Come and see," she called as soon as she saw Tevi enter below. "And I take back my scepticism. I think your story is entirely true. Almost." Jemeryl ducked back into the study and took her place at the desk in the centre of the room.

Tevi arrived shortly. She pulled over a stool and sat at the other side. "What have you found?"

"Abrak. She was a herbalist from the school at Ekranos." Jemeryl tapped on an open page. "That much, I could have guessed. But her real name was Lorimal."

"She's mentioned in your books?"

"Not nearly as much as I'd have expected. I'm surprised there isn't more about her, if only as a cautionary tale. But there's no doubt she's the one. She was last seen one hundred and fifty-two years ago, paddling a small boat and talking to the seaweed off a beach in Walderim. More than that, she's the only person in history who could have made the potion the way your story says. Everything ties in. Her speciality was potions producing permanent changes in the body. As a young woman, she was getting quite a name for herself, but then she made her big mistake." Jemeryl looked up from the book. "Did I tell you how herbalists work by watching the harmonics of auras and projecting their observations back though the underlying planes?"

Tevi's face screwed into a bemused frown. "Maybe."

"Lorimal wanted to improve the process, so she developed a potion to give her intrinsic empathy with plants. After she'd taken it, she could look at a plant and intuitively deconstruct its aura."

"She could do what?"

"She said the plants talked to her." Jemeryl was aware that she was being less coherent that usual.

"And she made a mistake?" Tevi was clearly struggling to keep up.

"The mistake was that after she'd taken it, she empathised totally with plants, and there was no antidote. Have you ever tried talking to someone who thinks like a daffodil?"

"My Great-Aunt Wirry?"

Jemeryl laughed. "I'm sure your aunt isn't in the same league. What happened to Lorimal was that she could no longer relate to humans. Your ancestors assumed that exposure had addled her wits, but she'd been like it for decades. After Lorimal took the potion, she carried on charging around the Protectorate, doing all manner of things that nobody could make sense of. Her only invention with any known use was a cure for mould that infects wheat in the eastern plains. One of the ingredients is a small amount of the farmer's own blood. Some say it shows the way her mind was running. Most herbalists use plant extracts to heal people; she used people extracts to heal plants."

"That makes some sort of sense."

"It's the only thing that did. Apparently, she once spent four months standing in a garden belonging to a weaver in Davering, acting like a rosebush. Don't ask me why she didn't starve to death. The book didn't explain, but it's no more bizarre than most of the other things she did. However, there's plenty of evidence to show she'd have been capable of creating your strength potion, complete with gender bias. Her abilities were phenomenal. It's tragic they were of so little use—from a human viewpoint."

"Why would anyone want her chalice?"

"Perhaps someone's got a turnip they want a chat with?" Klara said.

Jemeryl grinned at the magpie. "I'd guess it's more likely they're after some of her earlier work, though I can't find any information about what that was. As I said before, I'm surprised Lorimal is so overlooked. I only came across her name in a history of Walderim written by my grandfather, and he was more concerned with whimsical anecdotes than herbalism. Lorimal hardly appears in any other book."

"So it doesn't help us find who took the chalice."

"Lorimal's name is a good starting point." Jemeryl kept her voice level, even though her hopes soared at Tevi's use of the word "us." "The best thing would be for you and me to go to Lyremouth. There's bound to be more information in the Coven library."

Tevi's brief burst of enthusiasm died. Her eyes fixed on the desk, and she dug at the grain with her fingernail. "That's if I bother. I'm sorry, Jem, but you can't come with me."

"I have to."

"I don't want company."

It was the old stalemate. Jemeryl's patience snapped. "It doesn't matter what you want. I've been ordered to go."

Tevi looked shocked. "By who? And why?"

Instead of answering, Jemeryl kicked her chair back and stalked across to the window. She stared out over the valley. Ten days before, she would not have dreamed of telling the truth to a common, ungifted citizen. Now her emotions were so raw that the thought of losing face before Tevi was irrelevant. But would it help?

Jemeryl took a deep breath and turned back. "I wasn't told why. My mentor contacted me a few hours before you came to the castle. She told me about you and the basilisk. She said that when you left, I had to go with you. She also took the opportunity to tell me I'm a disgrace to the Coven."

"What!"

"Reports from the village have got back to Lyremouth."

"But the villagers have got you all wrong."

"It's nice you think that, but I wasn't able to convince my mentor. I've been removed from my post in the valley and ordered to help you on your quest. So I'm going with you, and that's the end of it."

"You have helped. You've found Lorimal's name. I could go to Lyremouth on my own and ask someone there to do the rest."

Jemeryl shrugged. "If I don't leave with you, I might as well go straight to Lyremouth anyway. They like you there in person when your case is taken before the disciplinary tribunal."

"You wouldn't be punished?"

"Disobeying a direct order? Of course I would."

"What would happen to you?"

"I'm trying not to think about it." Jemeryl reclaimed her seat at the desk. "But it isn't going to happen, as I'm going with you."

Tevi licked her lips nervously. "Perhaps you could come as far as Lyremouth. When we're there, I can explain that I don't want you with me."

"That will go down nearly as well as me deserting you."

"Why?"

"I was hauled over the coals for upsetting the locals. Now I've done the same with you. I don't know how." Jemeryl's head sank; her voice dropped as well. "Would it help if I said sorry?"

"You haven't upset me. You've been really nice."

"Oh, sure. I'm so wonderful you can't stand being in my presence."

"That's not far from the truth," Tevi mumbled.

"What?"

"Nothing."

Jemeryl buried her face in her hands. "Tevi, please. Tell me what I've done to offend you. Give me the chance to put things right."

"You haven't done anything."

"Tevi, come on," Jemeryl pleaded. "You can't stop me following you, but I can't stop you saying what you will to my superiors. If you're going to wreck my life, you at least owe me an explanation."

Tevi slumped backwards. Her knuckles were white on the tabletop. At last, she blurted out, "It's not you. It's me."

"What is?"

"It's me. I'm not fit company for any woman."

"Don't be stupid."

"No. It's true. The quest for the chalice was a way to exile me while saving my family the embarrassment of a public trial."

She's murdered someone. It was the first thought to shoot through Jemeryl's head, followed quickly by disbelief. There was no trace of malicious violence in Tevi. It must have been an accident, or a mistake, or something else. Who could tell what the barbarian laws of the islands might be?

In a whisper, Jemeryl asked, "What did you do?"

"It was what they thought I was going to do."

"Be sensible. Even Coven seers don't punish people for what they're going to do."

"They were right."

"If I'm any judge of character, you're a decent, honest person. I don't know what you think you were about to do, but I can't believe it was anything that bad, and even if it were, it wouldn't matter. The Coven leaders want me to go with you. I can't see them being put off by a crime that hasn't been committed yet, in a land outside their jurisdiction."

"Wouldn't they want to protect you from me?"

Despite the overwrought atmosphere, Jemeryl had to restrain the urge to laugh. "I think you'd have difficulty persuading them you presented any threat to me. I don't mean to imply that you're not a formidable warrior, but I'm a sorcerer. A dozen of you couldn't—" Jemeryl broke off. "Tevi, you're not making sense. What is this crime you're going to commit? How could you harm me?"

There was a long silence. When Tevi finally spoke her voice was a dull mumble. "I have a problem with men."

Jemeryl tried to understand. "I'm sure the same could be said for most women on your islands."

"No, it's different. I'm not sure how to explain." Tevi's eyes were devoid of fight and of hope. "There were slang terms on the islands, crude ones. I've not tried to find out what your words are for it. I thought it best to avoid the subject completely."

Jemeryl opened her mouth to speak but then closed it again. Tevi was finding things difficult enough without interruptions.

Tevi continued, picking her words deliberately. "I feel about other women the way a normal woman would only feel about men. In my heart, I can only..."

The struggle to say that much had left Tevi shaking. She leaned forward and rested her head on her hands. However, Jemeryl was no more the wiser. It was obvious that the confession had taken a lot of effort, but despite turning the words around in her head, Jemeryl could produce no interpretation that was not totally absurd.

"I'm sorry, Tevi. I don't understand what you mean." Jemeryl spoke as gently as she could.

"Don't play games with me." Tevi sprung to her feet, knocking over her chair. In three steps, she had reached the door.

Jemeryl could not allow Tevi to escape. A pull on the sixth-dimension tensors sent the bolt sliding into its socket and all of Tevi's superhuman strength could not get it to budge. After a few desperate attempts, Tevi let go of the handle and turned back.

Jemeryl was still seated. Quietly she said, "I'm sorry, but believe me, I'm not playing games. This is much too important to me."

"Jem..."

"I really don't know what you mean."

Tevi slumped against the door. She closed her eyes and swallowed. "I'm physically attracted to other women, not men. I fall in love with them. I can't help it. It's women that I want sexually. And right now, I want..." Tevi's words died in a grimace of pain. She twisted around to face the barred door, resting her hands on the wooden planks. "Please let me go."

There was utter, wretched despair in Tevi's voice. Jemeryl could not refuse. The bolt moved back, and Tevi tore open the door. Her footsteps pounded on the stairs and away.

Jemeryl stared after her. She was still not certain she understood, but Tevi's confession had struck a chord with something she had read earlier that morning. Thoughtfully, Jemeryl pulled her grandfather's book towards her and thumbed back several chapters.

The section she wanted was a lengthy extract from a two-hundred-and-fifty-year-old report by a Coven sorcerer named Bolitho. It had been made in the mistaken expectation of Walderim imminently joining the Protectorate. In the guise of an itinerant healer, Bolitho had travelled throughout Walderim while preparing extensive notes on the inhabitants. Some of his analysis reflected ideologies, fashionable at the time, that were no longer accepted. However, he had been a conscientious observer, and one of his findings seemed to offer the explanation Jemeryl needed. It took a few seconds to find the part she wanted, relating to gender stereotyping.

Jemeryl settled down to read.

❖

Inherent to a hereditary culture has to be belief in the inborn superiority of the ruling elite. Other groups have their value assigned on a descending scale, with the lowest sections relegated to subhuman status. In Walderim, the main groups to suffer from this have been women and migrant workers from the north.

The position of women is especially bleak, partly due to the widely held belief that instead of being distinguished by minor statistical variations, the characters of the two sexes are in some way diametrically opposed. In fact, the phrase "the opposite sex" is in common use. There is a refusal even to accept that a male sorcerer has vastly more in common with a female sorcerer than with an ungifted man (although I suspect that this will change once Walderim joins the Protectorate).

I had a conversation with one of their philosophers. He explained how the universe was divided into male and female principles. Male was active, light, hard; female was passive, dark, soft. We had this conversation sitting on the trunk of a fallen tree. I found a male and female wood louse in the rotten wood and asked the philosopher to illustrate these "universal" principles, using the wood lice as examples. The philosopher then accused me of being absurd!

The ideology results in a need to exaggerate any perceived gender difference into an unbreakable law of nature. For example, an inhabitant will state, "Men are taller than women." If I point out that only a small average difference exists, and the divergence is such that many women are taller than many men, I am met with animosity, as if I am being deliberately perverse.

This may at first seem amusing, but in practice, it is quite odious. People's lives are made miserable if their stature is such as to challenge the assertions about gender and height. It is as if tall women or short men have committed an indiscretion and are deserving of derision or censure. With personality traits, such as aggression or compassion, that are harder to measure objectively and seen as under the individual's control (despite the contradiction with the idea that they are fixed by nature), the extent of the assumed polarisation and culpability is intensified. It is a brave person who refuses to distort his or her personality by pretending to match their gender stereotype.

Some people in Walderim seem aware that their culture's gender stereotyping is artificial. Yet by adulthood, the beliefs have been ingrained on a subconscious level. However much they might value courage and independence, they are still more comfortable ridiculing an assertive woman than they are respecting her—since, needless to say, the majority of positive character traits are seen as male. For women to assume an active role in society, they will need to overcome the stigma of being "unfeminine."

The enforced divergence of the sexes has one inevitable side effect. It has been observed that everyone is romantically attracted to a narrow spectrum of personality type, centred around a few key traits. Since children in Walderim are raised to see the characters of men and women as diametrically opposite, it follows that anyone seeking a long-term partner will perceive their idealised mate as falling into an exclusively male or female pattern, and will even be unable to respond to the personality type if it is encountered in the "wrong" sex. I strongly suspect that few raised in this culture will be capable of falling passionately in love with persons of either sex.

This would be of no more than incidental interest were it not for strict local doctrines forbidding erotic relationships between people of the same gender. Such relationships are claimed to be deviant and unnatural.

During my time in Walderim, I have been discreetly approached by many with an exclusive attraction to people of their own gender, who wish me to "cure" them. I have been astonished by the strength of their belief in their culture's doctrine. They agree that people are right to despise them. They despise themselves.

The first time the request was made of me, I made the mistake of telling the man that while in the Protectorate, my own lovers had not been restricted to women. I suggested that he accompany me when I returned. Instead of the relief I expected, the man accused me of trying to turn Walderim into a "decadent" region like the Protectorate. To my astonishment, he told me in an impassioned speech that "some people still know what normal behaviour is." He then resorted to denouncing me to the rest of his tribe, claiming that I had tried to "defile" him.

I can conclude by saying that of all the things I have found in Walderim, this is the one that has surprised me the most. I was prepared to find people held in a state of subservience and those in power enforcing their beliefs on the less fortunate. However, this self-oppression has left me dumbfounded.

Even where people of different genders are attracted to each other, the result is less than satisfactory from a Protectorate viewpoint. As each partner has to conform to their own gender stereotype and may appreciate their partner only as the opposite stereotype, it seems impossible that they can ever really know their lover. The complaint "My wife doesn't understand me" is so common as to be a joke. It is all quite astonishing and very sad.

Eliminating the exploitation of migrant workers from northern Walderim is also likely to encounter problems...

❖

Jemeryl scanned the rest of the extract, but there was nothing else of relevance. At the end of the chapter were a few additional comments from her grandfather, which stated that the conditions described by Bolitho had largely disappeared from Walderim, although echoes remained, particularly among the lower social orders.

Jemeryl pushed the book away. "I guess that explains what Tevi was going on about. The clans would have taken their beliefs with them to the islands. And it explains her tortured attitude. It must be awful to believe that you're evil and depraved, and unable to do anything about it." Jemeryl spoke quietly. "Poor Tevi."

"So what do you do now?" Klara landed on the desk.

"I don't know. If Tevi has absorbed her society's morality in the fashion described by Bolitho, there's no hope of persuading her to change her mind. But it still doesn't explain why she doesn't want me with her. Although I suppose she might be worried that I'll try to seduce her."

"That's not a totally groundless fear on her part."

Jemeryl shook her head. "It doesn't match the feel of Tevi's words. It was as if she expected me to be shocked."

"Bolitho described a pretty strange mindset. Perhaps the island's culture is so ingrained that she has to accredit the same ethics to others, even when she must know they won't share them."

"Maybe. But there has to be some way around it."

"On to a new field of enquiry?" Klara said brightly.

Jemeryl considered the bookcase. She summoned a thin volume from the top shelf. "Somewhere in here is a section on the perpetuation of cultural ethics by transferred guilt, considered as an imbalance in fifth-dimensional perspective fields."

"I suppose you've got nothing about the utilisation of incomprehensible terms by sorcerers, considered as a nervous reflex under pressure?"

"No, but I might have a recipe for roast magpie somewhere."

Chapter Fifteen—Clueless

Night had fallen by the time Jemeryl finished reading. She had found a lot of ominous warnings, but very little in the way of helpful advice. Before leaving the study, she stood for a long while at the window, staring at the moon riding between ragged clouds. Talking to Tevi was going to be difficult, and Jemeryl had the nagging feeling that an important piece of information was still missing.

She left Klara in the study—the magpie's sarcasm would not help—and went in search of the islander. The castle was so silent, she could hear the thudding of her heart. When she entered the parlour, the only light came from the hearth. The chairs were all empty, but then she spotted Tevi sitting cross-legged on the floor, staring bleakly into the fire.

Tevi did not move at the sound of the door opening and closing. Jemeryl came to a halt a few steps into the room. "Tevi?"

There was no response.

"I'd like to talk to you."

"If you want. I'm finished with running," Tevi answered apathetically.

Hesitantly, Jemeryl slipped into a chair beside the fireplace. Tevi's eyes remained fixed on the flames, her expression one of absolute desolation. Jemeryl knew she was way out of her depth. All of her carefully planned questions evaporated. She was going to have to start talking, keep her words and tone as calm as possible—and hope.

"Tevi...what you said. I've been looking at my books and I think I'm beginning to understand, but I'm still unclear. I wonder if you... if we could sort things out."

The muscles bunched in Tevi's jaw. "What is there to sort out?"

"Well, from what you've said, on your islands men and women have strictly differentiated roles." Jemeryl spoke in a general search for inspiration. "What are your feelings about the way people relate to each other on the mainland?"

"It doesn't help, if that's what you mean."

"In what way?"

Confusion gave Tevi her first spark of life. "Pardon?"

"In what way doesn't it help? If that's not a silly question."

Tevi glanced in Jemeryl's direction as if to judge her seriousness. "It confuses me. All the men look and act like women. It's often impossible for me to tell them apart. But I've found it best not to make the effort. If I become too mindful that someone is a man, they usually end up complaining that I'm treating them like an idiot. So I try to act as if they're all women, but I can only push the pretence so far. Inside, I know they're not really women, and I'm not...attracted to them like women."

"That wasn't quite what I meant."

"Then what did you mean?"

"I've been reading about Walderim back at the time when your people left. Apparently, the Protectorate attitude to sexual relationships appalled your ancestors. I suppose you feel the same?"

"No...not at all. If anything, it's better than the islands. When I see couples like Verron and Marith, I think they're sweet. They treat each other as equals. They talk to each other. It must be nice to have a lover who can also be a friend."

Jemeryl ran her hand through her hair. Tevi's response tied in with nothing she had read, unless Tevi was wilfully sidestepping the issue as a defensive strategy, in which case things might get explosive if Jemeryl prodded too far. But she had to try. "So if there's a couple who are both the same sex, how do you feel about them?"

"You're asking me?"

"Yes."

It looked as if Tevi bit back her first intended retort. "If I met such a couple and realised...?" She shrugged. "It would hardly be my place to condemn them. I suppose I'd mind my own business and pretend I'd noticed nothing. Which shouldn't be hard. It's not likely they'd be brazenly advertising what they were doing."

Comprehension caught Jemeryl by surprise. Her eyes fixed on the ceiling, while her mind raced, adding together the odd comments and the conjectures. Everything seemed to add up to a coherent explanation. However, Bolitho's experience warned against optimism. Locked in her culture's inflexible beliefs, Tevi had been unable to see what was happening around her, let alone accept it.

"What else do you want to know?" Tevi broke the silence.

"Actually, I was thinking about tunnel vision. More as a metaphor than a medical complaint."

"What do you mean? My eyes are fine now."

Instead of replying, Jemeryl sat, reviewing her options—not that there were many. She had to take the risk of enlightening Tevi.

"But you still only see part of the picture." Jemeryl dropped her gaze. "Your confession this afternoon would have made no sense to me if I hadn't read a report by a sorcerer who visited Walderim as a healer, two hundred and fifty years ago. What you said reminded me of some odd requests for treatment he'd received from folk who complained they were sexually attracted to people of their own gender."

"You mean you can cure it?"

The intensity in Tevi's voice stunned Jemeryl. A few seconds passed before she found her voice. "I don't know. It would honestly never have occurred to me to try."

"What did this other sorcerer do?"

"He suggested they move to the Protectorate, where it wouldn't matter what sex their lovers were."

Jemeryl anxiously awaited the response, but instead of a violent outburst, Tevi only looked puzzled. "Why would he say that?"

"Because it was true, and it still is. Having an exclusive preference for one gender is a bit unusual, but no one is going to get upset about it."

Tevi stared in bewilderment.

Carefully Jemeryl asked, "You said you stayed with Sergo and her son, in their cottage. Who else lived there?"

"Her sister."

"Who told you it was her sister?"

"Well, maybe not her sister, but she was a close relative. They..." Tevi's words died.

Jemeryl held her breath, trying to guess which way Tevi's reaction would go. She wished Bolitho's report could give her more grounds to hope.

For a long while, only unspoken questions formed on Tevi's lips, but at last she burst out, "But you can't let the world run like that."

"Why not?"

"You need a woman and a man to have children."

"True, but were babies in short supply in Storenseg? Because the reverse problem is generally much more common. Even with potions to help prevent unintended pregnancies, most relationships in which the partners are of different sexes produce twice as many children as they're able to care for. Families hope some of their members will settle with a partner of the same sex to provide homes for the rest. For example, Sergo's son was born to her brother."

"But it isn't as..."

Tevi's voice faded as a confused kaleidoscope of emotions chased across her face, yet inflamed moral outrage did not appear to be one. Jemeryl decided to risk a few further comments. "When you made your confession this afternoon, I couldn't see why you thought it would upset me. What I now don't understand is how you could have spent a year on the mainland without noticing the way Protectorate families operate. It defies belief—even with the problem you have telling men and women apart."

"You're being serious? It's not part of—"

"Totally serious."

"But what do..." Again, Tevi's voice trailed away. She pressed one hand against her forehead. Her eyes would not meet Jemeryl's, but for the first time they seemed to be fully focused on the room around her.

Despite Tevi's obvious turmoil, Jemeryl was starting to relax. There were many other things they had to discuss, such as the quest, but they could wait. Better if Tevi had time to think, especially since there seemed a chance the islander might overturn her upbringing and reach a rational conclusion.

Jemeryl got to her feet. "I'm going to bed. Perhaps we'll be able to talk things through tomorrow."

Tevi nodded in a dazed fashion. Jemeryl left her as she'd found her, still cross-legged on the floor, still staring into the flames, but the expression of despair had gone.

❖

A quick check when Jemeryl awoke the next day revealed that Tevi was still asleep. There was no indication of how long she had sat up thinking or what the result had been. Hoping for the best, Jemeryl made plans for departure. Much in the castle would require careful dismantling.

Just before midday Tevi emerged from her room, looking rather sheepish. Jemeryl prepared lunch, limiting her comments to the mundane, and waiting for the other woman to open the discussion. It did not take long once they were seated.

"I've been thinking," Tevi said between mouthfuls.

"I'd rather thought you would. What conclusions have you reached?"

"That a lot of things fall into place. Things Kimal told me, jokes I didn't understand, things I heard and saw in the guildhall. Like a friend of mine, Cayell, talking of Big Papa and Little Papa. I just assumed 'Big Papa' was a wordplay on 'Grandfather.'"

"So now you've thought it over, how do you feel about the depraved behaviour of the Protectorate?" Jemeryl kept her tone light, although it was the most fundamental of the three questions she wanted to ask.

"I feel I ought to be shocked, but somehow, I'm not," Tevi answered thoughtfully. "There have been so many things we believed on the islands that don't hold true on the mainland. This is just one more. I'm not sure what it means for me, though."

The appraisal was much calmer than Bolitho's report had led Jemeryl to expect. With considerable relief, she moved on to her second question. "Might it mean that you don't object to my accompanying you on your quest?"

"I think I've...um. Sure, I don't mind." Tevi gave a half-shrug and started toying with the food. Something else was clearly on her mind. Jemeryl let her take her time. "Does everyone in the Protectorate take lovers from both sexes?"

Jemeryl had the impression that Tevi was skirting around her real question. She answered carefully. "That would be a bit sweeping. I guess we all have preferences. Some go for blonds, some for women, some for manual workers. It's not anyone else's business."

"What about you?" Tevi's eyes were fixed on her plate.

The breath caught in Jemeryl's throat. Her third question might be rapidly approaching. "Um...yes. As an apprentice in Lyremouth, I had affairs with my fellow students, both male and female. It wasn't important to me which they were," she said, adding mentally, *As long as they were tall and dark haired.*

"When we leave, do you still think we should start by going to Lyremouth?"

Jemeryl restrained her disappointment at Tevi's abrupt change of subject. There would be plenty more opportunities. Rushing things was unwise. "Yes."

"Is there anything we need to get ready?"

"Just a few extra supplies. If you go to the village, you can also reassure the locals you're safe and give them the good news that I'm going. Use my pony as a pack animal. While you're away, I'll clear up around the place."

"What do we want?"

"Depends on what's going. Use your judgement. Why don't you take Klara? If you get stuck, you could send her back with a message."

A short while later, Jemeryl stood on the battlements, watching Tevi ride down the overgrown path to the village. The ponies and rider disappeared through a gap in the outer walls of the castle. Jemeryl sedately descended the steps and entered the great hall. She paced to the centre of the room, and stood looking gravely around her at the piles of equipment. Then her composure broke, and a huge grin swept across her face. A volley of fireballs erupted from her fingertips as she indulged in a sorcerer's pyrotechnic display of delight.

❖

By early evening, the hall and study were empty—a considerable achievement even though one small sack was all she had to show for it. Jemeryl smiled as she deposited it on the table in the parlour. In reality, the bag was a gateway, rather than a container, through which items could be pushed into a suitable dimension. However, it was not quite so straightforward as the ungifted might imagine. It had taken only half a day to dispose of the equipment, but it would require much painstaking effort to unpack. Several reckless sorcerers had been killed by the impact of their belongings exploding through a carelessly opened dimensional gate.

There was still no sign of Tevi. Jemeryl was wondering whether to eat or wait a while longer when Klara flew in.

"Message from Tevi."

"What is it?"

The magpie fluffed her feathers importantly. "Jem. The villagers want to hold a party in my honour. They kept insisting, so I agreed. Unless you object, I'll stay here and bring the supplies up tomorrow." Klara spoke in a fair imitation of Tevi's lilting drawl.

"She's not coming back tonight?"

"That was the general drift of it. There's no point me carrying messages if you don't listen."

"I just wanted confirmation. I was looking forward to seeing her."

Klara put her head on one side. "Do you want me to go back and say you object?"

"Only if I can think of something plausible."

"You could join the party."

"I don't think that would be a good idea."

"Maybe not." Klara settled on Jemeryl's shoulder. "Never mind. She'll be back tomorrow."

Despondently, Jemeryl headed to the kitchen to prepare a lonely supper.

❖

Jemeryl sat in front of the fire, flipping idly through the book on her lap. Ruff and Tumble lay asleep by her feet, and Klara was perched on the armrest. This was the way she had spent most evenings since arriving in the valley. Tonight, however, she could not concentrate. Once again, her eyes drifted away from the text.

A rustle from Klara recalled Jemeryl to the parlour. Firelight glittered in the small black eyes, alive with the echo of Jemeryl's own intellect. Unlike the bears and squirrels, Klara was a true familiar. The bond was so close that, effectively, Jemeryl performed part of her thinking in the magpie's head.

Many sorcerers viewed taking a familiar as a dangerous affectation. The effort of maintaining the bond often outweighed the benefits, and there were tales of sorcerers rendered catatonic when their familiars perished unexpectedly, although in Jemeryl's opinion these stories were of dubious authenticity. Great care was needed in selecting a species.

Cats were virtually the only mammals worth considering, although many types of reptile and bird were suitable.

A magpie was an uncommon familiar, but Jemeryl was pleased with her choice. Klara combined acute senses with the useful abilities to fly and talk. A rueful expression crossed Jemeryl's face. Tevi's presence in the castle had made her realise how much she had fallen into the trap of treating Klara as a friend, even creating a sarcastic personality for the magpie. Talking to yourself was a bad habit, regardless of how you disguised it.

Jemeryl sighed and discarded the book. Thoughts of Tevi had dispelled all hope of reading but brought another idea to mind. In response to an unspoken command, Klara hopped onto Jemeryl's lap.

There was one further advantage to having a familiar. Klara was permanently available for mind riding. Jemeryl closed her eyes and blocked out her own senses. After a second of disorientation, she refocused on the room from Klara's viewpoint. For a moment she studied her own relaxed human face, devoid of expression in the trance, then she leapt upwards. Jemeryl's wings caught the air, and she flew out of the room.

Noise and light were spilling from the half-open door of the village hall. The gentle night breeze carried Jemeryl gliding over the huddled cottages and in through a large gap under the eaves. The magpie was invisible in the dark shadows beneath the thatched roof. She took a perch amid the rafters and settled down to watch, trying to ignore any pangs of guilt at such blatant snooping.

It looked as if the entire local population was squeezed in below. Spotting Tevi in the chaos was not easy, even with Klara's keen eyesight. Eventually, Jemeryl saw her, surrounded by a group of admirers. To judge by her actions, Tevi was recounting the tale of the hunt for the basilisk. The young mercenary was obviously the toast of the village. Jemeryl was amused to see Tevi's bashful response to the constant stream of people offering praise and patting her back.

Several young people were paying Tevi even more attention than the rest, their intentions clear. Jemeryl was unconcerned, even at the efforts of one especially persistent young woman. Tevi's reticence, combined with Bolitho's experience, reassured Jemeryl that competition presented no imminent threat to her hopes for Tevi.

The revelry got more boisterous as the night progressed. Bodies littered the edges of the hall, collapsed in drunken stupor. Children were sent to their beds. From her vantage point, Jemeryl saw Tevi squeeze through to where the beer barrels were stacked. As Tevi refilled her tankard, the young woman again appeared at her side.

The pair talked while they moved away to a clear spot. Tevi's neck was bent to catch what the shorter woman was saying over the hubbub. Jemeryl ruffled her feathers, hit by a twinge of jealousy. She did not need to hear the conversation to know that the villager was flirting outrageously. Whatever was said caused Tevi to look embarrassed, which she covered by taking a hasty gulp from her tankard.

"You're wasting your time, young lady," Jemeryl muttered. "At least, I sincerely hope you are."

Unaware of the watcher above, the unknown villager brushed blond hair back from her face. Her eyes danced with amusement as she stepped closer to Tevi. Jemeryl confidently expected the shy islander to back off. Instead, Tevi put her free arm around the woman and kissed her on the lips.

In a jarring storm of sensation, Jemeryl wrenched herself back to the castle, leaving Klara to return on her own. The dislocation made her nauseous. The parlour spun and then settled. Even before she was fully attuned to her surroundings, Jemeryl had lurched to her feet, disturbing the squirrels that had settled on her lap in her absence.

Jemeryl's first intention was to rush headlong to the village. Common sense stopped her before she had taken three steps. All knowledge of human nature told her that such an intrusion was highly unlikely to achieve good results. It was not possible to dismiss the villager and forcibly claim Tevi's affection—not by any method the Coven permitted. She had to leave Tevi and the villager free to do as they wished.

Jemeryl sank back into her chair. Summoning all her self-discipline, she tried not to think of Tevi or of what might be going on in the village hall. Her efforts met with utter failure. The night dragged by while the fire burned low. Klara returned from the village but wisely made no comment.

The image of Tevi kissing the villager kept slicing through Jemeryl's thoughts. Visions of what might follow stung like acid in the cuts. It became too much to bear. Jemeryl went to her stock of herbs and prepared a sleeping draught. *Tomorrow, I'll have Tevi back with me*, she told herself. *We'll leave the valley and the villager behind. It's pointless to sit up brooding. I'm going to sleep.* Her face crumpled. Was it too much to hope that Tevi was also sleeping, considering what else she might be doing at that moment?

❖

The honking of migrating geese woke Jemeryl at first light. She rolled over and stared at the ceiling. Memories of the previous night flooded back. Jemeryl pulled a pillow over her face in a futile attempt to block them out. There was no point trying to get back to sleep. She tossed the bedclothes aside and swung her feet onto the floor.

Tevi should be returning soon. It might be wise to prepare herself for the meeting. Although preparations would probably be as much use as hiding her face in a pillow.

Concentrating on sorting and packing was hard, especially as time went by with no sign of Tevi. In the end, Jemeryl abandoned all pretence of working and stood by an upstairs window watching the path to the village. An eternity passed before her vigil was rewarded with the sight of a lone rider leading a second pony towards the castle. Jemeryl leapt down the stairs and was waiting outside the great hall when Tevi finally arrived in the courtyard.

Even before the pony came to a standstill, Tevi slipped off its back and trotted over to greet Jemeryl, her broad smile reflecting obvious high spirits. "Sorry if I've kept you waiting, but I had a late night and I overslept."

Jemeryl needed all her self-control not to wince. "That's all right. I've been busy." It wasn't strictly true on either count.

To cover her threatened loss of composure, Jemeryl began unsaddling the ponies. The bears came to assist as porters.

Tevi seemed unaware that anything might be wrong. "You missed a good party."

"I doubt my presence would have added to the merriment."

"I suppose some villagers might have been unsettled."

"To put it mildly."

"I tried explaining that you're not dangerous."

"Did they believe you?"

"Perhaps if you'd been there..." Tevi paused. "I didn't put it in my message with Klara, but I was sort of hoping you'd come."

"You'd have been the only one." Jemeryl knew that the curtness of her replies would soon attract attention, despite her effort to control her tone.

"Are you all right?"

"Yes, I'm fine." Another lie.

"I suppose it must be a wrench to leave your home."

Jemeryl tried to force the tension from her voice. "It's not that. I had an unsettling side effect from some magic yesterday."

Tevi looked doubtful, but before she could speak, they were interrupted by a growl from Ruff. The bear had been dragging one of the packs to the kitchens, but a strap had caught on a tree root. A tug-of-war was now in progress.

Tevi darted over. "Hey, take care. There are breakables in the pack." She grinned at Jemeryl, her buoyant mood restored. "The villagers gave me two bottles of their best local wine."

"I wouldn't get excited. The stuff doubles as sheep dip," Klara said.

"It tasted all right last night. But I guess anything would after the cider." Tevi hoisted the pack onto her shoulder.

Jemeryl managed a weak attempt at a smile. "I made a start at organising the provisions. If you dump stuff on the table, I'll be along as soon as I've got the ponies stabled."

"Fine." Tevi headed towards the kitchen, humming cheerfully to herself.

Jemeryl buried her face in her hands. After several deep breaths, she let her arms drop and looked at the familiar stone buildings. She would cope. Tevi was back with her. Neither of them would set eyes on the woman again—or else, Jemeryl told herself, regardless of her Coven oath, there would be nothing left of the villager but a smouldering pair of shoes.

❖

The knapsack landed with a thud. Using her foot, Jemeryl shoved it into the corner and then turned to survey the room. Everything was packed. The parlour looked bare, devoid of personal possessions, although the fire still bestowed a cosy glow. This would be her last night in the castle. All that was needed was to saddle the ponies and ride out. Just as well, since Iralin's deadline to quit the castle expired on the next day.

At the other side of the room, Tevi was opening a bottle of wine, struggling with an implement that looked better suited for removing stones from horse's hooves than corks from bottles. Finally, the stopper came loose—a celebratory drink for the true start of the quest.

Jemeryl dropped into her favourite chair and stretched her feet towards the fire, using Tumble's rump as a footstool. She accepted a mug of wine and took a cautious sip. Contrary to Klara's remark, it was not bad, a touch sweet but very drinkable.

At first, their conversation was about the route they would take to Lyremouth, around the southern end of Whitfell Spur. The main Langhope Pass was still closed, and neither wanted to try the old pack route. Tevi recounted a few incidents from the journey with Harrick, although the account was unusually vague. Her mind was clearly elsewhere. Jemeryl refused to speculate about the subject that was occupying Tevi's thoughts. She would rather not know. However, she was not given the choice.

"Jem. Can I talk to you about something?" Tevi took advantage of a lull in the conversation.

After the briefest hesitation, Jemeryl replied, "Of course," trying to mask her reluctance. The topic had to be personal if Tevi felt the need to ask permission, and it did not require an oracle to guess what it was, but refusing would be neither polite nor tactful.

Tevi took a moment to gather herself. "Last night, I spent a lot of time watching the villagers. It wasn't hard to tell men from women once I stopped making assumptions. In fact, things were so obvious, I don't know how I'd missed it before. Like Sergo's son referring to 'my mothers.' I've heard the expression from other people but assumed they meant their ancestors—mother, grandmother, and so on. Or 'partner.' Verron and Marith always called each other that, so I should have known how the word is used in the Protectorate, but with Harrick and Rorg, I just thought they meant 'business colleague.'"

"No, a business colleague would be referred to as an associate, to avoid confusion," Jemeryl explained, although she was coldly certain that it was not mere linguistic usage that was concerning Tevi.

"Well, yes...but what I wanted to talk about was...at the party, lots of younger villagers were showing an interest in me. It's happened before, but I've always assumed the person was male and avoided them, or that I'd misinterpreted something, or in one case I...didn't react well." Tevi's expression shuffled between guilt and embarrassment. "But last night, there was one woman in particular. She was really keen, virtually chased me around the hall. Not that I minded. She was nice—fun to talk to."

Tevi was trying to look relaxed and failing. It wasn't just an idle chat. Jemeryl knew that anyway. She realised that an interested "Yes, go on," was called for but could not bring herself to say it.

"Her name's Kelly. She's a cheese maker from up the valley. Do you know her?"

"I don't think so."

"Blond hair, about your height, rather pretty."

"Oh." Jemeryl braced herself for what Tevi was going to say next. Suddenly, a hideous thought struck. She jerked upright. "You don't want her to come with us, do you?"

"No, nothing of the sort. It was just that she..." Tevi finished with a shrug.

Relief washed over Jemeryl. Listening to Tevi's account would be easy by comparison with a long journey, forced to endure watching Tevi with a newfound lover. It gave Jemeryl the strength to ask, "That she what?"

"It was...with her chasing me, I wanted to test my reactions, so when she asked me, I kissed her." Tevi swallowed. All pretence at nonchalance had gone. Her eyes were fixed on the floor. "It was all right. I felt conspicuous, but not immoral or anything. And nobody else batted an eyelid, except for her friends, who were making encouraging gestures to her. That's when I got worried. I realised this woman saw me as some great hero and lover. I didn't want to tell her the basilisk was a one-off thing, and I didn't have a clue about the other. So I made a joke about never trusting a mercenary's kiss and barricaded myself in a corner with the old folk until she left."

"You didn't spend the night with her?" Jemeryl blurted out.

"Oh, no. I didn't say I liked her that much."

Jemeryl's heart pounded. "So what is it you want to talk about?"

"It's just...like with the woman last night...about not having a clue..."

Jemeryl opened her mouth but could not force any words out.

Tevi continued haltingly. "Supposing...if there was a woman, and you really liked her, but didn't know how she felt about you, what would you say to her?"

"It would depend."

"On what?"

"On how sober I was, among other things." Jemeryl was amazed at how steady her own voice sounded. "We aren't talking hypothetically, are we?"

"No," Tevi answered after a slight pause.

"There's someone you have your eye on."

"Yes."

"Not another of the villagers."

"No."

"Or someone from Lyremouth or Treviston."

"No."

Jemeryl sat motionless, willing Tevi to look up, meet her eyes, and give a smile or some other unequivocal sign—in vain. Tevi remained staring at the floor.

There had to be more than one possible interpretation for why Tevi had chosen to say what she had said. *The way my luck's been running, she probably just wants me to recommend a few lines from a poem to put in a love letter home*, Jemeryl told herself. *But surely there's a chance that she's referring to me?* Her jaw clenched at the afterthought. *If not, it will be beyond bearing, whatever I do.*

Jemeryl got to her feet, walked to Tevi's chair, and then knelt so their heads were level. "What I'd say would also depend on who it was, how well I knew her, what situation we were in. Maybe I'd say nothing and let my actions speak for me."

Slowly, hesitantly, Jemeryl took hold of Tevi's hand, dreading that it would be snatched away, but the fingers she gripped tightened about her own. At last, Tevi raised her head, and their eyes met.

While red firelight flickered and danced over the room, the two of them stayed frozen in position. Jemeryl felt as if her entire life had been distilled into that moment. Tevi's gaze held her cocooned from the world. Nothing else ever had, or would, exist apart from the woman in front of her. She tried to speak, but her lungs were not working properly. Jemeryl cupped Tevi's cheek. She felt slight pressure as Tevi leaned into her touch. Then Jemeryl slipped her hand to the back of Tevi's neck and drew her forward into a kiss.

Tevi's mouth was soft, moving against hers, nuzzling, sucking, and then opening. Their tongues touched, and Jemeryl heard herself moan. She began to explore—at first tentatively caressing and then more fervently as her lips and tongue struggled to express the surge of desire.

Tevi's arms wrapped around Jemeryl, tightening and pulling her close, lifting her clear of the ground. She clung to Tevi's shoulders. Even through clothes, the firm body felt more real than anything else Jemeryl had ever touched. Somehow, they ended up sitting on the floor, squashed awkwardly between the chair and Tumble. Neither obstacle showed any sign of moving. At last, Tevi broke from the kiss. She rested her forehead on Jemeryl's shoulder, gasping.

"Dare I hope from this that I'm the woman you have your eye on?" Jemeryl's tone was not quite as light as she intended.

"I've wanted you since the moment I saw you." The thick cloth of Jemeryl's shirt muffled Tevi's voice.

"It's been the same for me."

"Truly?" Tevi sounded disbelieving.

"And you must remember I had a two-day head start on you."

"You really—"

"Yes."

Talk was inadequate. Jemeryl's lips travelled along the line of Tevi's jaw, detecting the faint tastes of salt and wood smoke. The smoothness of Tevi's throat became wet and slippery under Jemeryl's mouth. Tevi's hands trembled as they moved over her shoulders and down her spine. Jemeryl suspected that her own hands were none too steady either.

Jemeryl laid her face against Tevi's and opened her eyes. The chair leg was inches from her nose. She stared at it while forming the words she wanted.

"Would you like to share my bed tonight? I'll understand if it's too much, too quickly, and—"

She broke off as Tevi nodded sharply.

"You're sure?"

"Yes."

"In that case, perhaps we should move while my legs can still carry me."

Jemeryl wondered if they might be beyond that point already. Getting to her feet required both hands braced on the chair. She felt as clumsy as a toddler. Her knees were rubber. The stairs would have been impossible without an arm around Tevi's waist as support.

They stood kissing in the bedroom until Jemeryl gently pushed Tevi down to sit on the side of the bed. In a businesslike fashion, she undid the ties of her own shirt. Her hands moved to her belt but stopped. Tevi's gaze was transfixed on the gapping cloth. Letting her arms fall to her side, Jemeryl moved within reach. Tevi's hands slipped under her shirt, encircling her and pulling her close, while Tevi's face tunnelled through folds of material.

Jemeryl gasped at the touch of lips on her skin. Had it not been for the supporting arms, she would have fallen. She braced her knees against the bed frame. Her fingers burrowed through Tevi's dark hair, her grip firm enough to steer the warm mouth towards her breast. Tevi's tongue flicked across her nipple. Jemeryl heard a sound like the mew of a newborn kitten escape from her own throat. She guided Tevi to her other breast. Sensation flooded through her. Jemeryl looked down. Tevi's eyes were closed and shadow filled the hollow of her cheek as she sucked. By the time Jemeryl pulled away, she was shaking so much that it was hard to finish undressing and harder still to get Tevi free from her clothes.

The air was chill on exposed flesh. Jemeryl tugged back the bedcovers, pushed Tevi inside, and then snuggled in after. Jemeryl's senses were overwhelmed by the awareness of the body beside her; the texture of skin on skin; the whisper of breath; and Tevi's eyes inches away, staring into hers. She rolled back, pulling Tevi on top and letting the other woman's weight press her into the mattress. Jemeryl's fingertips investigated the contours of Tevi's back, while her thumbs rippled over the furrows of Tevi's ribs.

Tevi drew back, resting up on her elbows. She adjusted her balance so she could stroke Jemeryl's face. Desire was plain in her expression, and so was uncertainty. The doubts solidified.

"Um...you know what I said about not having a clue?" Tevi's voice was barely audible.

Jemeryl smiled in understanding. "You've never done this with a woman?"

"With anyone."

"Ah." Jemeryl considered the implications. "In that case, I'm afraid you might find it a bit of a disappointment. Most people do, the first time."

Jemeryl's smile broadened. She rolled over, so that Tevi was the one on her back, and began a series of light, teasing kisses, moving quickly over nose and eyes, dancing away from the lips, until Tevi grew more assertive and caught hold of Jemeryl's head. She clamped her mouth against Jemeryl's, claiming her in an ever-more-passionate embrace. Their legs entwined.

Jemeryl was swept along. Her paranormal senses intensified the message her other senses were providing. Tevi's aura was energised with the heat of desire. Her persona crackled with tension.

Jemeryl lifted herself on one elbow. The tip of her forefinger touched the hollow at the base of Tevi's throat. Jemeryl interwove the contact through the higher dimensions. When she snared the hub of Tevi's aura, she felt the jolt shoot through the body under her hand and Tevi gasped with the shock. Jemeryl's fingers traced the ethereal lines of arousal across Tevi's body, flaring around her breasts, snaking along her thighs and condensing in the pit of her stomach. Tevi's breathing grew ragged, as if air had to be dragged into her lungs.

Jemeryl's hand reached the elemental pivot between Tevi's legs, the focus now of both body and aura. Her fingers slipped into the silky wetness. Tevi's aura was overloaded, ready to erupt. Her body shuddered in spasms. Jemeryl guided the rising waves, moulding them to the rhythm of Tevi's breath. Gently, Jemeryl's fingers entered her. The surge through Tevi's aura matched the cry that broke from her lips. Tevi was close. It took only the final pressure to send her over the edge.

Jemeryl witnessed Tevi's climax in seven dimensions. Tevi's body arched. Her aura... Jemeryl shook her head, regretting the lack of words to describe the effect. If it were sight, it would be blazing blue light. If it were sound, it would be a trumpet. If it were taste, it would be raw alcohol. The experience left Jemeryl herself on the point of release, but it could wait—for a few minutes more.

Tevi buried her face in Jemeryl's shoulder. Slowly, her breath returned to normal. She rolled back and looked up. Her gaze met Jemeryl's with an intensity that burned through all the planes of existence. Jemeryl stared back into the pair of grey eyes she had created.

Abruptly, disconcertingly, Jemeryl's extended time sense intruded. The room broke into a kaleidoscope of seconds; then the world fell back into place. For better or worse Jemeryl knew, with a sorcerer's certainty, that her life would never be free of the consequences of that night.

The temporal shock when she had met Tevi—the Coven had provoked it, tinkering with time. It had been an attempt to manipulate the future, the train of events starting with the meeting in the castle courtyard, but was it cause or effect? Maybe she and Tevi had always been fated to meet, to become lovers, and the web of fate had dictated the Coven's action, or maybe it was the tampering that had entwined her destiny with Tevi's.

Whichever it was, Jemeryl did not care. Lowering her head, she lost herself again in the sensation of Tevi's mouth on her own.

Chapter Sixteen—Ordinary Folk

The pony's hooves clattered on the cobbles. Tevi made a final check to ensure that the load behind each saddle was secure. Two squirrels perched on the pony's rump watched eagerly, as if confident that nuts would soon form part of the game. Grinning, Tevi placed her hand on the bedroll and pushed it back and forth in an experimental fashion, testing that nothing would shake loose.

The straps and harness passed the test, but the squirrels complained noisily. Tevi stepped back and yawned, stretching her arms above her head. The joints in her shoulders cracked. The sun had not yet climbed high enough to appear over the battlements, and the courtyard was chilly. Her breath created white clouds in the dawn air.

Tevi flexed her neck, testing the way her body felt. There was a definite change, as if her muscles no longer fit together in quite the same way on her bones. Tevi's grin widened. Contrary to Jemeryl's words, she had not been disappointed—surprised once or twice, but most definitely not disappointed. Tevi pressed both hands against her cheeks. It was getting serious. She could not stop grinning, and her face was aching. She tried imagining what her mother would say, an exercise that normally removed any trace of a smile, but today, it only made her want to giggle. She had the feeling her feet were not touching the ground, that her life had shot off on an unfamiliar route, but she was not complaining.

The sound of Jemeryl's footsteps came from the doorway. The sorcerer appeared, wrapped in warm travelling clothes, with the two bears in retinue. At the sight of her, Tevi's insides turned to mush. Her first impulse was to rush over and sweep Jemeryl into an embrace, but Tevi hesitated, unsure of herself. Would it be overenthusiastic? Too immature? She waited for Jemeryl to join her before reaching out self-consciously and placing her arms around Jemeryl's waist.

Jemeryl planted a gentle kiss on Tevi's lips. "Everything ready?"

"Yes."

"Then it's time to go."

"Do we really have to leave today?"

"I was given a deadline to heal you and quit the valley. My time's up."

"Couldn't you tell them I suffered a relapse?"

Jemeryl muffled her laughter in Tevi's shoulder. "Don't tempt me. I'm in enough trouble with Iralin as it is."

Tevi started to turn away forlornly. Jemeryl pulled her back. "Believe me, I'd love to stay here in the castle, alone with you. But we'll be together until we find the chalice. With any luck, it'll take us months...maybe years."

"It might not."

"I'm sure we'll find a way to drag it out," Jemeryl said mischievously.

The tone put the smile back on Tevi's lips. After one last kiss, the pair climbed into the saddles. They rode under the heavy stone gatehouse and into the watery morning sunlight. Ruff and Tumble padded along behind, accompanied by an excited group of squirrels.

The trail led across the ruined outer ward before winding downhill between bushes and broken heaps of stone. Once they were well clear of the castle, Jemeryl reined her pony around. She closed her eyes and muttered softly while her hands made a series of sharp, cutting movements.

Before Tevi's eyes, a change came over the buildings. The solid timbers of the gate decayed and fell apart. Stones crumbled and fell. A crash resounded as a floor gave way; the boom echoed back from the surrounding hills. The squirrels fled in panic to the shelter of the nearest tree.

"Why did you do that?" Tevi was caught between alarm and surprise.

"Didn't I tell you the castle was a partial illusion? I just returned it to the state it was in when I found it. Else it wouldn't have been safe if the villagers came poking around once we're gone. Now the squirrels can have it all to themselves again."

Jemeryl turned her pony around and guided it down the trail, leaving Tevi staring in bewilderment at the ruins and trying to come to terms with the idea that she had spent the previous twelve days in a heap of rubble disguised by illusion. It did not make sense. She urged her pony to catch up with Jemeryl's.

"You can create a castle from a ruin, but we have to ride all the way to Lyremouth on horseback. Can't you make us fly there or something?"

"Magic isn't like that. Sorcerers can't make things happen out of nothing. We have to study the paranormal dimensions and use whatever we find there. For telekinesis to be effective, you need a suitable sixth-dimensional drift pattern. If you can coerce the essence to flow, then the mass in the three normal dimensions follows."

"What?"

"Flying isn't easy."

"The sorcerer in Treviston made a bottle of wine float in the air."

"You can force things over a short distance, but it's hard work. Usually, when a sorcerer makes things defy gravity, it's just to impress the ungifted. It would actually be less effort to move the items by hand."

"You mean it's not very useful?"

"It is sometimes. And if you're lucky with the currents, telekinesis can be impressive—but it doesn't happen often."

"Sounds rather haphazard."

"That's like a blind person saying sight is haphazard because it doesn't work well at night."

The trail passed through a breach in the outer walls. The bracken-covered hillside rolled down to the cultivated fields of the valley floor. The slopes above were covered in pine trees that ended in a ragged line a short distance away. Again, Jemeryl brought her pony to a halt and pointed to the trees. In obedience to her gesture, Ruff and Tumble ambled up the hill, shouldering their way through the coarse vegetation. When they reached the trunks, Jemeryl stood in the stirrups and clapped her hands three times.

As the sound faded, the two bears froze in their tracks; then Ruff shook his head and sneezed. Tumble looked at the branches above her head, whining softly. Back on the path, Tevi's pony fidgeted restlessly. The crunching of small stones under its hooves made both bears look around. Instantly, they spun back and pelted away into the woods.

Tevi watched them go sadly. "Will they remember us?"

"Just a few confusing details that will make them even more wary of people than normal, which is the way I'd want it," Jemeryl said firmly. "I'd hate them to wander up to a fur trapper and try to make friends."

"But Klara comes with us?"

"You bet, sweetheart," the magpie answered for herself, perched on the pack behind Jemeryl's saddle.

Jemeryl prompted her pony into a gentle trot down the hillside. "Come on. Let's go and bid our fond farewells to the villagers."

❖

Late afternoon, three days later, they reached the outlying farms surrounding the town of Rizen. A slow-flowing river looped through waterlogged meadows. In the dwindling light, flocks of sheep grazed on rough pasture. The ragged peaks of the Spur disappeared into low clouds to the west and a light drizzle was falling. The road forded several tributaries running down from the hills. Nobody else was visible on the road, although the track showed signs of much use. Its surface was furrowed with deep ruts from the wheels of farm carts.

Ahead of them, Rizen lay in a wide bend of the river. The heavy defensive walls were a reminder of the days before the area had taken allegiance with the Coven. The drizzle turned to rain as they approached the town gate. Tevi pulled up her hood, grateful that they would be spending the night under a roof.

Three guardsmen were sheltering beneath the stone arch of the gate. They were dressed in the uniform of the town militia, and their hands carried the mercenaries' red and gold tattoos. They paid far more attention to their own banter than to the approaching riders. Bursts of laughter echoed in the confined space.

Jemeryl halted her pony. "Could you tell me if the sorcerer is in town today?"

The sergeant broke off in mid-sentence and turned around, his mouth set in a self-important sneer. His contemptuous manner lasted a mere fraction of a second. As if incidentally, Jemeryl's sleeve was pushed back to reveal the black amulet on her wrist. At the sight of it, the sergeant snapped to attention. The other two guardsmen were only an instant behind him.

"Yes, ma'am. Sorcerer Chenoweth is in residence. Please, if you would wait a moment, I will arrange a suitable escort for you."

"Thank you, that isn't necessary." Jemeryl acknowledged the sergeant's salute with the faintest nod and rode on.

The abrupt change in attitude was not so easy for Tevi to ignore. *Of course. That's how people respond to sorcerers*, she reminded herself, feeling uncomfortable. The guardsmen's eyes looked straight through her. There was no response to her friendly smile. Tevi hesitated, tempted to speak, but then urged her pony forward to catch up with Jemeryl.

Substantial timber-framed buildings lined either side of the street. Above the doors hung the signs of a dozen guilds, but none denoted an inn. Tevi was about to suggest they look for lodgings when she caught sight of the red and gold swords of the mercenaries adorning a banner outside a tall building.

"I ought to call in at the guildhall," Tevi pointed it out. "I should check that Harrick left the payment. I suppose I'd also better explain about the basilisk. I didn't get paid for it, and I wouldn't want them to think I was cheating the guild out of its share."

"Don't be surprised if they aren't very pleased." Jemeryl gave a crooked smile. "As their name implies, the mercenaries don't go in for acts of charity. But while you're explaining it, I'll visit the town sorcerer. It counts as good manners to tell someone when you're in their area. I'll pick you up from the guildhall afterwards and we'll find an inn."

Tevi slipped out of her saddle and caught the pony's reins. "I guess I'll have to hand the pony over as well. It was only on loan. "

"Don't worry; we'll get another one."

"Right." Tevi shared a last smile before heading off in search of the stable block.

❖

Once Tevi was out of sight, Jemeryl continued riding along the street. A fair number of people were about, despite the rain. Most rushed by with their heads down, but those who spotted her amulet stepped aside discreetly, some bowing. Jemeryl barely noticed them. Her thoughts were locked on the imminent meeting with the Rizen sorcerer.

She was not looking forward to the conversation. Jemeryl had met Chenoweth on several occasions and they had not got on well. Jemeryl had found the other sorcerer uninspired and, frankly, not very intelligent. She suspected that Chenoweth thought her both arrogant and unorthodox. Iralin claimed that he had been the one to pass on the bad reports and Jemeryl was sure that he had been prompted more by a desire to upset her than concern for the villagers.

Chenoweth's home overlooked an imposing square. Jemeryl could not hide her scorn as she looked at it. The place was a monument to a weak imagination. In truth, it was a pleasant townhouse, built in the local style to generous proportions. However, Chenoweth had overlain it with illusion to the extent that it now appeared hideously incongruous with its neighbours. He had turned it into a caricature of a sorcerer's house. Animated gargoyles guarded the door and multicoloured smoke issued from the chimneys. If it impressed the local population, it implied a sad lack of sophistication on their part.

To Jemeryl's mind, Chenoweth was little more than an overrated witch, and she could not believe that Iralin would think him important enough to inform of the actions taken over the reports, but equally, he would be quite able to draw his own conclusions when he learnt that she was bound for Lyremouth. It was a safe bet that his response would be both smug and vindictive. Jemeryl chewed her lip, trying to work out the most tactful way of dealing with the situation.

Klara hopped onto her shoulder. "Don't worry. Just give him a quick summary of the relevant facts."

"Which are?"

"That he's an interfering arsehole who pays too much attention to the ramblings of morons."

Klara's suggestions were rarely helpful.

The guild master's massive forearms were laced with a network of scars. He crossed them in front of his barrel chest. "And you're quite certain you haven't anything else you'd like to declare?"

"No, sir."

On the other side of the desk, Tevi stood sullenly at attention. In the hour since arriving at the guildhall, she had come to realise that

Jemeryl's warning was well founded. The guild master had insisted she repeat her story four times, while his attitude had grown progressively more hostile. He clearly did not believe a word she said. For her part, Tevi was forming an intense dislike of the man.

The guild master gave her a long, hard stare. The only sound came from one corner of the room, where another guild official was rummaging suspiciously through the contents of Tevi's pack.

"Why didn't you complete your contract?"

"Trader Harrick agreed he didn't need me once we'd got over the mountains."

"Your contract said you would stay with him until Rizen. What gave you the right to change its terms?"

"By mutual consent, a contract may be amended."

"Don't quote the rules at me," the guild master bellowed. "I was living by them before you were born. Amendment of contract is only allowed in exceptional circumstances."

Tevi would have laid money he had been a bully as a child. "The lives of Protectorate citizens were at—" Her words were interrupted by urgent rapping on the door.

"What is it now?" the guild master shouted.

An apprentice poked her head in nervously. "There's a sorcerer to see you, sir. She says it's about the new arrival."

Tevi greeted the announcement with a sigh of relief. The effect on the guild officials was far more dramatic. They both froze with blank expressions of confusion while their eyes shifted from the messenger to Tevi and then to each other.

The guild master was the first to recover. "Don't stand there gawking. Show her up immediately." As the door closed, his glare fixed on Tevi. "I suppose you think this is your *friend*?"

Tevi felt herself blush at the emphasis on the word 'friend'. "Yes, sir. Jemeryl said she'd meet me here."

"Still sticking to your story? Well, maybe now we'll get to the truth."

Despite his continued belligerence, the guild master was noticeably unsettled. He got to his feet and stood, adjusting the set of his clothes and tightening his belt. As footsteps sounded outside, he combed his thinning hair with his fingers in a last nervous effort at personal grooming.

Suddenly, Tevi understood what the guild master had meant when he stressed the word "friend." An immense social gulf existed between a junior mercenary and a Coven sorcerer. In the castle, Jemeryl had insisted on acting like equals, but the rest of the world would not see them as such.

Tevi realised that referring to Jemeryl in terms more appropriate for a friend than a superior had prejudiced the guild master against believing her story from the start. Claiming that the Coven took an interest in her quest for a family heirloom had not helped. Judging by his reaction, the guild master had not even believed that Jemeryl existed. Now he evidently expected to have Tevi's account revealed as distortion, if not outright lies. However, Tevi did not have long to think things through. The door opened, and both guild officers bowed stiffly as Jemeryl swept into the room.

"How may we assist you, ma'am?" The guild master's combative tones were replaced by starched politeness.

Jemeryl did not answer immediately. Her gaze travelled very deliberately around the room. Tevi guessed that her own face held an expression of aggrieved irritation. Jemeryl could add it to the guild master's officiousness and his colleague's edgy sideways glances. Reading the situation would not be hard.

Jemeryl's eyes finished up fixed on the guild master. "Thank you, but my business is with Tevi." Her manner was condescending.

"On that subject, I'm pleased you've arrived, ma'am. There has been a little confusion. W—"

Jemeryl cut him off. "Confusion? Didn't Tevi explain?"

"We've had a version of events, but we're unsure of the accuracy. If—"

"You're surely not calling my friend's honesty into question?"

The guild master's eyes bulged in surprise. "Er...well...no, ma'am."

"Then what is the problem?"

"It's...we..." The guild master swallowed.

In the resulting silence, Jemeryl turned to Tevi. "You told them I want you to accompany me?" She sounded coldly offended.

"I've tried to."

Jemeryl looked back to the guild master.

"Um...no, ma'am. There's no problem."

Tevi was starting to feel uncomfortable. She had hoped that Jemeryl's arrival would resolve the situation with the minimum of fuss; but Jemeryl was clearly playing at baiting the guild master. Having recently been subjected to bullying, Tevi was unhappy to see it continued, even though her tormentor was the one currently on the spot. Yet despite her qualms, there was a point that had to be cleared up.

"They've refused me permission to leave town," Tevi said quietly.

"They've said what!"

"Ma'am, we didn't—" The guild master tried to get his explanation in.

Jemeryl spoke over him. "You told them we're on Coven business?"

"They said I had to stay here, regardless of who wanted me." Tevi tactfully refrained from quoting verbatim.

The guild master flinched.

Jemeryl stared at him. "You question my authority to claim Tevi's services?"

"No, ma'am. Of course not."

"But you won't let her come with me?"

"Oh, no, ma'am. But we didn't want her running off without authorisation."

"You want me to sign a contract for her employment? Of course, you are quite within your rights to do so."

While in Lyremouth, Tevi had been told that the Coven would only be asked for formal contracts in exceptional circumstances. When working for a sorcerer, the guild reimbursed its member from its own coffers. Tevi had not understood the ramifications, only that it was an indiscretion even to suggest charging the Coven. Despite this, Jemeryl held out her hand as if waiting to be passed a pen.

"Please, that won't be necessary. I'll sort out all requisite details." The guild master was half an inch from grovelling.

Jemeryl treated him to a glare that could have stripped the varnish off his desk. "So what is all this nonsense about?"

"We were just a little confused, ma'am. Your...friend's story was... unusual. We couldn't see why you'd need her services."

"You're surely not calling on me to account for my reasons?"

Tevi felt sorry for the guild master as he floundered in the face of the sorcerer's determination to put the worst interpretation on his every word.

"Oh, no, ma'am. There's been a misunderstanding. Your companion can leave at once."

The guild master clearly had the sense to realise that anything he might say would only make things worse. Both officials fumbled in their haste as they shoved Tevi's belongings back into her pack. In next to no time, the two women were outside on the street. Tevi had even been given back her pony. The guild master had personally promised to pay for it.

❖

Night had fallen while Tevi had been in the guildhall. The streets were deserted, and the rain had turned to sleet. Jemeryl created a small light globe and urged her pony forward. Its hooves splashed though the puddles dotting the wet cobbles. Tevi rode in silence, relieved to be out of the guildhall but deeply uneasy as she considered the events since arriving in Rizen and the consequences of Jemeryl's rank. Alone together in the castle, it had not mattered. They had become friends, without deference or superiority, and then lovers. Could this familiarity continue? Would Jemeryl want it to? Tevi found herself wondering just how Jemeryl saw their relationship.

Chenoweth had recommended an inn, a prosperous establishment, well situated in the centre of town. He had apparently also sent word to the innkeeper, since despite the weather, a member of the staff was waiting for them in the open yard. The stable hand rushed forward to assist the women, although once he had established which one was the sorcerer, Tevi received only cursory attention. She stepped back under the shelter of an overhanging roof and waited, studying Jemeryl.

Instead of her usual impish grin, Jemeryl's expression was aloof. She hardly spared a glance for the sodden stable hand. Her voice was a crisp monotone, leaving no doubt that she expected her instructions to be obeyed. Tevi's jaw clenched. It was hard to see any resemblance to the woman who had become her lover.

The ponies were left in the care of the stable hand, and two porters arrived to carry the baggage. Before Jemeryl and Tevi had reached the entrance, the door was pulled open by an anxious innkeeper. The lively hubbub of voices in the taproom, clearly audible from the stable yard, dropped to a hushed mumbling as Jemeryl stepped inside.

"We'd like a room for the night." Jemeryl's voice was cold.

"Yes, of course, ma'am. We're just having our best suite made ready." The innkeeper was clearly torn between nervousness and pride at his prestigious customer. His hands fidgeted with the cloth of his apron.

In Tevi's opinion, there was an excessive amount of fuss as they were led upstairs and along a wide hallway. The room they finally entered was large and elegantly furnished. Rich tapestries hung on the walls. The floorboards were scarcely visible between the rugs. Half a tree was burning in the huge fireplace. Opposite the entrance was a bay window that, in daylight, would command views over the river. Doors on either side gave access to further rooms.

The innkeeper stood anxiously as the sorcerer examined the accommodation.

"These are your best rooms?" Jemeryl's neutral tone could have implied anything.

"You are welcome to inspect any of the others."

"Don't you know which are your best rooms?"

"Y-y-yes, ma'am. These are. I'm afraid they're due for redecoration, but—"

Jemeryl held up a hand. "It will be satisfactory."

"Is there anything else you require, ma'am?"

"A bath before we eat. That will be all."

The innkeeper bowed and backed out. The second the door closed, Jemeryl's autocratic air vanished in her familiar grin. "Well, what do you think of it?" she asked with a sweep of her arms.

Tevi had been standing awkwardly at one side. She hesitantly left the position and wandered towards the fire. Her eyes shifted uneasily, taking in the whole room with the exception of the spot where Jemeryl was standing.

Jemeryl's exuberance softened into sympathy. "Were they giving you a hard time in the guildhall? I could tell as soon as I walked in that something was up."

"It's not that."

"What's wrong, Tevi?"

Tevi ran her hand over a long couch, fingering the embroidered fabric. "How much will it cost to stay here?"

"We won't have to pay. If I'm asked, I'll sign a receipt that the innkeeper can offset against his taxes, but I doubt that he will. It's taken as a sign of poverty to charge the Coven. Besides, he'll make it back. Saying that these rooms were good enough for a sorcerer will let him put two shillings on the price."

Tevi slumped onto a chair. Her eyes were fixed on the thick rug by her feet.

"What's upsetting you?" Jemeryl's voice betrayed growing confusion. "It's not really the money, is it?"

"No."

"Then what?"

"It's the way you behave with ordinary folk."

"The way I what?"

"The way you trample over people."

"I don't."

"You do. Not just in taking it for granted that you could have the best rooms free of charge. You were deliberately intimidating the innkeeper. You didn't even act grateful."

"It's the innkeeper who should be grateful to me," Jemeryl blazed. "I told you he'll recoup his money. Apart from that, ungifted citizens owe their prosperity to the Coven. Without us, they'd be living in mud huts, at the mercy of any magic-wielding tyrant."

Tevi was shaken by the angry outburst. But, instead of responding in kind, her manner was even more subdued as she said, "I know what the Coven does for people and I know all about poverty. On the islands, we worked from dawn to dusk. We regularly went cold and hungry. We saw one child in four die before its first birthday. And that was in the Queen's household."

"So what's wrong?" Jemeryl stood in front of Tevi's chair, glaring down.

"I'd forgotten how ordinary citizens jump when a sorcerer talks to them."

"Is that my fault?"

"You were playing it as hard as you could."

"Why are you bothered? I wasn't trying to pull rank on you."

"The effect rubs off. If it keeps up, I'm going to start calling you 'ma'am.'"

"Don't you dare."

"Is that an order?"

Jemeryl bit back whatever she was about to say and strode to the bay window, although it was too dark to see out. Raindrops were running down the glass, glittering in the reflected light from the fire. Tevi watched her lover's back, too overwhelmed by her own clashing emotions to speak.

At last, Jemeryl turned away from the window and walked back to Tevi's side. "Look, I know the bowing and scraping can be irritating. Sorcerers make people nervous. It's not that I want it." Her voice was deliberately gentle, as if she was working on sounding reasonable.

"You looked like you were enjoying the whole thing."

Jemeryl drew a sharp breath. She held it for a second and then let it out in a sigh. "Yes, you're right. I was."

"Why? You're not you when you act like that." Tevi could hear the pain in her own voice. It clearly got through to Jemeryl as well.

She knelt and took Tevi's face in her hands. "I'm sorry. Lording it over people is a bad habit that sorcerers get into. It's a silly game, and I didn't intend to upset you."

"You don't care about anyone else?"

"It's hard to," Jemeryl said, honestly. "There's a barrier between Coven members and ordinary folk. And it's not one-sided. Most citizens want to keep their distance. It would probably have worried the innkeeper more if I'd acted all chummy."

Tevi was silent for a while. "I don't feel like that."

"No. And I'm very pleased you don't. You're different."

"It made me understand the villagers' view of you...a little."

Jemeryl pulled a wry grimace. "Only a little? Well, take comfort that I'm not normally so bad. I had an unpleasant time with Chenoweth, and I've been taking it out on everyone else. I'm sorry. It was wrong of me." A corner of her mouth twitched. "Mind you, I think your guild master was asking for it."

For the space of a dozen heartbeats Tevi stared into Jemeryl's eyes, and then she glanced down, a faint smile catching her own lips. "Maybe just a little."

Before anything else could be said, there was a knock. Jemeryl stood and called, "Come in."

Four of the inn staff entered, carrying a large brass bath and copious amounts of hot water, which were taken to an adjoining room.

"Will you require assistance with your bath, ma'am?" The eldest servant politely addressed her question to a point several inches above Jemeryl's head.

"We can cope," Tevi answered quickly. However, the servant waited for Jemeryl's agreement before leaving.

By the time both women were clean and dressed in fresh clothes, a table had been set for them in their room. The glasses were cut crystal; the cutlery was solid silver. The dinner was an elaborate creation from the chef, complemented by vintage wine, but Tevi did not enjoy the meal. She felt awkward to be the centre of so much attention.

The waiters fussed about them to the point of irritation. Jemeryl was clearly making an effort to be friendly, but as she had predicted, the inn staff did not know how to respond and retreated into vacuous servility. Yet once or twice, Tevi caught unguarded expressions of resentment directed at Jemeryl and something closer to contempt aimed at herself. It was impossible to concentrate on Jemeryl and the food. She found herself straining to catch the whispered comments the waiters exchanged among themselves.

She did not relax until the door closed behind the last waiter taking away the empty plates. Her relief was short-lived.

"Let's go down to the taproom for a drink," Jemeryl suggested.

"Why?"

"Why not? We spent last night camping out and we'll probably spend the next few nights in the same way. We might as well enjoy things while we have the chance. There's a harper with a very good reputation who plays here."

"You could go on your own."

"Don't be silly. I want your company. I promise I'll be nice to people."

"If you really want to." Tevi's voice made her unhappiness plain.

Jemeryl grasped Tevi's shoulder. "What's wrong? Have I done something else?"

"Oh, no, it's not you." Tevi's head dropped. "I think Rizen has just been too much for me. If we go down to the tavern, everyone will be watching us. I don't think I can stand it. The waiters during dinner—they were acting polite, but you could tell they didn't like us. It brought back bad memories. On the islands, I was heir to the throne. Every move I made was watched, and I knew I never measured up. When everyone is looking at you with contempt, it..." Tevi's voice failed.

"The memory hurts that much?"

"I hated it...being seen as a joke when I failed. The one thing I liked about exile was being ignored."

Jemeryl placed her hand under Tevi's chin and turned her face so their eyes met. Her expression was caught between sadness and affection. "It's all right. I think I understand. I've got my own ghosts that haunt me from time to time. We can stay up here."

"No, I'm being oversensitive," Tevi berated herself. "We should go down to the tavern. I'll cope."

"We'll stay here."

"I don't want to spoil your evening. You want to hear the harper."

There was a glint in Jemeryl's eyes. "Don't worry. I'm sure you can think of a way to compensate for missing the music." With a smile, she lowered her hand and began to unbutton Tevi's shirt.

Chapter Seventeen—Forbidden Magic

The two women reached the brow of the last hill. Behind them were freshly ploughed fields of dark soil and hedgerows adorned with spring flowers. Ahead of them was Lyremouth. The sprawling mass of buildings and streets hugged the harbour under a pale blue sky. On the side nearest, close by the city, yet unmistakably distinct from it, were the buildings that housed the Coven.

The road was busy. The press of carts, riders, and pack animals made for slow progress, but at last Tevi and Jemeryl reached the point where the road split. The wider, busier fork headed into the city. The other branch, lined with oak trees, led across parkland to the Coven. They reined their ponies to one side, although it was impossible not to be in someone's way.

"Are you sure you don't want me with you, to confirm that the villagers were a bunch of childish gossips?" Tevi said.

"I'll be fine."

"If you're sure." Tevi dismounted and handed the reins to Jemeryl. The pony would only be a handicap on the crowded city streets. "I'll go to the guild and tell them what's happening. Hopefully they'll be more reasonable than the crew at Rizen."

"You should be all right. The people here have far more experience of sorcerers. But I'll collect you from the guildhall and rescue you again, if need be."

"Right. See you later." Tevi disappeared into the mass of people.

Jemeryl's face was pensive as she rode the last short distance alone. Persuading Tevi to separate for the meetings with their superiors had not been easy, especially since Jemeryl had not given all her reasons. The conversation ahead was likely to be unpleasant, and not merely because Iralin might want to re-launch her previous verbal assault.

Relationships with the ungifted were strongly disapproved of, although not completely forbidden. When strong emotions were involved, losing self-control was all too easy. The ungifted ex-lovers of sorcerers had a tendency to end up rather unpleasantly dead—or worse. This did nothing to improve the popularity of the Coven with the general population, and the authorities were keenly aware of the potential for trouble. Adding to this was the sentiment expressed by many sorcerers that it somehow demeaned their status if one of their number was willing to enter an equal relationship with a common citizen. Jemeryl knew there was a very real risk that somebody would make the attempt to separate her from Tevi.

Yet, despite her worries, Jemeryl gazed around fondly at the familiar surroundings. Only a few weeks ago, she would have said, without reservation, that the happiest period of her life had been spent there as an apprentice. Tevi had changed that. A confused frown crossed Jemeryl's face as she remembered her plans of returning to claim a place as a senior sorcerer. She was no longer quite so sure of what she wanted.

The stable block was unchanged since she had left, barring a new coat of paint. Even before she dismounted, the leading stable hand had come over, brushing loose straw from his clothes. The Coven would not be the Coven without Pym.

"Madam Jemeryl. It's good to see you back. Have you been recalled for more important work?" A smile of recognition lit Pym's weathered face.

"In a way."

"Something more exciting than rotting in a backwater?"

"It wasn't that bad."

"But the best of the action is here," Pym said pointedly.

"And what is the latest action?"

"Official or unofficial?"

Jemeryl's look answered the question. Pym laughed and proceeded to gossip amiably, listing a string of minor scandals involving Coven members.

"Nothing much has changed, then," Jemeryl said when the recounting was over.

"It never does, just the faces."

"I'm sure."

"Are you off to see Iralin?" Pym asked.

"Yes. And if you ever hear any rumours about her..."

"I'll keep them to myself. I'm not a fool."

They both laughed again, in recognition of Iralin's reputation for being someone it was very unwise to get on the wrong side of. As she left the stable, Jemeryl's smile faded—it was the unfortunate position that she now found herself in. She approached the door to Iralin's study with sinking spirits. Although Pym was renowned as the best source of gossip in the Coven, chatting with him had partly been a delaying tactic, but there was no sensible way to put off the confrontation any longer. Summoning her courage, Jemeryl knocked, half-hoping there would be no reply.

"Enter." Iralin's voice answered immediately. She was always there when you did not want her to be.

The senior sorcerer looked up from her desk. Her face hardened as she recognised her visitor. "Jemeryl. I hadn't expected to see you here. Where is the warrior you're supposed to be assisting?"

"We thought it best if we talked to our superiors separately."

"You have bad news?"

"Oh, no, ma'am. But Tevi hadn't told her guild masters she was quest-bound. While she's doing that, I can give you an update on what has happened."

"Tevi is the warrior's name?"

"Yes, ma'am."

"And what do you have to report?"

"I've made a start, but I need more facts. We've come to Lyremouth to consult the Coven library and to get more information from you."

Iralin shuffled papers on her desk for a few seconds before replying. "Precisely what sort of information were you anticipating?"

So far, the interview was going easier than expected. Iralin seemed more concerned with the state of the quest than anything else. It was too soon to relax, but Jemeryl was feeling happier.

"In order to find the memory chalice, I need to narrow down the list of people who might have taken it. It would help if I knew more about the previous owner."

Iralin's face showed no emotion and not much comprehension. The idea occurred to Jemeryl that her mentor had known little about the quest, and exposing Iralin's ignorance would not be tactful. Pretending to be better informed than they really were was a common failing among sorcerers—one frequently denounced by Iralin herself.

"Would it help if I gave a full report on everything that has happened, in chronological order?" Jemeryl suggested diplomatically.

Iralin nodded shrewdly—always a good cover. "Yes. It might be. You can take a seat while you do it."

Once settled, Jemeryl launched into an account of the events since Tevi had arrived at the castle. Iralin listened intently, giving Jemeryl the feeling that the older sorcerer was waiting for subtle clues that might mean more than was apparent. The story got as far as the saga of Abrak before Iralin interrupted.

"Like most folk tales, that's nine-tenths fantasy."

"I also thought so at first."

"Nobody has ever created a viable strength potion, as you should know. Are you suggesting that a lone shipwreck survivor could knock one out to order?"

"I've discovered the name of one sorcerer who could have done it, and the dates and other facts tie in. But I could find very little information about her. That's why I've come to Lyremouth. I think Abrak was actually a sorcerer named Lorimal."

The sudden absence of movement on the other side of the desk was what alerted Jemeryl to the name's impact. Iralin was frozen in something that looked like speechless horror.

"You know about her." It was a statement, not a question.

"Continue with your report." Iralin recovered her composure. She displayed no further reaction as Jemeryl continued the narrative.

"You've just arrived in Lyremouth?" Iralin asked, once Jemeryl had finished.

"Less than an hour ago."

"Have you spoken to anyone?"

"I met Pym in the stables."

Iralin caught her breath. "Did you tell him any of this?"

"Oh, no."

"This young mercenary. Will she be talking to anyone?"

"Yes...as I said. She's reporting to her guild masters."

"How much does she know?"

"About as much as me." *And it would be hard to know any less*, Jemeryl added silently.

Iralin pressed the backs of her interlaced fingers against her lips while she withdrew into her thoughts. She dropped her hands. "Get the housekeeper to allocate you a room and go to it. Apart from that, say nothing to anyone. You will be hearing from me shortly."

"Er... I'd arranged to meet Tevi at the guild house."

"We will deal with the mercenary. You needn't concern yourself with her anymore." Iralin's tone made it clear that she thought this to be the end of the matter.

"I thought I was supposed to accompany her on her quest."

"The situation has changed."

"I don't want to be parted from her."

"What you want is unimportant."

Jemeryl's stomach clenched, but she had to speak. "We're lovers. That's why I want to stay with her."

Iralin leaned back and studied Jemeryl dispassionately. "You must have realised that I recognised Lorimal's name. Possibly, you will soon learn why, but first I need to talk with others. Believe me when I say that this is a very serious matter. The stakes are far too high for a juvenile romance between you and this mercenary to count for anything. We will do what has to be done."

"Yes, ma'am." Unhappily, Jemeryl made her escape.

❖

The guild master with particular responsibility for junior mercenaries was in one of the courtyards, inspecting the new nominees. Tevi waited to one side until the group was dismissed before approaching. The guild master looked to be well into her sixties and her body was visibly weakening with age. Maybe this fuelled the impression she gave of viewing the existence of everyone aged under thirty as a personal insult to herself. Although Tevi had also previously wondered whether her attitude might be a result of her position in the guild, or simply her main qualification for it.

The guild master scowled at Tevi and snapped. "What is it?"

"Ma'am, I have a report that I need to make."

"All right. Let's hear it."

"It didn't seem important when I joined the mercenaries, but possibly I should have told you about my quest." Tevi began hesitantly.

She got no further before the guild master cut in sharply.

"You're quest-bound?"

"Sort of."

"Sort of? There is no sort of about it. Either you are or you aren't."

"It wasn't a proper quest. Just a chalice that had been taken from my family. But I met with a sorcerer and told her about it, and she thinks it's important. So we've come to Lyremouth so she can talk to—"

"Stop there." Again the guild master cut off Tevi's words, but this time her manner was changed; no less curt or decisive, but as if she had stepped back and slammed a mental door. "The Coven has become involved in your quest?"

"Yes, ma'am."

"Then it isn't me that you should be talking to. I'll make arrangements for you to see Tallard."

"Would he be interested?" Tevi was surprised by mention of the chief guild master.

"Of course, and in the meantime, I suggest that you keep this to yourself." The elderly woman put her hand on Tevi's arm, and surprisingly, her expression softened. "You're young and inexperienced. But take it from me, when the Coven starts tinkering it is seriously bad news all round. Tallard needs to know about it, and I don't." So saying, she turned and left.

❖

The next four hours trickled by while Jemeryl paced restlessly. The more she thought of Iralin's reaction, the more anxious she became.

"Do you have to keep marching about? How do you expect a bird to get any sleep?" a familiar raucous voice asked.

"How can you sleep at a time like this?"

"Exactly—I can't, because someone is stomping up and down, muttering."

Jemeryl sent a withering glare in Klara's direction and then balanced herself on the wide window ledge. The conversation with Iralin kept going around in her head. Obviously, the senior sorcerer had known nothing about Tevi, or her island background. Iralin had not even been aware that a memory chalice was the object of her quest and Lorimal's name had left her thunderstruck.

"If she's important enough to send Iralin into a flap, you'd have thought I'd have heard of her. Who was she?"

"She's a bad excuse to deprive a magpie of sleep." Pointedly, Klara stuck her head under her wing.

Jemeryl pouted at the magpie, but with any luck, a summons would come soon, and she would be getting answers. Jemeryl slipped down from the window and selected a volume from the bookcase at random. She settled in a chair and tried fruitlessly to focus on the printed words.

At last, the expected knock came. Jemeryl tossed the book aside and yanked the door open abruptly enough to surprise the young apprentice outside.

"Please, you've been summoned—"

"To Iralin's study. I know."

In her eagerness, Jemeryl jogged on her way there. However, the second she entered the room, her enthusiasm died as sharply as if it had run into a wall. Iralin was not the only one present. Two other senior sorcerers were waiting—the two most senior sorcerers of all.

Gilliart, Guardian of the Coven, sat with her back to the window. The hair sweeping from her hawklike features matched the white amulet on her wrist. Her expression was solemn, even by the Guardian's standards. Her deputy, Alendy, a stocky man in his late fifties, was on her left. Light glinted off his bald head. Iralin sat by her desk, staring grimly at its wooden top. All three appeared troubled, even frightened.

Nobody indicated that Jemeryl should take a seat, not that she had any expectation of being treated as an equal. She stood apprehensively. An interview with the Coven's three most senior sorcerers would be daunting at the best of times, and she had the nasty feeling that this was not the best of times. After her earlier desire for more information, she was starting to suspect that ignorance might be an enviable state.

Once the door had closed, Gilliart fixed her gaze on Jemeryl. "Iralin has told us your news, and we have decided on a course of action that will require you learning something of the background to the chalice." She paused briefly. "You know that the Coven forbids certain areas of magic. Nearly two hundred years ago, a young sorcerer, Lorimal, conducted experiments in one of these areas, more by naiveté than wilful disobedience on her part. Of course she was stopped as soon as what she was doing was discovered, but the Coven leaders at the time were guilty of an oversight. For various reasons, they assumed that she had made no progress, whereas in fact, she'd almost completed her work." Jemeryl's expression must have alerted Gilliart. "You have a question?"

"I merely wondered, ma'am, whether this was before or after she'd taken the plant potion."

"Before. And of course, once she'd taken it, she was in no state to question or volunteer information. It was only in tidying up her affairs, after she'd disappeared, that the oversight was discovered—rather too late. The decision was made to delete all references to her, to prevent anyone from copying her work, but all attempts to locate her memory chalice failed. The hope was that it had been destroyed with her."

The scarcity of information on Lorimal now made sense. Despite the situation, Jemeryl felt a degree of satisfaction.

"From what you have discovered, it would seem that someone has now found the chalice and is trying to retrieve the prohibited information. We can be certain the culprit is a member of the Coven, and the school of herbalism at Ekranos is the most likely location. We intend for you to go there and see what you can find out. Iralin will brief you further on what you need to know."

"Will she not be coming to Ekranos also—or someone else?" Jemeryl spoke from a mixture of bewilderment and apprehension. She had no idea how dangerous this forbidden magic was, but Iralin's reaction earlier implied that something very important was at stake. Were the Coven authorities really going to entrust the entirety of the mission to her?

"No. Unless the culprit is absurdly overconfident, they must be on the lookout. We're hoping that one junior sorcerer will not raise the alarm. We also want to minimise the number of people who know of the chalice. Sending you means that nobody else needs to be drawn in."

"What about Tevi?"

Alendy rejoined the debate. "She has played her part. Her continued presence in this is neither needed nor desirable."

Jemeryl felt her neck stiffen, certain that the "desirable" part was a reference to her relationship with Tevi. She had suspected that the Coven leaders would try to separate them, but she had not thought the move would be so soon or so blatant. Was the mission to Ekranos even seriously meant, or just an excuse to get her away from Tevi? Jemeryl could not believe that sending her on her own was really the best way to catch whoever had taken the chalice.

Her eyes focused on the floor while she considered her options. She was surprised at how easy it was. She could leave Tevi or she could tell the senior sorcerers that she would not go to Ekranos without her. The latter option would destroy any hope of advancement within the Coven, but the former was utterly unthinkable.

Jemeryl drew a breath, about to refuse to be parted from Tevi, but before she could speak, Iralin entered the debate.

"I'm trying to remember the exact import of the oracle we received on this matter. As I recall, it was that the best hope of success was if Jemeryl accompanied the warrior on the quest."

"Which she has done. And she has succeeded in finding out about what has happened," Alendy argued.

"But the quest is not over."

"The oracle did not say that the warrior's presence was necessary to the end."

"To my mind, accompanying someone on a quest does not mean abandoning them halfway through, once you think you've learnt everything from them that you can."

"I do not think their liaison is something we should encourage." Alendy made the reason for his objections plain, not that Jemeryl had any doubts before.

"I would not place the importance of separating them above that of succeeding in finding the chalice. Gilliart, I think the decision lies with you." Iralin appealed to the white-haired woman in the centre.

Jemeryl fixed her eyes on the Guardian, aware that her future in the Coven depended on the outcome. Her heart thudded against her ribs.

Gilliart sat, looking thoughtful, but then she nodded to Iralin. "You're right. We dare not take risks with ambiguous oracles. This warrior should go with Jemeryl to Ekranos."

❖

The chief guild master of the mercenaries was a thin, wiry man with sharp eyes. From what Tevi could remember hearing, he had originally been an assassin. But it was not this that caused her wariness when she entered his chamber. Even if he believed her story, Tevi was certain that he would not be pleased, and Jemeryl had not yet arrived.

Tallard stood by a window in his chambers, looking out. He did not turn when Tevi's name was announced. The seconds dragged by as she stood waiting in the middle of the room for him to acknowledge her presence. At last he faced her.

"When you were asked if you had any other commitments that might affect your ability to undertake work for the guild, you should have told us you were sworn to a quest."

Tevi swallowed. "I hadn't sworn to complete the quest, sir, merely not to return to my home until I had found the chalice. At the time I joined the guild, I had no reason to think that I would even attempt to complete the quest."

"You abandon your oath so quickly and start playing games with words?"

"No, but...." Tevi's voice died. Should she admit that, in disregarding the quest, she was following not merely the words, but also the spirit in which the quest had been laid upon her? While she debated with herself, Tallard went on.

"Normally, we would be considering disciplinary action. However, this is clearly not a normal quest."

"Yes, sir." Tevi jumped in eagerly. "If it hadn't been for Jemeryl, the sorcerer, I wou—"

"No, don't tell me. I have already learnt as much about this as I want." Tallard held up his hand. "If you're going to succeed in my trade, you have to be able to tell the difference between what you need to know, and what you need not to know." He walked forward slowly. "The Coven are involved in this?"

"Yes, sir."

"Then I'm better off knowing nothing more about it...as would you be." He was now standing scant inches from Tevi. "Do you have any idea how much trouble you're in? As I said, normally you'd be looking at a hefty fine from the guild. However, the chances are that any penalty we might impose would be nothing compared to what you've walked yourself into. You should never, ever volunteer information that carries any risk of getting the Coven interested in you."

He considered her in silence, while Tevi felt her skin prickle. Then he moved away. "I'm tempted to leave you to dig yourself out.

However, part of the oath that I've sworn is to safeguard the members of this guild, and not expose them to more risks than necessary for their work. And I do not renege on my oath as easily as you seem to do." His eyes returned to Tevi's, "Which is why I'm going to be kind to you."

"Thank..." Tevi's voice died with the sudden conviction that what Tallard considered kind was not what she would choose for herself.

"I've arranged for you to leave Lyremouth tonight, on a mission that will hopefully take you far out of the Coven's way. If they come asking for you tomorrow, we'll be able to say that you've left town."

"I'm sorry, sir. I don't want to go."

Tallard swung back. "Why not?"

"Jemeryl and me...we...we're..." Despite herself, Tevi stumbled over the word and could feel herself blushing.

"Lovers." Tallard's voice held a measure of contempt. "You don't need to say it. I can read it in your face." He shook his head. "You really are an idiot, aren't you? In which case it is even more to your benefit to be gone. And I'm not going to hear any argument."

Tevi's head shot up, ready to voice her defiance, when they were interrupted by a knock on the door.

"What is it? Tallard called.

One of the mercenary officials entered, carrying a letter. As he accepted it, Tallard's eyes darted to Tevi.

"You may not think it, but judging by the seal, this is most likely bad news for you."

Tevi kept her silence as Tallard proceeded to open the note and read. The ex-assassin's professional stony face showed no emotion. Tevi tried to match his calm, but her insides were churning. After a few seconds he looked up from the paper.

"It's too late for you. The Coven have asked me to find an excuse to send you to Ekranos, and I cannot ignore a direct order from the Coven. Even if it weren't for our oath of allegiance, it would not be a wise thing to do."

"Is Jem going there?"

"They haven't said in this note. And if they aren't telling me, then I'm not asking. Prying into the Coven's affairs is a very bad move...as you will find out, if you live long enough."

"Then how do I find out—"

Tallard cut her off. "I imagine that the Coven will make sure you are informed of what they think you need to know at such time as you need to know it." He scanned the note again. "Apparently they want you to take charge of a magpie on the journey. It will be waiting for you when you leave this room."

"That will be Klara, and they wouldn't send her to Ekranos without Jem." Tevi smiled in relief. "I don't care where I go, as long as I'm with her."

Tallard shook his head, his mask slipping enough to reveal a trace of irritation, and maybe also compassion. "You really are a fool. We didn't have you pegged as one when you were assessed, but love can be a bitch to us all."

❖

Tevi trekked across the quay towards the waiting vessel, the *Sea Eagle*, due to sail within the hour, bound for Ekranos. The sound of waves hitting the harbour walls competed with the dockside clamour. Tevi stopped to let a long cart trundle by, piled high with sacks. Klara was perched on her left shoulder; a large rucksack was slung over the other. The magpie was to play the part of Tevi's tame pet. She peered around with bright-eyed curiosity but, in accordance with the plan, gave no unusual display of intelligence.

A gangplank led to the ship's deck. Tevi waited for a group of porters before making her way aboard. Sailors clambered through the rigging above her. Still more were busy on deck, checking ropes and bolting hatches. One crew member stood by the rail—the ship's mate, judging by her shouted instructions to those overhead. Tevi gave her name and was directed to the sleeping area below deck.

A hatch gave access to the narrow galley, where a row of bunks disappeared into the gloom. Most had already been claimed and had belongings strewn across. Tevi picked a free one on the top row and dumped her rucksack on the pillow. It was her only baggage apart from a small satchel at her waist. The contents were her purported reason for travelling to Ekranos. Mercenaries were often employed for courier duties. The guild gave some assurance of their honesty, and they were able to defend themselves, should anyone try to misappropriate the items.

Before returning topside, Tevi looked around at the passenger accommodation. The space was cramped to the point of claustrophobia.

The only light came from the hatch. She hoped they would have good weather, since being cooped up with over twenty others did not promise to be much fun.

The scene on deck was unchanged. The landward side was a bustle of activity as the last preparations were made. Tevi found a seat out of the crew's way and took stock of her fellow passengers. One caught her attention, as clearly was his intent. The man was an elderly official from the Guild of Goldsmiths and evidently considered himself a person of great importance. To make everyone within earshot aware of this, he was standing in the middle of the deck, talking loudly at some unfortunate. His conversation amounted to variations on the theme that *he* had one of the two private cabins at the front of the ship. Tevi was delighted to learn this. The idea of being stuck with the goldsmith in the confined passenger galley did not bear thinking about.

Traders formed the majority of the passengers. A child from one party wandered over. His eyes fixed on Klara.

"You've got a bird on your shoulder," the boy said earnestly, as if the fact might have escaped Tevi's notice. "Is it a pet?"

"Sort of. Her name's Klara."

A woman detached herself from the group of traders—the boy's mother, judging from her age and the supervisory watch she kept on the child. She did not appear concerned about his talking to a mercenary, and rather than dragging him away, settled down and introduced herself.

"Well met, citizen. I'm Etta." The customary Protectorate greeting was delivered at a noticeably faster rate than normal. "My partner and I are traders, specialising in spices. Are you travelling with us?"

"Well met, citizen. Er...yes. My name's Tevi. I'm from the mercenaries."

"I could tell by your tattoos." Etta was a small dark woman who gave the impression that she was going at double speed. She continued without a pause. "We're based in Talimide. How far are you going?"

"To Ekranos."

"So are we, and beyond, through the Straits of Perithia to the eastern ocean. The *Sea Eagl*e isn't going that far, so we'll have to change ships. I'm hoping we'll have a few days in Ekranos. Have you been there before?"

"No." Tevi squeezed in her answer.

"It's a nice town; you'll like it. My partner comes from there.

We'll stop off and leave the youngster with his grandparents. He was going to stay with my partner's sister, who owns a farm south of town. She's a nice woman, but we're worried about her. Her health has been playing up. Mind you, it's the best place to be ill, with the school of herbalism on the doorstep. My cousin..."

Once Etta got going, there was no stopping her. Over the next ten minutes, Tevi learnt an awful lot about her family, friends, and their assorted idiosyncrasies. Etta spoke with a lilting accent and an enthusiasm that made it sound, if not exciting, then at least cheerful. It would soon get tiring, but given the choice between Etta and the goldsmith, there was no question whose company Tevi would choose.

By the time Etta got to her aunt's best friend, the cargo was loaded and preparations were complete, but the crew were still obviously waiting for something. The captain had come onto deck and was pacing impatiently in between pauses to scan the quay.

"Do you know what we're waiting for?" Etta broke off her recital.

"Could be anything." Actually, Tevi could make a good guess, but the plans, as far as they had been revealed to her, involved acting as if she and Jemeryl had no knowledge of each other until they met aboard ship.

"Probably the occupant of the other private cabin," Etta speculated. "Looks like someone important. I hope they're more fun than..." She indicated the goldsmith with a scowl.

At that moment, a disturbance broke out on the dockside. The captain rushed to the top of the gangplank. Several traders wandered to the railing, and the crew paused in their work. Tevi was glad that no one was watching her as she tried to appear nonchalant. Acting was not one of her skills. Fortunately, Etta's attention was completely taken with the sight of Jemeryl being welcomed aboard and escorted to her cabin.

The crew prepared to cast off.

Etta turned back. "A sorcerer. That'll put Master Goldsmith's nose out of joint. Mind you, sorcerers can be odd. The last time I was on a ship with one, he looked terrified the entire trip. Apparently, he was a seer. It was worrying. You kept wondering, 'What does he know?' Every time I saw a black cloud on the horizon, I thought, 'That's it; we're going down in a storm.' However, it was one of the smoothest voyages I've ever been on. Odd. But someone told me seers can be a bit..." She paused, searching for a word.

"Sensitive?" Tevi suggested, trying not to laugh.

❖

Four days out of Lyremouth, the *Sea Eagle* was making good progress. A steady wind filled the sails. Tevi leaned over the bow and watched the hull slice through the water, happy to feel the motion of the sea under her feet and the roll of the deck. A floating strand of seaweed was caught by the bow wave. It glistened and twisted in the surf and then was sucked under the glassy surface.

Footsteps made Tevi look over her shoulder. Jemeryl had climbed onto the foredeck and was casually strolling in her direction. Tevi pushed away from the rail and straightened.

"Good morning, ma'am." Tevi spoke respectfully. So far, they had scarcely acknowledged each other, making a show of being strangers.

Jemeryl's eyebrows rose at the formal greeting. A hint of a grin danced mischievously on her lips. "Good morning, citizen."

"Is there anything I can do for you?"

"Now there's a question." Jemeryl looked around, including the rigging overhead. No one was within earshot. "But we'd better take things in order. I'm thinking it's time for us to get acquainted."

"That's fine by me."

In fact, it was better than fine. The separation was having bad effects on Tevi's sleep. Each night, she found herself lying awake in her bunk and battling the temptation to try slipping into Jemeryl's cabin without being noticed. When she finally did drift off, Jemeryl played a prominent part in her dreams. Tevi was worried that she would call out in her sleep and wake her fellow passengers. Giving the likely content of any such outburst, there would be little chance of persuading anyone that she had been suffering from nightmares.

The ship's chicken coop was bolted to the foredeck. The wooden structure resembled a rabbit hutch. Its three inhabitants provided the captain and a favoured few with the luxury of fresh eggs. Their clucking was incongruous against the screech of seagulls. Jemeryl took a seat on the roof, looking out to sea, and indicated that Tevi should join her. Klara perched on the railing facing them.

"It's all right; we can talk. Klara will let me know if anyone comes near," Jemeryl said.

Tevi let out a small sigh. "Good. How have you been? I heard you weren't well yesterday. Seasickness?"

"I was fine. It was just an excuse to avoid eating in the captain's cabin."

"Isn't the cooking any good?"

"Oh, first-rate for aboard ship. It's the goldsmith that gives me indigestion. He manages to simultaneously grovel and boast."

Tevi laughed softly. "The problems that come with privilege."

"I've tried sarcasm to shut him up. I might have to move on to thinly veiled threats. How have you been?"

"Fine. But I miss being able to talk to you."

"Mmmm. Same here." Jemeryl's voice was soft. "And there's a whole list of other things I like to do with you that I'm missing as well."

Tevi glanced at Jemeryl. As their eyes caught, she felt her stomach flip over. She turned back quickly to the sea, trying to compose her face, just in case anyone else might wander by. She suspected that her expression would not be hard to read.

Despite looking away, her thoughts stayed with Jemeryl. "My guild master didn't want me to come with you. He thought it was unsafe for me. But I couldn't bear to be parted from you."

"Some of the Coven leaders wanted to stop you coming to Ekranos as well."

"I'm guessing that they weren't worried about my safety."

"Not directly. They are more concerned with the reputation of the Coven."

Tevi smiled. "Do you know what would completely amaze everyone back on my home island?"

"That you really are going after the chalice?"

"No. That with all the people unhappy about us being together, not one is concerned that we're both women."

"Well, it isn't exactly relevant to anything."

"That's not the way my people would see it." Tevi's eyes lost their focus as her thoughts drifted back to the islands and her departure from them. She had left with no idea of where she was going and no hope for the future, not even any idea of what future was possible. She would not have believed that, just a year later, she would have found a place for herself in the form of a guild that valued her as a warrior. Most of all she could not have dared dream that she would meet someone like Jemeryl. Now, whatever the future held, she had the hope that she would not be facing it alone.

Her thought moved on. "After we get the chalice. Do you think they will try to separate us again?"

"Maybe. They won't succeed." Jemeryl turned to fix her eyes on Tevi. "We're together for life. Nothing but death will part us."

"Can you be certain?"

"Yes." Jemeryl gave a wry smile. "And far more certain than I am that we'll find the chalice."

Tevi shrugged. "Who cares? The chalice isn't important to me. It never has been. I don't even—"

She was cut short by a hissed whisper. "Someone's coming." Raising her voice, Jemeryl continued, "Was it difficult to train the magpie?"

"Er...I got Klara from a friend when she was already tame." Tevi picked up on the cue.

"That was kind, to give her to you."

"It was a very good friend."

Jemeryl stood. "It's been nice talking to you. We must"—her face shifted through a range of expressions—"talk again." She sauntered away.

"Good morning, ma'am." The voice belonged to Etta.

Even before Jemeryl's footsteps had faded, her place on the chicken coop was taken by the talkative trader.

"She seems very pleasant, for a sorcerer."

Tevi made a noncommittal sound.

"You were having quite a cosy chat. I didn't interrupt anything, did I?" Etta's tone was hinting at something.

"We were just talking."

Etta was silent—a rare enough occurrence to make Tevi look at her.

"What is it?"

"I suppose she was the one who came over to talk to you?"

"Yes."

"Do you think she's nice?" Etta definitely had something in mind.

"What do you mean?"

"Well...a couple of times now, I've noticed her watching you. At first, I thought it might be trouble. I didn't know if I should warn you. But then, I thought, 'Aha. I know what *that* look means.' Now, I don't know how you feel about sorcerers. I mean, I think they're human like anyone else, but I know they give some people the creeps. One of my uncle's neighbours is a gardener at the school, and she says—"

"You think what?" Tevi interrupted, confused.

"Sorry, I'm rambling. Getting back to what I was saying, she's definitely got her eye on you. I think she likes you." The trader smiled slyly and nudged Tevi with her elbow. "I'd say if you're interested, play your cards right, and you're in with a chance."

Another two days, and Etta was not alone in speculating. Tevi was beset by advice from passengers and crew alike. There was little in the way of entertainment on the ship. Gossip was the main pastime, but opinion was sharply divided. Few expressed any great dislike of Jemeryl personally. Many more revealed a wariness of the Coven and felt that Tevi would be ill treated. "You can't trust sorcerers. They just use folk" and "Stick with your own" were typical remarks. Etta, with her enthusiasm, was in a minority.

Late one evening, Tevi was sitting on deck, playing dice with a group of passengers, when the door to Jemeryl's cabin opened. The sorcerer wandered across to the side of the ship and leaned on the railing with the apparent intention of watching the sunset. Tevi was aware that a lot of people were looking in her own direction, and it was not because they were waiting for her to throw the dice.

Unsubtle as ever, Etta dug her in the ribs. "Go on. Talk to her."

The anticipation on the faces about her was more than Tevi could take. She stood up, brushed the dust and rope fibres from her clothes, and strolled over to Jemeryl's side. A glance back confirmed that absolutely nobody was minding their own business. Etta's young son scrambled to his feet and bounced forward as if to join them. His mother grabbed his jerkin and dragged him back. At the same time, she sent an encouraging gesture to Tevi that was probably meant to be discreet.

Sighing, Tevi rested her elbows on the rail and turned her gaze out to sea.

"How are things?" Jemeryl asked.

"A strain."

"Why?"

"It's not so bad for you. I've got everyone on board giving me suggestions about how to deal with you."

"And what are the suggestions?" Jemeryl sounded amused.

"Most think I should avoid you, though they aren't too specific how I do it on a ship this size."

"You find it upsetting?"

"Yes." Tevi's frown deepened. "I don't understand people in the Protectorate. Even Marith, who was a really nice, sensible woman, talked about sorcerers as if you're some bizarre monstrosity. I've known people to credit more human emotions to their dogs than some on this ship do to you. They can't seem to see..." Her voice faded away.

"I think I know what you mean, but I've grown up with it, so I take most of it for granted." Jemeryl paused. "I wasn't popular when I was a child, back in my home village. It's the same for all sorcerers. The other children knew I was different. Some tried to pick on me. They soon learned not to, but even when they weren't being deliberately unpleasant, I was still isolated. Even the adults were very polite and very distant. As I got older and my powers developed, they started to treat me like...like a sorcerer. Probably wise. Children aren't good at restraining their tempers. We learn a lot about self-control at the Coven." Her lips shifted into a rueful smile. "It cuts down on the number of talking frogs around."

"A shame. I could nominate a few on board who'd be better as frogs." Tevi was not sure herself how much she was joking.

The two of them stood in silence before Jemeryl asked, "Would people be appalled if we made it obvious we were lovers?"

Tevi weighed it up. "Maybe a quarter would be, and there's an equal-size group who'd think it perfectly all right."

"And the others?"

"They'd claim to be against it, but privately they'd be delighted to have something exciting to gossip about."

"Perhaps we should give them their chance to be shocked."

Deliberately, Jemeryl slid along the railing so their shoulders touched. She then slowly moved her arm to encircle Tevi's waist.

Tevi half-expected a mixed chorus of gasps, boos, and cheers from the deck behind them. She put her own arm around Jemeryl's shoulders and pulled her close. A smile grew on Tevi's lips as the familiar feeling of total contentment washed her previous irritation away, and now at least they could go to Jemeryl's cabin and shut out the rest of the world for a while.

She was about to move away from the railing, when her eyes caught sight of an island, out on the horizon. For a second, her thoughts darted to Storenseg, but without longing. She realised that, even if the chance was offered to her, she had no desire to go back. The island was not home to her; she had outgrown it. Which meant, she guessed as she and Jemeryl left the deck, that in her heart, she was an exile no longer.

Appendix
The Legend of the True-Sighted Warrior
As Told By Villagers On The Eastern Flank Of Whitfell Spur

Once upon a time, there was a young and ambitious sorcerer who lived in a mighty castle in a valley on the east of Whitfell Spur. She was very gifted and adept in the magic arts and she was very beautiful, but she was also very reckless, for she had not yet learnt to temper her knowledge with wisdom. In her folly, she summoned a demon from the netherworld and tried to bind it to do her will.

At first, the demon was held by the power of the sorcerer's magic, and it taught her much that was arcane and wondrous to human ears. But the demon was ancient and well schooled in treachery and malice, and the young sorcerer was no match for its cunning.

One day the demon retrieved a mirror from the shadow-lands. "Look into this, my mistress," it said, "and you will learn much that has been hidden from mortal eyes. For with this mirror you may see all that has been, or is now, or is yet to be."

Eagerly the young sorcerer grasped the mirror and stared into its depths. Thus was she ensnared, for the demon lied, and there were no secrets to be seen. Rather, the life was sucked from her by evil enchantment and held in the mirror, and her body was turned to stone.

However, the demon knew that once the leaders of the Coven learnt of what had happened, it would not be allowed to remain in the land of the living. The sorcerers would come against it in force, and it would be banished back to the icy depths of the netherworld. Therefore, the demon cast another spell, so that all who set eyes on it would think it to be the young sorcerer.

Only one servant knew of what had happened. When the demon realised this, it drained the sense from the man's head and sent him forth, witless and babbling, to be scorned by all he met.

Then was the demon free to indulge its taste for evil. Soon tales of grim happenings spread. Farmers spoke of blighted crops and missing stock. Huntsmen found tracks of fell beasts stalking the woods.

When first these things were noticed, the villagers went to the castle, to beg the sorcerer to help them, little knowing that the one they addressed was not who they thought, but rather the source of the evil that afflicted them. To the villagers' dismay, the supposed sorcerer derided their fears, accusing them of acting like frightened children, and sent them away. When the complaints grew more insistent, the demon set wild spirits in the form of bears to keep guard on its home, and none who thereafter entered the castle left it alive.

And ever things got worse. Unclean things walked abroad and children were snatched from their beds. Evil lights played over the castle at night and even the air began to feel tainted. All went in dread of what else might befall them.

❖

Now, far to the west, beyond the setting sun, was an island, where lived a mighty warrior, beloved and revered by her people. For, by the strength of her arms, she had vanquished all manner of threat and bestowed peace upon her land. Yet for all the adulation of her people, the warrior felt a great emptiness inside, as if some vital part of her was missing.

Her family tried to comfort her and show how much she was valued and loved, but at last, the warrior could no longer bear the desolate longing. And so, despite the entreaties and tears of her kin, she set sail into the east, searching for that which would make her whole.

When she arrived in the Protectorate, she was hailed as a hero, and invited to join the Guild of Mercenaries as an honoured member. Many great and mighty deeds did she perform in the service of the guild. However, no matter how far she travelled or what feat of arms she performed, still the emptiness inside her never lessened.

And so it happened, one midwinter's day, that the warrior was trekking north along the western flank of Whitfell Spur, when she was hailed by an ancient seer.

"Hold a moment, hero," the seer cried, "and listen to what I have to say, for I know what it is that you truly seek."

"What do you mean?" the warrior replied.

"You seek that which will make you whole. Come, let me show you what it is that your life lacks."

At these words, the warrior felt her heart beat hard within her breast, for now she thought she might learn the cure for her dissatisfaction. The seer took a bottle of wine, and poured it into a chalice. The warrior drew close, unsure of whether the seer intended her to drink, but when she looked into the wine, she saw images form and then grow clear. And so, she found herself staring at the face of the sorcerer.

If the warrior's heart had beaten hard before, now it redoubled its pounding. She felt the blood seep from her face, and knew that she must meet this unknown woman, as soon as ever might be.

"Who is this?" she asked.

"One who needs your help. And to her aid you must go, before the month is out. Therefore I bid you, gather a band of followers and lead them across the Spur."

The warrior raised her eyes to the ice-scoured heights. Winter lay hard on the mountains, and storms raged every day. Yet her heart was not downcast, for her desire to meet the woman she had seen in the wine would have carried her through any trial. "I will do it," she said, and turned to go.

"Before you leave me, hero, there is more I must tell you," the seer said. "For there are three things you must know, although they may seem more like riddles to you."

"I have no time for games," the warrior replied.

"But if you do not find answers, you will not succeed in your quest."

"Ask away then, old woman."

"The first is to believe your ears when you have no eyes. The second is that a woodsman's axe may cleave through any deceit. And the third is that tears may melt the hardest stone."

"None of this makes sense to me," the warrior cried in dismay.

"You need not understand all now, but you must by the end, if you are to find what you seek." With those words, the seer vanished.

So the warrior gathered comrades who would help her cross the mountains. Few were willing to undertake the desperate venture, but at last, the gallant band set out. On their journey, they were beset by hardships that would have sent weaker folk fleeing to the safety of the nearest warm hearth, yet they prevailed by their strength and courage, and crossed the heights of Whitfell Spur in the heart of winter.

Thus, cold, tired, and battered, they arrived, unlooked for and unannounced, in the valley where the demon held its reign of fear.

❖

It happened that, at this time, the demon had called forth a hellhound, to make cruel sport with the villagers. The beast ravaged the district, and many good folk fell victim to its savagery. The nights were torn by its baying, and none dared set foot outside their homes after sunset.

When the warrior heard of this monster, she immediately resolved to slay it and remove its grim presence from the valley. However, at the sound of the hellhound's baneful howling, her band of followers, who had so gallantly crossed the Spur, lost their courage and fled, leaving the warrior to face the monster alone. Only two local youths would overcome their dread and help the warrior in her quest to hunt down the monster.

For twenty days and twenty nights the warrior kept on the trail of the hellhound, and at last she tracked it to its lair. Then she drew her sword and charged down on the beast. Long and dreadful was the fight, and the snow was churned red with blood, but at last the warrior dispatched her quarry, and cut off its head.

Then did the good folk of the valley breathe in peace and hope that their troubles were at an end. Alas, it was not to be. The demon was aware of its creature's demise, and immediately it claimed its revenge. The demon called on foul magic that it set upon the warrior, so that, at once, she was struck blind.

The demon then sent word that the warrior should be brought to its castle, and the villagers, still thinking that the order came from the lawful Coven-appointed sorcerer of the region, had no choice but to obey. With heavy hearts they led the blind warrior to the castle gates and left her there alone, at the mercy of the demon within.

The warrior now thought that her life would soon be over, but the demon did not so quickly pass by the chance to heap torment upon one who had stood against it. Rather than kill the warrior outright, the demon had her taken into the castle to be used as a slave, working at the demon's command from dawn to dusk. Many and cruel were the hardships she endured.

Yet the demon had miscalculated. Its spell of disguise meant that all who saw it would be fooled into thinking that it was the lawful Coven sorcerer. However, the warrior was blind and could not see the demon, and so she was immune to the spell. But she heard its foul tones, and the scratching of its claws on the stone as it walked, and knew it to be nothing human. Thus did she solve the first of the seer's riddles, for she believed her ears when she had no eyes.

The warrior now understood that the castle had been taken by some shape-shifting fiend. So she resolved to dispatch it from the lands of the living, and free the good folk of the valley from its cruel dominion, no matter how little hope there seemed that she might succeed, blinded and without weapons as she was.

❖

One day it happened that she was fetching wood from the store to feed the fires in the great hall of the castle, when her hand chanced on an old axe, half hidden under the logs. The shaft was worn and rotten with age, and the blade rusty and un-honed, but the steel was strong and the craftsmanship was true, and it might yet be returned to a serviceable condition.

As the warrior's fingers ran along the blunted edge, she remembered the second of the seer's riddles—a woodsman's axe may cleave through any deceit. "And surely," she said to herself, "there is some foul deceit at work here that needs uncovering." So she returned the axe to its place of concealment, until such time as she could return with a knife, a whetstone, and oil.

In the days that followed, the warrior carried on as before, working at the demon's command, and giving no hint of her plans. But at last she found what she needed. Then, at night she crept back to the wood store, and began working on the axe.

First, she honed the blade, until it was sharp enough to draw blood from even a stone. Then she oiled the steel, so that no rust would mar its keen edge. Then she took the knife and a length of stout oak, and carved a new handle for the blade, that would not fail her in the test to come.

By now, she was so familiar with the castle that she did not need sight to find her quarry, for she knew that through the hours of night, the demon would be in the great hall, feasting on the meat and ale which it demanded as tribute from the villagers in huge quantities—although the good folk had judged the privations this caused to be the least of their woes.

So the warrior silently crept up behind the demon, while it was at the task of sating its monstrous appetite. She heard the crunching of bone as the demon's jaws chewed through the carcass of its food. And she heard the slobbering gulps as the demon tossed back quarts of ale in each draft.

The warrior finished her stealthy approach, until she stood within smiting distance of her foe. And such was the noise of it eating, like a hundred pigs at a trough, that even blind, she could locate its head with ease. She hoisted the axe above her head, and then brought its keen edge slashing down on the demon's brainpan. Such was the force of her blow that she clove its head, straight through to its neck. Yet though it was a mortal blow, the demon was not so quick to die.

Knowing that it had not long left in this world, in fury, the demon raged and rampaged throughout the castle. It threw down walls, breaking stone from stone, and splintering mighty timbers with its claws, until the once-mighty castle was no more than a shattered ruin. However, the words of the seer riddle held true, and the demon could not long resist the honest magic of the woodsman's axe, unbinding the deceit of its own conjuring. With the coming of dawn, it faded from these lands, banished back to the icy netherworld, never to return.

❖

When she heard the demon run wild, the warrior had sought safety in the dungeon below ground, and despite all the demon's carnage, she was unhurt in the destruction of the castle. More than that, with the demon's final departure from this world, its foul magic was undone, and the warrior's sight was restored to her.

In joy, the warrior began to climb from the rubble-filled pit that was all that remained of the dungeon, when a beam of light from the rising sun fell though the carnage and lighted on the statue of a woman with the remains of a broken mirror at her feet.

"It is strange," the warrior thought, "to have a statue where none may see it."

Drawn by her curiosity, the warrior went to investigate, and when she looked on the statue, she recognised the one that she had seen in the seer's chalice. Yet, rather than a woman of flesh, there was no life in the statue's eyes, and the face before her was cold stone.

At this, the warrior thought her heart would break. For she now knew that this woman was the thing that was missing from her life, and without her, the warrior would always be unwhole. But it seemed that she was too late, and that the demon's foul magic had destroyed any hope of happiness for her.

"Alas," cried the warrior, "that you are not a living woman, for it seems to me that I would love you if we could but meet."

Tears ran down her cheeks as the warrior leaned forward and placed a kiss on the lifeless stone lips. As she did so, a single teardrop fell and landed on the breast of the statue.

Now was the meaning of the seer's last riddle revealed, that tears might melt the hardest stone. For, with the demon banished, and the shadow-land mirror broken, it took but one tear from the warrior to undo the magic and restore the sorcerer to life. And the first thing she saw, when her eyes were formed anew, was the warrior, standing close before her. And as she looked on the warrior's face, the sorcerer felt her own heart start to pound.

"Who are you? And what has happened here?" the sorcerer asked.

At first, the warrior was too amazed to reply, but eventually she managed to recount what she knew of the story.

The sorcerer looked at the warrior even more warmly, once she had heard all, and knew what she owed to the warrior's bravery. "You have restored my life," she said. "How may I ever repay you?"

"I want nothing in reward," the warrior replied.

"I cannot let you go empty-handed. But name your desire."

The warrior looked into the sorcerer's eyes, and said, "In that case, to name my desire. I took one kiss from your lips, when they were stone. To take another when they are warm flesh, I would count myself paid in full."

"That you shall surely have and more," said the sorcerer.

Then she took the warrior in her arms and kissed her soundly. And with the touching of their lips, their hearts were joined in such a love that would never fade, as long as they both might live.

"Now we must leave this valley," the sorcerer said. "For I must go to Lyremouth and tell the leaders of the Coven what has happened so that they may make amends to the good folk of this valley for the hardship they have endured by my folly. And I know not what penance might be put upon me."

"And may I go with you? For I would stand by you through whatever may come."

"Always and forever, my love."

So they left the valley, and went to Lyremouth.

When they heard the report, the leaders of the Coven pardoned the sorcerer for the harm her recklessness had let loose, as they judged her already more than amply punished and hoped that she might learn something of wisdom from her mistake.

And so, the pair went forth into the world and performed many great and good deeds for the advancement of the Coven and the Guild of Mercenaries, so that in all the annals of the Protectorate, no names are spoken with more respect and admiration than those of the warrior and her sorcerer.

Which is why we, who know the full true tale of what happened in this valley and how the two met, tell our story without names, that the reputation of the sorcerer will not be tarnished by this tale of folly from her youth, for she went on to become one of the greatest sorcerers of the Coven, and ever at her side was the warrior who had saved her. And thus were they heroes and true lovers together, for all the days of their lives.

About the Author

Jane Fletcher's novels have won a GCLS award and been short-listed for the Gaylactic Spectrum award. ***The Exile and the Sorcerer*** is the first book in her ***Lyremouth Chronicles***. The sequels, ***The Traitor and The Chalice*** and ***The Empress and The Acolyte,*** will be published by BSB in 2006. She is also author of the Celaeno Series—***The Walls of Westernfort, The Temple at Landfall*** and ***Rangers at Roadsend.***

Born in Greenwich, London in 1956, she now lives in south-west England where she keeps herself busy writing both computer software and fiction, although generally not at the same time.

Visit Jane's website at www.janefletcher.co.uk

Books Available From Bold Strokes Books

Chance by Grace Lennox. At twenty-six, Chance Delaney decides her life isn't working so she swaps it for a different one. What follows is the sexy, funny, touching story of two women who, in finding themselves, also find one another. (1-933110-31-7)

The Exile and the Sorcerer by Jane Fletcher. First in the Lyremouth Chronicles. Tevi, wounded and adrift, arrives in the courtyard of a shy young sorcerer. Together they face monsters, magic, and the challenge of loving despite their differences. (1-933110-32-5)

A Matter of Trust by Radclyffe. JT Sloan is a cybersleuth who doesn't like attachments. Michael Lassiter is leaving her husband, and she needs Sloan's expertise to safeguard her company. It should just be business—but it turns into much more. (1-933110-33-3)

Sweet Creek by Lee Lynch. A celebration of the enduring nature of love, friendship, and community in the quirky, heart-warming lesbian community of Waterfall Falls. (1-933110-29-5)

The Devil Inside by Ali Vali. Derby Cain Casey, head of a New Orleans crime organization, runs the family business with guts and grit, and no one crosses her. No one, that is, until Emma Verde claims her heart and turns her world upside down. (1-933110-30-9)

Grave Silence by Rose Beecham. Detective Jude Devine's investigation of a series of ritual murders is complicated by her torrid affair with the golden girl of Southwestern forensic pathology, Dr. Mercy Westmoreland. (1-933110-25-2)

Honor Reclaimed by Radclyffe. In the aftermath of 9/11, Secret Service Agent Cameron Roberts and Blair Powell close ranks with a trusted few to find the would-be assassins who nearly claimed Blair's life. (1-933110-18-X)

Honor Bound by Radclyffe. Secret Service Agent Cameron Roberts and Blair Powell face political intrigue, a clandestine threat to Blair's safety, and the seemingly irreconcilable personal differences that force them ever farther apart. (1-933110-20-1)

Protector of the Realm: Supreme Constellations Book One by Gun Brooke. A space adventure filled with suspense and a daring intergalactic romance featuring Commodore Rae Jacelon and a stunning, but decidedly lethal, Kellen O'Dal. (1-933110-26-0)

Innocent Hearts by Radclyffe. In a wild and unforgiving land, two women learn about love, passion, and the wonders of the heart. (1-933110-21-X)

The Temple at Landfall by Jane Fletcher. An imprinter, one of Celaeno's most revered servants of the Goddess, is also a prisoner to the faith—until a Ranger frees her by claiming her heart. The Celaeno series. (1-933110-27-9)

Force of Nature by Kim Baldwin. From tornados to forest fires, the forces of nature conspire to bring Gable McCoy and Erin Richards close to danger, and closer to each other. (1-933110-23-6)

In Too Deep by Ronica Black. Undercover homicide cop Erin McKenzie tracks a femme fatale who just might be a real killer…with love and danger hot on her heels. (1-933110-17-1)

Stolen Moments: *Erotic Interludes 2* by Stacia Seaman and Radclyffe, eds. Love on the run, in the office, in the shadows…Fast, furious, and almost too hot to handle. (1-933110-16-3)

Course of Action by Gun Brooke. Actress Carolyn Black desperately wants the starring role in an upcoming film produced by Annelie Peterson. Just how far will she go for the dream part of a lifetime? (1-933110-22-8)

Rangers at Roadsend by Jane Fletcher. Sergeant Chip Coppelli has learned to spot trouble coming, and that is exactly what she sees in her new recruit, Katryn Nagata. The Celaeno series. (1-933110-28-7)

Justice Served by Radclyffe. Lieutenant Rebecca Frye and her lover, Dr. Catherine Rawlings, embark on a deadly game of hide-and-seek with an underworld kingpin who traffics in human souls. (1-933110-15-5)

Distant Shores, Silent Thunder by Radclyffe. Doctor Tory King—and the women who love her—is forced to examine the boundaries of love, friendship, and the ties that transcend time. (1-933110-08-2)

Hunter's Pursuit by Kim Baldwin. A raging blizzard, a mountain hideaway, and a killer-for-hire set a scene for disaster—or desire—when Katarzyna Demetrious rescues a beautiful stranger. (1-933110-09-0)

The Walls of Westernfort by Jane Fletcher. All Temple Guard Natasha Ionadis wants is to serve the Goddess—until she falls in love with one of the rebels she is sworn to destroy. The Celaeno series. (1-933110-24-4)

Change Of Pace: *Erotic Interludes* by Radclyffe. Twenty-five hot-wired encounters guaranteed to spark more than just your imagination. Erotica as you've always dreamed of it. (1-933110-07-4)

Honor Guards by Radclyffe. In a wild flight for their lives, the president's daughter and those who are sworn to protect her wage a desperate struggle for survival. (1-933110-01-5)

Fated Love by Radclyffe. Amidst the chaos and drama of a busy emergency room, two women must contend not only with the fragile nature of life, but also with the irresistible forces of fate. (1-933110-05-8)

Justice in the Shadows by Radclyffe. In a shadow world of secrets and lies, Detective Sergeant Rebecca Frye and her lover, Dr. Catherine Rawlings, join forces in the elusive search for justice. (1-933110-03-1)

shadowland by Radclyffe. In a world on the far edge of desire, two women are drawn together by power, passion, and dark pleasures. An erotic romance. (1-933110-11-2)

Love's Masquerade by Radclyffe. Plunged into the indistinguishable realms of fiction, fantasy, and hidden desires, Auden Frost is forced to question all she believes about the nature of love. (1-933110-14-7)

Love & Honor by Radclyffe. The president's daughter and her lover are faced with difficult choices as they battle a tangled web of Washington intrigue for...love and honor. (1-933110-10-4)

Beyond the Breakwater by Radclyffe. One Provincetown summer three women learn the true meaning of love, friendship, and family. (1-933110-06-6)

Tomorrow's Promise by Radclyffe. One timeless summer, two very different women discover the power of passion to heal and the promise of hope that only love can bestow. (1-933110-12-0)

Love's Tender Warriors by Radclyffe. Two women who have accepted loneliness as a way of life learn that love is worth fighting for and a battle they cannot afford to lose. (1-933110-02-3)

Love's Melody Lost by Radclyffe. A secretive artist with a haunted past and a young woman escaping a life that has proved to be a lie find their destinies entwined. (1-933110-00-7)

Safe Harbor by Radclyffe. A mysterious newcomer, a reclusive doctor, and a troubled gay teenager learn about love, friendship, and trust during one tumultuous summer in Provincetown. (1-933110-13-9)

Above All, Honor by Radclyffe. Secret Service Agent Cameron Roberts fights her desire for the one woman she can't have—Blair Powell, the daughter of the president of the United States. (1-933110-04-X)